GASLIGHT

Book 1 of the Apex Society Trilogy

Rhone Atleshen

LONE SPIRE PUBLISHING

SERIES LIST

APEX SOCIETY

Gaslight ←you are here

Matchstrike

Burn

GASLIGHT

RHONE ATLESHEN

Published by Lone Spire Publishing
www.LoneSpirePublishing.com

ISBN:
eBook: 978-1-7355355-8-6
Paperback: 978-1-7355355-7-9
Hardcover: 978-1-7355355-9-3

Cover design by Candlelight Creative LLC
Interior design by Lone Spire Publishing

Library of Congress Control Number: 2025917785
Printed in the United States of America

First Edition: October 2025
10 9 8 7 6 5 4 3 2 1

Dedication

For every gaslit woman who's ever dreamed of watching
the lies go up in smoke —I've got matches.
We ride at dawn.

Content Advisory

Before you begin...

I write thrillers designed for emotional intensity. The characters and events in these pages aren't real — but the stakes are meant to feel real. My villains do bad things. My heroes are flawed, layered, and not always altruistic.

I hope you enjoy the ride, but your mental and emotional health matter more. In these stories, you'll encounter adult language, violence, and at times sexual content.
If you need to step away–*do it*.
My characters will still be here when you're ready.

For a list of potential triggers, visit the book's page at www.rhoneatleshen.com *before* you dive in.
Protect yourself.
Never stop reading.

Contents

Prologue   1
Moira: 4 Weeks Ago

1. Chase   11

2. Chase   23

3. Moira   33

4. Moira   43

Wilder Bro's Group Chat   49
-1-

5. Chase   53

6. Chase   61

7. Moira   69

8. Moira   77

9. Chase   83

10. Chase   91

11. Chase   97

12. Moira   105

13. Chase   111

14. Chase   117

15. Moira   125

16. Moira   131

17. Chase   139

Wilder Bro's Group Chat   143
-2-

18. Moira   147

19. Moira   151

20. Chase   155

Wilder Bro's Group Chat   165
-3-

21. Chase   169

22. Moira   177

23. Chase   187

24. Moira   193

25. Moira   201

Wilder Bro's Group Chat   207
-4-

26. Chase   211

27. Moira   219

28. Moira   227

29. Chase   237

30. Chase   247

Wilder Bro's Group Chat   257
-5-

31. Moira   261

32. Moira   265

33. Chase   273

34. Moira   283

Wilder Bro's Group Chat   291
-6-

35. Moira   295

36. Chase   299

37. Chase   311

38. Chase   317

39. Moira   321

40. Moira   327

41. Moira   333

Wilder Family Group Chat   341
-1-

42. Chase   345

43. Chase   351

44.	Moira	355
45.	Moira	363
46.	Chase	375
47.	Chase	387
48.	Moira	391

Epilogue   399
Chase: Several Months Later

Acknowledgements   405

About the Author   406

Read more Rhone   407

Sneak Peek: Matchstrike   408
Book 2 of the Apex Society Trilogy

PROLOGUE

MOIRA: 4 WEEKS AGO

H IS OUTRAGEOUS CHARM SLID into my DMs in a blaze of all-consuming persistence, powerfully funny and expectant. I could've blamed an isolated life for my momentary weakness with an online dating app. Still, the truth was that self-sufficiency had been my rusted armor since foster care. I longed to shed it, even as I forged a life as a freelancer who worked from home.

> Me: Guess who's officially a townie <3

Sending my text, I waited for the telltale typing dots of response before pocketing my phone with a sigh to continue unloading. I'd driven for days from Oregon to upstate NY. I intended to keep in touch with him, but my cell died outside of Akron–my charger lost along the way. When I finally located the cable, I mentally prepared for missed calls and frantic texts. Instead, when I powered up my cell, I found it eerily quiet. Losing an hour, I dove into the unpacking process in the hopes of

1

emptying the truck to return it and avoid another day of rental fees. But if he couldn't pick me up after dropping it off...then what?

Dean's brashness overwhelmed me during our long-distance whirlwind. Like clockwork, I woke each morning to a sweet text–some sizzling. He'd flood my phone with heart emojis if I were slow to reply. Once, he even had an extravagant bouquet of white roses delivered with a note that said, 'Check your messages, sweetheart.' Now, dropping the final moving box onto the heap in my tiny apartment, I scowled at the empty notification bar. It must be work, I reasoned. He hoped to hear about some promotion soon and was likely busy. But his last message was days ago–'Drive safe.'

Lifting my cell, I snapped a sweaty selfie and sent another text.

> Me: Done in record time and neeeeed a shower.
> Can't wait to see you. <3

All it took was a few weeks of Dean love-bombing me before I packed a bag for our first weekend. His lingering kisses and grand romantic gestures set the stage for six months of steamy video calls and reckless, exhilarating meetups in towns between my Oregon apartment and his Lake Placid cabin. The details never mattered—his intoxicating attention was a fairytale.

He called me his anchor.

Sex was like everything else–wild and overwhelming. He pushed my limits, swearing to pull me out of my shell. A promise he delivered on when he convinced me it was time to move.

It made sense on paper...even I could see that, 'You're portable, sweetheart. What's keeping you there?' I could freelance from anywhere after all. He was vital to his city's emergency services, and my social media work was... disposable. Any time my nerves wavered, he'd make me laugh at my silliness. His certainty always gave me a little shiver, but he wasn't wrong.

Now, stepping out of the rideshare I'd called to collect me at the moving truck drop off, taking in the towering pines I'd only ever seen in pictures, my paper-thin confidence faltered. I still hadn't heard from him.

Me: Surprise... I'm here!

Butterflies the size of pterodactyls swarmed my stomach as I climbed the steps of his wraparound porch and knocked. Faint classic rock drifted from inside, teasing a smile to my lips, but he didn't answer. My rideshare pulled away as I knocked again. Frowning at my phone, I hit the only number in my favorites–surprised to hear the ring coming from the side of his house.

"Dean?" I followed the ringing, threading between blaring music and the sharp crack of splitting wood. His voicemail whispered in my ear as I rounded the cabin, and found him...shirtless, sweaty, ax in hand, eyes locked on a tree stump with muscles coiled and jeans slung low. Every last nerve evaporated as my core clenched at the gritty lumberjack goodness of him.

"Hey, you," I spoke over the music, anticipating elation, but Dean never looked up. I opened my mouth to speak again, but paused when he smiled at the ground with an amused shake of his head.

"Moira, Moira. What a surprise." His odd smile never lifted as he grabbed the freshly split logs and tossed them into a pile. "What brings you to my neck of the woods?" The cool greeting snapped me right out of the mountain-man fantasy I was indulging in. I expected surprise, sure, but also...I don't know what.

Excitement, or at the very least...happiness.

"I called and texted earlier. My cell died, and I lost my charger, so I couldn't do anything until I got to my new place and - "

"Yeah, I got those. I was busy here." He loaded another log onto the platform and waved around with his ax as if his need to chop wood in the middle of summer made sense somehow. I started to walk forward, craving his arms around me, but hesitated again. The very air between us felt...off.

"Did something happen at work?" I halted my steps, suddenly worried he'd received bad news. "Did the promotion not go through?" He scowled at a fresh log as he reared back and split it with effortless precision—the crack splintered the air.

"Promotion is...on hold." He chucked the split logs to the pile and wiped his face with the shirt hanging from his back pocket before finally...finally...looking at me with an unreadable expression. "How are you?"

The cordiality of those three little words sent a wave of nausea through me. We'd talked about me moving here for so long. So why did I feel like an unwanted houseguest?

"I'm sorry if I'm showing - "

"Why?" He cut me off. "I never mind having company." He swung his axe and split another log with a crack that made me jump. "Want something to drink...a beer, maybe?" He left the ax buried in the stump and walked towards his house, unbothered by the gaping expression on my face.

My feet moved of their own volition, feeling like I'd made a horrible mistake. I entered the house as he turned down the music–that flippant smirk spreading across his face again.

"Moira, Moira." Anger flashed up my spine as he grabbed two beers, swiftly removing their lids and crossing to finally meet me. "Beer?"

"What?" I muttered. "Dean, I don't understand."

"What's to understand, you want the beer or not?" He shoved the cold bottle in my hand, sending the cap flying to the trash with a snap of his fingers. "God, you are so hard to read sometimes," he mumbled, turning his back to sit on a barstool as he palmed his favorite fidget, an old, time-worn zippo.

I sifted through the weeks leading up to my move. Planning all the details and letting Dean walk through my apartment for me via video chat. We'd discussed this ad nauseam, and he was thrilled for me to be here... wasn't he?

"I hoped you might be waiting for me at my new place." I grimaced at the skunky beer as I shook off my doubts and pushed forward.

"Why?" He smiled, taking a swig of his beer. "You said yourself your phone died. I couldn't have known you were gonna show up today, now, could I?" His cold retort was so far removed from the warm and attentive man who had once flown to Oregon just to surprise me with dinner. Even the lazy snick and snap of his lighter felt like a dismissal.

I'd asked him once why he fidgeted with that thing, and he'd claimed it was a hold-over from his former smoking days. I always hated it.

"Sure. Okay. I guess." I stepped towards him, clearing my throat and hoping I was misreading things. Surely his fatigue from chopping wood and the disappointment of a stalled promotion was feeding into this chilly reception...wasn't it? "Well...I got myself moved in and returned the moving truck just before they closed. I grabbed a rideshare and thought I would just - "

"Show up unannounced?" He mumbled around another swig. "Yeah, I figured that part out all on my own...sweetheart."

"Okay. Look," I huffed, done with tip-toeing around this awkward-ness. "I can tell something's up. I'm not sure what, but - "

Dean stood so quickly his stool screeched across the tile floor, stepping towards me so fast I had to stifle a yelp as he loomed over me.

"Look. Moira. Was there something you needed from me or..."

His words trailed off as he stared dead in my eyes, trailing his gaze down my body in a way that made my blood run cold. He never flinched...never blinked. It was not loving or warm; it felt predatory.

Dean...was predatory.

My free hand fisted against my stomach as the burning sting of tears welled in the corners of my eyes. I willed them not to fall with everything I had in me while he continued toying with that damned lighter.

"Why are you acting like this?" My voice was weaker than I wanted it to be. "We talked about this—me coming here." Dean's eyes burned through my defenses, leaving me naked and humiliated as he licked his lower lip.

"Moira, Moira." He grumbled, "What am I gonna do with you?"

"Stop saying my name like that!" A flush rose on my cheeks, embarrassment giving way to anger. "Just tell me why you're - "

"No need to get hysterical, sweetheart." Dean flicked my chin with his thumb as he brushed past my shoulder and headed towards the door, the final metallic snick-snap his private joke at my expense.

Traitorous tears fell as I raced through every detail to figure out where I had gone wrong. I had allowed Dean to push my boundaries time and again, convincing myself it was good to branch out and break free from my solitude. But surely I didn't concoct this relationship in my head. The faster the memories came, the darker his intentions seemed until I settled on the only conclusion that made a sort of sick and twisted sense.

"You," I whispered past the lump in my throat, willing my words to be more than a whimpering plea as I turned to face him. "You played me."

"Aw, come on now, Moira. I thought we had a lot of fun." He slid the glass door open and stepped outside as he continued. "We never really talked specifics, right?" He half-shrugged, all but dismissing me. "I'm sorry you don't see it that way."

"No. NO! Dean." I stomped back outside behind him. "We made plans...for *months*! You knew I was coming; you WANTED me to come."

"Did we talk about all that?" Dean crossed to his axe. "I can't recall. I mean, God, you did text and call a LOT."

"No! You called, you texted, you flew out to see me and - "

"We had fun, sweetheart. You...were a lot of fun. If you thought it was more than that, well...that seems like a you problem." The bastard casually lifted a log to the platform as if chopping wood after eviscerating my life was old hat.

"A YOU PROBLEM?!" I tried to step before him, but he brushed past me like I was nothing. "You made me move across the country. I changed jobs for you. I gave up my entire life because you said, 'You couldn't come to me.'" I waved angry air quotes in his face even as I inwardly cursed the hope I felt that he'd remember he wanted me.

"I think what you remember is your old job was already ending, and I offered to help you find a new one," He tossed his hands out to the side with a shrug. "'Cause I'm a nice guy like that. You chose to move out here when I told you I wouldn't come in that direction." He reached for his axe before finishing. "If you got some mixed signals, then..."

"Dean, NO!" My last shred of dignity screamed to stop begging, but the words escaped anyway. "We were more than that!" Dean swung his axe so close I flinched as the crack stung my ears.

"Might wanna steer clear, sweetheart." He smirked as he reared back for another swing, and I swear I heard a laugh rumble out of him when I stumbled. "Look." He huffed as he tossed the axe to the ground and grabbed the split pieces. "I can see you're going through something. I don't wanna make this about me, but you're kinda putting me on the spot."

"I'm putting YOU..." The venom dripped so effortlessly from his lips.

"You were fun. But that was it. You made this wild decision to move out here." Stopping his work, he straightened his back and locked his gaze on me. "And now you show up at my door and act shocked that I wasn't...what?" Dean's face held a now-familiar dead-in-the-eye stare that sent chills down my spine. Moving only a fraction, he put his face so close that I tasted the sour musk of sweat mingled with the beer on his breath. "What did you think was gonna happen here...sweetheart?" His voice was taunting, and I had to clench back a fresh wave of tears and bile.

"No. It was more than that...*we* were more than that." Anger gave way as humiliation surfaced with the words I couldn't say, 'You said you wanted me.'

"I took pity on you." His face was soft, and in any other scenario, it might have seemed caring, but now it was suffocating. Dean slipped one rough hand down my cheek, wiping at my shame. "I was helping a woman with no friends. But frankly, I got my own shit to deal with and I can't carry you anymore." Hooking a finger into the collar of my shirt, he tugged me towards him and laid his forehead on mine. "And it's not fair of you to lay more of your problems on me when I was just helping you clean up your mess."

The whispered cruelty was tender as reality crashed down around me—I was a fool. I thought I'd won some fairytale ending after a life of solitude.

I deserved to choke on it.

A fresh sob escaped as I dropped my forgotten beer. I looked down and watched as it spilled over the top of my foot, creating a sour river between our feet.

"Guess you'll be expecting me to clean that up too, won't you...sweetheart?" I choked back the bile when he kissed my cheek and brushed past me. "I'm due for a poker game in the city. Let's not make this awkward."

He called me his anchor... didn't he?

So why did I feel like I was suddenly adrift?

1

CHASE

911 Central Dispatch: 911 Central on open channel. We have a reported structure fire at the Branson Heights apartment complex. 2200 block Sequoia Avenue. Requesting immediate response.

Firefighter 1: Lieutenant Wilder here. Engine 1 and Rescue 2 en route, ETA three minutes.

911: Copy, Lieutenant. Engine 1 and Rescue 2 responding. Stand by for updates.

Firefighter 3: Ladder 3 en route. Any info on access? Over.

911: Rescue Units 1, 2, and 3 responding. Police should be arriving now. PD, can you confirm the crowd size and access issues?

EMT: Dispatch, this is Unit Alpha 20. En route to Branson Heights. Requesting an update on any confirmed injuries or urgent needs.

Police: Dispatch, Sergeant Wilder pulling up. Flames visible from the third and second floors. We've got multiple cars here and road closures in place. Evacuations underway.

911: Copy that PD. Fire and EMT units will be there shortly. Can you confirm fire status?

Police: It's contained to one building. But the flames are up top. We've got injuries already.

911: Can you detail any injuries?

Police: Multiple burns, possibly smoke inhalation. We need medical.

EMT: EMT pulling in now. Notify County ER, multiple fire-related injuries with smoke inhalation inbound soon.

Firefighter 1: Dispatch, police perimeter is secure, EMTs are working. Battalion 1 on scene and assuming Command. We're heading in.

Dispatcher: Copy that. Boots on the ground. Dispatch standing by for further coordination. Godspeed, gentlemen.

The Branson Heights fire was exactly what I didn't need tonight. Not that any fire is ever good, but my team shouldn't have been in play. But the nearest station was down a rig, and, well, here my crew was. I loved the job, loved helping people. If I were being totally honest, I loved the adrenaline high of running into a burning unknown. Tonight, however, I was coming off a 4-day shift that ended with a review board grilling that had sucked the life out of the past month. I was mentally exhausted, and the paperwork for tonight's fire would have me out until sunrise.

This was our fourth fire in as many days, which in a town as small as ours was saying a lot. We held a population barely over two thousand, and most of our fire stations were half-served by volunteers. Even the review board asked if I believed the issue at hand was related to an uptick in fires. I told them I wasn't sure, but the question nagged at me even as I looked up at the smoke-spewing structure.

I could tell the fire started on the third floor, as the roof was framed in flames and covered by billowing black smoke pouring from the uppermost balconies. ALL those fine particulates from the mixture of wood, cloth, and paint would be mixed with the pollutants of whatever accelerant was soaked into the roofing materials, creating intense fumes. I grabbed my face mask and slapped our latest probie on the shoulder to jog his memory—his face showing me the adrenaline made him forget that smoke inhalation was the single largest killer in a fire.

"Chase!" Grabbing my ax, I turned towards my brother's voice bellowing over the roof of a squad car. "We pulled the residents back to the far corner of the lot. Sam's there now." Troy, the 'older' of us all, was a Sergeant with the Police Department. He'd been on the force as long as I was with the fire department, but he rose quickly in the ranks due to his no-nonsense work ethic. He always followed every rule to the letter. He never shied away from late nights, overtime, or weekend work either. Not that it was a big surprise.

The three of us were technically the same age, but Troy was always the most responsible, the most reliable, and thus 'the eldest.' My brother Sam was an EMT and the de facto' youngest' of us, and I fell into 'middle brother' status, hovering between Sam's recklessness and Troy's do-gooder impulses when we were growing up. We were always thick as thieves, even serving together on a tour in the Marines and returning home simultaneously to pursue our chosen fields. I was drawn to be a firefighter, and so the Wilder brothers had their hand in all of Essex County, New York's emergency services.

"How'd the review go?" Troy watched the scene as he waited for me to respond.

"Fine," I answered, scanning the empty building as my team prepped the hose. "All good."

"Formal charges?" He cocked an eyebrow at me, but I shook my head.

"None of them wanted to pursue it."

"Fired, I hope?" Troy inquired further. "Or temporary suspension?"

"Officially...Conduct Unbecoming. No severance, no pension, full-stop." I answered dryly. "Better than nothing, though not what the bastard deserved."

"Oorah," Troy said with a nod.

"Oorah." I nodded back in kind.

"Think he'll retaliate?"

"His grudge ain't my problem. That asshole kept a video library of sexual conquests in his office laptop in the same place as field training videos. He got busted trying to blackmail women with it. I couldn't care less if he's pissed... he's lucky I didn't knock his teeth out."

"Your nose is clean," Troy said matter-of-factly.

"It's all good, man," I smirked and cocked an eyebrow at my brother. "I only cold-cocked him that one time, and Chief could hardly be mad since his niece was one of the women being blackmailed." Troy's silent fist bump was answer enough that he had my back.

The three of us always had each other's backs.

Growing up orphans, my brothers and I had a thick bond that was unshakeable. From Nonna's place to the Marines, we looked out for one another. We were so locked in, with efficient, shorthand communication, that our CO drafted us into a special ops branch for field missions that required a surgical approach. So, while the current mess with the review board was messy, I never doubted that my brothers had my back.

An odd noise drew my attention back as I scanned the third floor again. The smoke reduced visibility until the flames appeared as tiny peaks of vibrant orange licking across the roofline before slipping beneath the haze, but I was pulled to look again.

"We know everyone's out, right?" I looked at Troy, who shook his head.

"The residents didn't know. They said the smoke got to them before the heat, though."

Shit.

If the smoke reached them before the fire, none of them would be able to identify the source or the origin, or if it started with a now-missing resident. I made the quick call and yelled back at my crew.

"It's Marginal at best—definite extension into the attic. Smoke first, and the source is unknown. Note the roofline before we..." Electricity trickled up the back of my neck as the faintest sound of a high-pitched scream rang out over the roar of the fire. I froze, and Troy turned too, seeing my attention go rigid. With full focus back on the fire, I quickly scanned the windows until a flick of blonde hair flashed past a window.

"Third floor!" I barked, bolting towards the stairs.

"WAIT!' Yelled my probie. "We're still stretchin', Lieutenant!"

There was no time to wait for the pipe to arrive. That much smoke wasn't pouring out of nothing. Wherever this blaze originated, it was burning rapidly and intensely. Whoever was behind that window was too close to the catalyst. If the heat didn't take them down, the smoke sure as shit would.

I took the stairs two or three at a time, and a deafening crack popped to one side of me. My pipeman yelled on my radio.

'3rd floor balcony is pulling off the building, Chase.'

I had to move faster. If the balcony gave way, then the damage had already extended to the subfloor's structural elements. I blasted past the second floor and radioed back to my team: "Open doors on 2. Seems to be mainly smoke. I'm pushing to 3. Someone's up there."

'Copy. Sending a runner to clear 2. Pipeline's ready. Where we putting the stick?'

My mind raced as I reached the top of the third floor, trying to decide where they should place the ladder. All doors were open save for one, and I breached it without a second's hesitation.

Rookie mistake.

The door split, and a gust of heat slapped back so hard I nearly fell down the stairs–I had found the origin of this blaze.

"Shit," I yelled into my radio. "3rd-floor front corner unit just handed me my ass!"

I got my bearings and noted that the kitchen of the small apartment was gone, having been engulfed in flames. I yelled across the open space towards the lone closed door on the other side of the room.

"FIRE DEPARTMENT. IS ANYONE INSIDE?"

The oppressive heat was so close that even in my protective gear, I was roasting as I slowly worked my way across the space. I called out again, but no one answered, and I feared I was too late. Inching my way forward, I ignored the creaking moans under my feet and the balcony doors hanging at the wrong angle. The muffled shouting of a woman's voice caught my attention again, and I quickly closed the distance to the door. I took the smallest beat to assess that no active flames or smoke were coming from under the door, but the knob wouldn't turn. Leaning into it with my shoulder, the cheap hollow core banged back into the wall. I quickly sighted a woman huddled in the far corner, cradling one hand while trying to hold her soot-covered shirt over her mouth and nose. When she saw me, she nearly lunged at me, but I held up a hand to stop her.

"Whoa, whoa, whoa, lady!" She froze at my raised hand, abject terror in her eyes. I didn't want to add to her fear, but soot rimmed her nose, and I began calculating how much smoke she had already inhaled. "I'm here to help, but don't move! Is anyone else here with you?"

"No... I'm Alone!" Her panic was palpable, so I kept my instructions short.

"Okay. I'm getting you out. But we have to be careful." I paused long enough to make sure her eyes were on me. "Don't move. The floor is weak. Stay under the smoke. I'll come to you. Nod if you understand." To her credit, the woman stepped back against the wall and nodded as she slid down to her knees, again cradling her hand as her wide eyes took in the flames through the splintered door behind me. "Okay. Good job. What's your name?" I tried to keep her focused on me while I moved as quickly as possible, testing each step for spongy warning signs of a hole opening.

"My name... I'm...Uh." A crack sounded on my right, and her eyes darted again around her. Her chest rose and fell rapidly as she took in the scene and more smoke.

"Hey! Eyes on me. Don't look at the fire." Another groaning crack told me more of the building was collapsing, and time was running out. "C'mon. Tell me your name!"

'Main stairwell compromised.' My team bellowed in my helmet's earpiece. *'Moving the stick bravo side.'*

"Copy. I have a live one up here. Coming out of the remaining window." With the stairs gone, this rescue was no longer about getting her out...but getting us both out.

"No. You can't!" Her scratchy voice screamed as she held up her cradled hand to reveal an angry, blistered palm. "The door...it was locked...and the window." She was sobbing, eyes wide despite the heat and smoke's stinging effects. "I tried to open it...but it's too hot. I think it's painted shut!"

I was impressed that she had the wherewithal to convey anything to me, given the panicked state she was in. More so that she'd tried to break the thing with her bare hands.

She was a fighter.

"Don't worry about that. I got some great gear and big gloves, and I'll do all the heavy lifting." As I edged near the window, I saw the ladder coming far too slowly. I stretched out my hand to the woman crouched on the floor. "Come on." She grabbed my glove and stood, immediately burying her face into my coat. "Okay, miss. I'm going to break the glass now. Don't be alarmed if a sudden rush of heat comes at you. It's the fresh oxygen drawing the fire. But my crew is right outside, and my gear will protect you." I stripped off my coat to wrap it around her. "Nod, if you understand."

"But...what about you?" Her eyes darted around the room, even as she pressed her body against mine, white-knuckling handfuls of my undershirt. I faintly noticed a thumping in my abdomen and realized she was pressed so close that her heart was beating wildly against me.

"Nod, if you understand!" I bellowed, needing to know she was hearing me. We had seconds left. Her eyes locked onto mine, tears welling as I swiftly shattered the window. True to form, the fire gushed through the bedroom door, sending a blast of heat straight at us. The woman buried her face in my chest and screamed. Instinctively, I wrapped my arms around her and put myself between her and the heat source, barely registering a nagging sting on my shoulder. Looking out the window, I saw my team moving on the ground, preparing to make the climb up—too slow. Turning back to the woman now swimming in my coat, her eyes locked on mine as her lids fluttered. She swallowed gulps of air, faster and faster—her panic her undoing if I couldn't get her out soon. Before I could do or say anything more, her body tensed, and then she collapsed like a ragdoll.

"Goddamnit!" My brain went into overdrive, imagining all the ways her oxygen was being compromised. We were on borrowed time before she had a serious compromise to her airways— if I wasn't already too late. Then, because the universe loved to make things extra interesting, the flooring under my right boot shifted, and my instincts screamed. She was unconscious, and I couldn't wait to hand her out the window to my crew, who hadn't made it high enough yet. Holding the woman with one arm,

I slung a leg out and rested it on the top of the ladder. Then, I tossed her over my shoulder and climbed out to distant shouts of profanity below me. I moved as fast as possible to get us both clear of the heat.

The last thing I saw was a wall of fire move through, right next to where we had been standing, as a fresh blast of heat flared out of the shattered window.

2

CHASE

"SHE PASSED OUT JUST before I got us out." I handed the woman off to my brother Sam and his team, watching as they carefully laid her on the stretcher. "There's a burn on her hand."

"I've got airway. You check the hand." Sam commanded as he went to work, removing my coat from the woman and tossing it at me. "Check the legs for additional burns."

"On it." His partner answered. "Starting a line."

Sam's communication was concise and direct—his team a well-oiled machine moving seamlessly around the woman. Entirely in his element, Sam commanded a respect I was grateful for as the echo of her words rippled through me. 'I'm alone.'

I couldn't pin down why it clung to me, and so I found myself mesmerized by Sam and his process. He worked swiftly but with expert care, listening to her airway while cradling her head with his free hand. I saw the way his lips moved as he assessed her vitals, murmuring under his breath. Stepping closer, I listened as he dictated everything he did as if soothing a small child with simple narration. Only then did I notice her pinched brows, as if she wasn't entirely unconscious, and it made sense. He knew she was trying to wake up, and he didn't want her to be afraid. Something in his words, his tone, soothed me too, as adrenaline flooded my brain, replaying our narrow escape.

"He's good at what he does." Troy had walked up beside me, pulling me from my thoughts.

"Has he always talked to people like that?" I watched on with no small amount of pride. "When he's working on them?"

"I've seen him on a couple of calls. He's different with different people. But yes." Troy gave a nod at our brother. "Especially women and kids. The elderly. People are usually scared when he shows up, and he works to put them at ease."

Sam was an orphan, too. Nonna adopted him last, hence his status as baby brother. Impulsive, fun-loving, and effortlessly charismatic, he was always the smallest of us until puberty exploded him into a giant man-child. Always a lady's man, he had an ease about him. A trait that made him well-suited to his job as an EMT. He was never rattled, no matter what chaos was going around him. Not like Troy and I. Troy was always so taciturn, and I always came off like a giant asshole, a hazard of spending too much time hiding out at the gym.

Sam was bandaging the woman's hand as his partner swiftly cut her top down the middle, flipping the sides out and exposing her breasts. I knew it was to place monitoring leads on her. I knew it was necessary. And yet, as her free hand twitched reflexively, it felt like an intrusion. My feet were moving before I realized what I was doing.

"For fuck's sake!" I lunged, pulling at her shirt and wrapping it across her body.

"Whoa, Chase." Troy pressed a hand on my chest, pulling me back with a side glance at Sam. "They're just doing their job."

"At least load her in the rig so the whole goddamn town isn't watching you strip her," I growled, ignoring how crazy I sounded as all my instincts screamed to shield her.

"What's with you?" Troy pulled at my elbow. A stab of searing pain shot down my arm, and he didn't miss it. "What the hell is this?" Troy spun me to look at my shoulder, then tipped his head to Sam, who sent over one of his team to check me out.

"When I broke the window, I shielded her from the blast," I mumbled, only then feeling the full extent of pain. The EMT pulled my shirt to the side, sending stabbing pain down my back as I hissed at the inconvenient reminder that firefighting was just like combat. The hum in my blood commanded action first, but all the feelings came after the adrenaline crash.

"Come on," Sam tipped his head to his ambulance. "You're both going for a ride." I turned back to the fire and saw another rig had joined my team, bringing more than enough able bodies to finish dousing the already dwindling fire.

"You're out, Wilder." Yelled the Battalion Chief on the scene. "Get that shoulder treated."

Walking to Sam's rig, my chest tightened at the sight of Sam placing oxygen tubes up the woman's nose—a silent plea echoing that I'd gotten her out in time. Her whole body was marked by the dingy grey smudge of soot and ash, except for the cuff of her pants, which showed a crazy, glittery pink leopard print above her bare feet. A flash of color that made me wonder if the rest of her apartment was filled with pink and glitter, too? Or was this her go-to comfort outfit in a home she felt safe in before fire destroyed it all?

"Go on," Troy nudged. "I'll swing by to get you when I'm done here."

"Yeah, man," I noted the tight quarters in the ambulance and scanned the scene around me. "Is there another rig?"

"Bullshit!" Sam snapped from inside. "Get your ass in here, and let me look at you." He then locked eyes with his partner and tipped his head towards the cab. "She's breathing well on her own. No signs of internal swelling for now. I got this. Make room for my brother." The man secured the final strap on the gurney and stepped out the side door. With a final shove from Troy, I climbed into the freshly vacated spot opposite Sam.

The woman lying between us seemed at ease for now, the crease in her brows gone, and for the first time, I wondered how the aftermath of a fire rescue felt to civilians. Maybe it was riding the rig for the first time, or maybe it was her eyes as she looked at me and asked, 'What about you?', but I was lost in the idea that her whole world was going up in smoke and she was too out of it to fully know yet. Sam pulled me from my thoughts with an elbow tap.

"Lemme see that shoulder."

"Is she gonna be okay?" I twisted awkwardly in the belted confines of the narrow seat, leaning as best as I could for Sam to make quick work of cutting my shirt. Sam sat back and rummaged for supplies just as the ambulance rocked over a bumpy stretch of road that had me testing my hand on the side of the stretcher to steady it. I never knew how rough these rides were, and every jostle of the unconscious woman's head had me silently cursing the state of the blacktop around town.

"Again." Sam barked impatiently, twirling his fingers at me. "Now."

"It's fine," I growled, ignoring the tight stretch of my skin as Sam tugged at me. "What about her?"

"You're second-degree, at least. Put this on it." He doused a giant pad with some kind of gel and icy cold saline and stretched across the rig to plop it dripping down my back. "Let that sit 'til we get to the ER."

"Great," I growled through the sting, jerking my head impatiently at the woman whose brows had pinched together again. "Now...*Her*. Is she gonna be okay?" Sam cocked his scarred eyebrow at me before answering.

"The smoke damage seems superficial. They'll assess her more at the hospital, but her SATs are good, and she's breathing easily on her own."

"And her hand?" I reached to lift her injured hand, but Sam beat me to it, flipping it up to inspect the bandage on it.

"Better than your shoulder, it'll sting for a while. Hands and fingers tend to be more painful. The ER will determine if she has any other injuries."

"So... she's okay." I breathed, leaning forward and resting my elbows on my knees, studying her features.

Even with the black smudges around her slender nose and the tear streaks down her ash-covered cheeks, there was a sort of raw beauty that made me want to see more. The woman's hair was dingy from the smoke, but looked blonde in color. Those perfectly arched eyebrows I kept studying seemed the same color, and I wondered if her eyes were blue to match. I let my eyes slide to her mouth and the small cupid bow of her top lip. I had seen those lips scream and cry, but I wondered what her smile looked like. A notion I had never had before with anyone I'd helped in a fire, and one I could only attach to that word, still sounding like a gong in my head.

Alone. She was alone.

Despite my brother's reassurances, I wanted to see her be okay with my own eyes. I needed her to show me if her eyes were the blue I was imagining or some surprising shade of brown or green. My whole body hummed with a need to see her open her eyes. Just once. Just enough to see she made it.

"Chase, do you...know her?" The question snapped me out of my inner battle, and I looked up to find my brother watching me with an odd half-smirk.

"No. Why?" His only answer was a down at my hand, which I had rested on her forearm at some point. I started to remove my arm when a soft, scratchy voice squeaked between us.

"Where–" A forced and breathy huff cut her short.

"Ma'am." Sam sprang instantly into action, pulling out his pocket light and examining her. "You are safe in the ambulance with Essex County EMS. We are on our way to the hospital. You were pulled out of a fire. Do you remember what happened?" He moved gently around her, careful not to jostle her while rapidly checking her vitals, and I was grateful for his care.

"The fire," Her eyes fluttered, and she rocked her head back and forth as if trying to clear the confusion and sleepiness. "My door...it was locked...I couldn't–"

"It's okay," I answered. "I got you out, and my brother says you're gonna be okay."

"You..." Slowly, she turned her face to me, her bloodshot eyes flickering open and closed before flashes of recognition wisped across her face, and she bolted up. "Oh My God... the fire!"

"Whoa, Ma'am." Sam tried to coax her shoulders back down to the stretcher as monitors alerted her spike in heart rate. "Try to remain calm."

"I can't..." She clawed at the oxygen tubes on her nose. "I can't breathe." Her ragged breathing grew wheezy as Sam tried in vain to both calm her and replace the oxygen tube.

"She's going into shock." He ditched the nose cannula for a full-on mask, kicking against the front wall and yelling at the driver. "We need to hustle here!" He tried to secure the face mask despite her grappling to remove it. "I know you are scared, ma'am. But the oxygen will help. Focus on my voice if you can. You are safe now."

All my training would have told me to stay out of the way. I knew I should have let Sam do his job. But I moved before I even knew what I was doing, reaching up and placing my hand gently on top of hers as she scrambled for purchase against the mask.

"That was pretty brave of you to warn me about the window, you know." I did my best to match Sam's tone, soft and low, as she stilled. I slowly lowered our hands to her lap, trying to help anchor her in the present. "But you never did tell me your name."

"You." Her eyes stopped darting around the ambulance as she turned her face to me again. "You came for me. You..." Tears welled in her bloodshot eyes again, and my chest tightened. "You found me."

"Of course I did, silly." I half smiled, trying to keep her attention on me as Sam maneuvered the mask over her nose and mouth. "But right now, you need to lie back and let Sam help you." Her eyes slid drowsily over to Sam, who gave her a gentle smile.

"Ma'am. I'm going to help you relax back again so your body can rest. You've been through a big ordeal, and I need to resecure your IV." Sam nodded down at her hand, where she'd nearly ripped the IV off in her panic. When she followed his eyes, her breathing sped up once again at the fresh blood welling on her skin, and my brain scrambled for anything to try and help her calm down again.

"Come on now, are you gonna finally tell me your name?" She turned at my voice and locked her bloodshot gaze. I took my free hand and gently cupped the back of her head, guiding it back to the gurney.

"Or shall I call you 'Fancy Pants' in honor of those ridiculous glittery leopard things you're wearing?"

"Moira." She whispered with a scratchy huff of what sounded like a laugh. "Moira Vanderbilt."

"Wow. A Vanderbilt, eh?" I leaned my elbow on the edge of the gurney, afraid that if I took my hand away from her head, she'd panic again. "Fancy Pants indeed." Another breathy laugh sounded, and out of the corner of my eyes, I saw Sam relax back as her heart rate evened out.

"I'm not fancy. I promise." She held my other hand as she continued. "How...did we get out? I don't..." Her eyes scrunched together, forming that familiar sooty 11 between her brows. "I don't remember..." Her words trailed off with a breath.

Sam gave a subtle shake of his head, indicating I shouldn't go there, and I had to agree. She'd already panicked twice since regaining consciousness. She was finally getting good oxygen, and her IV was precariously stable but wouldn't sustain another fit.

"So, how did you end up with a name like Moira Vanderbilt if you aren't fancy? Vanderbilt sure sounds like the name of hoity-toity aristocrats?"

"Not likely." She mumbled, fatigue dragging her lids down in slow flutters. "At least not that I'd know. I never met my birth parents."

It was crazy how that one phrase shared a novel's worth of details. She didn't say parents; she said birth parents.

She was adopted.

But then I remembered her declaration of being alone, and I thought maybe orphaned was a better word.

Watching her drift in and out, I suddenly saw this frail woman in a completely new light, and with it came new questions. Would there be anyone to call for her? If she needed help recovering, would she have a support system? Would she be alone at the hospital, too?

"We're here." Sam's voice dragged me out of my thoughts, and I glanced first at the woman...at Moira...and noted that she seemed asleep. "I'll get her unloaded and then take a better look at that shoulder."

"Please." Her mumbled voice came through the oxygen mask despite her closed eyes. "Please don't leave me." She squeezed my hand, and the band around my chest tightened.

"Ma'am," Sam answered. "We're gonna take good care of you."

"No." The strain in her words grated, her knuckles white with the force of whatever energy remained in her smoke-addled body as she clung to my hand and pleaded. "Please! Don't -"

"I'm not going anywhere." The words fell out unbidden, and yet they felt right. Needing to confirm them for myself as much as she did, I wrapped her shaking hand in both of mine and repeated them. "I won't leave you, Fancy Pants."

"Dude," Sam placed his hand on my forearm. "I got this. You need -"

"You heard me," I mumbled to Sam, never taking my eyes off Moira's as her breathing slowed and her eyes fluttered against the sleepiness she was fighting. "I'm. Not. Going. Anywhere." I emphasized every single word as I ignored Sam's concern and instead noted how my declaration visibly relaxed her. She took a deep breath, clutching my hand to her chest, before slipping into unconsciousness. All I could do was stare as she went under again—a tiny, frail thing. She was scared and alone, and I knew...to the marrow of my bones...I couldn't leave her yet.

She needed me.

3

MOIRA

P AIN.

Before I even surfaced from the fog of sleep, I felt it—bone-deep and all-consuming.

It throbbed through my legs, my arms—even my guts twisted in protest. My head was murky sludge, complete with waves of nausea rippling through me. Memories balled up in my throat as my ribs stabbed their presence.

I wrestled with myself, trying to come awake or stay asleep, taking stock of my situation through closed eyes.

The beeping equipment and distant, muffled footsteps on the tile flooring created a soundtrack to my hazy state.

Emotions I didn't want welled up inside me. I yearned to be dragged back down into the dreamless sleep where I could hide a little longer. I wasn't ready to face the brutal reality of all I had lost.

A fire.

I swallowed the pins and needles in my throat and decided coughing was not advisable. My eyes were itchy. I tried to rub them, but felt a tight pull on the back of my hand. I reached to investigate the sensation only to find my other arm tethered by a thick band.

Is that a blood pressure cuff?

Pulling past the restraint, I curled my fingers to relieve my eyes from their burn, and my palm screamed in pain—a sensation strong enough to make me still again. I let my mind drift to new sensations and found a plastic tube draped around my cheeks, with stale air gently blowing in my face. It was dry and chafing.

Turning my head, I tugged against what I now knew was a nose cannula, and I used my other hand to pull at its feeder tube until I was free of it. Inhaling the sour tang of cold antiseptic, a wave of nausea rushed through me, and I cringed as my mind flooded with memories.

The smell woke me up from my bed. My bedroom door was stuck, and it was extremely hot. Then there was him: some man, a fireman. I remembered his arms around me as he shielded me from the heat. Then there was a gap — a blackness. Then there was the ambulance.

He asked me my name.

He held my hand.

Ripped from my reverie, someone gently slipped the oxygen tube into place, and I froze. I was not alone. Was that a nurse or a doctor?

"Boy, you really don't like that thing, do you?" A familiar voice mumbled next to me. I couldn't piece it together, and my mind filtered through all the sensations, and my eyes fluttered open. The blinding overhead lights were intense, and I lifted a hand to shield myself from their harsh glare, hissing as the screaming palm made itself known again. "Oh hey. Lemme turn those down for you."

The voice grew a little louder–a man, soft and familiar beside me.

"You've been out of it for a while, so take it slow." My ribs protested when I tried to sit up, even as my eyes adjusted to the dimmed lighting. Then his hand was there, pressing the button and raising the bed. "I'll sit you up. Just try not to move. Do you remember where you are?"

"There was... a fire," I forced, wincing at the pain in my throat. "My apartment...did everyone get out okay?" I flopped back against the bed with exhaustion from that shuffling movement. My head pounded in agreement, but I was determined to see the face attached to whoever this voice belonged to.

"There you go...surprising me again." His voice was deep and smooth, with a timbre that trailed calm in its wake. "You wake up in a hospital, and your first question is about everyone else." His huff of laughter enticed me to open my eyes, slower this time, so that they could adjust.

I looked to my right, blinking away the sting of dryness as my vision cleared. There he was, the voice that drew me into the light.

"Huh...." He mumbled. "River Blue." Clean-shaven with an almost military-style buzz of dirty blonde hair, the man leaned forward, knees on his elbows.

The firefighter.

His position limited me to only seeing his upper body, but the grey t-shirt he wore stretched across what appeared to be a massively wide set of shoulders. I let my eyes wander slowly across his face, taking in every detail of his strong jaw and the gentle dimple in his chin before finally landing on his eyes.

"How do you feel?"

"Like I was hit by a truck," I squirmed, trying to find a comfortable position for my throbbing ribs.

"Last night would've been a huge adrenaline rush to your body. The hangover of all that will linger a day or two." He added quickly, "But from what they tell me, you are otherwise okay and don't have any major injuries, though."

"Being bodily flung out of a burning building will do that, I guess." I quipped. Humor...ever my faithful shield.

"I didn't have much time to make the trip down very soft." He smiled a sheepish grin that teased a set of dimples hidden away. "Sorry about that." He lifted a hand to wipe a tear that I never realized was drifting from the corner of my eye. He was gentle despite his size, and when he feathered his finger against my cheek, a part of me fractured at the tenderness.

"You." I could barely finish the words as emotions swelled inside me. "You saved me."

"Hey now, Fancy Pants." He leaned his massive shoulders over me, wiping another tear even as a scratchy laugh escaped at the ridiculous moniker I now remembered. "Don't go giving me a big head. My brothers will never let me live it down."

"That's right, you have a brother. The EMT." Another stinging tear escaped, and he didn't hesitate to stroke his hand along my cheek as if trying to capture each tear before it reached the pillow.

"Yeah. That was Sam." He said softly. "My other brother, Troy, was there too, but you didn't meet him. He's a Cop." The warmth of his hands grounded me as he spoke–his voice a low lullaby.

"Three of you, eh?" I tried looking at him through eyes that stung. "You *all* saved me." My eyes closed with a surge of pain in my head that brought a powerful wave of nausea. "I still can't believe it."

I played through my patchy memories of the ambulance ride before heat rushed across my cheeks. Snapping my eyes open, I lifted the hospital sheet, looking at a clean gown and bare-naked legs.

"Fancy Pants!" I blurted past the throbbing wave of pain cascading through me. "Where are my - "I couldn't finish as I pressed my eyes shut against my pounding head, willing my stomach not to leap from my body. I wasn't sure if my blush showed as I peeked one eye open and spied the man next to me.

"Uh. Yea. Your clothes were...wrecked." He glanced at my sheet-covered body, and a faint pink rushed up his neck.

"But," I darted my eyes down my body and back up to his, the movement making my head throb harder. "I'm not wearing wrecked clothes now."

"Well, yeah." The man said before his eyes went wide, finally understanding where my thoughts had gone. "Oh—yeah. No, I didn't—God, no. *I* didn't take your clothes off!" He scrubbed a hand down the back of his neck. "Sam kicked me out to deal with my shoulder. I wasn't here when the nurses took care of you." He sat back down but scooted his chair close enough to keep his elbows on the edge of my bed. "The nurses and staff here handled you...I mean, helped you." His blush deepened until his ears were blazing red.

"You're shoulder?" I lifted my head to see but couldn't make out any bandages.

"Don't worry." He gently placed a hand on top of mine, and the warmth sent a wave of relaxation coursing through my body. "The nurses here are great. They took excellent care of you, getting you cleaned up and changed. I'm sure your things are in a bag somewhere, though I doubt they'll be salvageable. That kind of smoke damage tends to be permanent."

With a sigh, I let out a little laugh and let my head flop back on the pillow. Huge mistake as it sent a blinding burst of pain that turned my stomach upside down.

"Guess you can't call me Fancy Pants anymore, then."

"I dunno." He smiled. "It kinda goes with that mouthful of a name of yours, Moira Vanderbilt."

"And you're shoulder?" I repeated, hoping to distract myself from the headache. "Is it bad?"

"Naw." He tipped his head back to his shoulder, where the edge of bandages peeked from under the collar of his shirt. "I'll get a week or two off work, but I'm good."

"You got hurt...saving me." Tears stung my eyes again, my emotions riding a razor's edge of restraint. "I'm so sorry."

"I didn't become a fireman thinking I'd never see a little heat, Fancy Pants. It's an occupational hazard."

"Do I get to know your name at least?" I spoke slowly, remaining very still so as not to jostle my head and begging my stomach to get the memo. "Or shall I call you 'Big Guy'?"

"I'm Chase." His massive hand wrapped gently around mine in a mock handshake. "Chase Wilder. At your service."

"My hero's name is Chase." As the words left my lips, drooling nausea crept up my throat, and all my efforts to contain it were lost. "I think.... I'm gonna..."

I managed to lean off the side of the bed seconds before my stomach heaved, giving me only moments to suck in a breath before launching a second wave, then a third. Skull-crushing heaves brought dizzying pressure, and I was grounded only by Chase pulling my hair out of the way, rubbing my back, and murmuring something unintelligible as I tried to halt my body's attempt to turn itself completely inside out.

"Try to take a slow breath if you can." His voice was comforting as he reached the call button on my bedside. "Rm 112 is awake and having some ... pretty severe nausea."

'On our way.' Answered the voice on the speaker.

My last heave was a fruitless, dry one that tightened my stomach into knots. I panted from the exertion as I sat back on the bed, clutching my ribs that screamed reminders at me that I should not have moved so fast.

"Oh my god. I can't believe I just did that in front of you."

"That was likely the concussion." The chipper voice of a young doctor clipped into the room. She strolled over, glanced at the floor beside my bed, and stuck her head out in the hallway to call for a cleanup. Then, rounding the other side of the bed, she immediately clicked on a bright pen light and flashed it into my eyes.

"Concussion?" I winced back, trying to escape the sharp glare.

"You've been through quite an ordeal, Ms. Vanderbilt. You are lucky to have been pulled from that building when you were." She gave a curt nod to Chase before continuing. "If Lt. Wilder had been a minute or two later, you could be looking at severe smoke inhalation, a miscarriage, or worse."

My brain struggled to catch up—the word miscarriage echoing in my skull.

"As it is, you have a mild concussion. You'll endure a day or two of a sore, scratchy throat as you recover fully, but you and your baby should be just fine." She grabbed her tablet and clicked her nails on it a few times. "Since you were unconscious when you arrived, we don't have all your medical information. Did you have morning sickness before the fire?" Looked quizzically over the rim of her glasses like an impatient teacher waiting for her student to answer a pop quiz.

"M...m...Morning sickness?" No, no, no, no, no

"Well, they *call* it morning sickness, but really, it can happen *any* time of day." The doctor pushed forward, smiling obliviously at my confusion. "Do you have any of the typical 1st-trimester symptoms? Dizziness, fatigue, nausea, and so on?"

"I..." My mouth opened and closed like a fish out of water, but my brain scarcely made coherent thoughts as I pilfered the past few weeks.

I'd been feeling overly tired and had little appetite, but surely there was another reason beyond pregnancy. It was stress, anxiety, and my trademark dehydration since I hardly remembered to drink water on a good day...but a baby?! I knew the doctor was waiting for an answer, but my god. How? I was so careful. Wasn't I? I stared down at my stomach, as the news washed over me, and I asked the most idiotic question I could have at that moment.

"Am I.... I'm pregnant?"

"You didn't know?" The doctor asked, clicking on her tablet again. Her eyes flicked briefly up at Lt. Wilder and then back to me. "In that case, I'd like to keep you one more day, perhaps." She glanced at my vitals from a monitor, tapping on her tablet again as if she hadn't just blown up my life. "I want those headaches to subside, and I'll have OB give you a quick look to confirm everything. Do you have any questions for me before I leave?"

I had a lifetime of questions, but couldn't voice one as I did rapid period-math. I hadn't started since I moved, so that's four weeks... Before that, it was at least three weeks, or was it four? Had I started packing yet?

"Maybe she needs a minute, Doc," Chase said. "Kinda seems like you just dropped a bomb on her."

I had no words. Just shock and complete disbelief as I turned and laid eyes on my other hand being held in the giant hands of the man who had saved me...or saved us?...from a fire in an apartment. I had barely even made a home for myself, much less a baby.

The bleak reality washed over me as I crumbled into a million deep, jagged, broken shards.

Homeless, jobless, alone, and ...pregnant.

"Is there someone I can call for you? Someone who can come stay with you?" Chase asked. His expression was soft and clear, and I locked onto it like a lifeline.

This man had saved me, had stayed with me.

This man who didn't know anything about me and yet held my hand now, my hair before, without flinching.

A hero, no less, with a family and brothers. He was a full, whole, good person, and he was holding my hand with no judgment in his sad, blue eyes. Eyes the same color as mine.

I realized then what he meant before.

"You have river blue eyes, t–." My sob choked off the last word.

I'm not sure why I said it, but his expression shifted. It was subtle. A feathering in his jaw, a passing expression of some emotion I barely had time to register, much less understand, before it was gone.

"The baby's father, perhaps." He said, "I could call -"

"It's just...me," I said, barely above a whisper.

No one to call.

No one coming.

Just me.

And now...us

4

MOIRA

I FELL APART, THEN.

I'm not sure how many minutes passed as I sobbed at the news that I was pregnant. Minutes where I clung to the hand of a stranger who was the only other soul sharing this private and intimate knowledge with me.

I fell, and I fell, and I fell.

I don't know why Chase never moved. He sat next to me, held my hand, and murmured soothing, low words I barely registered as my world broke. I was so grateful for his warmth as I cried until I was empty of tears and my body burned from the exertion of it all.

Then came the shame.

Chase tried to make small talk while I gathered my slivers of dignity, but he wouldn't leave. He seemed almost conflicted about it until I claimed exhaustion, which seemed to convince him to go home.

I said goodbye to him, knowing I'd never see that kind man again, then took stock of my situation.

I had barely been in my place for a month. The job I'd moved out here for turned out to be a total bust, and though I was careful with my spending, I was already draining my savings as I searched for work. I had renters' Insurance, but how would I contact them without a phone? I needed my laptop, which had been on the kitchen table. It was almost certainly toast. While I hadn't had a chance to get details on the fire and the amount of damage, it was clear from the size of it that I'd likely lost everything.

Stupid girl. The thought echoed in my mind. Stupid, lovesick girl, hoping for a fairytale from a man who thought of her as nothing more than a plaything, and now where are you?

I didn't have any family, and being new in town with no job, I hadn't made a single friend. Where would I live with no discernible income? Even reputable hotels required proof of active credit cards for long-term stays, and my cards were most definitely melted to oblivion. Perhaps a budget motel that didn't need a credit card would suffice while I waited for Insurance to start replacing things.

I allowed myself to wallow for exactly one more minute, random monitor beeps marking the time, as I contemplated the utter mess I was in. A mess I'd made for myself that I needed to now clean up for myself...and my baby.

I raised my chin defiantly and squared my shoulders.

"You got yourself *into* this situation, Moira. You can get yourself *out* of it."

I paged the nurse and asked for a notepad and pen. When she brought it to me, I asked if she could pull up the number to my insurance agency from her cell. As I waited, I began making a list.

- Call Insurance and start the Claims Process.

- Find a hotel.

- Replace Essentials.

- Get a new phone/laptop.

- Secure Job.

- BABY...

Baby...dot...dot...dot. I wrote it in big, bold letters, and each dot I stabbed sounded in my head like a gong.

I hadn't realized I was pregnant, but now, thinking back, I wondered. I was exhausted and didn't have much of an appetite, but I assumed it was due to the emotional stress of everything, with the job falling through and the break-up. Even my history of occasionally irregular periods had me second-guessing. Still, as I now sat staring at those four tiny letters, I realized how wildly foolish I'd been.

What did this mean? What would I do? How would I possibly raise a baby when I was homeless, unemployed, and alone?

My heart ached to think of a baby coming into the world in such dire circumstances, and I instantly felt a pang of understanding and sorrow for the young mother who had once given me away. I never knew her name, only that she was young and lived in a homeless shelter and opted to give me away for a better chance at life. I'd never harbored resentment towards her, but I now felt a sense of shared burden.

Was I her now?

The intrusive thought sank in as reality weighed down on me. My short list suddenly held so much more importance in the wake of this news.

I was pregnant...and alone... and homeless.

Despite a lifetime of fighting to be self-sufficient, I was in the exact place as the stranger who'd made me, and if my life could perpetuate this cycle despite all my efforts, then how weak was I

I had many things to decide on and almost no time, as I was already so far along, perhaps as much as eight weeks. The whole world felt like it had shifted on its axis. Yesterday, I was living my life, starting over, in a new territory. Today, I was in charge of making decisions for another person's life while watching my tenuous grasp on my own come unraveled. My thoughts swam around like this for the better part of an hour before an older OB doctor came in with a resident student at his side. His questions were blessedly brief before he quickly got to the information I longed for.

"Your hCG levels look good, and if your dates are accurate, you are likely 10 weeks along." His questioning tone had me blushing at my sad lack of bodily awareness. "My concern is with the fire..." He let his words trail off as the student nervously shifted next to him.

What he wasn't became crystal clear. I was still early in my pregnancy and now had endured the strain of being pulled from a burning building. Maybe he was sparing me by not stating what I knew to be true, and the sting of that delicate consideration of my indelicate calamity hurt more than I could bear.

He thought I loved this baby when the truth was, I had barely come to grips with the idea that I had a little passenger on board.

Was I upset about the risk of losing a baby when I'd barely recognized I had one?

And by that logic, if I wasn't upset about losing this baby, did I deserve to be its mother? It's...his....her?

Stupid, stupid, girl.

"Will I lose the baby because of the fire?" The doctor looked at me with a soft smile, unruffled by my blunt question, before leaning one hip on the end of my bed and gently patting my foot.

"Ms. Vanderbilt, you are built of tougher stuff than this. I suspect you and your baby can endure just about anything. Since you are neither bleeding nor experiencing any cramps, we have no reason to believe you are at risk of miscarrying at this time." His smile crinkled the corners of his eyes, giving him a soft, grandfatherly quality. "For now, I suggest good rest, good food, and plenty of hydration," he nodded at the resident with him, "and let's see if the sonogram machine is fixed and get her on schedule for some measurements, shall we?" He turned back to me, "small town problems. One machine in the building, and it's on the fritz." He turned back to the resident. "Pull an AFB, progesterone, and Estradiol to help narrow down calculations, and let's run a full thyroid, iron, and vitamin panel to make sure mama is healthy too." The resident nodded, and the doctor looked at me with genuine kindness in his eyes. "Let's see what these labs look like, and we can go from there. Until then, good food, good rest, and hydration." He gave my foot another pat and left.

Looking down at my belly, I whispered the single biggest word in all his instructions.

"Mama."

Gently, I rested my hand on my stomach and took in a heaving gulp of air as the tears began. I wasn't just some stupid girl who had fallen for the wrong man. I wasn't just some silly plaything with no brain in her head. I wasn't helpless, and...I wasn't alone.

I would never be my mother, but I was now and forever A mother.

Right now, at this moment, no matter what else happens in the future, I was unequivocally, and forever, someone's mother. Some tiny, beautiful soul was woven into me. I would never be alone again. All the doubts and self-pity fell away in that single beautiful thought. I had a baby, and we were gonna get through this together.

I tore off the first page, crumpled it, tossed it toward the trash can, and started a new list.

'Plan for Baby and Me'

1. Expedite Insurance Claims Process.

2. Secure a Job with Benefits and a Maternity Leave Policy.

3. Find OB.

I redrew the picture of my life. The way I planned it, the way it was, the way I wanted it to be.

From here on out, it was no longer just me.

From now on, everything would be us–me and my baby.

WILDER BRO'S GROUP CHAT

-1-

ME: I need to bump spaghetti night.

TJ: Is it your shoulder?

Samoa: It's his dick.

ME: Don't be an asshole, Sam.

Samoa: I heard you didn't leave the hospital for 24 hours.

TJ: But it's not your shoulder?

ME: I'm fine. The woman I pulled from the fire needs some help.

Samoa: From your dick?

ME: Jesus Christ, Sam!

TJ: You stayed with the woman all night?

Samoa: Finally! Boyscout grows a pair.

ME: We're skipping over Sam still tapping the nurses if he knows when I left?

TJ: Sam is a man-whore. Old News.

Samoa: Don't hate the player.

TJ: Tell me about the girl.

Samoa: pretty, blonde...fiery hot ;-)

ME: You're an asshole, she was scared. You saw her in the ambulance.

Samoa: Yeah, man. I get it. It's hard to pull out sometimes...

ME: Stop.

TJ: Stop.

Samoa: WITH YOUR DICK!

TJ: You walked into that one.

ME: Fuuuuuccckkkk

TJ: Alright. Dinner in a few days. Check-in with me before then. Make sure Sam sees that shoulder again.

Samoa: Yes, Grandpa.

ME: and you walked into that.

TJ: Really? Grandpa again? You're better than this.

ME: He's really not.

Samoa: You need to live a little, TJ. Boy scout here is pulling more tail out of burning buildings than you've seen in the better part of a decade.

TJ: We don't all think like you, Sam.

Samoa: With your Dick?

ME: JESUS!

TJ: Dammit Sam!

5

CHASE

I BARELY SLEPT AFTER I left the hospital, replaying everything in my head on a loop of doubt and second-guessing, and it bothered me more than it should have.

I'd never gotten so attached to someone I'd helped before, and it made no sense. But something about the desperate way she clung to me hit me deep. I tried to ignore it—chalk it up to adrenaline and that one gut-punch word: orphan.

But it was more.

No one had ever expressed selfless concern for me beyond my Nonna and brothers. And since Nonna had been gone for several years, I had grown wholly unaccustomed to the gentler side of compassion.

But she did...she worried about me in that fire.

I'd split that night equally between nodding off in the uncomfortable armchair and replacing the oxygen tube Moira squirmed off in her sleep. Twice, I considered how ridiculous I was being and even rose to leave in the hopes of saving face. But then she'd move or fidget with the oxygen again, and I couldn't go. So, I watched over her, making small talk with the nurses and, in between catnaps, I studied her face.

The nurses had done a solid job of cleaning her up. Her hair was freshly cleaned and splayed across her pillow in waves of pale-yellow gold. Her nose, once soot-framed, was clean and perfectly straight with tiny, sand-colored freckles across the bridge. The slight curve above her top lip only served to highlight her symmetry. I catalogued her features, including the tiny moon-shaped scar on the back of her thumb. Boredom found me wondering what caused it. Her body was covered by the sheet, but I imagined it to be small and soft with rounded hips. I imagined more than I should've. Everything about her seemed fragile–Not breakable but precious. Then she opened her eyes, and my stomach dropped to see that her eyes were a perfect, dusty, river-blue.

Like mine.

I was lucky to grow up in Nonna's house with my brothers. But being an orphan means that somewhere, quietly, you always wonder where you come from. In those early years, I'd sometimes catch myself wishing I shared something visible with my brothers—some tiny thread that made me feel like I belonged. We were all different in skin tone, build, everything. Troy had dark brown skin and warm, soulful eyes like Nonna. Sam was lighter, with green eyes and a soft jawline. And me? I was pale, lanky, and weirdly angular for years—scrawny until testosterone kicked in and gave me this square jaw and cleft chin that didn't match anyone else.

Nonna used to say my eyes reminded her of the deep river eddies near her childhood home in southern Colorado. She said they carried stories—mine, hers, maybe someone lost between. I never saw anything special in them.

But when Moira looked up at me, blinking back the hospital lights, and her eyes—that exact same river blue—met mine, it stopped me cold. It wasn't about family. It wasn't about resemblance. It was something else. Like I'd been looking for a place to land and found it staring back at me.

I told myself it was just nostalgia—that it was Nonna's old stories tugging at my gut. Not the way Moira's brows pulled together when she frowned, or the flicker of worry in her voice when she asked if I was okay.

And then my brothers came in hot, razzing me for spending the whole night at her bedside.

Moving dinner was a mistake.

We had a weekly dinner tradition since Nonna passed away three years ago. Not once had any of us missed one. If we were broke, we kept it small. If one of us was sick, the other two moved it to their place and drove them bat-shit crazy with cough medicine and soup. If one of us were too busy at work, we'd grab a pizza and join them, but we never, ever skipped. My asking to move it was understandably huge. If I were being honest, I surprised myself even considering it.

But the fire destroyed everything this poor woman owned.

She didn't even have someone to call to sit with her.

How could I leave her?

I was already holding one of her hands from being sick, so it was perfectly natural to hold her when the doctor let it slip that she was pregnant. Despite her momentary silence, I clocked every fleeting expression that drifted across her face. The way her eyebrows rose and then scrunched together, the way her jaw dropped, and the way she slowly gazed down at her belly.

I had a front-row seat to her unraveling, and it felt like I was intruding.

Then the crying began, and I couldn't leave her. Each tear felt like a ten-ton boulder in my chest and my body wrapped around her, folding her into me as if we'd been together our whole lives. Her sobs wrecked me, and, in my panic, to give her comfort, my Nonna's memory floated to the surface. Specifically, the words she said during my first night in her care when I was a scared and lonely little boy adjusting to my 3rd foster home.

'Let the tears come. They will heal you. But you are stronger than this, and you are now and forever never alone. I'm here. I've got you now. I'll take good care of you forever.'

I don't know if my words registered as I whispered them into the top of her head. She cried so hard. I almost didn't realize what I was saying until it was out, but there was no unringing that bell. I'd just promised a complete stranger I'd take care of her, but I couldn't bring myself to regret it as the need to protect her flooded my better senses.

In the end, I gave her the space she asked for, but I couldn't get her out of my mind. Not as I left her room or made my way home. Part of me, and not a small part, wanted to run back in there and park my ass in that damn uncomfortable chair and stay until she was released from the hospital with a clean bill of health.

Then what, idiot? Stalk her home, too? What home? She has no home.

My brain was in knots of want and need and confusion as I showered, took a nap, and then texted my brothers the can-of-worms declaration I knew I would pay for later.

I didn't care.

Glancing down at my phone, I noted it was about dinnertime at the hospital and grabbed my helmet. Surely Moira would enjoy a non-hospital meal.

I picked up a pizza from my favorite shop in town, only to give the teenage boy outside a chuckle at my expense when I tossed him a whole pie after realizing it was too big to carry on my motorcycle. I considered different food options as I approached the hospital, but my mind became stuck in a cycle of indecision. Does she have food allergies? Can she eat takeout if she's pregnant? Does the baby need vegetables or meat? What do babies need at all...like....ever? By the time I walked into the diner across the street from the ER, I was in a flop-sweat when the hostess approached me.

"Can I help you?"

"I need a few meals to go," I scanned the diner, eyeing different plates of food and wondering what would be easiest.

"Great. What can I get for you?" She handed me a menu and whipped out a notepad.

I started to answer, but couldn't seem to make a decision, still drowning in all the things I didn't know about this woman, her child, and their respective needs.

"Sir?" she asked again, no doubt noting the thousand-yard stare I was sporting.

"I'm uh.... taking food to a woman in the hospital, but I don't know what she likes."

"Hmm..." She nodded as her pen tapped the notepad. It might as well have been a ticking bomb for all the anxiety it delivered.

"I just met her, and she's pregnant." Suddenly, worried about over-sharing, I tried to back up. "It's not mine! I mean, it's *obviously* not mine; I *just* met her." I kept talking, words pouring out like a giant, helpless idiot. "But she's alone, and I wanted to make sure she eats well," my brain screamed, stop, knowing full well I was seconds away from unloading my entire childhood history to this stranger to justify my utter panic at ordering food. Still, I just kept talking—like a total dick.

"The hospital has food, but I hear it's not good. She needs something better, but I'm not sure what she likes and... "

I stopped rambling when I noted the smile on the hostess's face. Embarrassment rushed up the back of my neck.

I debated the merits of just running out of the building and using the waiting room vending machine instead.

"If I may suggest?" She slipped the menu from my hand and returned it to the stand.

"God, yes." I huffed.

"My stomach was a little fickle when I was pregnant with my son. Some days, I could barely eat anything, and other days, I was ravenous. Since your connection with this woman is..." She cocked up an eyebrow at me, "New?"

"Yes!" I shouted. "New." God, I was such an idiot.

"I recommend you buy two meals, one heavy, the other light." She gave a nod and a wink before adding, "Let her nose decide which she likes best."

"Her nose?"

"Trust me." She laughed, scribbling on her notepad. "Her nose."

I left there with a grilled chicken Caesar salad, dressing on the side, and a bacon double cheeseburger, fully loaded, along with fries and onion rings. I tossed in a few bottles of water and a side of bread, hoping for the best, as I strolled back to the hospital.

As I neared the elevators, the gift shop window caught my eye. It was filled with colorful items I'd never paid any attention to before. Still, suddenly, envisioning Moira's room, I wondered: Who would bring her flowers, balloons, or cards?

Would anyone congratulate her on the baby?

Not entirely sure what I was doing, I found myself snagging a small pink and blue stuffed elephant, a little basket of white roses with pink and blue ribbons, and a massive set of balloons. The stares I drew as I walked down the hall to her room had me second-guessing all my life choices–No doubt my brothers would find out courtesy of the small-town gossip mill.

But I blew past everyone and walked into her room all the same.

6

CHASE

W HEN I LEFT, MOIRA was exhausted, tear-streaked, and more than a little shell-shocked. I was mentally prepared to find her lying in bed, oxygen on her face, asleep perhaps. I was not prepared to see her sitting up, bright-eyed, and laughing with an elderly doctor.

"Knock knock." I paused at the open door, unsure if I was intruding.

Moira turned and looked at me with a broad smile that lit up her face like never before–it took my breath away. Her eyes were no longer bloodshot but sparkling. Her hair was piled on her head with little wavy strands framing pink, healthy cheeks, and her laugh...God, I could listen to it all day, even if I was still a little scratchy from the smoke. It was infectious, and I couldn't help but smile in return.

"Chase!" Her hands clapped as she turned to the doctor at her side. "This is the fireman I told you about."

"Hale, the conquering hero!" The doctor crossed to me, reaching out a hand to shake mine. "Good job there, Lieutenant?"

"Wilder, sir." I set the flowers and elephant down next to my helmet and returned his offer for a handshake. "Just doing my job."

"Job indeed." He gave a quick glance at the food and gifts. "I'm Dr. Richard Burner, Obstetrics. I was checking in on Ms. Vanderbilt."

"He's agreed to take me on as a patient!" Moira was beaming, and everything inside me relaxed at the sight of it.

She should smile like that every day.

"Well, I could hardly say no to a smile like that, now could I." The doctor gave her a pat on her foot. "Hopefully, we can get that sonogram machine here soon, but I will check on you once more before you leave. Remember my instructions." He lifted a finger expectantly.

"Good food, good rest, and hydrate." She recited, bobbing her head and offering a salute.

"Such a good mother already. And clearly in good hands with meals delivered by men built as big as this one." The doctor nodded up at me. "You're a damned house." I tried to laugh, ignoring the heat creeping up my neck. I was never comfortable with people noticing my size first, or the misconceptions that came with it, so I was relieved when he pulled the door closed behind him.

Turning to look at Moira, however, I lost all capacity for thought as I shuffled around the room, moving my helmet, the flowers, and the elephant closer to her bed. I ran my hands up and down the back of my neck, considering all the ways I could stick my foot in my mouth. I know you told me to leave, but I decided you needed food...and gifts...and please don't run away screaming even though your new favorite doctor just called me a fucking house.

"Hey there." Moira's voice rescued me from my awkward silence.

"Hey," I mumbled back, lifting the bag of food. "I thought you might be hungry, so I brought dinner." I rolled the tray table next to her and set the bags on top. "I got a few options since I wasn't sure how your stomach was feeling." I opened the first bag and pulled out the salad and bread, pausing for her reaction.

"This is very kind."

She smiled, but it didn't quite reach her eyes, and I was not okay with half smiles now that I had seen how her big, full smile glowed. I opened the second bag, watching as Moira closed her eyes and took a big, long drag of the savory aroma of bacon and cheese.

"PLEASE say whatever is in that bag we can share!" Her eyes opened, laser-focused on the greasy cheeseburger I pulled from the bag.

"Actually...I got this for you," I slid the burger to her side and pulled out the sides. "But I might steal an onion ring."

"DEAL!" Moira clapped her hands like a kid at Christmas, digging in before I finished unpacking the fries.

Watching the woman eat was fascinating. At first, it was the utter glee in her eyes. After the first few bites, however, it was the moan that had me shifting in my seat. Then there was the little wiggling dance she did after combining an onion ring with the burger for what she called 'the perfect bite'. That clinched it – she was adorable.

As we ate, we chatted about easy things, and I was mesmerized by her conversation. To hear her speak free of panic and fear was soothing. As if she uncoiled the knot inside of me, I hardly realized I had.

"What is that look?" She gave a slight smirk, her brows pinched in concentration.

"Look?"

"You have a look." She swirled a finger at me between swigs of water. "A sorta half-smile that hides your dimples. What are you thinking with that look, Fireman Wilder?"

"I, uh..." Think you're adorable. I love it when you laugh. I'm not sure what I'm doing here. I wanna feed you more burgers. I think I might be crazy. "Don't think I've seen anyone enjoy a meal so much before. That's all." I gulped my water to hide the smile on my face.

"Oh...yeah." She shrugged, dragging the last fry through the ketchup. "I hadn't been able to eat much the last few days before the fire and then..well..you saw what I was like last night." She gazed downward, eyes flickering briefly in hesitation before seeming to shake off. "They gave me the good meds in my IV about an hour before you got here with the cheeseburger of happiness, and my stomach was like, 'hell yes!'"

"Cheeseburger of happiness?" I couldn't help but laugh as she tossed the last fry in her mouth with a defiant chomp.

"There are those dimples." She smiled softly. "You should do that more, ya know." She suddenly looked at her tray, full of empty wrappers and containers, and gasped, her hand over her mouth. "Oh God! We were gonna share the onion rings. I ate the whole thing! I'm so sorry."

"Are you kidding? I was only gonna *eat* them. You celebrated that meal like a returning war hero. Those rings lived their *best* life with you." Moira burst into a big belly laugh, head tossed back in a carefree moment that had her eyes nearly squeezed shut from the brightness of her smile. My chest thumped with that familiar tightness again, and all I wanted to do was push forward, hoping, praying, she'd laugh one more time. "I wouldn't dare miss that little wiggle dance you do." She laughed again—the infectious sound rippling over me until she leaned back with a sigh of contentment.

"Thank you for that, too, by the way." She gestured to the elephant and flowers.

"It's nothing," I started to clean up the trash in the hopes of hiding my embarrassment.

"You've done so much...too much." She glanced down at her hands... that damn shadow clouding her eyes again. "I don't know how I can repay you."

I hated how she looked down at her hands, fidgeting and unsure.

"No one should have to be in a hospital room without flowers and gifts, right?" I said, willing my voice to sound as nonchalant as possible in the hopes it would take those shadows away so she could laugh again.

Then came more silence, and the misunderstood teenager in me reared his scrawny head, wondering what we could talk about or if I should leave now. Glancing down, I recognized a stack of blank forms hidden under the food bags and smiled at the new conversational course.

"I see fire administration came by with the Victim Assistance Statement."

"Ugh. Yes." She ran her hands over her face before shoving the tray away. "I don't wanna do them."

"Paperwork is indeed the worst...but they're kind of important." I organized the forms, tapping their edges to make a tidy stack. "They help expedite your insurance claims if you have a full and detailed accounting of what happened." Moira bit her lip; those eyebrows scrunched above a grimace that was new...and confounding. "If you want, I could help get them started. I mean...I *was* there." I let out a small laugh, hoping to bring her around, but Moira just looked at me, then the forms, then let out a big sigh.

"I just... don't see why I need to. It was just a silly apartment fire, right? One of the nurses told me that no one was badly injured or even mildly hurt other than me...and I'm okay." Her face twisted in a sort of frantic excitement as she continued. "I didn't have a very big policy anyway, so it can't slow things down much, right? Besides, I can clean up my own mess."

"Well, yeah." I ran a free hand across the back of my head, wondering why she was so uncomfortable with paperwork. "I could just fill in the easy stuff if it'll help. Then you can fill in the details before signing your name and - "

"NO!" Moira snatched the papers from my hand. "No names!" Out of the corner of my eye, the flickering of her heart rate monitor showed quickening spikes as she swiftly shuffled the papers back into a tidy pile. I had spooked her. "I'll try later, maybe, but I just..." Tears welled in her eyes, and I was moving without, resting on the edge of her bed and covering her shaking hands with my own.

"Moira." She stared at our hands but didn't speak. "I'm not pushing you...or rushing you." I couldn't figure out what I had said or done to upset her, but her eyes took on a distant look as if lost in memory or thought. "I'm sure you are overwhelmed...and for good reason. Forget the paperwork for now. I'm sorry if I was pressuring you."

"No." She sniffed at the tear that trailed down her nose. "I'm sorry. It's not you...I just can't..." She hesitated, her face scowling in concentration as if wrestling with something, before she shook her head. "I just don't want my name in the papers or news. Ya know?" She wiped away her tears and squared her shoulders, finally looking me in the eyes. "It's a small town. Finding work here will be much harder if I remind people of this."

"Oh." Relief washed over me at something I could fix. "These forms aren't released publicly...to anyone."

"Really?" Her eyes were desperate, pleading even. "They stay...private?" I couldn't have been more thrilled than I was at that moment to put her mind at ease.

"Absolutely! These stay *strictly* in the fire department. They only leave our hands if a criminal investigation is opened, and then they have to go up the chain of command to the police, but that's it." Her face went pale, and her mouth dropped.

Shit. Undo it, undo it, you idiot!

"But even then, we'd never release your details to the press or public in any way. Your information is limited to city personnel only."

I wondered what I had said that had her in a panic. For that matter, I wondered what I said that made her feel relieved, and now apparently had her frozen again. The back and forth of it all was so confusing, and I had never wished more to have Sam's smooth moves with the ladies. I gave her hand a little squeeze, silently willing her to smile again.

"Hey, Fancy Pants, come back."

7

MOIRA

THE IDEA THAT MY name would be attached to this fire sent me into a tailspin of self-loathing. I'd already spent the better part of a month climbing out of the pit of humiliation I'd dug for myself at the realization I truly knew next to nothing about Dean, his full job included. I'd been such a trusting fool. But if my name came across Dean's desk, as a city employee possibly privy to the files, he would no doubt come sniffing around to gloat and then find out about the baby.

Cold fear slithered across my skin to think of Dean wanting a piece of my baby's life after summarily discarding mine.

My embarrassment worsened against the kindness of this ginormous hero of a man who had come with food and gifts, expecting nothing in return. How could I explain that I wasn't even sure what branch of city services my baby-daddy worked in? More than that, how could I begin to explain that my name on that paperwork could trigger a landslide of potential events I was not capable of handling?

I frantically tried to rein in the rush of emotions crawling up my throat. I couldn't fall apart, not again, not on this man. My lungs tightened as I willed my breathing to steady despite my racing heart. Seconds pounded by, and the dizzying lift of hyperventilation threatened to make this show a double feature as I closed my eyes and took slow, deep breaths. Then I heard Chase's voice in my ears—warm hands sending waves of relaxation up my arms.

"Come back."

Those two simple words, in his low timbre, were enough to claw my way out of the void I was spiraling into. The gentle squeeze of his hands grounded me to the room, to me, and slowly, my heartbeat steadied as I looked into his big, blue, pleading eyes. I allowed myself to rest in the comfort of this handsome stranger who risked everything for me. A handsome stranger who came back to me a second time and sat patiently as I panicked. Just one moment of imagining what my life might have been if I had found a fraction of this support growing up...before...or since.

Come on, Moira. Letting a man put us together is what put us here.

"Whew. I'm sorry." I forced a half-hearted laugh out, fanning my face to regain composure and put the slightest bit of space between us. I prayed he wouldn't notice my shaking hands or the blush my daydream had brought on. "Must be the exhaustion and hormones making me so emotional."

"Good news!" The nurse interrupted our moment, sending Chase back into his seat as she happily checked the vitals on my machines. "I just got the orders that say if you continue to improve overnight, you'll be checked out of here tomorrow."

"Really?"

"Yep. Your headaches subsiding was a good sign. And I can clearly report you're eating and drinking well now." She gestured to the trash can of empty food containers.

"I figured she might stomach something *not* prepared in the hospital." Chase offered with a smile.

"Good call." The nurse gave him a friendly elbow nudge. "Dr. Burner wants one more set of labs, but as long as they are good through the morning, you should be free to head home."

Home. Where was that now?

"Is your throat still bothering you? Eyes stinging?" the nurse continued.

"No, actually. My eyes feel great." I gave a small test swallow to confirm and added. "My throat feels better, too, though it's still a little scratchy sounding."

"That will resolve in another day or so." She noted a few things on her tablet and handed me some Tylenol. "And your hand?"

"Still throbs if I try to use it," I answered, tugging at the edge of the bandage to try and peek at the blisters. "I'm hoping that will get better soon?"

"Each day should improve, but it'll be a nuisance for a week or so." She tilted her head with a sad smile when I grimaced at the idea of a two-week healing period. "I know it feels like forever, but it will fly by." She gave my arm a little pat and turned to leave.

"This is great," Chase leaned forward, elbows to knees. "So..." He drew out the word until I looked over and saw the questioning expression on his face. "Why does your face not seem happy to be free of terrible food and interrupted sleep?"

"I'm fine." I deflected with a smile. The last thing I needed was the pity of a man determined to play hero, to a woman facing eviction in 24 hours from the only place she knows she has a bed to sleep in. "This is great."

"Lemme guess." He gave that half smirk that barely showed his dimples. "Afraid you won't find a place to get new fancy pants?"

"Ha. Ha." I chuckled dryly, noting the way he stared me down, waiting for me to give a better answer. I needed to work on my poker face. "It's just...I called the insurance company and started a claim using the hospital's phone. But I don't have a new cell phone yet, and I have no clue what hotel to check into without my ID or credit cards, which all need to be replaced." His face went solemn, and a muscle twitched in his jaw. I couldn't bear a charity handout, so I smiled widely and added, "I'll be fine, though. It's just a matter of figuring out the logistics. But I'll get it handled."

"Maybe I can help?" And here came the pity I so hoped to avoid.

"No, really. I meant what I said earlier. You've done *so* much for me already." I tried to sound optimistic, to put a cheery spin on a ridiculously complicated situation even as I squared my shoulders in resignation. "I'm a big girl. I can clean up my own mess."

"Moira," Chase whispered my name, his eyes so soft they looked like he was breaking inside, and it nearly broke me. "Losing your stuff in a fire isn't some mess you made that needs cleaning. I don't mind helping. I could grab you a new phone, or help line up a hotel so it's waiting for you."

His sincerity stripped away my false bravado–being rescued sounded amazing. His face was so sweet, so open. And part of me wanted him to do everything he suggested and more. Another part of me wanted him to put his big, warm hands around mine and tell me how he would swoop in and save the day.

Stupid, foolish girl. Don't you ever learn?

"You are too kind.... but I'm working on a plan even as we speak." I focused on the notepad and paper lying beside me on the bed. "I've made a checklist of things to do and have managed to handle a lot of it using the hospital phone." I lifted the list and waved it triumphantly in the air. "I bet by tomorrow I'll be ready to reboot my life."

I hoped to show off courage I didn't have. I couldn't... wouldn't...be someone's pity project. I could save my damn self. For me and for my baby, I could do this.

"At least let me give you a lift to your hotel, then?" Chase's sheepish grin, with the hint of those dimples, almost had me nodding in agreement, but I held firm.

"I'm good. Besides, I can't imagine me and the elephant would fit well on the back of whatever crotch rocket you rolled in on." I teased, tipping my chin at the helmet perched in the corner.

"I'll have you know I ride the only respectable thing on two wheels, a Harley."

"You mean the giant muscled fireman rides a giant muscled motorcycle?" I gaped in mock surprise. "Shocking."

He laughed as he pulled his phone out to show off a huge black motorcycle. Clearly, it was his pride and joy with the number of photos he had, but the lack of women in the pictures made me happier than I had a right to be. A thought I almost got lost in until his phone rang, pulling us from his photo album.

"It's my brother, Troy. I'll just be a minute." He stepped out, and I perused my checklist.

I started the renter's claim process, but still wrestled with the Fire Victims Assistance paperwork. Despite my fears, the insurance claim was the lynchpin to replacing my documents and, thus, gaining access to my money. I needed that claim done, and the form could expedite it, but it could also bring Dean around. Thinking of him felt gross, so I pushed him away and moved down my list.

Dr. Burner was a trusted OB, and I felt good checking that box off my list—other items were still unfinished. Before the fire, I landed a final interview with the city library for a part-time position. It barely paid the bills while I worked on side contracts, but it wasn't nearly enough for an overnight reboot with a baby. Not that I could do anything about it until I replaced my cell phone and laptop, both of which were crucial to my freelance work and both unavailable from this room. The familiar cycle of frustration tugged at my mood, and I tossed the pen and list to the tray with a huff.

I was antsy, and my body ached from lying in bed all day. I stood slowly and stretched my legs for a little walk around the room. I dragged my IV pole to the window to admire my first official baby gift. I took in the little features of the blue and pink plush as I imagined my baby and I playing on a blanket. I imagined tucking my baby into bed at night with their little elephant watching over them. I imagined my baby with wispy blonde curls and big blue eyes, like mine.

River Blue. Chase has those eyes, too.

My imagination had entirely too much fun indulging in that line of thought.

Shaking my thoughts free, I turned to the basket of flowers—an abundance of baby's breath and tiny white roses. My stomach flipped as a memory tugged me back to Oregon and Dean's flowers. My heart sank at the intrusion of Chase's gift, turned ugly by the man who called me his princess while lying through his teeth. He abandoned me, reminding me of just how alone I was in this world.

"Alone except for you," I breathed, caressing my abdomen. "I'm never going to be alone again, am I, baby?"

Chase reentered, closing the distance in three easy strides and towering a full head taller than me.

"I figured you needed it." He smiled and flicked the elephant's ears, his dimples on display. "And it's pink and blue, so if you have a boy or a girl, it still works."

"It's adorable." I stroked the elephant's trunk. "I'm glad I have this to start my reboot."

"You mentioned that word before...reboot."

"I moved around a lot as a kid, and sometimes bringing my stuff with me wasn't an option."

"Foster kid?" He never flinched as he gazed down at me.

"Yeah... how'd you know?"

"I was in the system, too, before I got adopted. I moved once or twice that I remember. But I knew other kids who moved even more."

His scrutinous gaze held no signs of pity, and I was grateful for that, even if it had me squirming.

"Well," I pulled away, strolling back to the bed. "I saw other kids fall apart every time they had to relocate, and I decided early on to look at those moves as a chance to reinvent myself. Like a reboot. I could start over in the new place with a new me–be whoever I needed to be."

"Focus on the road ahead, not the one behind."

"Exactly! And I guess it just sorta stuck with me into adulthood, such as it is." I shrugged a little with a sigh as I waved around the hospital room with a huff of laughter at how untenable my situation seemed. "Now that everything has *literally* gone up in smoke, I'm about to put those skills to the test. New clothes, new apartment, new everything, and fun new challenges like a lack of ID or cash!"

"Fancy Pants 2.0?" Chase smiled, and I couldn't resist smiling back, drawing on his boyish optimism to fill in the cracks where my confidence waned.

"Exactly...Fancy Pants 2.0."

8

MOIRA

"I NEVER KNEW WHO my birth parents were," Chase casually dropped. "Just that they ended up in jail, and that's how I ended up in the system."

He spoke so easily about his background, but his eyes gave a haunting look I was all too familiar with. We foster kids were always a little untethered in the world.

"You looked for them?"

"Not really. Nonna took me in when I was five. She gave me a great home and my brothers." Chase smiled at the mention of his family. "I was luckier than most."

Luckier than me.

"Were you all adopted?"

"Yeah." Chase leaned back in the chair like he had nowhere else to be. "She adopted Troy first...took him right from the hospital as a newborn. She closed her home for a few years until a social worker called and told her about me. She brought Troy with her, and he told her I had to come home with them. We were both five, and, in his eyes, that made us best friends."

"Aw. That's sweet."

"It took me a while to settle in, but after that, Troy and I were thick as thieves. Then Sam came along. He wasn't in the system like us. It was some long-distance friend or family arrangement. Nonna called Sam her cherry on top, and we gained another brother."

"You all seem pretty close," I remembered moments of the way Sam and Chase spoke in the ambulance. That, coupled with Chase's smile, made it an obvious statement.

"Troy and I made Sam's life hell for a while with endless pranks." The dimples were on full display, and I was mesmerized by them. "He might have been the same age as us, but he was smaller, and we never let him live it down."

"Wait," I began doing the math. "He was the same age...as you both?"

"Yep. We arrived at Nonna's in different ways, but our birthdates only differ by a few weeks."

"Oh...Wow!" I could hardly imagine having a home with siblings, much less siblings close enough to be glorified triplets.

"Troy and I deemed Sam the baby brother because he was the smallest of the pack." Chase leaned into his usual posture–elbows to knees in a full man spread. Those massive shoulders pull the seams of his shirt like they owed him money. "We sorta shoved him to the sidelines at first. Right up to the day he came out of school with a busted lip."

"Uh oh." I smiled, suspecting where the story was going.

"Some kid in his class decided they could tease him for being small, too. Sam's mouth got the better of him, and the bully nailed him right in the kisser." Chase threw a mock punch at his mouth. "We had the rule to meet by the monkey bars to walk home together, and when Troy and I saw Sam's face...." He shook his head, his hands lifted as if a bomb had gone off.

"Game over?"

"Oh yeah. Sam pointed him out. Troy pinned him down and bloodied his nose and I spit in his hair."

"Ew...gross!" I laughed.

"The kid had it coming. He was way bigger than Sam!" Chase's voice was almost melodic with happiness. "We told him he'd better never touch our brother again."

"Was your Nonna angry?"

"The school called her, and we were all lined up in the hallway outside the principal's office when he arrived." His eyes went distant as he dove into memory. "She looked at Sam's lip and then at Troy and me, both sporting scraped knuckles." Chase smiled in pride at his balled-up fist. "She talked with the principal and then walked us home in dead silence. We thought for sure we were dead meat as we did our homework and our chores. None of us dared to speak through dinner even... until she brought out a huge plate of cookies."

"Wait...Cookies?" I didn't bother hiding my smile as he nodded and continued.

"Chocolate chip for Troy and Snickerdoodle for me. She plopped a heaping pile of them on the table and said, 'In this family, we always protect one another. We defend one another. I'm very proud of you two for sticking up for Sam. That bully had it coming.'" Chase sighed, lost in the warmth of the memory.

"And after that, you were inseparable," I mumbled, almost to myself, promising my baby that if they were ever caught defending someone... I'd make them cookies too.

"Did you ever find your birth parents?" Chase voiced the question all foster kids ask each other at some point and I spit out my stock answer.

"Bio-mom was a homeless teen who bolted before filling out a birth certificate. I went straight from the hospital to the orphanage."

"Damn."

"Yeah...my name, as you so enjoyed, was assigned to me by a Scottish social worker who followed me around the South Oregon system through my early years before retiring when I was 5. After that, I had a new case worker every year, it seemed."

"No long-term placements?" His eyebrows pinched with the kind of look that made you feel read down to your DNA.

"My first placement ended when my fosters got pregnant with their own child and sent me back to the orphanage." I shrugged to affect a nonchalance I didn't feel in the hopes of bypassing the pity this story usually got me. "Then I had a few homes I don't remember much about. By the time I was 6, I was accustomed to staying packed for quick departures."

"No shit?" He asked, his face awash in an expression that looked about as deflated as I felt. I hated sharing my sordid foster journey and all it's pathetic gritty nuance.

"Once the cycle of moving started, the transition felt easier than staying put. One girl I met along the way taught me how not to see the moves as a negative...To take whatever the next stop is as a fresh start until I aged out to live on my own." I sighed, remembering that one friend who eventually disappeared with my favorite hoodie when she aged out a year before me. "It wasn't a *bad* lesson to learn, all in all."

"But you did that." Chase took on a surprised look of admiration. "You've made a life for yourself. Considering where you came from, that's sort of a miracle."

His kind words sent a bolt of shame through me.

I wasn't some miracle of self-reliance and grit.

I was the stupid girl who'd fallen head over heels for the first man who showed an ounce of attention. A stupid girl who upended her life with a whisper of a fairytale ending that I thought would make my whole wretched life seem like it had meaning.

I was a fraud.

"Thanks...I guess." I tucked a strand of hair behind my ear and mentally sifted through ways to change the subject.

I didn't want to unpack the entirety of my life story. Especially if it led to 'and what moved you here.' I just couldn't face that humiliation. Chase was so considerate but so inquisitive. There was no way he wouldn't ask me how I ended up in his town, and I knew I couldn't lie. Not in the face of his heroism and his kindness. I was never so relieved when the nurse came in to talk about discharge paperwork.

"I'd like to be here when she leaves," Chase stood, accepting the papers the nurse handed off as if he were family. I felt instantly irritated at feeling like I was being bypassed. "Do you know what time she'll be ready?"

"No!" I blurted, hoping to cut the answer short and regain some agency. "It's not necessary. I already have a ride worked out." Big fat liar felt worlds better than helpless fool. Still, Chase's face held the briefest hint of pleading, and I found myself softening. "I appreciate the offer, though."

"Well, either way, these things usually go slow." The oblivious nurse volunteered. "I'm guessing nothing will happen before lunchtime."

9

CHASE

WHEN TROY CALLED EARLIER, I told him how nervous Moira was about the paperwork, and he offered to find out if there was a reason to push her on it. I was grateful for the help, but made sure to end the call before he asked why I had spent another day at the hospital. He'd be right to ask—hell, I kept asking myself. What was I doing here again? 'Can't stay away' sounded more like a punchline than a plan, and even she seemed to be half-shoving me out the door. When my phone chirped, it came a voicemail and a short text.

> Troy: There's news.

Ever the efficient communicator, I took his text cue to step out and listen to the voicemail since Troy was never one for redundancy.

'I asked around, and sure enough, the fire was the final straw in a growing arson concern. Your team and mine have scheduled official meetings, but it seems your busy schedule lately might not be a coincidence.

There's more, but...see that the woman completes the Vic. Asst. forms.' I figured that would be the end of the message, but I heard his breathing hitch before he added. *'Be careful with her, Brother.'*

Troy was a man of few words by anyone's accounting, so his last line was weighty. Troy's love and concern for us leaned more towards mother-hen than it did fraternity hijinks. He never pried into our personal lives, but was always nearby. He was a lot like Nonna in that way. But 'be careful with her' was unexpected.

Was he worried about me being hurt or me hurting her? And for that matter, which of those options made sense of the mess I kept returning to? How would he not be worried about me, or her, when I hardly knew what I was doing? Hey guys, I pulled her from a fire and she begged me not to leave her and now, I can't leave her alone cause I'm addicted to her laugh and want her to steal my food forever. Fooooreverrrr.

Forever?

Shoving insecurity aside, I focused on the larger piece of his message. Arson hadn't been uttered in my town ever in my life. This...was huge. I started to text Troy back when Moira's voice cried out.

"No!"

I bolted, fearing I'd find her gasping for air or bleeding somehow. Instead, I saw her frantically righting an overturned water bottle gushing across her tray.

"Shit shit shit!"

"Dammit, woman." I heaved a sigh of relief. "You almost gave me a heart attack." I grabbed a wad of paper towels from the nearby sink and helped her clean the tray. "You *really* didn't wanna do these forms, did you?" I teased, noting how the water dripped off the corners as I lifted them. "There is no saving them now."

"I *swear*, it was an accident." She tried helping me, but only seemed to spread the mess.

"How are you making it worse?" I laughed.

"I'm sorry!" She leaned back on the bed, chuckling as I frantically tossed the forms in the trash and finished drying the water from the tray. "Guess now is as good a time as any for you to learn that I'm a klutz."

She tossed a wad of soaked towels into the trash can, missing by a mile, and sticking them to the wall. Her nose scrunched in a grimace, but her eyes danced as she laughed again.

"You keep smiling like that, and I'm pretty sure it'll never matter what you spill," I muttered as I trashed the giant spitball. In an instant, her smile dropped, her gaze too, down to her hands to fidget with her nails.

"Oh. I... I'm sorry." I crossed to her bedside, leaning on the edge again, hoping to bring back that peaceful smile. "I was just teasing." I rubbed the back of my neck, scrambling for something to say that didn't make me sound like an idiot. "You're gonna learn real quick—I suck at saying the right thing."

"No, no. It's not you." She reached her unburned hand out towards me. Such a small, simple gesture, but I couldn't help the thundering of my heart as I answered her silent request by reaching out my hand in answer. "You have been great, Chase. I'm just a little in my head." She seemed content to sit and hold my hand, though her eyes went a little distant as if lost in thought and I both hated and understood it. She'd been through a lot, and that was without knowing her fire might have been intentional.

My mind wrestled with that word from Troy's text. Arson. I remembered every second of entering her apartment, the way the fire engulfed her kitchen, but her bedroom door wouldn't open. That triggered a question I couldn't hold in.

"Hey. You mentioned you couldn't open your bedroom door when the fire started, and you had tried." Moira's eyes concentrated on me, but she was calm, so I pushed forward with as casual a tone as possible. "Was the door too hot to open, or was it locked?"

"It was warm, that's for sure, but I think it was locked."

"And you didn't notice the smoke before that?"

"I fell asleep with music playing on my phone. It wasn't until I turned the music off that I heard a cracking sound."

"No smoke alarm?"

"Maybe the fire melted it?" Moira shrugged quizzically. "I smelled the fire before I saw or felt it." Her nose scrunched again, a look of mild nausea on her face.

"The smell?" I asked, my attention heightened. "Was it like gasoline or burning plastic?" Both were common accelerants for electrical or household fires, though living in an apartment didn't bode well for having a gas can lying around.

"No, it was sour, or," Her nose wrinkled up with the memory. "Like rotten eggs...but stronger, it made me gag."

Shit. Sulfur.

"Was that when the smoke hit?" I kept my tone light, impersonating my best Sam to avoid overwhelming her despite the urgency growing inside of me. If the investigation was looking into arson, Sulfur would definitely narrow the field of possible accelerants and thus could lead to a probable suspect.

"The room was a little smoky, but when I went for my doorknob, it was locked. I tried banging into the door with my shoulder and hitting the knob. Then I ran to the window, but it wouldn't open either." The thousand-yard stare returned as she relayed the whole sequence of events. "I could see people running in the parking lot. I screamed for help and banged on the glass, but none of them heard me. I tried to open the window, but it wouldn't budge. I ran back to the door, but when I grabbed the knob," She lifted her bandaged hand and stared as she saw through the gauze to the burn. "I went to get my phone, but the smoke was so thick I started to gag, and my eyes were stinging. I tried the door again, but it was *so* hot. When I got back to the window and tried to smash it, I wasn't strong enough and no one could hear me...I couldn't see anything..."

Her eyes welled with tears, and I felt like an immediate asshole when I only then noticed the tremble in her hands and her bottom lip. I didn't want her to have a panic attack, and I hated that I'd pushed as hard as I had.

"Hey." I inched closer, placing my hand on top of hers as her fingers splayed across mine. "You did everything you could. And you *did* get out. That's the important thing. You're safe, and so is everyone else."

She remained quiet, taking a few deep breaths to calm herself, and I sat there staring like a mute idiot, torn between needing info about the fire and wanting to pull her into my arms. She let her head drift back to the bed, grimacing as if her head hurt, and I wanted to kick my own ass for making her relive everything. Guilt had me vowing to never push her so hard again.

"Do you need me to call the nurse?" I asked, channeling Sam's EMT voice again. "For your headache."

"No." She whispered. "It seems only to come back when I cry, which is delightful since I can't seem to stop doing that."

And I'm the asshole who made her cry this time. Never again.

"I, uh," I fumbled for some way to fill the void, afraid that the silence would highlight how supremely awkward I felt. I glanced at the bed next to her and saw her slightly damp notepad with a partially finished checklist. "You must be relieved to get out of here tomorrow. You've only got a few things left to check off."

"I mean, who wouldn't be happy to be out of the hospital?" she said, her smile yet not reaching her exhausted eyes as she grabbed the water-blotched checklist.

"I meant what I said about wanting to help you out, even if it's just to give you a ride." I gave her a half-smile while jotting down my number on a napkin and handed it over. "Call me if you need something before discharge or if something changes. I'm just 15 minutes away, and I am on leave from work, so... I'm so bored." I saw the polite decline on the edge of her mouth, her eyes pleading, and I couldn't stand it if she denied me again when the urge to take care of her was damn-near suffocating me. "You'd be doing me a favor just by asking honestly. I don't do well sitting around...and I promise not to bring the Harley."

Moira considered me momentarily, her eyes gazing back toward my injured shoulder.

"Does it still hurt?" She looked down at her hand then. "Mine throbs sometimes but mostly feels sort of tight and stinging." She wiggled her fingers. "They tell me I'll heal fast."

"Honestly," I let her subject change slide, not wanting to push her as I tipped my head towards my shoulder. "I can't count how many burns I've had."

"Occupational Hazard?"

"The itchy phase is the worst, but I have a special cream I use...that all of us use...at the station. Sorta of a trade secret. I could bring you some when I come get you tomorrow." Again, her blue eyes seemed to rake over me, considering how to answer. I did my best to keep my face neutral, not to push, despite every instinct in me wanting to be closer, to grab her hand again, to sit on the edge of the bed with her.

"Yeah. Okay." She said the words while stifling a small yawn, and I again felt terrible for keeping her up when she needed rest. Still, I couldn't ignore the little internal boost from her soft compliance that I could come tomorrow.

It was a win, a small win, but I held onto it for dear life.

"I'll go let you rest." I crossed to grab my helmet and moved the elephant and flowers a little closer to her. She didn't smile. That bugged the shit out of me. C'mon. Just one more smile. "I plan to be here by noon tomorrow. Harley-free." I added a scout salute at the last minute, which gifted me a sweet little laugh that reached all the way to her eyes.

That laugh? Oxygen. And I was already addicted.

10

CHASE

I PULLED MY BIKE into the engine bay and walked into the main living quarters of my firehouse. It was late enough that the crew was already done eating; everyone sat around watching the game or playing Xbox, except for the rookies cleaning up the dinner mess. I noted a half dozen areas in disarray in my few days off, but had to let it go as I angled towards the chief's office.

"Hey, Lieutenant." A recruit waved with his towel from the kitchen sink. "Aren't you on leave 'til that shoulder heals?"

"No shit, dude." Answered my main ladder guy, who looked up from the TV. "That window pull was squeaky tight. You know if the girl's okay?"

I pondered how to answer best without giving away that I'd spent every free moment by her side. God knows I'd catch 50 shades of hell. Luckily, my Chief's voice boomed from his office.

"Go the fuck home, Wilder, let someone else rescue a damsel once in a while."

"Sorry, guys. I shrugged and headed into the Chief's office. "Gotta be quicker on the draw next time."

Fire Battalion Chief Brandt Jacobs had been in my life since I was a kid and was about the closest thing to a father figure I'd ever had. He did an elementary school fire safety presentation at my school. I was the quiet kid who never raised my hand, but he noticed me. He pulled me into his presentation, letting me demonstrate the Stop, Drop, and Roll maneuver repeatedly until the whole room was applauding. Then he gave me a toy fire hat and a plastic badge that I got to wear all day, much to the awe of my classmates. When school was out that day, his rig was sitting out front, and my brothers and I got to hitch a ride home on the big truck.

In Little Boy Land, that made us celebrities. I wanted to be a fireman when I grew up.

Back then, he was just a rookie, but I called him Chief from day one—and the name stuck. He followed up with me and my family periodically, inspecting our home for fire safety and occasionally attending Little League games that his station supported. He even helped Nonna with car repairs and small tasks around the house, and once he got married, we all got to know his wife, Carol, who was a yoga instructor. As I grew, so did his mentorship. I spent my high school summers cleaning the station and working out on their gym equipment. I sometimes stayed there on weeknights to do homework, even, and the whole crew took me in as an honorary mascot. When I enlisted in the Marines, Chief and Carol were with Nonna to send me off, promising to hire me when I returned. With so much behind-the-scenes knowledge, everyone assumed I'd breeze through fire school. Instead, Chief rode me harder than anyone. He seemed to be the only person who saw my awkwardness for what it was — a deep desire to protect the people I loved. Protection I wasn't given before, Nonna...and protection I hardly knew how to channel, with muscles growing faster than brains.

"Protocol says you're off duty 'til a medic clears you, Wilder."

"I'm just swinging by on my way home," I said, clasping his forearm in mine. "Wanted to check in."

"I heard you did well at the review board. Sorry, I couldn't be there in person." He waved his hand in the air. "My family connection and all."

"Nah, it's fine." I shrugged him off. "I knew I was in the clear."

"We *all* knew that kid." He motioned to the chair across from his desk. "Nasty business, that was. 6 women video recorded without consent, maybe more. What a piece of shit."

"Anyone find out what his endgame was on that?" I grumbled, my skin crawling at the thought of how many women my former colleague was working over.

"Naw. Just a pervert with a temper and a kink for blackmailing women after he bedded 'em. I can't believe my niece didn't see him coming... she's so smart." Chief shook his head in disappointment. "But that's not why you're here...is it?"

"What's the news on the Branson Heights fire? Word is that an Arson investigation has been opened up."

"You and your damn brothers." Chief swigged his coffee. "If I didn't like you so much, I'd have your brother's badge for sharing interdepartmental news." He leaned back with a sigh, rubbing weathered hands across the bald expanse of his head. "I have been riding the rig longer than you've been alive, Wilder. I've never seen so many fires in such a short time."

"You mean the four we had before Branson?"

"More." Chief tossed a manila file folder across the desk at me. I opened it to seven fires, some in neighboring counties. "You think these are all the same guy? The arsonist." The word was bile in my throat.

"We don't think...we know. They all have the same propellant residue."

"Gunpowder," I said, wishing I were wrong.

"How'd you know?" Chief leaned onto his elbows with a withering stare and me in his sights. "I hadn't told the police that yet."

"It's why I'm here." I sighed. "I've been at the hospital with Moira."

"The vic from the 3rd floor?"

"She said she smelled sulfur, really strongly, and that it was the smell she noticed first, not the heat or even the smoke." I leaned my elbows on my knees, fighting to push back the memory of Moira cowering in a locked and burning room. "Since it hit her nose first, the point of origin had to be nearby or connected by ductwork?"

"What else does she say?" The chief's tone shifted – all business.

"Everything is sketchy. She didn't hear or see anyone in her place, but I'm pretty sure her kitchen was the origin by the way it was engulfed when I arrived."

"Actually... I've got a team working the site, but all evidence points to gunpowder in the electrical panel behind her kitchen wall." He took the file back from me. "She didn't hear anything?"

"She was sleeping... didn't notice anything until she got up and smelled sulfur...then she realized she was trapped." Trapped and terrified and still somehow capable of worrying about me. So fucking strong.

"Till you," the Chief stared at the file before him. "Ya did good, Wilder. It was a solid save. Even if you did run in half-cocked. The whole fucking team was scrambling to get a goddamn ladder up in time."

"I couldn't wait...you saw that roofline."

"Yeah. Yeah. I know. In my younger years, I'd have done the same." He lifted his coffee, grimacing at the bare bottom of it, and stood. "Walk with me. What else do you know?"

"Almost nothing. My shoulder sidelined me pretty fast, and Sam had me in his rig once my boots hit the ground. I was at the hospital all that night. Only went home long enough to shower before going back up there."

"You went back...to the hospital?" He pulled the collar of my shirt, peering down my back. "The guys told me the burn wasn't that bad."

"I'm fine," I shrugged off his hand. "I was—"

I hesitated, unsure what to tell the Chief about why I was at the hospital and trying to tamp down the flush of heat reddening my cheeks.

"Holy Shit, kid." Chief topped off his coffee with a smirk and walked back into his office. "It's the girl."

"It's nothing."

"Fuck me, it's nothing!" He chuckled with his wry smile. "I'd heard about some *big* dumbass biker walking into that woman's room with dinner and flowers, but I just KNEW it couldn't be *my* big dumbass biker." He placed his hand across his chest as he continued. "Not my stoic, workaholic, ever-diligent, buttoned-up Chase who'd never been seen so much as *speaking* to a woman, much less bringing bunnies and balloons." His eyes sparkled with delight as he added. "Wait 'til Carol gets a load of this."

"It was just one elephant, not a bunch of bunnies." My face instantly heated when the Chief's eyebrows shot up in gleeful joy. "It's not—Jesus, Chief. It's not like that."

"The hell it is." He gave me a full-faced grin, laughing til he ran out of air before he turned more serious. "She's gotta be a looker, but she's also involved in a case now, kiddo. She tell you anything else useful?"

"A few things that sounded off," I sat back in his office, glad to be away from the station's gossip mill.

"Alright." He pulled out a pen and opened the file folder. "Shoot."

"She never heard a smoke detector, but the complex has updated inspections on file."

"Mm-Hm." He kept scribbling, so I continued.

"And she said her bedroom door was locked from the outside. Not the inside. It was still locked when I got there. I had to bust it in." I leaned over, trying to read his notes. "And her window... it wouldn't open. I was gonna go by and see if it was painted shut?"

"Fuck you will." He eyed me over the rim of his glasses. "You steer clear and rest that arm. I need you 100%." He looked back down at his paper. "She do the Vic. Assist. Forms, yet?"

"No. She's sort of...spooked by 'em. That's weird, right?"

"Eh." Chief flicked a hand through the air like swatting a gnat. "Fires are scary. Paperwork can feel overwhelming. I'll send one of the ladies up front to visit her, see if they can get 'em from her." He leaned back and rubbed his hands over his face again. "Alright, Wilder. Go home. I don't wanna see you back in here until that shoulder is cleared. Carol'll have my ass if you hurt yourself on my watch doing something stupid."

"Yeah, okay, Chief." I stood to go, but he yelled behind me.

"And Sam can't clear you! I want you cleared by someone who hasn't been drunk on my sofa!" As I waved goodbye to the rest of the crew, I dropped a text to Troy.

> Me: Work or home?

> TJ: Last-minute meeting. Meet me at home.

11

CHASE

"Yo...Chase. Wake up, dude." Sam tapped my chest to wake me.

"Holy hell," I rubbed my hands over my face, trying to clear the fatigue tugging at me. "I must have conked out." Sitting up, I stretched my neck, which screamed in resistance from the most uncomfortable nap of my life. "What time is it?"

"7. Troy's grabbing food. Told me to check on you."

"I'm fine...just bored waiting, is all." I clicked the remote, turning off the game I failed to watch.

"More like you haven't had a good night's sleep in a week, and that hospital chair didn't do you any good." Sam slapped my boots off the coffee table and sat beside me on the couch. "Lemme see that shoulder." His travel medic kit plopped to the floor in front of him.

"It's fine," I grumble, trying to wave off his hands pulling me forward. "Which of your chicks at the hospital snitched on me?"

"Fuck off." Sam snarked as an electric bolt of pain sliced across my back when he removed the bandage. "I do end up at the hospital myself, you know...occupational hazard and all. I saw you with my own two eyes."

"And you didn't say hello?"

"It seemed like ya'll were having a moment." A shadow of the gentle concern I'd seen in the ambulance flickered across Sam's face. "She was crying."

My mind was instantly back in her heartbreaking sobs, my arms wrapped around her, wanting more than anything to take away her pain. I was so lost in the memory that I almost missed Sam's warning to 'hold on' before he rubbed something blisteringly cold across my shoulder. I couldn't help the hissing curse as the pain radiated down my back.

"You've not changed the bandage since this was put, idiot. It got too dry. You gotta keep it moist, man." I knew he was right. When you get a burn, you cool it, clean it, and keep it covered and moist while it heals.

"Holy Shit, Sam. I think I fucked up." I rubbed my face again, racking my brain about how I had gotten so twisted over a woman that I'd forgotten basic wound care. "I don't know what's wrong with me."

"I grabbed this from your place." He handed me a clean shirt and started repacking his kit. "And yeah, I've never seen you so distracted. Not by any rescue...*ever*." Sam strolled into Troy's kitchen and tossed over his shoulder, "Tell me about her."

I hardly knew where to begin.

She's beautiful and all alone. Her laugh makes my heart pound out of my chest. Nope. Can't tell him that. She's pregnant by some douche who left her alone, and now I'm drawn to protect her, care for her, care for her baby, and murder the abandoning asshat. Nope. Can't tell him that either.

"There's not much to tell." I lied, accepting the beer Sam shoved in my hand. "She's new in town and just lost everything she owns in a fire." Guilt tugged at me for withholding so many of the thoughts and feelings in my head, but before Sam could ask for more, Troy walked in with Pizza.

"Good. You're both here." He flopped dinner on the table and strolled through to his room, no doubt to stow away his weapon. When he returned, Troy tipped his head my way but addressed Sam. "Shoulder?"

Sam, already shoving in a slice of pepperoni at the bar, gave a thumbs up.

Troy grabbed a beer and a slice, then looked me over silently. Always the quietest of the three of us, Troy was a man of few words. Most people thought Troy's quiet contemplation was a cop thing. It wasn't. Troy took time to gather his thoughts and consider all angles before interjecting, even as a kid. He was slow to speak, but his mind was always working, and his words held considerable weight when he released them. I could see how it benefitted him during interrogations, though; I would just about spill anything to end the scrutiny I received now.

"Out with it," I said at last, preparing to be grilled about hanging at the hospital or nagged about my shoulder.

"We have a problem." He said at last. "Several, in fact."

"What's going on?" Sam asked, replacing my empty beer with a new one as he pulled up a chair.

"For starters, I can confirm that the recent fires are classified as Arson," Troy smoothed his tie, then continued. "Each has the same propellant residue and other similarities. An investigation is officially opened and underway."

"I figured that was coming," I slumped back in my chair with a slice of Pizza. "Have we ever had an arsonist? A real one...not like kids pulling stunts?"

"Not in recent history." Troy opened his beer and took a swig. "There's more. You gave Chief details about the Branson Heights fire earlier?" I nodded in agreement. "You told them that the woman -"

"Moira." I clarified.

"Right." Troy nodded, and I ignored the look my brothers shared as Troy finished his statement. "You said her room was locked."

"Yeah. I had to bust it down...like the door locked from the wrong side."

"You weren't wrong. The knob had, in fact, been reversed. That is what sealed the connection between all the fires." Troy wiped his hands on a napkin, crossing his arms across his chest and leveling Sam and me with his big brother gaze. "Your chief called my Captain the second you left his office. Each fire had a point of origin near a bedroom or bathroom with locks on the wrong sides."

"You mean someone started the fires on purpose?" Sam growled with the same anger that grew in the pit of my stomach. "And messed with the lock on this woman's-"

"Moira," I corrected again before chugging the last of my beer.

"Right. Sorry man. Someone started the fires on purpose and locked Moira in." Sam paused. Troy nodded confirmation. "Do we think *she* was the target?"

"Fuck!" I stood so fast my chair fell back to the floor as the visual of Moira cowering in her smoky room rushed to the surface.

"Sit down, Chase." I could hear Troy's request, but I needed to pace through this conversation–my body demanding action.

"Is there a suspect list?" I asked, ignoring his hand hovering over my vacated chair.

"So far, there is only one person of interest." Troy stood in my path, halting me from pacing with a raised hand. "Sit. Down." His face was neutral, but each word carried that familiar 'big brother' tone that had me sitting as if Pavlov himself had rung the bell.

"Can you tell us who it is?" Sam tossed me a tumbler of bourbon I hadn't seen him pour.

"I am in an unofficial capacity–not on the team investigating the Arson." Troy turned his gaze to me. "I was given command to see what Moira knew....because of you."

"Me? What can I do? I'm sidelined with this shit!" I grumbled as I cocked my chin to my injured shoulder.

"There's more.... It's Jensen." My whole body locked as two parts of my world collided. In the distance, I heard Sam drop the f-bomb as I slugged back my bourbon in one pull.

"How the hell is Dean Jensen connected to the Branson fire, TJ?" Sam voiced the question even as all my alarm bells fired off. I was too foggy to nail down a connection between my administrative board review and Moira's fire, but I had a sick, sick feeling.

"When you busted the window to get Moira out, it pulled enough of the fire away from the point of origin, and the blast hit your shoulder." I nodded my understanding, fist clenched around my empty glass. "Your crew had direct access to the room where it started, just long enough to preserve a partial print."

"And?" My stomach rolled, and my subconscious brain already connected dots I didn't want to face.

"Every fire's origin was very near to a female." Troy waved a hand, halting Sam from pouring another bourbon. "All early-to-mid-twenties. Blonde hair. Single."

Troy paused, his face shifting sympathetically just enough that I was already shaking my head.

"No way." I raced through what I knew of Moira's baby, realizing she'd shared next to nothing about him, and there was every chance that Dean Jensen was her baby's father.

"All of them were in Jensen's videos." Troy had his hands lifted placatingly, even as I tried to pour myself another bourbon. "And the print appears to be Jensen's."

"Fuck." My blood boiled through the whirl of booze. "He can't be connected to Moira, though? I don't think she even lived here when all that was going down." I held onto a whisper of that hope, begging the universe not to have tainted such a beautiful creature with someone as vile as Dean Jensen. In the same breath, all my instincts rose to the front of my lizard brain, begging for his blood.

"The theory is, Jensen used fire to scare the women who threatened legal action against his blackmail. Perhaps even the reason they refused to press charges." Troy rested his hand on me, but I jerked away, rubbing my face as Moira's tears burned in my memory. "Has Moira said if she knew Jensen at all?"

"No...I only know she's here, *alone*, and..." I trusted my brothers completely, but disclosing Moira's baby to them felt like a violation. I focused on the empty glass in my hand and shook the encroaching fog from my head as I scrambled for whatever else I could offer. "She was freaked out by the Vic. Assist. forms, though, paranoid about her name being attached to the fire...or people thinking she had anything to do with the fire." I ran my hands across my face again, fatigue nagging at my memory. "I just thought it was the shock, but now..."

Anger rose inside me, and I had to clench my fists at the idea that Jensen did such a horrible thing to someone so good. Moira was kind and beautiful, and he was a monster. No wonder she hesitates to trust me...I was a firefighter just like him. God, did she think I was like him, too?

"Was anyone else hurt or killed...at the fires?" Sam's question sounded distant again, and I could hardly face him as I imagined all the ways Jensen could have killed Moira if I hadn't reached her in time–if not the fire, then the smoke, or the collapsing structure.

He could have killed Moira. And the baby. Holy Shit. He nearly killed her baby. Did he know about the baby? My stomach flipped at the thought. Was that why he went after her with the fire? Did she know he set fires? Is that why she wasn't with him? Cause he'd treated her like all these other women.

"The other fires were smaller...vacant," Troy answered. "Til now."

"Fucking hell." Sam sighed. "And they think he videotaped them having sex and then blackmailed her, too? To that girl from the–"

"Moira!" I stood abruptly, and the room spun. "Her *name* is Moira."

"Whoa, whoa, hey." Troy was on his feet in an instant, shooting Sam a glance. "How many drinks did he have?"

"It ain't the booze. Dude hasn't slept in days." Sam slid up under my arm, taking more of my weight than seemed entirely necessary as I trudged to wherever he was leading me. "He's been at the hospital every day, all night, even. He might as well have poured gasoline into his veins."

I swayed on my feet, and I was prodded to the couch, as the desire to clarify that she wasn't like all those other women...she was special.

"If Jensen did this...he can find her again." Fear gripped me even as the earth began to sway. "I have to tell her, to warn her. You gotta arrest him, TJ."

"We already searched his house, and I requested a unit to stay by her room. Don't worry." Troy slowed my drop to his couch.

"That bastard." I could hear my slurred words, but didn't care. She was Moira, and she was alone, and she needed me.

"Yeah, man." Sam's ambulance voice was in full swing. "Let Troy take a shift while you grab some shuteye." My boots fell off. "You can't rescue the damsel if you can't stand up, ya teetotaler." A pillow was shoved under my head. The room grew dark.

Sam's voice really is relaxing.

12

MOIRA

I BARELY SLEPT THAT night as my mind mulled over everything I still needed to figure out. Primarily, where I would go when I left the hospital, when I had no money, no credit cards, no car, and no clothes. When the morning finally came, someone from the fire department visited to discuss the Victim Assistant forms. I had to admit they'd been ruined, but the kind woman handed over a fresh set, encouraging me to complete them as soon as possible. I told her I would, then promptly abandoned them on the deep windowsill, with my few belongings – an elephant and that damn basket of roses.

As kind as I knew Chase meant them to be, the reality was that my heart sank every time I saw them, and I hated that. I hated that something intended for good was turned sour by Dean and our sordid history.

"Knock, Knock!" An overly chipper nurse entered even before I could answer. "I've got a surprise for you, Ms. Vanderbilt."

"For me?" I sat up in my bed, noting the movement didn't hurt as much as before.

"I have official discharge papers, earlier than anticipated." She handed me a stack of papers that included follow-up instructions and discharge notes.

"Oh wow. I wasn't expecting these until I saw Dr Burner again."

"He was pulled into a delivery-turned-c-section, so he's unavailable. However, the OB fellow on the floor saw your labs and has cleared you to go." She slid another piece of paper into my hand. "Dr. Burner requested you get an ultrasound and schedule an appointment in his office within 2 weeks. His contact info is included."

"Oh, okay." I stared at the bags hanging off the nurse's elbow. "And the other surprise?"

"Yes!" She practically clapped with glee. "We have a closet here of things that patients leave behind." She set the bags on the bed for me to look at. "Mainly clothing that is in good condition and has been washed for use, should someone need it. A few of us found some items we think will be your size. There are some T-shirts, a pair of jeans, and even some sneakers." She leaned forward in a mock whisper. "We sprang for socks and underwear at the gift shop, so you aren't wearing a stranger's skivvies." Sitting back with a laugh, she stretched out her hand, offering me an envelope. "And we got a little something for the baby, too."

"I don't..." Opening the envelope, my words fell flat as I took in cash and a gift card to a department store in town. "How..."

The gift card was worth $100. Wildly more than I had at present and so incredibly needed as I navigated the coming days. But the cash–easily 200 bucks or more if I could count through the blur of tears.

"It's a small town. Your apartment fire was *big* news. We couldn't imagine going through that and being new here. We wanted to let you know that not all of Lake Placid is as scary as it seems. Some of it is quite beautiful and filled with good people." My heart shattered into a million tiny pieces as the gratitude washed over me. I'd never been on the receiving end of such generosity, and to have it now was almost too much to bear.

"I can't possibly repay this." The nurse held her hand up and shook her head.

"It's a gift." She gave my shoulders a kind squeeze before standing again. "Kickstarted by an anonymous donor who contributed the first $100.00. No repayment needed."

"A Donor..." I sighed, smiling at the thought. "Chase did this, didn't he? The fireman who has been visiting me? He's the one who saved me." The nurse mimed a key, locking her closed lips and giving me a wink.

"I'm sworn to secrecy." Then she leaned in and whispered. "But between you and me, the giant biker is a step up from the silver fox who slid in the anonymous Benjamin."

My heart sank.

"Did you say...silver fox? As in, the gentleman who brought the money was an older gentleman? Dark stubble...Grey at the temples?"

"He visited late and didn't want to interrupt your rest." She nodded in clueless glee as my world crashed around me. "Just inquired about your condition and then offered up the donation."

"My condition?!" I clutched my belly. "Did you tell him I was pregnant!?"

"We never divulge patient health information." Her eyes narrowed with concern. "All he said was he hated that you'd been in a fire, and he wanted to check on you. We informed him that you were stable and likely to be discharged today."

"Okay." I took a few deep breaths as the nurse walked to the edge of my bed.

"I take it you don't want Mr. Silver-fox knowing about the baby." Her eyes held no judgment, and I was ever so grateful for it.

"I'd like it if Mr. Silver-fox didn't know I even existed, much less that a baby is on board," I swiped a stray tear from my cheek. The nurse considered me, her eyes grazing my face, and then my hand resting on my belly. When she finally spoke, it was in a very matter-of-fact tone.

"Ms. Vanderbilt, I have to ask, do you feel safe leaving here?"

Shit shit shit.

Nurse Chipper was suddenly no-nonsense, thanks to my stupid tears triggering safety alarms in her brain. I couldn't bear a bunch of people sharing in the shame that was my life, and all I wanted to do was hide under the blankets. I could tell by her worried expression that I needed to proceed with caution, or else security could be up here wanting me to file assault and battery charges when really I was a victim of my own poor judgment.

"I'm okay. It was just a bad breakup." I offered a half-hearted smile in the hopes it would calm her down, but her scrupulous gaze was relentless. I needed to tap dance a little faster. "I didn't even know I was pregnant til the fire.... I need time to process everything before I share the news."

"Ah. Okay." She seemed hesitant but turned to leave, stopping just short of the door. "For what it's worth, I've had my share of bad breakups, too. So I hope my advice isn't out of line here, but if it helps..." She paused until I nodded for her to continue. "Silver-fox slid in at night, left without a word, and had you in a panic at the mere mention of him. Giant biker guy brought you gifts, set by your bedside, held your hair

while you puked, and fed you dinner with cartoon hearts in his eyes."
She gave a little shrug of her shoulders. "Seems like an easy choice to
me."

Her assessment was overly simplistic but brutally accurate. Chase
had done all those things. He'd sat by me that first night while I was
unconscious. He didn't know a thing about me, but he stayed. He
didn't have to, and his job didn't require it, but he chose to help
comfort me. And when my world went sideways, and I broke apart, he
just sat there and held me while I cried. He could have left after that,
but he returned once and had promised to come again.

From where I'm sitting, it seems like an easy choice, too.

Instantly, I hated what I'd let myself imagine. There was no choice.
Chase wasn't an option. I didn't need options.

I needed a reality check.

Yes, he pulled me from the fire–that's his job. And sure, he went a
little over and above after that, maybe, but it wasn't declarations of love!
He hadn't even spoken words that would allude to anything beyond
basic human compassion. A concept so far removed from my life that I,
apparently, could hardly fathom a world where people did nice things
like donate clothes to someone whose life literally went up in smoke.

Chase wasn't Prince Charming from a fairytale ...he was a fireman
with a killer follow-through.

Anger rose to my cheeks as I took stock of where I was and what
I was doing to myself. Again! My emotions pushed impractical ideas
into my head, distracting me from the reality in front of me, and I had
to stop and take stock of what I had.

My checklist for rebooting my life was incomplete, but I now had
some clothes, a gift card for necessities, and a wad of cash. A wildly
better position than just a few minutes ago. This wasn't the time for

self-pity, and it sure as hell wasn't an opportunity to moon over a man who showed a modicum of decency.

I was no one's pity project.

Frustration and embarrassment flooded me, and all I wanted to do was get up and make a clean break from this place before Dean came sniffing around again. Sitting straighter, I squared my shoulders and rang the bell for the nurse's station.

'Yes?' came the disembodied voice.

"Can I get the number to a local rideshare company, and get my IV removed? I'm ready to dress so I can leave."

'I'll send someone in right away.'

"It's high time we hit the road and make a plan," I whispered to my baby, even as I looked across the room at the little stuffed elephant with a pang of sadness. "Just you and me, kiddo."

13

CHASE

THE MORNING LIGHT SLICED into me with groans from a sore neck born from a couch entirely too small for me. All it took was a few stressful days with too little sleep, and all 6'4" of me crashed, taken out by a few beers and a glass of bourbon.

"Morning, sunshine." Troy smiled over his cup of coffee, though his eyes never left his phone as he scanned the news.

"I'm gonna kick Sam's ass," I had to force a swallow around the hangover fur coating my tongue.

"Now, now. He poured...you drank." He gave a side glance at me. "Let's not blame the bartender for the sitting fool's thirst." I scowled at the platitude Nonna'd say when one of us was drunk while on leave from the Corp. Not that she ever said it to uptight, control-freak, Troy.

"Aren't you supposed to be off today?" I flicked a hand towards his crisply ironed dress slacks, starched dress shirt, and perfectly pressed tie.

"Event meetings, " he grumbled. "I *loathe* the day I was voluntold to liaise for the town council's event team."

"That's what you get for being so damned anal." I rubbed my eyes to clear the sleep. "More work."

"Drink up." Troy nudged a cup of coffee towards me. "I'll start breakfast to soak up the rest of the booze."

I could hardly complain. Troy made a damn good cup of coffee and was no slouch in the kitchen. By the time I finished the first cup and used the bathroom to rinse my face off, the whole place smelled of fried ham and eggs, and toast wasn't far behind.

"Where's Sam?" I slouched into the kitchen chair, head hanging between my hands.

"He stayed an hour or so after you passed out. Called the hospital to make sure Moira was okay and confirmed the uniform was outside before leaving."

"I should apologize," I might as well have been talking through a mouthful of rocks as dry and gravelly as my throat felt.

"For being a cheap date?"

"I was an asshole. I lost my shit."

"You did." Troy never minced words, but his tone told me he was winding up a big brother's lecture.

"I don't know what came over me," I offered, hoping to lessen the whipping I had coming.

"So, we're swimming *this* river now?" Troy handed me a heaping plate and a fresh cup of coffee before joining me.

"River?"

"Where you pretend you have no clue why you lost your fool mind last night," Troy let his hand drift back and forth as if dancing to his now lyrical voice. "And I sit and watch as you dance around the truth that is painfully obvious to anyone with eyes."

"So I'm dancing in a metaphorical river?" I shoved more food into my mouth, wishing he'd get to the point.

"Deniiiiiaaaaal." He drawled. I started to protest, but he raised his hand and cut me off. "When have you ever sat bedside of a fire victim, much less brought them meals? I do not believe your department budgets for stuffed elephants and balloons, either."

Fuck. I knew the balloons were too much. I was too much.

"It's not like that -"

"It *is* like that. And what's more... I'm glad."

Mouth open, fork full of eggs hovering mid-air, I froze.

I expected a chastising lecture about responsibility. A nagging finger wag about professional decorum or ethics. After all, I had never yelled at my brothers over a woman, or gotten drunk over one, so I expected endless teasing. I was not, however, expecting 'glad' to fall from my monosyllabic big brother's mouth.

"Chase." Troy leaned his elbows on the table, staring me down with that same intensity I'd seen a million times growing up. "You're a good man. Great firefighter. Damn solid brother. But for all those great qualities you let me and Sam see, you've never been one to wear your heart on those sizeable sleeves of yours. We've seen the distance you put between you and the world." Troy's unusually prolific words poured out as I gaped openly, stripped bare. "I understand where that protective action comes from. I remember what it was like for you in those early days when you wrestled away guilt over your birth parents' arrest." He flashed a rare, toothy smile even as his voice softened. "So the random hook-ups you have enjoyed never went anywhere because even you feared if you got attached, and failed someone, they'd leave. But god knows, for all those massive muscles you work out, it's your heart that wrecks us all."

"Dammit, man." I choked on the lump in my throat, as Troy summarily stripped away all my walls, laying bare the part of me I never told anyone. I'd tried to save my parents from arrest, and I failed, and they were gone, and it broke me.

"I don't know if this woman will last the hour or the week or if she's the one for you for the rest of time. But something in her has reached into that outer shell of yours, and if the world gets to witness even a small fraction of that soft underbelly, then yes, little brother....I am glad." Troy leaned back and tipped his cup towards me in a toast. "You deserve happiness."

"Jesus Christ." I crushed my fingers across my scrunched-up eyes at hearing my brother use the word soft to describe any part of me. "I don't know how she's gotten under my skin, but I can't seem to stay away from her."

"Then don't." Sitting back, I could only marvel at the encouragement I was getting on an issue I barely recognized I needed support in. I hadn't given myself time to figure out what Moira was to me, much less what to say about her to my brothers, and yet Troy saw past all of that and gave me...his blessing.

"What time is it?" I padded my pockets, looking for my phone.

"Just after 11. Why?" He slid my phone across the table.

"She's getting released. Told her I'd help her settle into a hotel until her claims were processed and she was back on her feet." I looked around for my boots and found them near the couch.

"An active investigation is just the sort of thing most insurance companies use to postpone policy payments."

"Yeah. I know." I slid my boots on and found my keys on the coffee table. "Can I borrow your Truck?" Troy tossed me his keys without question, taking mine and my helmet in return.

"Let me know how it goes." He called behind me as I paused at the door.

"Thanks." I kept my back to him, not trusting my face to stay cool.

"Go... get her," I swear I could hear him smiling.

14

CHASE

I BARELY REGISTERED THE drive to the hospital or riding the elevator as I wondered what I could do for Moira. I promised her a ride to a hotel. Then what—leave her like none of this mattered? The idea made my chest ache, but I had no plan. Above all, I had Troy's words in my head telling me to go get her. Get her and do what...say what? 'Hey Moira, I'm obsessed with you, and my brother said it was okay, so can you just move in with me now we'll be platonic roommates, but also, you're soooo pretty.'

I felt like a bumbling idiot by the time I walked towards her room, instantly annoyed that the police officer who was supposed to be watching over her was instead flirting at the nurse's station at the end of the hall.

"Shouldn't you be down at 1214?" I growled in passing.

"She's fine. "He trailed behind me. "She was napping last I checked."

I turned the corner into her room, and my heart sank. Her bed was empty, and her gown was on the floor. I looked to the windowsill and found no elephant, flowers, or balloons. Even her notepad was gone.

"Oh, Shit." The officer grabbed his radio. "Dispatch, I've got 10-57 on the Fire Vic at General." His voice trailed behind me, blood pumping in my ears, as I neared the bed to find a folded piece of paper with my name written on top.

Dear Chase,

Your offer to help me when I left the hospital was too kind. You are a good man and have been incredibly generous these past few days that we've spent together. But I have to figure this out on my own. I am feeling much better, and I found my way to a hotel. It'll be just a few days until insurance kicks in, and then I'll reboot!

I don't have words to thank you for all you've done. You were soft and kind to me when the world was hard and scary.

I'll forever be grateful.

Wishing you all happiness,
Fancy Pants 2.0

Her polite words shredded me into a thousand pieces. 'Too kind...on my own...reboot.' She was pushing me away and running, but she called me good and soft. Words that I'd only ever heard from Nonna growing up and then Troy this morning, and I wanted to hear them from Moira's lips, not the flimsy piece of paper.

The nurse and police officer returned as I stared at the note, reading it over and over as they tried to figure out what happened. She'd left, and by the way the nurse was freaking out, she'd done it without signing final papers.

But... 'Wishing you all happiness.' It was a knife to my heart, and I couldn't deny how gutted the casual sign-off left me.

"How the hell did this happen?" I crumpled the note in my hands in a blistering attempt to control the hurt boiling inside me.

"I swear I was right outside." The cop answered radio chatter in his ear. "I don't know how she slipped out when I was between her and the elevator."

Did she give the staff the slip?

"Who picked her up?" I asked the nurse, hoping against hope that she had a friend who'd come to her aid.

"No," She said breathlessly. "She hasn't had any visitors except you and the gentleman last night."

"What?" I snapped my head up, locking onto the nurse as I crossed the room in two strides. "Who visited her last night?" The nurse blanched at me, eyes wide, and the uniformed officer wedged his shoulder in front of me.

"Hey, man." I barely registered his hand on my chest. "I've already radioed in. We all wanna find her. Let's calm down."

"Who was it?" I growled

"I don't know." The nurse took a step back, squaring her shoulders and leveling her eyes at me. "I wasn't on shift; I only have the logs. Someone came around midnight, inquired about her condition, and offered an anonymous monetary gift. We added the money to the pool we'd started for her." My fists clenched as worry built to a fever pitch, envisioning a thousand ways this could go bad.

Still, I couldn't ignore the armed officer between me and the nurse, and I knew I had to gain some control before he mistook my worry for anger.

"Can you please see if anyone who was here then is still here now?" I forced the words as flat and calm as I could, desperately hoping it was anyone other than Jensen. The nurse looked briefly at the officer, who nodded approval. She left as my phone chirped a text.

TJ: I just heard. I'm on my way.

Samoa: What's going on?!

Me: Moira's gone! Your guy wasn't watching her.

TJ: I'll be there in 15 minutes.

Me: Some anonymous guy saw her last night...for her!

Samoa: I'm close, TJ...gimme 5.

Me: She left me a note. I have to find her... what if it was Jensen?

TJ: I'm coming. Just wait.

Pocketing the phone, I scanned the room one more time. She'd left nothing else behind.

"Sir, the night shift has gone home," I growled at the news.

"Can we call them in?"

"Sir." She took a deep breath, steadying her voice. "We're doing what we can—but patients walk out all the time. She'd been cleared on all medical fronts, and even though the officer didn't see her leave, I couldn't do what you asked anyway." After a moment's hesitation, she added, "You aren't her emergency contact."

That. Cut.

I stepped into the hallway and looked towards the elevators. The officer would surely have seen her if she'd gone that way. Turning in the opposite direction, I saw the stairwell and started walking. At the bottom, the closest door out of the building was the main revolving one in the lobby. Exiting quickly, I scanned the parking lot in hopes of seeing anything that might tell me what car she left in, but there were no cars lined up to talk to. I was about to go back and find my truck when Sam's SUV pulled up.

"Hold up, man." He hollered as I climbed in and showed him the note.

"She said she was going to a hotel, but without credit cards or ID, how is she going to do that?"

"Any chance we're waiting for TJ?" Sam sighed.

"Sam! She didn't just fucking walk out of here?" I thumped the note in his hand, thinking, by some miracle, the intensity of her words would bleed through to him too. My heart was pounding, and I was a breath away from bolting to my truck. "I have to find her."

"Alright...what do we know?"

"Her ID and cards burned in the fire. She was still waiting on insurance to process."

"Right. So, she won't be staying at any big chain hotels."

"What does that leave?" I scanned the sidewalks as if I might see her walking down the street in her hospital gown, tugging along a basket of flowers and trailing balloons.

"There are some...cheaper motels out by Highway 86 to Wilmington." Sam flicked a side glance at me. "We can start there and work our way back towards town."

"Fuck." I slumped into the seat. "How would she even get that far on her own?"

"I don't know her like you do, man." Sam was calm, and that familiar soothing tone slipped seamlessly into place as he continued. "But she managed to survive a fire and walk out of the hospital, slipping past a posted officer. She sounds pretty badass."

"She's alone, Sam. I promised her I wouldn't leave her alone." I couldn't bring myself to care about Sam's expression when I let the words fly. I was nearly in a panic.

"Dude. I've never seen you like this over a woman before."

"Jesus, Sam," I warned. "I got no bandwidth for bullshit right now."

"Don't get it twisted," Sam never taking his eyes off the road. "I'm happy."

"Jensen was here... I know it." And I had failed to protect her, and she ran without me.

"We don't know that for sure, right?" Sam tried to reassure me as we drove through town towards the first in a small string of motels that ran along the road leading off the highway. "This motel is the best of the bunch, and that's saying something," Sam warned. "Shit gets progressively seedier from here."

I went to the front desk and inquired about a blonde woman who may have checked in earlier today, but the zit-faced kid behind the counter just said he hadn't seen anyone since he clocked in at midnight.

And so, it went for the next motel...and the next. Each one progressively worse, and each time my heart thudded, the failure in my chest that had I just stayed with her last night, she wouldn't have been alone for Jensen's visit... wouldn't have been alone trying to fend for herself out here.

"No way she's out here. No fucking way."

"Look, man, I take calls out here on a pretty regular basis. The past three motels were cheap but mostly on the up and up. These last two, however," he nodded at two small facilities on the other side of the intersection. "Well, I usually am out here for one of three reasons." He held up a finger as he rattled them off. "OD, Assault, Prostitution, or some combination of the three. If she's here-."

"If she's in there—I'm dragging her out myself."

15

MOIRA

THE DRIVER DROPPED ME off at a hotel he deemed most likely to accept me without ID, provided I paid with cash. Grateful as I was, my hope flickered at the sight of the Traveling 'Otel and Spa–its neon M long since burned out. The word 'spa' seemed suspect when the letterboard offered low 'rats' by the hour, but I reminded myself that this was temporary. Walking in, I pushed forward, ignoring the overflowing ashtray and the stains on the worn, thin orange carpet squares.

"Excuse me, sir." The old man behind the front desk hardly glanced sideways before returning to the game show blaring from his tiny TV. "I was hoping I could rent a roo -"

"ID and Credit Card under the window." His scratchy voice barked, cane thumping the scuffed plexiglass that separated us.

"Yes...Well... that's the thing." I adjusted my bags and looked around for a place to set the flowers and balloons, but the counter looked like it hadn't seen soap since the Reagan era. "I was in a fire. Or rather, my *apartment* caught fire. I wasn't on fire, obviously." I nervously chuckled at his vague disinterest. "I am waiting on my insurance company to replace all my documents, including my ID and Credit Cards. But I have—"

"50 bucks a day." He cut me off with a grunt. "Three-day minimum. Up front." I began the mental math, and my stomach lurched.

"Is there a discount or -"

"Cash gets you 25 a night." He smirked even as he turned his full attention my way. "No refunds."

I'd counted my cash in the car—an even 300. The driver took 35, and at 25 a night, I'd barely have enough for a week after calculating food costs. Normally, I could scrimp on one meal a day, but with a baby...

I have to do better than this. I have to be better than this.

"Could I negotiate a partial down payment now with a promise to pay the rest in a week or two? Maybe a half-pay cash rate...in exchange for free website or social media work. I'm in between jobs, but I have a new job starting soon, and my background is in - "

"Lady, do I look like I need a fancy website?" He turned back to his TV, summarily dismissing me, and I was drawn back to the very second I had last felt so humiliated.

Of course...It was Dean.

The moment he walked away, discarding me like an unwanted solicitor. Or rather, the two seconds after that when I realized I had no car and no way back to my apartment. The humiliation was suffocating as I glanced at my phone to find no cell reception—no way to call a car. My options were to crawl back to Dean and endure the humiliation of hearing him rescue me again... or...

The ultimate walk of shame was a mistake, but given my self-flagellating independence, I was unwilling to rescind.

I felt confident I'd find a gas station where I'd have a signal to call a rideshare. Still, the walk itself was a degrading march soundtracked by every passing car witnessing my debasement. It was the single most humiliating moment of my life...until now.

"Please." My voice was barely a whisper as I closed my eyes and begged the universe for just one God damn break.

"25 is my final offer. Take it or don't."

"She won't!"

Even without turning around to see him, I knew, to my core, who owned the low growl behind me. Chase sounded like he might rip someone's head off, yet it was the same voice that woke me up that first night in the hospital. That felt like ages ago, as if the pity ride to this godforsaken shithole had shifted through a lifetime.

"She *doesn't* need the room. She *has* a place to stay." The comforting familiarity of Chase's warmth at my back made my whole body prickle, just as embarrassment hit me like a fever, shame a close second.

How long was he standing behind me? How would I possibly explain what I was doing in a place barely above a hostel? Did he just witness me holding everything I owned, negotiating ways to lower the already embarrassingly low cash-pay offer I'd been given?

"Moira." His voice gentled, and my heart hurt. "You can't stay in a place like this." His hand rested on my shoulder, tugging me to turn towards him, but I couldn't.

"I know this looks pretty lame, but..." I willed my voice to sound lighthearted...confident even, despite my inability to face him. My cheeks flushed with embarrassment and restraint, and if I looked into his eyes, I would break. As it was, it was all I could do to fight the brimming tears as I scrambled to explain my pathetic failure at self-reliance. "This is temporary... until my insurance comes in, and - "

"Stop." He tugged at me again, and I yielded, turning to find his pleading blue eyes looming down at me. His hand slipped from my shoulder, smoothly sliding the bags off my arms while his other hand rested on my waist. "I told you I'd help you, and that includes making sure you never spend a night in a shithole like this."

"Hey." The grump behind the counter thumped his cane on the plexiglass. "This is my shithole."

"Can it, Ernest. You know this place is a breath away from being demolished for the betterment of humanity." I craned around Chase's broad stance to find the owner of the familiar new voice.

"Ms. Vanderbilt." He gave me a wave, grabbing the bags from Chase. "I don't know if you remember me. I'm Sam."

"The brother." I looked back at Chase. "From the ambulance?" Chase nodded, studying my face as if cataloging every feature.

"I'll take these things to the car and try to head off TJ," Sam mumbled to Chase. "He's wicked pissed."

Panic choked me at the thought that someone was angry.

"I'm so sorry! I wasn't trying to cause problems or - " I looked from Sam back to Chase. "I didn't get anyone in trouble, did I?"

"He's not pissed at you." Chase lifted his now free hand and held it palm up in invitation. "There was a guard at the hospital. The fact that you gave him the slip is what Troy's pissed at." His dimples came from under the scruff on his cheeks when I let my hand slip onto his. "And he told me to wait at the hospital. I didn't. So, he's likely pissed at me, too." He studied our hands for so long that I found myself looking at them and marveling at the size difference between us. Then imagined his hands on other parts of my body, and I had to slam that door shut.

"I can do this on my own." I let my gaze slide to the floor. "If I can just get through the next few days, the rental claim will pay, and my job will start soon, and then I'll - "

"The renter's claim will take a while. There's more to explain. But I'm making sure you have a safe place to stay that's cleaner than this dump." The man behind the counter grunted. "You *will* come with me. You will *not* argue." He hooked a finger under my chin and forced me to look up at eyes that somehow held a ferocious compassion. "Please...let me help you."

His voice was firm but not unkind, and that combination sang to my battered ego. My hero, again, offered shelter from my doubts as he laced our fingers together and let him walk us away from Grumpy Ernest and The Traveling 'Otel & Spa.

16

MOIRA

CHASE'S BROTHER PLACED MY piddly possessions in the back of his SUV as Chase opened the back door for me. I climbed in as one of their cells rang, and I watched the two men hover around the cell in a clipped conversation. When Sam slipped into the driver's seat, I looked out my window, expecting to see Chase climb in next to him. Instead, he opened the back door and sat next to me, offering a quick scowl in the rearview mirror to his smirking brother.

Grateful as I was to be leaving the row of rundown motels, I became acutely aware that I was in a car with virtual strangers...and had no idea where I was being taken. I glanced at Sam, focused on the road, then at Chase, sitting stiffly next to me. Neither of them seemed overly chatty, but the silence was more than I could bear.

"So," I exhaled, trying to sound more casual than I felt. "What happens now?"

"We're gonna get you settled into a way better place to unpack and rest or grab a shower if you need to." Chase glanced briefly out the front window before turning back to me. "Then after that, I'll take you shopping for whatever else you need."

My initial question about where this 'better place' was evaporated at that last declaration.

"You don't need to take me shopping!" Chase held up a finger, silencing me in a gesture that might have seemed belittling if not for the boyish dimples returning in a smirk. I made a mental note to build up a little armor against those bastards.

"We could do this back-and-forth, where I offer help, and you tell me you don't need it, and then you write me notes and take off, and I have to call my brothers, and then we all search you down," Chase said, a wry smile in his eyes.

"Ahhhh, that old chestnut." Sam teased from the front seat, his eyes never leaving the road. "A classic."

"Or," Chase lowered his hand, palming mine in one fluid motion. "You can make *both* our lives - "

"And mine!" Sam lifted a finger.

"So much easier by just accepting the help we both know you need." He nudged my hand back until both our hands rested in my lap." Let me do this for you." I looked down at the deeply personal gesture and saw his pinky lightly graze my belly. A secret nod to the baby that only he knew about and a less-than-subtle reminder that this wasn't just about me anymore. Like it or not, I had no way to properly care for either of us at this moment, and that pill was hard to swallow.

We drove the rest of the way in silence past the nicer hotels lining the highway and into the small downtown area of the town I'd been living in but realized I'd hardly seen. I hadn't left the apartment much after I moved, and the drive to a motel in an Uber was too stressful, with counting out money and making life choices. Now that I wasn't panicking, I noticed the town green anchoring the small business strip—quaint, like a postcard that dared you to dream.

Normally, town centers had gazebos or benches, but this one had a charming old church at its center. Pristinely landscaped with trimmed flower beds and shaped evergreen bushes. The building practically begged you to come inside. Was it historic, the site of some old battle? So much history was written in this part of the country, and my chest tightened to think of living in a place long enough to have a history of my own. Then we passed a park where mothers chased toddlers, and I swallowed thickly at the realization that it could be me one day.

Before long, Sam turned down a street of tiny homes lined up in a row, each with manicured lawns. Some had picket fences around them; others had wrap-around porches. The setting was idyllic as large trees dappled shade across the narrow sidewalks, and again, emotion choked me. Maybe I could have this for us one day. I slipped my hand across my belly. I'll even get you a swing from the tree, and...we could have a home. My imagination built a beautiful picture with trick-or-treating at Halloween and hanging lights for Christmas. I imagined birthday parties on the lawn and flowers in the spring. All the things I never had and all the things I wanted to give my child...if I could ever get my life together enough to be a better mother than what I'd been given.

The streets finally curved into a cul-de-sac of three near-identical houses, each with narrow front yards and thin gravel driveways running along its sides. Sam pulled into the house at the end and parked his SUV in the driveway of a small cottage, devoid of decorations, which made it appear to be a rental property.

"This looks nice," I took in the narrow walkway leading to three steps and a small, covered porch with a single white front door.

"Yeah, it's okay, I guess," Chase spoke from where he stood outside his door, hand extended in invitation. "But you're staying over here." He cocked his head back over his shoulder at the house in the middle. A small grey cottage with white trim. It had two small windows with black shutters flanking a wooden door painted deep red. "That's Sam's place," Chase pointed to the house we parked at. "We're neighbors." He pointed across to the third house that was nearly identical, save for a Navy door. "That's our brother Troy's house over there."

"You're neighbors?" I watched Sam pulling my things out of the SUV.

"It's not as weird as it sounds," Sam answered. "We're so busy with work that this makes it easier to handle our side biz." My brain struggled to take everything in as Chase tugged me to his porch, where he opened the front door and guided me inside.

The petite, open-concept craftsman featured a combined living room and kitchen, with an island separating the two spaces. Although there was a single door in the corner and a short hallway off the far wall of the kitchen, the rest of the home was wide open, with a big rustic beam spanning the high ceiling, giving the small space a spacious feel.

"Where do you want these?" Sam squeezed in behind us.

"In the bedroom," Chase dropped my hand, leading Sam back through the corner door.

Standing alone, my brain finally clicked the pieces together that Chase hadn't just taken me to some vacant rental house. He had brought me to his home where, apparently, I was expected to stay. Looking around from where I stood, I saw no other doors to indicate a second bedroom, and I began to wonder about sleeping arrangements, but my brain short-circuited with questions I didn't know how to ask.

Would Chase sleep on the couch, or would I? Perhaps he would be with his brothers, and I would be here alone. The idea of sharing space with Chase felt like lighting a match near a gas leak, but staying in a strange place alone was downright terrifying. Or it would have been had the jolt of the front door slamming into my back not pulled me out of my thoughts.

Off balance, I turned to find a huge black man with intense eyes bearing down on me. He was broad and tall, his face stern as he scowled at me with an intensity that had me stumbling back. He stretched his hands towards me as the leather straps holding two ginormous guns came into view. Yanking back, I bumped into the end table with a yelp as the floor flew up to meet my backside, only then seeing the police badge clipped to his belt.

"Whoa!" Chase stepped between me and the man, placing one hand on the man's chest, and turning towards me, splayed across the floor. Then he delivered a hard whack with the back of his hand to the armed man. "Way to scare her, asshole."

Protective nature or not, I couldn't imagine Chase slapping an armed cop unless it was someone he knew.

"Don't let Troy scare you." Sam scooped me off the floor like I weighed nothing. "He's got zero concept of how broody his ass is, but he's harmless." Confident I was steady on my feet, Sam crossed to what I then realized was their brother. "You could've left the hardware at home, though."

"My apologies, ma'am." Troy stretched a hand towards me, but Chase knocked it away with a scowl, stepping between us like a human wall. "I tried to catch you before you fell, but-"

"Are you okay?" Chase shifted a worried glance to my belly, and I understood he was worried about us both. "You fell." He mumbled the last part so softly that I barely heard it, and I was grateful, for the second time, for his discretion.

"I'm fine," I breathed, embarrassed as the realization of who this was washed over me. "I'm sorry I'm such a klutz." I strained to peek around Chase. "You must be Chase's *other* brother?"

"I should have announced myself properly," Troy nodded. "I wasn't expecting company." He extended his much less menacing-looking hand to me a third time. "Sgt. Troy Wilder. Police officer and Chase's brother."

"Moira Vanderbilt," I shook his hand, willing my heart to settle. "You must be the final piece of the Wilder Brothers Protection Agency." I gave my throbbing backside a little rub from where I landed on the hardwood. "I didn't see your badge at first...only man-wall, then guns...hence the clumsiness." I glanced up at Chase. "Sorry if I startled you."

"You don't have to apologize." Chase glanced at my belly with unspoken worry on his face. I touched his arm, bringing his eyes back to me.

"I'm okay," I whispered, soft enough that if anyone else heard it, they didn't let on. "I promise."

"Ms. Vanderbilt," Troy's voice pulled us both to face him. "Were you aware you left the hospital *without* signing final discharge papers?"

"I didn't realize. I apologize. I can go back if I need to finish something." I glanced at him and Sam. "I wasn't trying to be sneaky." I looked back up at Chase. "I was trying to be efficient."

"There are things we should discuss." Troy continued, glancing at Sam, who subtly shook his head. "But I suppose it can wait until you are more settled."

I opened my mouth to insist we could discuss things now, but Sam interjected.

"It's been a weird day." He looked at me with kindness in his eyes. "It would be good for you to get some solid rest. How about we talk over dinner?" Sam looked at Chase and added, "Tomorrow?"

Suddenly, Chase's face broke into a huge smile.

"Absolutely." Chase looked to Troy, who offered a resigned sigh and a nod.

"6 Sharp." Sam finished, "Chase, you got the drinks this time."

I was still trying to piece together the unspoken conversation between the three of them as the brothers filed out. Sam spouted health directives like 'make sure you hydrate' before Chase closed the door, even as I stood, mouth open and hand raised. Gaping like an idiot and wondering why I felt like my voice in these decisions had just been swept under the rug.

17

CHASE

HAVING MOIRA IN MY house was surreal.

My space was always small and, for the most part, decorated with only the items that served both function and form. I thought it was good enough until Moira, in simple jeans and a pink t-shirt, somehow lit up the space with her raw beauty. Her stunning blonde hair hung loose around her shoulders, and I imagined her fresh-faced in the morning, hair splayed across the pillow and gazing sleepy-eyed at me as we basked in –

She was here because she needed protection. I needed to remember that.

Clearing my throat, I extended my hand around the room.

"Would you like a tour?"

"No." Moira's voice was harsh, her answer blunt. I turned to look at her, seeing a Medusa-like glare so intense that I thought steam might come out of her ears. She was...angry. "I wanna know what all *that* was?"

"All...that?" I wondered if she was still mad at Troy knocking her down, but she seemed okay then.

"You said you'd help me find a place. Not... trap me in *yours*." I opened my mouth to answer, but she kept going. "Then Sam just moved my stuff in, while Troy tells me the hospital was looking for me?" Again, I tried to speak, but she wasn't done. "Then suddenly you all go mute for 'things we need to discuss,'" she flashes air quotes to the room, but never pauses. It was impressive. "With your weird glances, and now we're having what...a family dinner tomorrow?"

"I promise," I jumped in quickly, hands raised in surrender. "It's okay."

"It's not okay when there are decisions that involve me...that I'm being left out of." Her face was stern, brows pinched, and dammit if it weren't the cutest thing I'd ever seen.

But she had a point. As much as I didn't want to worry her about Jensen and arson and all the things that were genuine threats to her safety, she deserved the respect I hadn't given her when I cave-manned her here.

"You're right," I let my hands drop and sat back on the arm of my couch. "I was so worried about finding you that when I did, I sorta missed a few steps." I kicked myself for my subpar communication skills, wishing, as always, that I were as smooth as Sam.

"Like maybe having a conversation?" Moira's arms crossed even as her brow smoothed. "About why *here*?" She waved to the room as I considered her words, wondering how to explain that I'd never considered any other option than my place.

"I don't know how long your insurance stuff will take...or when your job starts," I scrambled through as many reasons as I could think of to explain my insanity. "But your voice is still a little scratchy...and until that smoke works its way out, I don't feel safe leaving you alone." Her face was unreadable, and I couldn't tell if she was buying the thin truths I was lobbing at her. "I'm on med-leave for a few weeks...and there's an EMT next door, so here seemed smart." I left off the benefits of a police officer flanking us when her maybe ex was maybe stalking her. "If you stay here, I'll be able to sleep, worry-free." The little eleven appeared between her brows once more, and she opened her mouth to protest, but I added quickly, "And if you totally hate it here, we'll find you a hotel that doesn't have hourly rates tomorrow...I swear."

She continued watching with an ice-melting intensity, and I mentally prepared to pack a bag if I needed to get us adjoining hotel rooms.

"You asked if I wanted a tour, then." Just like that, the argument was done. She never said she agreed with my plan or was still angry. She didn't address my blatantly bullheaded move to get her here, nor did she kick me square in the balls and run off, which I very likely deserved. It was a win I would take.

The tour took a whopping 5 minutes. My house was small, but I invested in the task with diligence, and Moira...followed me. In the bedroom, I paused, letting her take in the space, spinning slowly to survey the dresser where her things sat.

"Where will you sleep?" She looked unflinchingly into my eyes, and I couldn't tell if hers held worry, regret, or fear.

"My couch is stupid comfortable, according to my brothers. They've both slept on it." I smiled, hoping to see her smile back. "Seems only fitting I take a turn."

Moira considered me silently, eyes distant as if thinking so hard it gave her a headache. I worried she would fall back into telling me she didn't want to be an imposition, or wanted to repay all this, or didn't need any help at all, and would kick me in the balls if I tried to hold her.

She needed to know about the investigation and the delays the additional red tape would cause her insurance claims. I needed to tell her about Jensen and that we suspected a connection with her. For that matter, I needed to tell her about Jensen's connection to me. But all I could think of was that furrowed brow, knit so tightly together that the two little lines between her eyes formed that adorable 11.

I wanted to run a thumb across that brow, smoothing away her worries.

I wanted to see her smile again.

I couldn't bear to tell her how much harder this all got for her. I couldn't stand to be the one to lay even more worries on her shoulders. And I couldn't give her a reason not to trust me. Not yet, at least. I wanted to give her as much peace as possible for as long as possible.

"Why don't you grab a shower?" I stepped toward the bedroom door, grabbing the knob to close it behind me. "We'll figure out where to get some things you need...and make a dinner plan. Okay?" Before she could argue, I backed out and closed the door.

Wilder Bro's Group Chat

-2-

ME: What was the hospital fallout?

TJ: Security tapes show she walked right out.

ME: So not sneaking out.

Samoa: Shout-out to the officer of the year.

TJ: Top-Tier work indeed.

Samoa: Have you told her about Jensen?

ME: No.

TJ: She hasn't said who visited her last night?

ME: I haven't asked.

Samoa: Dude.

ME. She needs rest.

TJ: She needs the truth.

ME: Can we give her a few days to recover?

TJ: We need information she may have.

ME: One day then...She's been through so much.

Samoa: I'm with Boyscout. She looks like she's about to fall over.

TJ: I'll hold off on what I can. But I'm limited. If Jensen was the one who visited her...

Samoa: He's dumber than we thought.

ME: And my chief? I can't go there now. Not without her knowing.

Samoa: I'm going to the station tomorrow for cross-training. I'll see what I can find out.

ME: Don't say anything about her being here.

Samoa: Understood.

TJ: She seems lovely, brother.

ME: And so different from me.

Samoa: Not SO different.

TJ: Tread carefully.

ME: I know. She's fragile. I'm trying to give her space, not crowd or push her.

Samoa: He means with you, dipshit. Be careful...with you.

TJ: I've never seen you fall so hard. And now she's staying with you.

ME: Better here than some shitty motel alone. Not with Jensen out there.

Samoa: Again...I'm with Chase.

TJ: Proximity complicates things.

Samoa: He knows, Grandpa.

18

MOIRA

I WASN'T SURE WHO cleaned me up after the fire, but even the one brief pseudo-shower I'd taken at the hospital hadn't removed the feel of smoke and grime off my skin. So, when Chase suggested a shower and left me in his room, the temptation was too strong to pass up, awkwardness be damned.

Stepping into Chase's shower, with the heat high enough to steam the room, was pure unadulterated bliss. I lingered, letting the hot water pound away the tension in my neck and shoulders. Turning, I leaned my hands against the wall as the water rained down on my head, sending a curtain of serenity surrounding my face. I knew there was still so much to do, and so many unknowns to consider, but at that moment, I needed the sound of the water drowning out the world.

It was the first time in days that I had enjoyed such a solitary moment of peace.

Only when my fingers pruned did I lather up, letting the bubbles drag the last of the hospital antiseptic down the drain. Drying off, I realized I had no comb or brush. Only Chase's toothbrush and deodorant were on the counter, and there was no medicine cabinet to speak of. Under the sink was bare, save a few cleaning supplies. There was no basket of travel toiletries, no collection of stray things left behind. It was truly as if there had never been a woman, or anyone, in this space at all. It was hard to believe a man with muscles for days had never had a woman leave something behind.

Not that his love life was any of my business.

I shook the thought away, finger-combing my hair and padding into the bedroom. As I dressed, my eyes drifted to the dresser drawers. I had never been one to snoop—privacy in foster homes was not always a given, so I respected people's space. However, my curiosity grew as the voice in my head reminded me; If we're staying here...probably smart to check for serial killer stuff.

Creeping to the dresser, I opened each of the six drawers. The first held neat rows of perfectly rolled socks and boxer briefs; the second contained tidy stacks of tanks and muscle shirts, while the third was filled with stacks of athletic shorts. Next, I found pristinely folded t-shirts of varying designs in black, as well as two drawers of jeans. Everything was folded and stacked, free of any ropes or weapons.

I closed the drawers with a sigh, but my eye was drawn to the sliding closet door. I figured, after seeing his bathroom and all his drawers, a peek in his closet couldn't do any harm. I slid the door open, finding a few dress shirts, Henleys, and hoodies. There was an impressive selection of leather jackets in shades of black-ish grey, and, below them, an array of sneakers and giant biker boots. There were a few small shelves with magazines about firefighting and motorcycles, but I was drawn to a single photo, framed in bright silver, sitting on top. The photo was a few years old based on Sam's hair growth and Chase's slightly smaller frame, but there was no doubt that it was him and his brothers. They were in a restaurant, surrounding an older woman with weathered skin and a huge smile that crinkled her eyes as she cradled a giant cake.

This must be Nonna.

The differences in the guys was fascinating. Sam was baby-faced and had a clean-cut head of hair that would almost classify him as preppy in comparison to the tousled-haired lumberjack I'd met. Troy wore a traditional police uniform in the photo, and he didn't have the goatee he sported now. Chase had short hair, but not the current buzz trim, and he smiled so big that I could practically hear the laughter radiating from him. His body language looked so relaxed, carefree even, as he leaned into Nonna with Troy's arm draped over the top of his shoulders. I had seen glimpses of his smile and lighthearted nature at the hospital. The surprising little elephant and the way he made silly jokes to cover up the fact that he was fussing over me. But there was no sign of that light in his house, I realized.

Replacing the photo to its perch, I closed the closet and scanned the room with a pang of sadness. His place was devoid of any evidence of the messy, good things I would expect in life with brothers who were so close. No family heirlooms, no past girlfriends littering the way, no hobbies save the stack of free weights on the wall. Nothing to tell me about this man whom I was now, inexplicably, living with. As if he too lived portably...ready to uproot at a moment's notice.

Dressing quickly, I grabbed the toothbrush the hospital gave me and returned to the bathroom. Wiping the fog from the mirror, I had no choice but to look at myself. Shampooed hair and clean skin were about the only two good things to note in my appearance. My eyes had purple circles in the inner corners. My lips were dry, and my hair hung limply down my back. My collarbones were peeking at the edges of my slightly too-large shirt collar. I couldn't help but clock the bruises I had been avoiding in the teeny hospital bathroom mirror: bandaged hand, IVs in my elbow, deep purple splotches licking my ribs.

It was a sobering moment as my hand drifted from ribs to belly, stroking the flat hollow of me that housed a tiny baby. Still safe and warm and snug inside me, I forced air into my stomach and pushed my belly forward, imagining what I might look like in a few months. Exhaling in a gush, I looked at my drawn complexion and felt that tug of shame pull at me again.

Stupid, foolish, girl...in such a mess because I trusted a man, and look how far that got me.

19

MOIRA

I COULDN'T IGNORE THAT I needed a few things to hold me over to my insurance check, and Chase seemed almost eager to take me shopping. I convinced him to take me to the store where I had a gift card. We enjoyed a pleasant trip overall, especially his laughter as I gave the shampoos the sniff test to see if they made me nauseous. I kept my clothing selections basic so that my money would stretch. As I walked towards the registers, I felt pretty good about my practical choices. Seeing Chase scowling down into the cart, however, had me questioning myself.

"What's wrong?" I looked inside the cart, but everything looked normal.

"It's just," he tugged us to a stop in the middle of the aisle, his face contorted as he chose his words. "Don't you need more stuff?"

"More... stuff?"

"Well, yeah." He ran his hand up and down the back of his neck, his face showing an adorable blush.

"Are...are you embarrassed?"

"No... it's not that. It's just," He blew out an exasperated breath before gesturing to the cart. "I always kinda got the impression y'all need more... *stuff*."

"Y'all?" I fought the urge to smile as his face reddened further.

"Girls."

"Stuff?"

"Well, yeah. I thought girls liked lots of soaps and gels and lotions and stuff." His face reddened even more.

Soaps and gels and stuff," I repeated, struggling not to laugh as he squirmed. "For girls."

"WOMEN!" He shifted on his feet. "Not girls. Women! Don't y'all like lots of makeup and perfumes...no, you probably can't stand the smell of those...but clothes and shoes. Women *like* shoes." He reached in and lifted the pair of neutral ballet flats I tossed in. "You only have one pair."

"And you think I need more?" It was mean to keep him squirming, and I was just about to let out a laugh when his head looked like it was about to pop.

"You skipped over half the aisles!" Even Chase looked startled by his outburst.

Then he closed his eyes, took a deep breath, and started pointing down the central aisle.

"You didn't go down the aisle with the hairdryers and stuff at all, and I know you need at least that, if not a curling thing or a straightening thing. And you barely glanced at the four different rows of makeup." He pointed in the other direction and continued. "Flats are great, but you need a good pair of sneakers if you wanna exercise and stay healthy for the baby, and the weather will be getting cooler soon, so a pair of boots would be smart." Then he lifted the clothing items in the cart. "And I can see you are trying to keep it simple with your clothes, and that makes sense, I guess, but you didn't even glance at the maternity stuff or bras and shit. You need a sweater 'cause nights are cold, and I *know* you like a wild set of pajamas, but you walked right past those and..."

He paused then and stared at me, wide-eyed and a little worried, as I marveled at the level of thought he'd given to my choices. His shoulders slumped a little as he dropped the clothes back into my cart. I couldn't tell if he was mad or sad, but it broke my heart to consider either, and I found myself feeling a little guilty for enjoying his earlier squirm.

"Wow. There is a lot to unpack here." I rested my hand on his arm, waiting until he looked me in the eyes. "I'll start from the top." I pointed to the basket. "I don't get fancy in the soap department. I grabbed one pair of shoes because I'm keeping my wardrobe at a minimum so that when the insurance check is cut, moving isn't monumental, and I won't even need maternity clothes for months still." He didn't seem convinced, so I tossed in an extra bit of truth to help him understand my plans. "And yes, I *normally* would use a hair dryer and a little more makeup, but I don't want to crowd your life while I try to reboot my own." He winced, and I tried aiming for a joke. "And I was never much of a gym rat, so the sneaker aisle is safe from me, but..." I winked as I lifted a few items to show the bottom of the cart. "I snuck a bra in when you weren't looking, so... I'm good."

He scanned the cart, and then my face, but he seemed hesitant still. I opted to share a little financial info to hopefully help him understand that I was being practical.

"The gift card I have will only go so far. I plan to chip in on groceries while I'm at your place." He immediately opened his mouth, but I held up a finger and pointed it directly in his face, "No argument on that, buster. I pull my own weight."

"Moira." Chase rested his hand on top of mine, looking at me with an urgency that belied his soft words. "Insurance companies are fickle. There are things you can't plan for or predict. I know staying with me wasn't your original plan or even your plan B, but I want you to stay with me as long as you need to." His hand slid to my arm, and my whole body felt the move like it was electrified. "I know that means moving stuff around, and I'm more than happy to have your company, so please....Crowd me."

"Chase." I tried to argue but stopped, realizing I never had a good plan A or even a mediocre plan B. Chase was my only plan, whether I liked it or not, so...what was I arguing for?

"I insist." He grabbed the cart with one hand and laced his fingers through mine with the other. "Now...where are the weird pajamas?"

20

CHASE

MOIRA'S INSISTENCE ON MAKING herself small in my life landed in my ribs like an anvil.

I didn't have words to describe how badly I wanted to see her things in my bathroom, her clothes in my closet. I wanted her snacks in my kitchen and baby items in the living room. I didn't want less....I wanted her to take every inch of space she deserved in the world.

She barely agreed to a few more things, but I saw the muffled laugh when I insisted on the gaudiest pair of pink lounge pants available. At the checkout, I saw her doing mental math with a scowl, but I had zero intention of letting her pay for anything. I whipped my card out so fast she didn't have time to protest, and when she argued, I used her logic against her.

"You said you wanted to chip in on food...well, there you go. Groceries on you for a while." I gave her a wink, knowing full well I'd never let her use that card on me. I thought she was done fighting me, but the next battle arose when I bought her a new phone at the cell phone store.

"Chase. I can get my own phone!"

"I'm sure you can and will," I spouted my prepared counterargument. "But they'll want an ID, and you don't have yours yet. Use this one until things settle down, and then you can get your account going again." I left out how much I liked that Jensen couldn't track her—and that now, I could. I didn't know for sure yet that Dean was the one looking for her, but I wasn't taking chances with her safety and knowing I could find her if I needed to settle something in me. She accepted the phone with a begrudging sigh but smiled sweetly when I programmed her into my phone and me into hers.

I could have lived on that smile all day.

I hadn't missed the yawns she hid, so I opted for drive-through burgers, knowing she had to be completely exhausted. A fact she proved when she didn't argue with me handling the bags, and she went inside empty-handed. It took me two trips to unload everything, and I found Moira sitting on the couch. She had a pensive look on her face, and the stuffed elephant in her lap looked like a shield.

"Why was Troy upset I left the hospital?" She asked.

I had hoped to prolong the peaceful little bubble a little longer, but my brother's words were in my head: she needed the truth. I couldn't bear to give her all the nasty details about Jensen's activities, nor risk her pulling away from me if she learned I was mixed up with him. I wanted to continue being a safe place for her, so I chose my words as honestly as possible, but carefully.

"There is reason to believe your fire is connected to other fires. An officer was placed at the hospital to make sure you were safe and had no unwanted visitors." I crossed to sit next to her on the couch. "That's part of why TJ...Troy...came over in such a rush."

"Am I in *danger*?" Her chin quivered, but she fought the tears with a determined scowl. "Is *that* why I'm here?"

"Anytime there is any kind of investigation about a fire, it instantly delays insurance claims until policyholders...like you....are cleared of involvement."

"So... they think I did it?" She whispered, her eyes big and round.

"The department is clearing all the residents' involvement as fast as possible to expedite claims." I rested a hand on her knee, needing her to believe my next words. "No one believes you caused this."

"Then why the police detail?" Moira turned, facing me with a determined look in her eyes.

"We think this fire might have been different, and they're looking into it with more detail. More care."

"Why. The. Police. Detail?" She stood pacing around my small living room as I scrambled for the right response. "You didn't come careening down the road checking hotels and motels just cause I left early...did you? Sam wasn't driving, Troy didn't barge in here, just cause they're nice guys...did they?"

"Moira, please come sit." I could hear the clipped frustration in her words, and I worried about the concussion, her headaches, and selfishly...how mad she'd be at me if I fucked this up.

"Why was a cop at the hospital, Chase?" A tear slipped down her cheek, and it was all I could do not to whisk it away with my hands...or a kiss. "Tell me the truth."

"My brothers *are* nice guys..." I swallowed hard, hating that Medusa scowl in her eyes leveled on me with a 'just try me' expression. I had to give her the truth...even if it hurt. "We believe the arsonist was targeting you. And we haven't captured him yet. So yeah, I called my brothers, and things got a little intense. We *may* have...overreacted a little."

"Him." Moira froze, back ramrod straight, as her eyes took on a thousand-yard stare. "You know who it is... don't you?" If her body language hadn't told me, the absolute wash of pale that flooded her face would have. She was terrified. And fearing that I was right about the Jensen connection, so was I.

"You are safe here, I promise." I reached for her hand, gently giving her fingers a tug toward the couch. "Please, sit down."

"Who is it?" She crossed to the couch, tucking one leg under herself and returning the furry pink and blue shield to her lap.

"We suspect it's..." I hated how far she was from me. Effectively curled into a ball on the far end of the couch, my next words would possibly be everything or nothing. "A guy named Dean Jensen."

The cringe that washed over her was tangible; clenched fists, eyes closed, wave of nausea inducing, and brutal. I waited as she turned her face away, taking a breath either to calm her emotions or possibly resist vomiting, either felt like viable options since, above all, I knew I was right.

"You knew him," I stated, feeling the need to take my own deep breath when she gave an almost imperceptible nod.

"Dean and I met online nearly a year ago. I'd never really done online dating, but I figured it could be nice to have someone to talk to, so I created a profile and started swiping. Dean popped into my DM's, and we hit it off. At first, it was easy getting to know one another. He seemed genuine and earnest, texting me daily. Then, every night, we'd video chat and sometimes even watch movies together that way. It all seemed so normal." She picked at her nails, keeping her eyes glued to the task as she talked. "He didn't even flinch when he found out I was a foster kid. No pity eyes or 'poor you.'"

I knew those pity eyes and the relief of seeing someone react in virtually any other way than to feel sorry for the cards you'd been dealt. Jensen needed to bleed for using that to manipulate her.

"He flew out first...so we could hang out over a long weekend....a perfect gentleman...barely tried to kiss me even." The vision of that asshole kissing her cut like a knife, but I didn't dare breathe a sound for fear that she'd stop talking. "After that, we flew to places in the middle of us, or he'd come to Oregon again, and each time, he'd encourage me to try new foods or do some new activity. He only tried to push me into something I didn't want once and..." She flicked her eyes nervously at me for a second, leaving her sentence unfinished and me white-knuckling a barely tamped-down rage as I imagined all the ways that story could have ended. "Anyway, in between all the travel and texting, he got more demonstrative about his feelings. He talked about how great our lives could be if we had more time together and how perfect we were. I questioned how fast things were moving, but he just kept telling me, 'Don't go looking for red flags, sweetheart.'" She shook her head, muttering 'Asshole' under her breath. "He pushed for me to move in with him, but when I pushed back on that one, he suggested we should take the next step and move into the same town at least. He told me he couldn't leave his job as easily as I could move mine since I worked from home, and God, I was so stupid!"

"No."

"YES! My contract was ending...he helped me find a dream job on the East Coast...it even offered a relocation reimbursement after I'd made it past probation." She rolled her eyes before adding, "Even *that* was too good to be true."

"The job didn't work out?"

"Nope." She gave a sardonic laugh despite the tears flowing down her cheeks. "Apparently, the company itself never existed. On my first day, I tried to call for login information and got a dead number. Emails all bounced. And when I started digging around, even their website was a shell. I was completely scammed...like a chump," she gave a half-hysterical laugh to the room and declared, "and there goes *any* hope for maternity benefits." A sob cut her words off, and I reached for her then, but she shook her head, holding a hand out to stop me as she took a deep breath. "By the time I arrived in town, I couldn't reach Dean. I was even worried about him when I finished moving my stuff in and hadn't heard from him." She stood up again, pacing as I wondered about the timing of his sudden silence, my stomach in knots at the likelihood that I caused that when I confronted him at the station a little over a month before her fire. "I was so stupid."

"No, Moira." I sat on the edge of the couch, fighting equal urges to wrap her in my arms, and hunt down Jensen to squeeze his throat til his eyeballs pop.

"Oh, I was!" She started gesturing to the room as she vented. "Of *all* the people who should have known not to trust someone who had all the right words at all the right times, you'd *think* it'd been the girl who'd been dumped by not one...not two...but no less than *eight* foster families." She looked dead in my eyes then and held up her fingers. "Eight!"

The number shocked the hell out of me. I'd barely been in three different homes, and still, I fought impostor syndrome, whispering my life was temporary. I couldn't imagine the damage that comes from being shuffled around that many times. Yet, here she stood, spilling her guts in an inspiring display of courage.

A courage that Jensen tried to break.

"Dean arranged the apartment, paid for my moving truck... I had no doubts in my mind when I loaded up my entire life for a job I'd only communicated with via email...no doubts about moving to a state I'd never set foot in before, and for what!" She was screaming, tears streaming down her face, and it only fueled my hate for a man I already wanted six feet under. "The childish sparkle of an idea that people like me *really* could have the fairytale endings you see in the movies?"

A gasp escaped as she fought a full-body sob. It was enough to have me on my feet when she turned and looked right at me, eyes fallen so dark that my heart broke with her.

"The worst part was when I finally found him...he acted like he barely knew me." She donned a mocking man's voice and gestured angrily." 'What brings you to my neck of the woods...unannounced...', 'Was there something you needed from me or...', 'No need to get hysterical, sweetheart.', 'We had a lot of fun.'" The picture her words painted made my skin crawl, and I began to get a little descriptive myself in all the ways I wanted the man to suffer.

She stopped pacing, shoulders slumped, eyes locked on the elephant in her hands.

"I wasn't his girlfriend, I was...just some overreacting, pathetic, sad-sack orphan." Her final confession, muttered more to the ground than to me, gutted me. "His poor, pitiful, little plaything." Finally, so low I almost couldn't hear it, he whispered. "Guess that's what I get for being so hard to read."

"The Fuck." I closed the gap between us, wrapping my arms around her even as she folded into my chest and sobbed. I tried to will my strength to her while plotting painful ways to make him pay for what he'd done. "You aren't hard to read...that asshole was just illiterate."

"I was such a fool." She sobbed into my chest, tears as hot and fresh as if the betrayal was yesterday, and in the dark corner of my mind, I had to wonder if she had loved him. Or, worse, loved him still. After all...he was most likely the father of her baby, and asshole or not, if she wanted him in her baby's life, who was I to stop her? Who was I to her at all? My stomach clenched at the idea she shared such intimate feelings for someone who was an evil bastard, but I shoved them aside, focusing on her.

"Jensen was a master manipulator. A vile woman-hating prick." I stroked her hair, hoping what I was saying was sinking in. "Anyone who can go to those lengths has some serious issues. Add in the questions around your fire, and yeah, Troy made a good call. I'm glad the cop was there." She shook her head in agreement, the sobs slowing. I pulled back enough to look into her deep, river-blue eyes, drinking in the exhausted trust she offered me and swearing to myself Jensen would never hurt her again. "You being here with me now is also a good call."

"That's why I'm not at a hotel." Moira pulled back, wiping her cheeks and putting a distance between us, which I hated.

"Where could be safer than crashing with a fire-fighter, between a top-shelf EMT and Essex County's finest police officer?" I gave a forced grin, trying to lighten the mood despite my stomach still roiling from her story. "But don't tell my brothers I said that... they'll get a big head."

Her face turned pensive again, thoughts spinning despite the exhaustion etched in her whole body. She'd shared a lot tonight, and I was strung out from it, and that was without being pregnant and still healing from what she endured. I wanted to help her find some peace tonight, some rest. My mind went to the trick Nonna used anytime one of us had a hard time sleeping.

"What do you say, we wash away the bad taste of this with some hot chocolate? We can find something on TV to watch and let it all simmer." I smiled when she nodded in agreement and crossed to the couch, her legs curling beneath her as she donned her elephant barrier once more.

I'd build a fortress of fluffy elephants if it meant she'd never feel ashamed again.

WILDER BRO'S GROUP CHAT

-3-

> ME: Any updates?

TJ: It's not even been a day.

Samoa: Just got to the station. Heard they pulled a partial print.

> ME: Did they run it yet?

TJ: They'd need us for that, and I don't see anything yet. Patience brother.

Samoa: For real, dude. We left you last night.

> ME: Chief tell you anything?

Samoa: Chief's locked up tighter than Troy's asshole. I'll keep my ears open.

ME: Maybe if I call the chief.

TJ: NO.

Samoa: NO.

TJ: Right now, no one is looking to you for Moira.

Samoa: How'd you work that?

TJ: I told them she was placed in protective custody at an…undisclosed location.

Samoa: Well done Grandpa.

TJ: Has she told you anything else?

ME: She knows there's an arson investigation. She guessed it was Jensen.

Samoa: and the rest?

ME: I gotta tread carefully here. That asshole did a real number on her.

TJ: You can't lie to her, brother. Not even for the right reasons.

Samoa: He knows.

ME: I can't lose her go.

Samoa: We know.

ME: What the fuck am I doing?

TJ: Seems kinda like falling in love.

Samoa: Indeed it does.

21

CHASE

TROY WASN'T ONE FOR emotional declarations or grey-area polic-
ing, and this made two in as many days, along with a vague declaration on Moira's whereabouts. Surprising as that was, I found his
words...comforting. I kept people at arm's length, I knew that. I had
coworkers and a few friends, and had engaged in one-night stands more
times than I cared to admit. But I never fully connected—no real bonds,
except my brothers.

Then Moira.

The way she clung to my hand in the ambulance and leaned into me
when she found out she was pregnant was revelational. She let her whole
heart show in the face of massive shocks, and it was me she needed. That
courageous vulnerability broke through my walls, and I couldn't fathom
a world in which I didn't share oxygen with such a fiercely feminine
creature. That same courage had me tossing and turning on my too-small
couch all night as I wondered why she hid that part of herself over and

over. Like she needed me to prove her strength when all I wanted was to let her be soft.

Several times, I thought I heard her awake, tossing and turning, and I wondered if she needed to talk or needed space. Warring between those two had me wound tight as a spring. I finally got up when the ache from my shoulder made coffee more appealing than sleep. I tried to keep my footsteps soft until I heard her turn the shower on, and only then did I slip into my bedroom to grab a change of clothes, feeling strangely self-conscious, tiptoeing through my own house.

When she called out that she was done, I slipped into the bathroom from the back hallway, not wanting to invade her privacy. I turned on the water, and as I waited for it to heat, I took in the other changes to my space: new bottles in my shower and a second toothbrush on my sink. I expected to see her hair stuff and makeup, but found them still in the bags under the sink. I made a mental note to find her something better to keep those in when I heard Moira's voice.

Curiosity devoured propriety as I carefully cracked the door, peeking in on Moira. She sat on the edge of my bed, dressed only in a t-shirt, with the visible curve of her hip peeking from its edge. Her wet hair curtained her face, but I could tell she spoke in a soft, almost lyrical cadence, down at her hand resting on her belly.

"You know, baby, I am so sorry you are having such a rocky start in life, but I promise...you won't ever have to know Dean or deal with him in any way. I'll keep you safe now and forever and forever." A swirl of conflicting emotions squeezed my chest at overhearing something so tender...but I was too enthralled to walk away. Moira continued talking, even as she looked up and gazed out the bedroom window. "I'll get us medical benefits...and find you the best pediatrician. I'll get a little house like this too, as soon as I land a real job. We can have a swing on the porch and window boxes on the front for flowers. I'll find a great neighborhood where we can play in the yard...and I'll make sure you have a great school."

Leaning my head on the door frame, I exhaled through the wave of emotions that flooded over me. Relief, to my core, to hear her promise to avoid the man who'd put her through hell. The worry about her being emotionally attached to that waste of skin gave way to shame that I hadn't given her more credit for what she had overcome. Of course, none of that rose to the surface faster than the shock of wanting to sit by her side, caressing the skin on that hip as she held her belly. I wanted to see her smile at her baby and...I wanted more than anything for that voice, that peaceful, easy melody, to speak to me after we shared an intimate moment of our own.

By the time I got in the shower, the water was cold, and frankly, it served me right. My unwanted hard-on needed the reminder that this woman was not wooed here by romance but thrust here by circumstances beyond her control. The shallow release as I spilled my guilt across the tile wall did little to relieve the ache to hold her, but it did strengthen my resolve to keep her with me...to keep her safe. Toweling off, a text alert chimed a message from my Chief.

> Chief: Stop snooping. I can't disclose anything...
> this is now a criminal matter.

I sighed, shaking my head that clearly Sam wasn't as subtle about his snooping around as we had hoped.

> Me: Do we have a lead on Jensen?

> Chief: Got a lead on the woman from the fire?

I wasn't sure how to proceed. Troy had left Moira's whereabouts specifically vague, as much for her safety as anything else. But if I disclosed that to the Chief, would he share it up the chain? More than that, would he give me a single shred of information if he knew I was in such close proximity to her, given my already messy entanglement with Jensen? He texted again before I had a chance to respond.

> Chief: We gotta unpack her connection to Jensen...but I'm guessing she won't turn up for a day or so more, right?

That last 'right' confirmed what I suspected. Chief Brandt knew she was with me. Still, if he was fishing, I needed to redirect his question. I tried to pivot the chat to the fire itself.

> Me: Branson Heights cleared for inspection?

> Chief: Maintenance secured the rear stairwells. Forensics has been through it, too.

> Me: So I'm clear to check it out then?

> Chief: You can't go in an official capacity when you're on med-leave.

It wasn't exactly a no, and I decided not to press the issue.

> Me: Understood

> Chief: And no one is scheduled to work there today.

The additional disclosure was the closest thing to a thumbs-up I was going to get, and I was taking the win.

> Me: You're the best...you know that?

> Chief: And you better be fucking alone when you go.

> Me: Understood

My Chief always had my back in life and on the job—but I wasn't sure where he stood on Moira until just now, and it was a silent encouragement that helped spur my burgeoning plan along.

We needed answers—about the fire, Jensen, and what tied him to Moira. I also wanted to cement Moira's place here with me, to help her feel secure, like she wasn't a burden. I hoped that seeing the burnt building would give her enough closure to stop fighting my help, as well as shake loose a few details that might help capture Jensen. Gears spinning, I walked into the kitchen just as Moira closed the fridge.

"You *do* realize protein powder isn't real food, right?"

"I eat at the station when I'm on shift or with my brothers when I'm not working, but honestly, I'm very rarely not working."

"Fair warning, I'm a girl who likes snacks so much that my hangry resembles a feral animal under a bridge. My gift card is burning a hole in my pocket, so how about you let me buy some provisions to save us both?" I had to laugh at the visual of her adorable face scrunched up like a hissing kitten. Going to the store seemed like a great segue to my quickly forming plan.

"Wanna grab a bite to eat first, then we can go see if anything at your place survived the fire before grocery shopping? We can grab the drinks for tonight, too."

Her eyes went wide in surprise.

"I can see my place?" The pitch in her voice went up a solid octave as she began bouncing on her toes, rapid-fire questions coming one after another. "Did anything survive the fire? Is my car okay? Will my insurance claim process now?"

I had to hold my hands up in surrender to get a word in.

"Yes...I don't know...and I'm not sure." Her excitement all but deflated at the last one. "Nothing has moved that would expedite insurance red tape...this is a sort of side favor."

"Of course, red tape takes longer."

"It's okay. You have time; there's no rush here." I reassured her, already missing the bouncing sparkle in her eyes.

"But this is a favor?"

"Chief and I go way back. I think he has an inkling of our arrangement." She nodded her head, eyes going distant in thought. "I'm hoping that being in the space will jog your memory about any details that might help move the investigation along." My fists clenched as I silently added, 'And help us nail Jensen to the goddamn wall.'

"If anything survived, can I take it?" Her voice was soft, almost hopeful—and I hated the hard truth I had to give her.

"Between the fire, the smoke, and the water... it's unlikely anything is salvageable." Her face fell so hard I could have sworn it hit the floor with an audible thud. "We'll look, but the goal is to jog your memory. If you remember anything important, I can relay those through Troy to the team investigating in a way that keeps your whereabouts secret."

"I need to be...secret?" Her hand moved to her belly, and dammit if I didn't burst with a swell of pride at her protective instincts.

I walked to her, fighting the urge to place my hand on top of hers in a sort of solemn pledge as she glanced down at her belly, and I gave her the only words I had.

"Absolutely nothing is happening to either one of you with me around."

22

MOIRA

A S MENTALLY AND PHYSICALLY exhausted as I was, my mind wouldn't stop replaying all that Chase and I had shared. I accepted that Dean was a gaslighting, egomaniacal narcissist. And that, for my part, I'd ignored red flags and my better instincts for misguided romantic notions. But facing the possibility that he was an arsonist had me tossing and turning all night.

I played through everything in the past through this new filter; Chief among them, I had no idea who Dean was. I built him up to having a stable desk job running a critical city service, like some low-level politician. But could a politician commit arson?

Shame burned through me as I thought back on all the times I'd accepted his evasions about his life. I then began playing through all our texts and chats, measuring what I knew about the father of my baby.

I knew he liked his cabin and being outdoors.

I knew he liked high-adrenaline things like rock climbing and sky-diving.

I knew he had poker once a month with 'the guys,' but who were they? Were they work buddies? Why didn't I ask more questions? I managed to drift off in the wee hours of the morning, but woke up with a new question screaming in my brain.

Did Chase know Dean?

It'd been nagging at me with the way Chase chose his words carefully about Dean. And he was so eager to have me in his home, rather than a hotel. It didn't quite add up to the 'I just want to help you get on your feet' message he was pushing. He could help me find a hotel if all he wanted was to buy me time until insurance money came through. His reaction to Dean, to all of this, felt overly intense for a random guy who happened to be faster up the burning stairs.

I waited until we'd eaten and were driving across town to my apartment to ask, knowing he'd be trapped in the car and couldn't deflect or distract me.

"How well did you know Dean?" Chase's eyes never left the road in front of us, but I saw his jaw clench and unclench twice, and it was confirmation enough that I was right, so I pressed on. "You are a firefighter, after all. And your brothers are a cop and an EMT. It's a small town." I was practically sitting on my hands to keep from fidgeting as I watched his grip tighten on the steering wheel, tension electrifying the air. "Surely you knew him, maybe even knew we were dating, right?"

I stopped then, letting my words hang to see how Chase would pick up the ball I'd volleyed. The minute that passed felt like an hour before he spoke.

"I know him...knew him...but we weren't friends." His tone was even, almost lifeless if he hadn't added such vehemence at the end. His anger was clear and present, but I still wasn't sure if the anger was at Dean as a person, or if the dislike was solely because of the fire and his connection to me.

"Why didn't you say anything, then?" I willed my face into neutrality, hoping to hide the anxiety blooming in my stomach. I wanted to clarify, but frankly, I wasn't sure I'd like his answer.

"I didn't have a reason to...at first. You never said his name in the hospital...and I only learned about the arson investigation a day or so later." His pause felt heavy, and I could tell he had more to say. "It was your fire, your statement about the fire, that helped put things together."

"Me?" I jerked my head back in surprise, unsure what I could have said about my fire that would've connected me to Dean...when Dean wasn't even on my radar for the fire. Watching Chase again clench and stoically hesitate to speak was becoming unbearable, and my patience finally snapped. "What aren't you telling me?"

His long-resigned sigh was heavy.

"I don't know everything. I've been out of commission for a few days. But the locked door on your room and the window that wouldn't open were similar to other fires."

"Other fires....Wait, my locks? I thought they were just jammed from the fire." I hated that my voice cracked, emotions overpowering my will to appear strong and capable, as so many words bounced around my brain.

Chase apparently didn't miss it either since he immediately pulled the car to the side of the road, flipping on hazards and turning to face me.

"I've been out with my shoulder, so I'm only getting bits and pieces right now." He reached his hand across to me slowly and rested his fingertips just at the edges of my own. "I'll share what I can."

His face was an absolute vision of soft concern. His eyes, open and clear, hardly blinked as he worried over my feelings. His mouth, relaxed but closed, never wavered. There was no belittling smirk or sneer, no quips to make me question myself. Everything about him was so terribly genuine, and I couldn't help but hold it up in stark contrast to Dean. Dean, who was never without a charming, disarming, disembodied smile to shine a distracting light on things for an emotional sleight of hand.

The question still rang in my head from earlier, so I pulled at the one nagging worry that plagued me most.

"But you and Dean...you *aren't* friends?"

"No." His words held zero hesitation and seemed genuine. But then, hadn't I believed all the things Dean told me? "I could never be friends with a man who could treat women like that?"

Women, plural. That had shame rising.

Of course, I knew Dean wasn't a snow-white virgin when we met, but knowing how easily he discarded me, the knowledge of him being with other women made me feel cheap. Like I was just the next notch on his bedpost. Tears stung as I closed my eyes and willed them away. I wanted to know if Chase and Dean were friends, and I had my answer. For good or ill, I had no choice but to trust it. If I let myself think too much about anything else right now, I'd fall apart, and I had no room for falling apart.

"Okay." I nodded, focusing my eyes forward. "Good enough for now."

"Moira, I want you to know that–"

I shook my head, shutting down any more discussion on the topic before I lost the battle of tears I was holding back.

"It's okay. Let's get this over with."

Chase eyed me for another minute before pulling back onto the road with a soft but resigned sigh.

Pulling into my apartment complex was jarring. The two front buildings were business as usual, with cars parked in their reserved spots and people milling about on balconies or stoops. The picture grew bleaker the further back we drove, and my heart sank as we entered the ghost town that was my building.

The epicenter of the fire was plainly evident by the sheer volume of black, ash-covered soot that clung to my building's charred skeleton. Even the cars still parked at the building's base were blackened and melted—one of them mine.

Chase jumped over a curb and pulled the SUV down a burnt path around the backside of the building. Things looked more intact back there, more of the natural wall color peeking through the smudge and soot, and a tremor ran through me at the realization that the damage was far worse on the side of the building where I lived. Chase parked and then grabbed a duffle bag from the back seat.

"Before we go in, let's slip these on." He dragged out two plastic jumpsuits complete with foot booties, gloves, and a plastic hood. "Buildings are filthier than people realize, post-fire. All the ash and water combine to form a nice, thick sludge that drips from everywhere. If you don't cover yourself from head to toe, there is no way you aren't getting dirty." We donned the protective gear, and after a brief moment of levity as he helped cuff the ridiculously long sleeves and pant legs to fit me, we headed to the rear door of the building.

"Now...this is where I need you to pay attention." Chase turned serious, his tone all business. "This stairwell has been structurally cleared, but there is no other way in or out. We are going *directly* to your apartment and *nowhere* else. I move first, and you follow my footsteps *exactly*.

If I say we stop and turn back, you don't argue. No hesitation. No looking back. Got it." I nodded my understanding, anxiety rising with the severity of his words. "I wouldn't bring you here if I didn't think it was safe, but I won't take anything for granted. We're looking at the bare minimum." I nodded again as he squeezed my arm and led me inside.

Chase checked each step with his full weight, first with one foot, then both, making our ascent painfully slow. I appreciated his caution, but it was eerie to watch nonetheless. The black film of doused flames coated absolutely everything. And the silence of the building felt otherworldly. No faint sounds of someone's TV or distant laughter, not even cricket or bird song, were heard. It was like crawling through a burnt-out husk, and I was surprised at the sorrow it brought to imagine all the displaced lives from what...maybe my bad dating choices? I had to shake away that deprecation before the gritty black depression tugged me down with it, just as Chase nodded at a door barred by yellow tape.

"Mechanicals room." He pointed his flashlight. "That was the point of origin. It's directly behind your kitchen." I swallowed hard around creeping memories as we entered the back hallway—my apartment door on the left. "Remember. Go slow, step where I step. And if I so much as get a whiff that something feels unsafe, we immediately work our way back out." He waited for confirmation before we stepped into a level of destruction I was not prepared for.

Natural light flooded the blown-out front windows of the living room. My feet squished into the mud that used to be my carpet, and each step took us deeper into an acrid cloud of sulfur and smoke hanging thick in the air. The couch and coffee table were half-burned, half-smoked...the stack of magazines I would read on a lazy afternoon, little more than ashes. The kitchen was entirely gone, with a melted fridge door and cabinet doors hanging half off their hinges— if hanging at all. I didn't bother looking to see if my dishes survived. I rarely cooked and had little need for them. I was momentarily sad to see the small table and chairs I once owned were trashed, but then I remembered I owned nothing. The apartment came partially furnished, and none of this was really mine, save for the brief sunny mornings when I could enjoy a cup of coffee curled up around my laptop at that tiny two-seater table.

Now, a tiny two-seater pile of kindling.

Sadness settled around me at how transient and small my life was.

"My laptop...it was here." I pointed to the outline on the table where a ghostly sootprint sat next to the shattered remnants of my favorite mug.

"Maybe the investigators have it, what with an arson investigation and all." He glanced back at me with a hesitant look on his face. "I'll see if Troy knows." I had to swallow past embarrassment at the idea of someone seeing all my private documents. Not that it held a collection of anything scandalous, but there were more than a few steamy and even X-rated chats between Dean and me. If someone were investigating him, they would surely read those. Mentally, I chastised myself for holding onto them at all when clearly he deserved to have everything burned in effigy like my whole life had been.

In the bedroom, Chase held up a hand, halting me at the door as we glanced at the bathroom and closet.

"It doesn't look like any of your clothes are salvageable and ..." His voice trailed off as my heart pounded in my ears.

The bed I'd been sleeping on was blackened and saturated. The walls were a stark painting of a burning crime scene, and there, in the far corner, the corner I cowered in. Torrents of memory and sensation came rushing forward.

"I hated the quiet." Chase turned to see me, but I only registered it in my peripheral vision as I stared at the tomb of my room. "I blasted music when I needed a little pick-me-up. I needed that a lot in the days following Dean. I was sleeping with music blaring on my phone. I woke to a sour smell...It was *strong*." I had to clench my teeth to stop the bile from rising as I tasted the memory of that sour now, with the knowledge that Dean could have done this... to me. "I couldn't imagine how I'd been sleeping and...the door wouldn't open, and I wondered why it was stuck. I was so dense; it took me so long to realize the real danger I was in."

"Not dense," Chase responded to words I didn't realize I'd spoken aloud as my heart raced. "The heat hadn't made it in here yet."

I tried to smile in response...to feign a semblance of being together and calm, even as I saw the blown-out window and felt the air whoosh from my lungs.

"I ran to the window." Tears stung my eyes as if the blinding smoke was back. I pulled in a breath, desperate to make myself calm down. "But you,"

My hand reached out of its own accord, and Chase was there.

"Moira." He held my hand in his, his other hand on my back. "This is too much... I'm sorry....we should-"

"No... I'm okay." My eyes scanned the space again, memories of my escape playing out in vivid, high-def, technicolor, full-body real-time. "You saved me." I breathed through a sob. "I'm only okay 'cause you saved me."

"Just doing my job."

"NO!" Chase's smile faltered at my snapped command. "Don't discount how amazing you were.... Or are." Sorrow and gratitude moved me, lifting my hand to his cheek, even as I felt the heat of the blast he shielded me from as if it were still present. "You saw me in the window; no one else did. You ran into a burning building, busted down my door..., *You* rescued me...you saved my life when he..." I grabbed his hand and pressed it to my belly, no longer fighting the tears that streaked my cheeks. "You saved *both* our lives, Chase!" The torrent of emotion, fear, and memory that I channeled into this single declaration overcame my earlier anxiety as I looked into his eyes. "You might think that's *just* a job, but it's not," I willed my voice to remain strong a moment more before it gave way to emotion. "You saved...what I didn't know I had...from a man who tried to steal it all away."

Gasping for air, I worried I had said too much as he stood blinking at me. Then gently, Chase slid his hand from my belly to my waist, tugging me close enough to rest his forehead on mine. Closing my eyes, I leaned into him as I let go of all the feelings attached to the charred carcass of my life and gave peace a chance to sit within me.

"Please... don't cry." His low voice was smooth as velvet, resonating all over my body. I tried to calm my breathing, lingering in the space he had created that was separate from the bleakness that surrounded us. It was a silent, sacred thing...this space we'd embraced, and I soaked it into my bones as his breathing synced with mine. Unsure of how long we held the moment, Chase broke the silence first.

"I'm not...good with words." He started, and I immediately shook my head.

"I didn't say all that for you to feel obligated... I just wanted you to–"

"Lemme say this." He squeezed my hands, which somehow had made their way to his chest and were wrapped in his own. "I want to be better with words...but you have to know," He pulled back, waiting for me to focus on his eyes. "Saving you was pure instinct. But staying with you is as easy as breathing. Having you move in was the most natural thing in the world. You fit into my life, and I don't know what's going to happen from here, but I won't...I don't...regret a single second I get to spend with you, if for nothing more than this moment right here." He ended his declaration by resting his lips against my head, and I felt it all the way down to my toes.

Not good with words, my ass.

23

CHASE

I PLANNED THE TRIP to Moira's apartment tactically: go in, scan the scene, then leave. Like an idiot, I failed to consider the emotional impact, and Moira's tears caught me off guard. I scrambled to put her back together, but her emotions shifted from a near panic-attack into a declaration about me saving her. Then she grabbed my hand and pressed it into her belly, and before I knew what I was saying, I spilled my damned guts.

I should have been embarrassed for pining over how she fits into my life, but I wasn't.

When we left, her hand found mine, like it belonged. I held it all the way back down to the truck, and she didn't pull away. Afterward, I suspected her mind was still wandering through memories as she'd grown quiet. I wanted to know where her head was taking things, though.

"That was your first fire scene, I take it?" Moira nodded, but seemed steady, so I continued. "Most people are surprised by either how much damage there is or by how little damage there is...depending on where their imagination goes."

"Honestly, it looked about like I expected...sorta...I guess." Moira paused, as if choosing her following words. "I think I was more surprised at how *little* of me was there to begin with."

"How little?"

"I was mentally going through my things when we arrived, wondering what would have survived and what condition it would be in. I considered trash bags to haul it out and wondered if regular detergent would get the smoke smell out." She paused, and I held my tongue at the silence...waiting for her to take a breath or two. "But I had almost nothing there. No pictures on the walls, no favorite books stacked in a closet. There was no special dish that had a memory attached to it or even a favorite sweater or old stuffed toys that I would mourn the loss of."

She turned towards me and grew more animated.

"Did you know that I had an entire truck, a small one, but still an entire truck that I moved here with? But looking around today, I saw none of my flair or style. How crazy is that? To have lived a life so small that when it all went up in flames, there was nothing to mourn." Her voice grew soft again. "How pathetic a life so unlived that my most cherished item was a laptop...and that elephant you gave me."

I might have soared at the thought that she loved that stuffed toy I got her, but damn, it hurt that she felt her presence weighed so little when she took up all the oxygen in my life.

"Given that you had eight foster homes growing up, you said yourself you became good at prepping for a reboot. It makes sense that you would default to a minimalist footprint in case life required you to be suddenly mobile."

"But, I don't want that for my baby!" Moira's voice was so firm that I nearly pulled the car over again, fearing I'd made her angry. "I want my baby to have roots...big ones! Where we never move, and we own gobs of ridiculous tchotchkes. And there should be marks!" She lifted a finger, pointing defiantly to no one in particular. "Juice spills and scuffed tables so that, when they're adults, we can look back and see evidence of a life well lived. I want our life to be big and noisy so the whole world knows we exist...ya know!?"

"Shit, woman," I laughed, marveling at her ferocious expression like she was just willing the universe to take it on the chin. "That's about the ballsiest thing I've ever heard anyone say." She shared my laugh, and I could see her relax back into the seat.

"You don't think I'm crazy for wanting spilled juice and tchotchkes?"

"I'm not sure what a tchotchke is... but no." I slid my free hand across the cab, lacing my fingers between hers with a warmth of ease that felt honest and fitting. "Maybe it's a foster kid thing, but I think you basically described my dream life." She curled her fingers around mine, and all I could think of was how great my place would look full of table scuffs and fingerprinted walls. So much better than my sterile, efficient existence.

"The burned laptop is cramping the job search a bit, though. Working off my phone is getting me by, but I need to fill out papers. My job starts in a week. It's part-time, so I'll still have to find more permanent work...and benefits."

"You never told me where you are going to work?"

"The library...on the main street. They need branding and social media work. That's what I do." I loved learning more about her and immediately integrated her into my real estate business with my brothers, making a mental note to discuss her services with them. "They don't know how long they'll need me, but hopefully long enough to buy a new laptop and get online again."

Our real estate business was something we sort of fell into, but we all agreed it was a good, long-term project for us. My brothers and I enjoyed investing in the town we loved, but none of us were particularly tech-savvy, so it hadn't flourished as much as I knew it could. Moira's skills could be a perfect fit to fill a need we didn't know we had, and part of me loved that maybe she could share in this with us. We finished the drive with a quick grocery trip for drinks and a few more snacks, then loaded everything back into the car and headed home.

"So...this dinner tonight?" Her eyebrows lifted as she let the question hang unfinished.

"Yeah...My brothers and I enlisted in the Marines after high school. Nonna hated seeing us leave and made us promise to video call once a week."

"Sounds like a reasonable request...after abandoning her and all," Moira smirked.

"Other than when we were in theatre, we gathered round the camera to call as much as possible."

"In...theatre?"

"It sorta means in the field of action. My brothers and I were tagged as a team capable of executing quick, surgical strike-type missions. We'd have to go dark...no communication...for those." I saw a flash of concern cross her face, and I wanted to sidestep whatever her next question might be. Being a Marine was in my past, and I never felt compelled to dwell on the sometimes brutal work we did. "But those were few and far between. Otherwise, we called each week as expected."

"Awwww," Her sing-songy voice was light, and it made me feel light to hear it. "Ya'll were good boys for your mom."

"When we'd come home on leave, she'd make this *huge* celebratory Spaghetti dinner. Like...*massive*. Heaping bowls of pasta, a vat of sauce she'd cook all day, garlic knots...from scratch. And always some chicken parmesan or meatballs."

"Growing boys need protein!" The laughter in her voice was enough for me never to want the story to end.

"We'd eat 'til we were stuffed, then hang out all night catching up until after Nonna went to bed. She'd wake up the next morning and find us passed out on couches and floors, usually hungover...whole place reeking of garlic."

"That sounds kind of amazing."

"It was." I agreed, letting myself feel the warmth of that memory and the bittersweetness of missing my Nonna. "Once we all finished our tour, the tradition kinda died out. We were starting our careers and getting involved in the community through real estate activities. Then Nonna got sick."

"I'm sorry." Moira's hand moved to my leg—her voice instantly soft and warm. "You don't have to tell me anymore if it - "

"No... it's okay." I let my hand rest on hers, loving the connection. "My Nonna was way too old to be raising three rowdy boys. It's why we called her Nonna and not Mom. The whole town treated her like a grandma...everyone called her Nonna. She cooked for *everyone*, and there wasn't a person within a 10-mile radius who hadn't received one of her homemade pies if they were sick. That's how we first got to know my fire chief and even Troy's police chief. Nonna was big on holiday cookie deliveries to first responders."

"She sounds perfectly magical."

I paused, remembering how Nonna was never too tired to stay up when I needed a late-night pep talk. And I know she's the reason both my brothers and I would never turn down a phone call or text from one another, no matter the day or night. She might have been older in the parenting department, but her love dug deep. It lived in us.

"She was diagnosed with late-stage ovarian cancer at 72. It was rough but not long. She passed within months." I'd hardly realized I'd parked us back home until Moira unbuckled and slid closer, leaning her head on my shoulder. I couldn't resist leaning my head to the side and resting my lips gently on the top of her head. I wanted to kiss her, deep and real, but given the emotions of the day, I wasn't entirely sure it would be welcomed, so I kept going with my story.

"After she passed...We wanted to do something in her honor and realized we all missed the weekly dinners."

"And spaghetti night was born." Moira finished for me. "It sounds like an amazing tradition."

24

MOIRA

LEARNING ABOUT CHASE'S NONNA felt special. I tucked away the sweet memories like precious gems—happy he'd had a life like that, even if a little sad that I never had such a happily-ever-after with my childhood.

It didn't take long to put away the groceries before we took the short walk across the shared lawn to Troy's. I planned to carry some of the drinks, but Chase swooped in, tucking the case of beer under one arm and dangling the seltzers in the same hand, freeing his other hand to move back to mine. He handled the bulky weight of the drinks as if they were nothing. I found myself more than a little impressed at the corded muscles moving under his t-shirt, but was pulled forward more by the most mouth-watering aroma.

"What...is that heavenly scent?" I closed my eyes, inhaling the delicious tomato and garlic, and exhaled on a moan.

"Looks like Baby likes garlic bread." Chase smiled, nudging open Troy's door with his foot. "Hey guys, sorry we're late; We had to put some groceries away at home first."

"You mean Moira doesn't want to live on protein bars, leftovers, and sadness..." Sam mocked a look of shock on his face. "You don't say?!" Chase dropped my hand to punch his brother in the shoulder as I took Troy's place.

It was clear, both men enjoyed things neat and orderly, but where Chase's home was neutral and almost staged to look vacant, Troy's home was the picture of warmth with overstuffed upholstered furniture and blankets over the back of every chair. His coffee table held tidy stacks of books and magazines that invited you to sit and read, and the full-wall entertainment cabinet was filled with family pictures that drew me in. There were framed report cards, news clippings of high school stories, and photos of braces, graduations, and everything in between. Intermixed in it were childhood medals and trophies and a smooth wooden bowl filled with ticket stubs and the buds of dried flowers. Vacation photos had themed frames, and there was even a pedestal holding a signed baseball from some Little League game. I felt like I was looking at a museum of Chase's life, and I wanted to touch and hold every single piece.

"It's the family memory, it seems." Troy's voice pulled me out of my revelry with a jump. "Sorry if I startled you." He handed me a beer, and not knowing what to do at that moment, I accepted it with a smile before turning back to the photos.

"These," I said, lifting a hand and waving it across the expansive shelves, "are amazing."

"I pass it every day; sometimes, I forget what all is here." Troy lifted the signed baseball. "Sam threw a perfect game for this. Nonna insisted he find and sign the ball for her."

"And this one?" I pointed to a photo of the boys happily plopped into a muddy pit. Troy lifted a photo with a chuckle.

"There was an unseasonable amount of rain. The backyard was a swampy mess, much to our young delight. Nonna discovered us tunneling through the mud, trying desperately to build a mud hut where her best winter bulbs had been planted."

"Oh goodness...was she mad?"

"Oh, she was furious. Epic mess...the flower bed never recovered." Wistfully, Troy set the photo down. "But first, she insisted on a photo before turning the hose on us all."

"This cabinet is beautiful."

"These were Nonna's things...before she passed. We couldn't bring ourselves to let them go." Troy eyed the shelves, his eyes taking on a distant sheen as if lost in memories. He lifted a photo of the three of them at a ceremony for Chase in his dress uniform, clean-shaven and stunningly handsome. "I suppose I've added to them through the years."

"These are all great." I sighed, brushing my fingers along a photo of a younger Chase. "Chase's house is so," I hesitated to finish, worried it would sound critical instead of curious.

"Sterile?" Troy answered with a bemused look in his eyes. "My brother forgets these memories are as much his as ours." Troy's smile dropped just a fraction of a second, but I didn't miss it. "I keep everything in the hopes he'll one day find the freedom to embrace it." His face looked nearly sad, and a pang of guilt washed over me that I'd caused that.

"Well, your cooking smells AMAZING," As if on cue, my stomach growled.

"Let's set up the table and chairs," Sam announced, as the three of them moved into a seamless dance. Chase and Sam slid the huge couch out of the way before carrying the round kitchen table to the middle of the living room, four chairs appearing from nowhere.

"You rearrange for dinner?" I whispered when Chase came by.

"The kitchens are too small for us all; this is easier." He winked, grabbed the beer from my hand, and whispered. "Lemme get you a seltzer."

"Thanks." I mouthed at his flash of dimples as he walked away. I wondered when and how to tell Sam and Troy that I was pregnant, with Dean's baby, no less, but decided tonight was definitely not the time to wrestle with that beast. I was kind of exhausted, and still unpacking the continual revelations this day had brought.

"Can I help with anything?" I followed Troy into a narrow galley kitchen, inhaling the aroma again. A giant pot of sauce simmered on the stove, making my mouth water. I was ravenous. "I don't want to be in the way, but I can carry out food or chop a salad."

"NO RABBIT FOOD," Sam bellowed from the living room, causing Troy to roll his eyes.

"I have the cooking well in hand." Troy handed me a stack of napkins and a basket of steaming garlic knots. "But I'll take help carrying out the bread if it won't hurt your hand." I lifted my hand, wiggling my fingers in a show of good health.

"The bandage is nearly unnecessary, but Chase insisted," I noted how little the movement stung. "His firefighter-miracle-goo was fantastic."

"Better safe than sorry," Troy slid the basket of bread into my non-injured hand. The buttery garlic wafted its steamy goodness to my nose, and it was all I could do not to steal a roll before we started dinner. Setting the bowl on the table, I must have been openly salivating since Chase's hand darted into the basket and popped a roll into my open mouth.

"Baby wants?" He mumbled under his breath, "Mama gets."

He dropped a swift peck to the top of my head before grabbing a second one and eating it himself. I might have dwelled on the meaning in his kiss more had my mouth not clamped down around heaven-sent buttery joy, sending me into a full-on, moaning, mouthgasm.

It was that good.

Knowing that Chase knew I was hungry and did something about it, and even joined me, made it all the more delicious. My imagination chose that moment to gift me multiple scenarios of Chase feeding me in a sensual, core-clenching way, and I made a mental note: research pregnancy hormones–because that bread should not have been that erotic.

"Score." Sam snatched a roll from the basket, jolting me from my lusty carb-inspired fantasy. "I'm starving."

"I better go see what else I can carry in," I mumbled around my mouthful, but barely made two steps before Troy came out carrying a giant bowl of pasta topped with meatballs and sauce–Chase following with extra sauce and a block of parmesan on a grater.

Just as coordinated as before, Chase dropped the plate to the table, smoothly producing a seltzer from some back pocket in his ridiculously snug jeans, just as Sam smoothly slid my chair behind my legs, and Troy sat across from me. I swear, these three moved like a dance team.

"This all looks amazing. Thank you...all...for including me." I glanced at Chase, who had a boyish smile on his face. "Chase told me a little about this tradition. I hope I'm not intruding."

"Nonsense," Troy answered without a glance as he began serving. "We make too much food, and it's no trouble adding a fourth chair."

"Besides, you moved in, so it's kinda your dinner tradition, now," Sam mumbled around more bread.

"Dude." Chase shot a glance at his brother as his cheeks flushed a little pink. It was adorable, and I was tempted to tease him about the blush before Troy cleared his throat and spoke.

"I take it you are settling in okay," Troy passed me the extra sauce, and we began dinner.

Chase and I took turns sharing what we had accomplished in our short time. Both his brothers teased Chase about his insistence that I buy more things, and it was sweet seeing them like that. I couldn't remember a time when I'd sat so comfortably around a table with someone. Not performing for a date or a job, but enjoying easy conversation with people who share history and genuinely enjoy each other's company.

It was bliss...until we got to the part at my apartment.

His brothers listened quietly as Chase shared how it looked. He mercifully left out my total emotional meltdown, which I made a note to thank him for later. They didn't ask many questions, but Sam's eyes did cast a look my way that felt less like 'you poor thing' and more like 'damn that sucks,' and I loved that distinction. Troy was blissfully all business and used that to segue into his department's work with the arson investigation.

"Dean Jensen has officially been listed as a person of interest." Troy leaned back in his chair, smoothing down his perfectly straight tie. "There is an APB out for him." Chase's arm draped across the back of my chair, and I leaned into the silent support he offered.

"No warrant?" Sam asked. "I thought they lifted a print that put him on the scene."

"The print was only partial, and not as conclusive as we'd need given our lack of evidence." Troy looked at me then, addressing me with direct but gentle words. "Not a dead-end, just a momentary hold-up while we search. We are working on your hard drive as well in the hopes we can find a lead."

My mind went instantly to the steamy messages between Dean and me, and my heart skipped a beat.

I was never overly exotic with my language, but I did at least try to reciprocate the provocative things Dean would send. At the time, I felt bold, brave even, for pushing outside of my comfort zone. Now, however, knowing Troy and his team...people who knew Chase...might read those, had embarrassment warming my cheeks. Still, I worried that speaking up might force Troy to hold back for my sake, hindering a criminal investigation. And I barely had the bandwidth to dwell on my spectacularly poor man-choosing skills that netted me an ex-honey turned possible arsonist and baby-daddy.

It was all just a little too humiliating. So I let myself lean into Chase's thumb, caressing my shoulder while they talked.

I let the words flow around me as I daydreamed back to a happier moment–Chase and I shopping, holding hands in the truck as he told me about his childhood. Slipping my hand to my belly, I imagined a future dinner table with spaghetti traditions, and I wondered if it could ever be this beautiful with just the two of us. I caught Chase's animated face from the corner of my eye, and I wondered what it would be like if it were the three of us around my future table. A vision I lingered in a little too long, when I suddenly realized Chase and his brothers were all staring at me as he happily declared.

"And that's why I think Moira should marry me, ASAP."

25

MOIRA

"WHAT?"

The word echoed in stereo as all our jaws dropped, and my world tunneled to those ridiculous dimples as I scrambled to replay whatever I missed that led to a proposal.

"Dude," Sam had both hands lifted in surprise. "Did you just say you want to get *married*?"

"Chase." Troy looked at me with hands reaching towards Chase, "You *cannot* be serious."

"Hear me out," Chase said to his brothers before turning sideways in his chair, legs manspread around me and caging me in with his giant body. "You need insurance for a variety of reasons." He flicked a glance at my hand resting in my lap. "You're burned hand will need tending, and you still aren't 100% clear of the smoke damage to your lungs. You're still scratchy in the morning...who knows what could crop up."

"She's been cleared by the hospital, Chase," Troy gestured to my hand. "She told me herself, the hand is all but healed."

"She's a picture of health, brother," Sam added. "The lingering scratchy voice doesn't mean anything."

Chase held a hand up, silencing them, his gaze locked on me as all the unspoken things about my baby and this pregnancy sounded like a gong on my brain.

"I've thought this through." His brothers leaned their elbows on the table as Chase laid out his plan. "We file the marriage license, just paperwork. It gets you on my insurance, fast-tracks your birth certificate, unlocks your bank account faster, and gives you access to mine in the meantime—just in case." He paused long enough to flick another silent glance at my belly before continuing, "Needs arise while the investigation and renter's policy and job situation resolve themselves."

Chase's animated ranting was reminiscent of the store when he desperately tried to convince me to buy more clothes, and I wondered why he was desperately trying to convince me now.

"Chase," I shot a nervous glance at his brothers. "This is crazy talk. *Surely* you don't mean for your first wedding ever to be to a stranger you *barely* know?"

"I never said wedding," Chase responded with a confident wink. "It's paperwork...a workaround to keep you secure while the red tape slogs forward." He looked at Troy and added, "Arson investigations like this can take months, ammiright?" Troy blinked in surprise before taking a breath and finally conceding.

"Chase is *technically* correct. These investigations can be unpredictable in terms of timing." Quickly, he added, "But well-intentioned as my impulsive brother might be, you have options beyond marriage here, Ms. Vanderbilt."

"Is this even legal?" I shifted my gaze from Troy to Sam's and then rested again on Chase's face, which held an expression I could only measure as cautious hope. "I won't want to do something illegal...and I won't let you do something illegal to help me." Chase's hand, which I hadn't realized rested on my knee, gave the smallest squeeze in response. "And what about your brothers?!"

I shouted a little more abruptly than intended as my adrenaline began to peak under the shock of Chase's idea.

"Don't worry," Sam gave a cocky smirk. "You don't have to marry us, too." Troy rolled his eyes and smacked Sam on his shoulder with the back of his hand.

"What she means is, will our brother's crazy plan compromise us, idiot?"

"I won't ask you to do that," I answered Troy's question, looking back at Chase but still speaking to the room at large. "I won't have you all lying and putting your jobs or yourselves at risk just to clean up my mess. Chase, this is crazy...we can't."

Chase flinched as if I slapped him, but I held firm. His idea was insanely far-fetched, and my heart pounded in my ears as the unspoken threads of conversation passed between the brothers. I used the time to plan my words for a firmer decline, but Sam finally broke the silence.

"I'm not a lawyer, but from what I know, insurance fraud only occurs when someone intentionally provides false information to obtain benefits to which they are not entitled. Ammiright?" He looked at Troy, who gave a reluctant nod of his head.

"That is the technical merit of it, if not the spirit of the law," Troy's eyes went a bit distant in contemplation. "Marriage between two US citizens isn't as heavily scrutinized as it would be for someone trying to immigrate. One could argue that marriages of convenience happen daily for all sorts of reasons like tax reduction, corporate mergers, and the like."

"So unless Moira is secretly a Canadian citizen trying to smuggle in drugs through a super elaborate, arson-investigated wedding scheme...you should be in the clear!" Sam sat back, folding his hands behind his head with a knowing smirk.

"Moira," Chase took both my hands in his. "I won't push you...and I know I'm springing this on you, and we haven't talked about it at all before right now, and that makes me kind of an ass, and I'm sorry for that too. But from where I sit, it's a quick solution to about half of your current problems. Marrying me gives you instant security, a financial safety net, and allows you more breathing room for everything else to fall into place." He nodded to Troy. "Add that to the safety of a police officer next door, and I feel a whole lot better about your general well-being."

I waited for his next statement, but no other words followed. No more discussion between the brothers about the technicalities, and no more persuasive arguments from Chase. Just awkward silence, as seconds or minutes ticked by; it could have been years, given the way my heart was racing. I realized with jolting clarity that they were waiting for me. To agree or to disagree or even to have a single coherent thought in my head, I didn't know.

I was the pin in this whole grenade, just waiting to be pulled, for good or ill, all over all of our lives.

"Troy?" I looked at the 'eldest' brother, wanting to know his opinion. "What do *you* think?"

"Ms. Vanderbilt," he began, but I interjected.

"Please, we're discussing marriage...I feel like you can call me Moira now."

"Moira," Troy sighed, sliding his elbows on the table until his hands were spread wide. "I find the idea utterly lacking in sanity...but I must admit his logic holds water. Investigations like this can move at a glacial pace. We could find other ways to help you should you not wish to tie yourself to such a foolhardy man... his plan does offer the most instant protection in all the ways he claimed." Troy didn't so much as hint at any malice or sardonic surprise in his words.

"Sam?" I lifted my brows to the Cheshire grin next to Troy. "I assume you're on board."

"Oh, it's batshit crazy!" He laughed, his eyes going soft when he looked at Chase before coming back to me. "But hell yeah. You'll be covered on all sides, and I get a sister. What's not to love!"

'What's not to love?' Both of them held my gaze as the words echoed, without a hint of sarcasm. In fact, every syllable they'd said rang with honesty, and all that was left was to measure the weight of the man before me. Chase, who still sat perched, eyes wide in cautious hope, still held my hands. He'd already done half a dozen miraculously kind things without a single ounce of hesitation. And while I had vowed never to be the helpless fool waiting around for someone to rescue me, this didn't feel like a rescue.

It felt like air.

I silently compared him to Dean, and there was no comparison; the two were polar opposites. Where Dean had tried to remove my agency, leaving me miserable and alone...Chase surrounded me with options, choices, and people to protect and watch over me. Sam's mild amusement, Troy's smiling resignation, they both spoke of men who were willing to come alongside Chase and me in this plan to offer even more support. Even still, doubt may have crept higher if not for Chase's hopeful gaze at my belly. This wasn't just about me.

I steeled my nerves. I could do this, trust them, just this once...for my baby. There was a belonging here that I needed, and with a final declaration, I promised myself that I wouldn't be foolish. I wouldn't fall. This wasn't a fairytale romance. This was a pragmatic stop-gap solution to help make my next reboot...the final reboot. I could do this. We could do this.

"Okay."

WILDER BRO'S GROUP CHAT

-4-

ME: Located Jensen yet?

TJ: No.

ME: His cabin?

TJ: Vacant. We haven't given up.

Samoa: Can we help?

TJ: Moira can.

ME: She hasn't been in contact with him at all.

TJ: That wasn't how I meant.

Samoa: Surely you don't mean she should try to contact that asshole.

TJ: Of course not, but it might be time for her to come make an official statement.

ME: No! She's just now beginning to relax here.

TJ: Has she told you anything...at all?

ME: There was one weird comment ... Jensen had a monthly poker game.

Samoa: And that's weird because...?

ME: I worked with him for years. He never mentioned poker ...but did take a day every month to go to NYC. One of those was the day I found his recordings.

TJ: Purpose of his trips?

ME: He never said...but he never missed it.

TJ: I'll pass it along...but you need to press her for more if she can't come in.

ME: What about her laptop?

TJ: We have a specialist from the NYPD's cy-
ber-crimes unit assisting.

Samoa: Why are we looking at Moira's laptop?

TJ: A hunch. Moira is smart. Her being conned
seems outside of Jensen's...proclivities.

Samoa: So you think he recorded her, too?

ME: MOTHERFUCKER!!!!!

TJ: We aren't speculating anything, merely seeing what we can salvage from any messages between them that might help us find him.

ME: Jesus, TJ...if he recorded her...I'll kill him.

TJ: I'll use the utmost discretion, brother. But her
help would move things along.

ME: I won't push...but I'll try.

Samoa: She seemed relaxed at dinner.

TJ: She did fold in nicely.

ME: I wish she'd relax more here.

TJ: Meaning?

ME: She keeps all her stuff in bags…won't just settle. It's making me crazy.

Samoa: Have you made space for her?

ME: Dude, I've got nothing BUT space.

Samoa: You live in a hermetically sealed show home. No woman unpacks into that.

TJ: Sam would know best here.

Samoa: Hell yeah, I do.

ME: Fine…what do I do?

Tj: Make Space?

Samoa: and TELL HER it's for HER, Boyscout.

26

CHASE

M Y MILITARY ID AND Moira's birth certificate secured a marriage
license, and within three days of spaghetti night, Moira became
my wife. My chest squeezed as I signed the marriage certificate, unsure
whether it was the finality of the paperwork or the possibility that I
wanted it to be real. On the morning of our appointment with the judge,
I worried I had pushed too hard, but the smile on her face when she
signed on the dotted line made me wonder if she desired more as well.
Something that seemed to resonate as our lives ambled forward into the
day-to-day in a routine formed like muscle memory—easy, quiet, and
damn near perfect.

I'd wake up and make my coffee on the porch (the smell of it turned
her stomach). Then, I'd make her this tea concoction she seemed to love
called a London Fog. While she drank her tea, I'd shower and dress, and
while she was cleaning up, I'd make us breakfast. It was all so domestic,
and maybe the most fun I'd ever had in my house. With me on leave and

her not yet started at her new job, we used our time to do a little sightseeing. She loved our few drives around town and admitted to spending zero time acclimating here since her move. As such, we made each day an adventure, and honestly, I was excited to show her all the things I loved about my town. It would have been perfect, except for one thing.

"More sightseeing today, or have you finally decided to get back to your life?" Moira eyed me over the rim of her tea as I tracked a delivery on my phone. "I'm a big girl, you know. I can entertain myself if you need to go to work or do whatever you did before I arrived on the scene."

There it was...the reminder that she felt like a burden. I hated that she acted like a lingering afterthought when the truth was that she was the antidote to my otherwise dull life. It drove me crazy since I couldn't ever find the right words to make her believe that I wanted her in my life. But, following my brother's advice, I had a plan today.

"C'mere." I pocketed my phone and grabbed her hand, leading her into the bedroom. She froze at the door with a stiff jerk, something I noted but didn't draw attention to as I continued over to the dresser. "I realize I haven't been the best host, and I need to make better space for you." Opening the three drawers on the right-hand side, I waved a hand over them. "For you."

Her shoulders relaxed, and she stepped closer, peering into the empty drawers like she expected a nest of snakes.

"Where are your T-shirts and jeans?" I had to stifle a grin at her admission of snooping.

"I needed to purge a little. I donated some stuff and consolidated the rest." I slid my closet open and showed the empty hangers into view. "You have room to hang whatever needs hanging, too."

"Oh...I couldn't possibly - "

"Stop!" I turned towards her and her wide eyes, and felt like an ass for raising my voice. Swallowing down my frustration, I forced my voice to calm. "Look, I know this arrangement wasn't ideal for you...or even planned. But you are here now, and I want you to be comfortable." I took her hands in mine, watching as she took in the closet and then our linked hands before finally looking at me. "You aren't a burden, Moira, or an imposition. You aren't even a mild annoyance."

"I know, but," her expression said she didn't know. "It's just that–"

"No, Fancy Pants." The nickname brought a small huff of laughter despite the shine in her eyes. "You are a breath of fresh air." I tugged her closer. "As much as this was my house, it wasn't much of a home before you. I want you to make it your home." I gently wiped away the lone tear trailing her cheek, fighting the urge to declare how much I wanted our marriage to be more than the slip of paper I tucked away in a fireproof lockbox under my bed. "Believe me when I say I want you and your stuff here. Take up space, make a mess, and *stop* walking on eggshells!" I paused then, remembering what my brothers said and hoping she'd be on board. "And today, when we go out, we're picking up whatever we need to get your stuff out of the damn plastic bags and into a proper spot." She laughed then, and it was a big, full laugh that went all the way to her eyes. "And you *won't* argue with me. We're getting tchotchkes!"

"Okay. I promise." I was about to pull her in for a hug, but my doorbell rang. "Sam or Troy," she asked.

"That is the surprise I got for you." Opening the door, I signed the delivery ticket as the driver unloaded two huge boxes into my living room.

"Surprise?" Moira scanned the large boxes, both of which held no indicators as to their contents.

"Let's call it a...wedding present." I winked and gestured to the large rectangular box, "This is a new desk here. And that one over there is a chair." I started opening boxes as I kept talking. "You mentioned your job was temporary, but that you normally work from home. I figure the living room is plenty big for a desk in the corner... I grabbed you a chair that reviews said had good back support, too. You should be able to use it the whole pregnancy." I rambled on, opening boxes and laying out pieces for assembly as I laid out the plan for Moira's new home office space, mentally calculating which tools I'd need. "When we go out, we'll get stuff to organize the space, and if the light from that window glares on your monitor, we can get curtains." I gestured back and forth from the desk to the corner of the room and back as I rambled on. "And until you find something more permanent, I was hoping you'd help me with the real estate stuff. We're terrible at marketing our rentals and.." I turned to look at her, and my heart sank.

Moira...was crying.

No, not crying, sobbing.

Tears streamed as her hands covered her mouth, muffling shoulder-shaking heaves as she cried. I opened my mouth to say something, but froze. I thought I had done something good that showed her that I wanted her here.

But clearly, I didn't.

Clearly, I broke her.

Dammit! She's leaking!

I replayed everything I'd said, debating the merits of throwing myself at her feet in apology to make the tears stop. I wondered if I should repack the furniture, or perhaps fling it into oncoming traffic. Kneeling in a pile of cardboard, helplessly watching as she cried, I waited as long as I could before doing the only thing I could think of.

Reach for her.

"God. Fancy Pants. Please. Tell me what I did wrong." I held her to me, wrapping my arms around her and holding her until she relaxed enough to melt into me. "Do you hate the desk or the chair? I'll return them both. Did I push too hard or too fast? I'll slow down, I'll fix it, I'll do *anything*...but...please, stop crying."

"No." She shook her head frantically back and forth. "You didn't do anything wrong."

"Then...why are you crying?" I held her back enough to look at her eyes, wiping away another tear that welled at the edges of her beautiful lashes.

"No one has ever done anything like this for me. Ever. Not the house, or the marriage, and even this damn desk. And it's all wonderful, you are wonderful. Still, with these pregnancy hormones, I don't know if I have room for any more of your giant acts of kindness, cause I'm about to burst with how freaking happy this stupid chair is making me." She gave me a teary-eyed half-smile that would have unraveled me entirely if there hadn't been another knock at my door...and my head nearly exploded.

"Um." I thumbed over my shoulder with a half-shrug. "If I tell you this is your new laptop...are you gonna cry again?"

"What?!" She pushed past me, flinging open the door and snatching the box out of the deliveryman's hands. "CHASE WILDER! You did not!?" I signed for the delivery as she unwrapped it with the ferocity of a wild animal. "A MacBook!"

"I read they were good for media work, and with insurance delays slowing your replacement, I figured–" Her excited noises were music to my ears as she turned it on, fired it up, and genuinely clapped with happiness. "And laptops are portable, so you can take them to your new–"

Before I finished my sentence, Moira spun and flung her arms around my neck, pressing her perfect lips against mine.

The world went still.

I didn't breathe–didn't dare as I wrapped my arms around her and lifted her off the ground, deepening this gift from heaven. The softness of her molded into me, and it was intoxicating. I slipped a hand under the edge of her shirt, feeling the soft skin of her back, and my cock twitched. Every fiber of my body sang its praises, even as I calculated how many more laptops I could reasonably buy if it meant this kind of reception.

Moira pulled back, sliding slowly to the ground even as I kept her pressed against me and the bulge in my pants. I wanted to soak in as much of her as I could before the shock wore off. I pained at the very idea of her withdrawing from my reach, but I didn't dare squeeze her closer for fear of freaking her completely out, so I just stood there...praying for time to stop.

"Sorry...I um..." The flush of pink in her cheeks was adorable, and I was encouraged that she didn't look horrified. "I mean...Thank you." She studied my face as if searching for words, and I was more than content to let her linger in my arms while I swam in her shining blue eyes. "I can't begin to tell you what this means to me." Her voice was barely a whisper, but the way her lids drooped when she let her eyes drop to my mouth had me longing for another kiss.

"If it means I'll earn another kiss like that, I'll empty every damn drawer in this house and buy you all the furniture you could dream of." She let loose a big belly laugh that made my heart clench, even if she took a step back, the moment slipping away. "Did you catch the engraving?"

"I was in such a hurry to fire it up." She turned and lifted the laptop to read 'Property of Fancy Pants.' Hugging it to her chest, and leaning into my chest, my arm around her waist as I pressed my lips into her hair.

Yep. As many laptops as it takes.

27

MOIRA

Dear Ms. Vanderbilt,

We received the statement from Officer Troy Wilder regarding your cleared status concerning the fire at your apartment. Unfortunately, we are still unable to process your insurance policy claim(s) until we receive official confirmation of a resolution regarding the arson case from all parties involved. Once the investigation is closed, we will evaluate your claim and process it within the terms of your policy.

We apologize for any inconvenience caused by this delay, blah blah blah.

Signed,

Douche-Canoe Automated Email Creator

I FINISHED OFF MY tea with a scowl as my insurance company all but confirmed the whole investigation had to close out before they'd pay up. Troy warned me this was likely, and it made sense in a warped way since Bureaucracy loved anything that delayed payout. Still, here I sat. I was squatting in someone else's house. Driven in someone else's car. Eating someone else's food.

A guest in my own life.

My 'paper-marriage' helped me secure a few identifying documents. Still, my bank demanded a government-issued photo ID to replace cards and checks. That meant I needed a new driver's license. Chase had already done so much for me, up to and including the computer I was currently sulking in front of. I knew, if I asked, he'd be more than willing to drive the 2 hours round-trip to the DMV. I knew he'd wait around while I filed for a license.

I couldn't bear it. The idea of asking for one more thing from the man who'd done so much was just a step beyond what my already battered ego could tolerate. I felt lost in my days as I scrambled for something that felt concrete, and somewhere inside, a voice screamed that I needed to do something about it.

It wasn't rebellion—it was survival. I needed one damn thing I could do on my own.

Today was the first day of my new part-time job at the local library. Having already been in the building twice, my new supervisor told me today would be extra short, and that's when my plan hatched. Double-checking my bag, I confirmed I had the bus schedule and all my documents on hand, including the initial fire report, my Oregon Birth Certificate, and my shiny new marriage license. Once I finished my work, I'd bus my way to and from the DMV before Chase returned to pick me up at the end of the day.

I was psyched to get my pretty new license for Mrs. Moira Wilder...or Mrs. Moira Vanderbilt-Wilder? I hadn't figured out where to go with my last name, unsure as I was about how long the marriage would last. That was the lingering question in my head as I deposited my cup in the sink, noticing steam rolling from the cracked bathroom door.

Chase habitually entered the bathroom from the hall side despite my reassurance that he could go through his bedroom. The door was cracked open, and, shaking my head, I moved to shut it just as the water cut off. I froze as the metallic slide of the shower door and subtle floor creak indicated he'd climbed out of the shower. I turned to leave until I heard the soft, low hum of Chase's voice—a gravelly baritone that floated out with the steam. Drawn to the warmth of his gentle singing, I relaxed against the door, inadvertently admiring the shape of his foggy reflection. His broad shoulders were impressive, but the dark shading of his tattoo had my full attention. I couldn't see details in the steam-muddled mirror, but it seemed to cover the entire left half of his body from shoulder to waist. I shouldn't have spied, but any desire to preserve decorum was silenced by the devil on my shoulder waving a marriage license and screaming, 'Do it for the spank-bank!'

And I let her win...just for a second.

My imagination filled in delicious details as I stole a longer look that I knew I'd revisit in my dreams. Maybe it was tribal, all black, and swirls of abstract shapes. Or perhaps it was artistic, his body a canvas for detailed line work. I imagined a lighthearted collaboration of pieces from his youth and his time in the Marines, even wondering if it wrapped around his back as well. Wishing for an unfettered view, I leaned against the door, my core clenching as I envisaged Chase's ink dipping low. I imagined him naked, swirling ink dipping below the fabled V of muscle that his towel clung to while I—

The door slid open, and I fell face-first into Chase with a yelp.

"Oh God... I'm..." Words failed as I clung to Chase's strong, damp arms. "I wasn't...I mean, I didn't mean to." I tried to stand and smooth the front of my dress down, even as embarrassment burned my cheeks for drooling over him like a slab of beef. "The door...it was cracked, and I went to close it, but I heard...and then I saw..."

Chase's eyes darkened as he steadied me without a hint of embarrassment. Gone was the lighthearted, boyish smile, and in its place was the seductive upturn of lips that had my blood boiling.

"You...have a lot of tattoos," I gulped.

"If you wanted to look, Fancy Pants," Chase took a half step back, standing for inspection. "You only have to ask". My jaw fell open when he winked, elevating one tattooed arm slightly in front of himself, while the other held his towel closed. "Want to know about them?"

I nodded, it's all I could do, and he guided my hand to his inked pectoral.

"This is my latest addition...part of the half vest I've been building out." Chase watched my fingers trace the heavy black swirls covering the bulk of the muscle. "This one," He guided my wrist, sliding my fingertips to his impressive shoulder and the USMC ink complete with Semper Fi ribboning. "A Marine Corps addition. It hides a scar from my time in service." I leaned closer to see a small, puckered circle. He twisted, allowing me to see its twin on the back side, and I winced when I recognized the bullet hole. "It wasn't that bad." He reassured my unspoken question softly.

I looked back at him, hoping my eyes conveyed what my voice couldn't. Fearing that if I spoke, my growing lust would be further fueled by this primal sense of pride at his bravery.

"This one here," He twisted his arm, sliding my fingers to his bicep, displaying three thick, black chevrons stacked perfectly one atop the other. "These were first. My brothers and I got them on our 18th birthday."

I was a breath away from Chase's body, feeling the remnants of steam and heat wafting off him as my hand slipped back to his ink-covered torso.

"And this one?" I cleared my throat, trying to sound more confident than I felt as I grazed my hands across his abs like a whisper. "Does it go..." I swallowed hard, watching my fingertips drift down his ribs. "Does it go around your back...or...lower to your leg..."

My questions were a weak excuse, but my mouth moved before my hormone-soaked brain could rein it in. Suddenly aware of what I was doing, I pulled my hand back in embarrassment, preparing to retreat as Chase cuffed my arm with his giant hand, holding me to him. I looked up at his face to find lust-filled eyes bearing down on me as his towel dropped to my feet.

Sweet. Musclebound. Goodness.

"You are very welcome to inspect any part of my body at any time...*wife*." Slipping his newly freed hand beside my jaw, he tangled his fingers into my hair as the title 'wife' branded into my psyche.

He pulled me in, tilting my head back even as he tugged at my waist until I could feel the hard length of him pressing into me. It was all I could do not to drop my eyes and drink him in. Lowering his head, caressing my cheek with his nose, he whispered, "But only if I get to see yours too."

Time...stopped.

Chase captured my gasp, claiming my mouth in a bruising kiss, sliding his tongue across my lips and exploring my mouth until I was breathless and aching. A simmering growl rumbled out of his chest before he released it into my mouth, sending a bolt of lightning straight through me. All my higher brain functions stopped as my pussy clenched around a painful emptiness as the man kissed me stupid. Then, in one swift move, he lifted me off the ground by the back of my legs, forcing me to cling to his shoulders as he wrapped my bare legs around his waist and pressed me against the bathroom wall, my dress bunched up around my waist. The kiss grew impossibly deeper, and waves of pleasure washed over me. I heard a distant moan that I barely recognized as mine when his hard cock pressed against my entrance with only thin cotton panties separating us.

"God, woman," Chase growled between the kisses across my jaw and down my neck. "You are heaven on earth."

I wanted to respond, but couldn't make words as my body came alive in his arms, seeking contact and pressure. Held aloft by his hands cradling my ass, I rocked against him, desperate for a friction that I couldn't find. As if he knew what I needed, Chase lowered me just enough that his cocked pressed against my clit, and I gasped at the sensation. My arousal slipped down my walls, soaking my panties as Chase ground his hips back and forth. Time slowed as my world narrowed to him in the cradle of my thighs, with his tongue lingering on my neck.

"You are even more delicious than I dreamed." He mumbled, tugging the neckline of my dress aside to expose my shoulder so he could kiss and nip at my collarbone.

"Oh God..." I panted as heat bloomed low in my belly. "You're so..." strong, gorgeous, sexy as hell, the man of my dreams; words flashed through my mind but failed to launch as he shifted his movement, rocking up and down against my pussy with growing intensity. "Oh God," a fever radiated up my spine as he nested in the spot I needed, making me feral as I writhed in his arms in shock at how intense this was. His hands gripped the globes of my ass in a way that would surely leave marks, and the hint of pain only heightened my pleasure. "Chase...please."

"Yes, Moira." He growled into my neck, grinding and sliding his dick up and down against my soaked pussy.

My body coiled–a powder keg ready to ignite as his mouth lingered in the spot where my neck met my shoulders. Shivers fired through me when he nipped me there, and I arched against him with a whimper.

"Fuck yeah, wife." Chase ground his cock against me faster, nipping at that spot again. Each nibble sent a fresh bolt of lust to my core, and I couldn't stop my nails from digging into his shoulders as I tried to match his hips' movement. "So perfect," He squeezed my ass again, sliding his cock across my swollen, dripping sex. "So perfect...with me."

Without warning, Chase bit down on my shoulder, hard, and I shattered like glass in the sun.

"Yes! Yes, yes, God, yes!" Waves of pleasure rocked through me as the most surprising and intense orgasm of my life exploded.

His mouth came back to mine, swallowing my final cries of ecstasy before he gave an audible grunt of his own, jerking against me until hot cum soaked the upper edge of the panties I was still wearing.

He never released my mouth.

Kissing me through my climax, through his own, and even after, we stayed pressed against the wall, my legs wrapped around his waist, as he lingered in my mouth. When he finally released me, it was only to lean into my neck again, panting, as we came down from what was by far the most erotic moment of my life.

"I wasn't even inside you, and still..." He let me slide slowly down until my feet touched the ground, and he gazed into my eyes with an expression I could only describe as drunken adoration. "Absolute, fucking, perfection." Brushing his thumb across my cheek, he wiped away tears I didn't realize I'd shed and whispered. "I hope those tears aren't regret."

"Not even a little," I whispered, letting his warmth sink in just a little longer as aftershocks rippled through me.

"Good." His fingers trailed across the outline of my breast, and my nipples instantly tightened as if protesting their neglect. "'Cause if you felt that good and I wasn't even inside you..." He let his sentence trail off, unfinished, but I knew what he meant, closing my eyes and imagining the possibilities.

How much better could it be?

"I don't want you to be late," Chase said with a sigh as he planted a kiss on my forehead. "I'll let you have the bathroom while I get dressed." He grabbed his towel from the floor, swiping it across my lower belly to clean most of me off before leaving me jelly-legged, mystified, and thoroughly satiated.

I had never come so easily, so fast, with absolutely zero penetration, and the only thought left in my head was...more. I promised myself I would be pragmatic, but standing here reveling in the memory of Chase calling me his wife, I knew 'pragmatic' was precariously close to being thrown out the window because his kiss felt like forever, and my heart wanted that promise a little too much.

28

MOIRA

I MIGHT HAVE SPIRALED about what we'd done if Chase hadn't held my hand the whole way to the library–his big, warm lifeline pulling me away from anxiety's edge. As it was, I enjoyed a peaceful drive, lazily watching the last days of summer roll by. Even still, I didn't want to leave with no words spoken between us, and I debated how best to convey that I was more than okay with everything we'd shared. I considered playing coy, but figured a little honesty, wrapped in my faithful shield of humor, was the best path. Gathering my things, I paused at the open car door.

"Hey, Chase?" He looked at me, brows raised in worry. "I really...*really* like your tattoos." I couldn't hide my smile when his eyes went wide, and his dimples framed that grin I loved. Closing the door with a wink, I strolled in for my first day at my new job.

The library's ad for social media work appeared on my news feed while I was still in my apartment. It was part-time, but the pay scale was just enough to cover my rent for a month or two at most. At the time, it provided financial breathing room until something better came along, so I accepted the slightly boring position as a stopgap measure. Walking into the building today, however, I felt a sense of excitement as my pregnant nose decided books smelled like a warm slice of heaven. Walking past the rows of books, I let myself linger as I inhaled the tomes of wisdom flanking the main walk up to the front desk. My eyes drank in the warm colors, and I was nearly tempted to drag my fingers along the bumpy spines just for the whole sensory experience.

But I had work to do, so I resisted the literary ASMR and focused.

As expected, my first day was short, and the time flew by as they set up my workstation and shuffled me in and out of meetings with various department heads. I took dutiful notes, smiled, and charmed my way through it all, memorizing as many names and faces as I could before saying my goodbyes and activating my plan.

There was a bus stop just outside the library. Walking out just in time, I caught the bus that had only one stop between me and the DMV. I planned to pop in, handle the driver's license issue all by myself, and be back at the library before Chase picked me up. A flutter of pride rose within me as I imagined his surprised face when I showed him what I'd done.

A host of other emotions immediately followed that I wasn't prepared to put titles to.

Sneaking around felt a little like lying...and lying to Chase felt so wrong. Still, I reminded myself this was a good plan as I grabbed a seat in the back of a mostly empty bus. Leaning against the window, I watched the scenery go by, letting my mind wander through the picture of my life.

The way I planned it, the way it was, the way I wanted it to be.

I had a job and was well on my way to accessing my money. That meant I wouldn't depend on Chase as much...not that he minded. If this morning was any indication, he was in no hurry for me to leave. I couldn't help but smile as I imagined what life might be like if I stayed. I saw Chase helping me build a crib and fussing over me and my baby...or would it then be our baby? A question I hadn't let myself think on as I rested my hand on my still invisible bump.

I mean, it was clear he had feelings for me, but what feelings exactly? Were we long-term, or was this lust? Would he accept me in his life with another man's baby in my belly? For that matter, could his brothers? If not, what did any of the rest of it matter? I was head over heels for the little surprise growing inside of me, and if Chase couldn't accept the baby...he couldn't have me.

It was as simple as that, painful though it was.

The bus hissed its next stop, and my eyes drifted closed as I played out scenarios in my mind, like regaining my footing and politely thanking Chase for all he'd done, as he repacked my things to move. That picture stung, so I shifted it to him–celebrating my wins and congratulating me. I reminded myself that I didn't need him to reboot my life. Still, I didn't like the taste of that either.

I was trying to figure out what that meant when a rough hand slid on top of mine.

"Moira, Moira." My eyes snapped open just as Dean's bulk dropped onto the seat beside me, his arm curling around my shoulders like it belonged there. "How's that baby of mine doing?"

"No!" I yanked my hand free and shoved him hard, but his body was a wall. He casually crossed one leg and hooked his foot around mine, caging me in as he laced our fingers together. "What are you..."

"Shhhhh, now, honey." Dean smiled, flashing a glance up at the driver, who didn't see me flinch as he draped his heavy arm across my waist, effectively pinning me. "Let's not make a scene. I just want to talk."

"I *don't* want to talk to you!" Fear cracked my voice as I tugged against the sweaty weight of his cologne—all musky pine and gasoline memory. "How did you even know I was here?"

"You mean, how did I know you were at the library, or how did I know you were taking my baby on a bus?" He smiled at my belly, possessively circling it with his thumb. Bile surged into my throat. "I came to visit you at the hospital. You had such a scary ordeal...I was worried about my princess." He looked into my eyes, concern worn like a mask to hide the monumental asshole. "They wouldn't let me talk to you; you were resting and didn't list me as your emergency contact." He cocked his head to the side and gave his best playful pout. "I was hurt, sweetheart. But I did overhear that you had a library job, and well... I'm a patient man." His sing-song voice was baiting me, but the smile he flashed had too many teeth.

He was enjoying this.

So, I spat in his face.

"Get the fuck away from me, you arrogant bastard." Dean constricted around me, his arm tightening, his leg anchoring like a predator setting his next trap. Cold reality set in. "You set that fire, didn't you?"

"Such language." He lifted his hand with a chuckle, wiping spit from his face. I used the moment to grab my cell phone and swipe to Chase's number, but Dean's hand covered the screen and pressed the phone to my lap. "I admit our last meeting wasn't ideal, so I'll let that little stunt pass. But you never told me about the baby. If I had known, then..."

"What?" I snapped, looking across the aisle but finding that seat empty. "You would have acted like a human being instead of gaslighting psycho?"

"Gaslighting psycho?" Dean laughed, as if we were sharing an inside joke. The bus driver glanced up, smiling, and my stomach sank. To him, we looked like lovers as Dean nuzzled my cheek. "Boy, you have pulled out the big words, haven't you?" He tightened his grip and buried his face in my cheek like a man in love. "What am I gonna do with you?"

"I hate you. I don't want you." My voice shook, not from fear, but fury. My eyes darted from window to aisle to rearview mirror. The bus was empty. I was truly alone with him — and trapped.

"You don't want me?" The mock hurt in his words was insulting, and vomit churned in my guts as he spoke. "Let's not be dramatic. We had a lovers' spat, but there's a baby now. Our baby deserves a father, doesn't it?"

"Not you." I snapped back. "A feral dog would be a better father to this baby than you."

"Better than any daddy you ever had." Dean looked me dead in the eyes as he fired that little arrow. "Aren't I...sweetheart?"

"I don't want you." I declared as firmly as I could, though my voice was barely a whisper. "Not in my life, not in my baby's life, and -"

"My baby, you mean." My vision tunneled as he gave me a dead-eyed smile. "Where are we going today on this shitty bus? Your library job was short-lived. Did you lose that one already?" He waved his hand in a casual gesture. "No matter. I got a buddy in the city who is gonna hook me up with a job, and it pays way better than that promotion I was working for. I've already got a place for us. We'll get settled, and I'll make sure you and the baby have all you need. You won't even need to leave the house." His voice was velvet-wrapped control, but I didn't miss the threat.

We'd never leave him again.

"You think I would *ever* come back after the way you treated me? I could never trust you or love you after the way you made me feel." I squirmed against him, trying to free my leg so I could stand and make a move to run off the bus. "You left me out in the middle of nowhere,

Dean. You made me walk all the way back to town, in the dark. Do you know how long that took me?"

He smiled, wide and snake-slick, and I knew if I didn't do something quick, I'd be screwed.

"Let's not fight anymore." His palm flattened over my belly, digging his fingertips in. "It's not good for my baby, sweetheart."

"Stop calling me that!" I yelled, alerting the bus driver.

"Hey man," The driver asked. "Ya'll okay back there?" Dean didn't flinch. Instead, he reached calmly for his ankle and laid a gun in my lap.

"You know, my fiancé here is pregnant. I think she's getting a little road sick." Dean offered an apologetic smile to the driver. "I hate to be an inconvenience, but is there any way you could maybe drop us off at the next intersection? She could use the fresh air."

Blood pounded in my ears as I sat mute, eyes locked on the driver's reflection.

Look at me. See me. Ask me what I need.

"Yeah, man, sure." The bus driver pointed ahead with a slight smile. "There's a pharmacy at the next main light. I can drop you there."

"Perfect. I appreciate it." Dean smiled down at me, fingers gently stroking over my stomach with the gun nestled in his palm as a tear slipped down my cheek. "See, sweetheart. I'll take care of you and our little family."

"Not a gun...please..." My voice cracked, and I hoped the emotion would sink in and soften Dean's grip on my hands. "Don't hurt my baby."

"Our baby." He nuzzled his nose against my cheek and whispered into my ear. "Dry those tears before this bus stops. You raise an alarm with that driver, and I'll blow his brains out before I let anyone come between us."

My stomach rolled again as sour bile burned my throat. I couldn't take my eyes off the gun sitting so casually against my baby as a singular thought played in my head like a broken record: do whatever he wants...but get that gun away from my baby. Dean had all the strength and a gun, and I had nothing but my bag, a cellphone I couldn't use, and a baby in my belly that needed me to be smarter than this. I had no power but to cooperate, obey, and pray I could find some other way out. The intersection came into view, and I took a deep breath, exhaling slowly as I willed my tears to stop.

"Good girl." Dean kissed my cheek, and the bus brakes hissed. "Now, get up and act like you love your baby daddy." He stood up, stepped forward, and stretched out his hand. I hesitated, glancing behind me, hoping for literally any other option. "Better sell it, sweetheart." He nodded down at the gun resting in his belt as he covered it with his shirt.

I had no other choice. Grabbing my bag, I painted on a smile and walked to the front of the bus.

"I hope you feel better soon." The driver said with a tip of his hat. "My old lady had terrible morning sickness. She said lemons helped."

"You hear that, sweetheart?" Dean tugged me to a stop with that malicious smile plastered to his face. "We should get you some lemons." He stepped in front of me, exiting first and turning to help me down like a perfect gentleman. I managed a stiff nod to the driver as I exited into Dean's waiting arms. He turned us quickly, arm around me in mock concern, as the bus pulled away. "Now I have you back in my life, what say we move to the Big Apple, eh, Sweetheart?" His grizzled beard slid down my neck, and my stomach clenched. "That is, unless you need actual lemons first. How has this first trimester been? I've missed so much. Tell me everything about Junior here."

Dean's disgusting show of concern sparked an inkling of an idea. It was slim, but all I could think of. Clenching my abdomen, I leaned over with a groan.

"What is it?" Dean scanned around us. "The baby?" Using my already sour stomach and a quick jab of my finger to the back of my throat, I threw up my entire breakfast across Dean's boots, making sure to aim directly towards the bastard's jeans, soaking the bottoms of his legs.

"Goddammit!" Dean jerked back, disgusted—just enough for me to bolt.

Pumping my legs with all my might, I ran towards the pharmacy at the other end of the parking lot. I could hear Dean screaming behind me, but I never looked back. I lost my bag and phone at some point, but I stayed focused on the building in front of me. If I could make it close enough that someone might hear me, surely someone would help. My legs burned, but I never let up as I inhaled a deep breath, preparing to scream. Suddenly, a thick arm clotheslined my waist, halting me so fast my feet flew off the ground and all the air whooshed out of my lungs.

"Where did all this feisty energy come from, sweetheart?" Dean panted in my ear as he squeezed around my middle. "Maybe if you were a little more like this in the bedroom, I might have fucked you a little longer before ditching you in the Adirondacks, eh, baby?"

His words tipped me beyond the point of fear, and I slipped around with every ounce of strength I had and slapped him across the face with a deafening crack. It was a desperate move, born of anger, and sent pain jolting up my arm.

It was impulsive...and a mistake.

Dean wiped blood from his lip, rage sparking in his eyes as he reared back to hit me.

I mentally prepared for the blow as cars and flashing lights swarmed, sirens screamed, and a freight train of screaming fury barreled straight for Dean.

29

CHASE

IT WASN'T PLANNED OR romantic, nor how I would've chosen to give her that kind of pleasure for our first time, but it changed everything.

Feeling her hands trace over my tattoos sparked something alive in me. Swallowing her moans, feeling her wet heat against me, while hearing her beg me to take her over the edge had me blowing my load like a goddamn teenager. Just the thought of being inside her, claiming her baby as my own, left its mark.

I was hers.

Driving her to work, I worried that her silence but her playful departure was enough to put me at ease and give me a hard-on. I was now counting down the seconds until I could hold her in my arms, surprise her with another gift to celebrate her first day of work, and bring her home to bed the way I was aching to. The way my wife deserved.

She was mine.

Pulling up to Sam's, I honked the horn, and he came lumbering out.

"Get in loser, we're going car shopping,"

"'Bout time I got my ride back." Sam snarked as he climbed in. "You tell her you were buying a car yet?"

"I want to surprise her...but thanks for letting me hijack your ride."

"She's not a motorcycle fan, eh?" Sam's joke aside, I had to bite my tongue. I didn't want to give away her pregnancy secret, even if the truth was I'd never allow Moira to ride during the first trimester without confirming with her doctor that it was safe.

"I've arranged for the dealership to have a few models lined up, and the paperwork is half done. This should be fast, and then you get your car back."

"And you get to add another peg in your little plastic car as you play the game of life?" Sam twisted his finger into my dimple the way he used to when we were kids.

"Fuck off." I swatted his hand away, not even minding the teasing. Moira loved my dimples.

"Look, man." Sam ran his fingers through his unruly beard. "I like Moira, I do. And I'm happy she's safe, and you two seem to be connecting."

"Buuuuut?"

"I won't lie—I worry." Sam held up two fingers as he continued. "You've known her *barely* more than two weeks, and you've spent hospital nights at her bedside, moved her into your house, married her, and now you're buying her a car."

And dry-humping her up against the bathroom wall while imagining it was my baby in her belly.

"Yeah. Okay... It's fast. But there's just something about her, man."

"Oh, we're all getting that," Sam's words made it clear he and Troy had both discussed this. "Just...be careful, man." He huffed a resigned sigh. "As much as I want her to be safe and happy, I want that for *you* even more. This chick comes with serious baggage, being wrapped up with Jensen, and all."

"That isn't her fault!"

"Whoa, I know, dude." Sam lifted his hands in surrender. "I'm not blaming her for that piece of shit's actions." He waited until I took a deep breath before continuing. "But you're falling hard. I can see it...Troy can see it...hell, an idiot could see it as much as those big-ass dimples show up. But bro, she might not be ready to fall with you." He sighed then, his voice taking on the soothing tone from his ambulance. "I don't want to see that giant heart of yours be cannon fodder on her road to stability."

I knew my brother meant well, but the truth in his words stung. I pulled into the dealership and started scanning cars even as my mind mulled over Sam's words, unable to help my brothers understand the connection I had with Moira when I was barely able to define it myself. I wanted forever...but did she?

"I get what you're saying," I said as we waited on paperwork in the sales guy's office. "But my life has been upended in the best possible way, and I'm ready for whatever comes next." For everything that comes next. I thought to myself. "I won't lie and tell you that I don't worry, though. She's been through so much, and she's so damned determined to be as independent as possible, which is driving me a little nuts." It made my heart ache to think she might push me away even after this morning's wall grind. "I'm trying not to push her...but–"

"You're so happy you're losing your damned mind?" Sam smiled without a hint of judgment on his face. "You're 'get married and make babies' kind of happy?" I was already nodding in agreement when Sam's phone rang. "Huh, that's weird." He lifted the phone, and I leaned over as he answered. "Hey, Moira, what's..." his voice trailed off as he leaned forward, eyes narrowing as he listened intently. Scowling at the phone, Sam hit mute and put it on speaker, letting us listen to a muffled, masculine voice.

'I admit our last meeting wasn't the best, so I'll let that pass. But you never told me about the baby. If I had known, then...'

'What? You would have acted like a human being...'

My whole body went rigid at the sound of Moira's angry voice. Leaning in, I strained to hear the more distant voice to try to figure out who she was talking to.

'Gaslighting psycho? Boy, you have pulled out the big words, haven't you? Moira, Moira. What am I gonna do with you?'

"That's Jensen!" I shot to my feet, and Sam grabbed my shirt, pulling me back down.

"Shut the fuck up. We need to figure out where he is. Call TJ?" Ignoring Sam's command, I pulled up the tracker app on my phone. "She's on the feeder road out of town." Standing again, I didn't look back as I barrelled out to Sam's car.

"Dude. Fuck." Sam yanked the keys out of my hand. "I'll drive. Keep this line open, tell TJ where we are going." I fired off a text, sent a ping to Troy's phone with my location, never taking my focus off the voice coming through the speaker.

'I don't want you. Not in my life, not in my baby's life, and–'

'Our baby, you mean.'

I wanted to reach through the phone and throttle him even as Sam shot a look of clear surprise in my direction.

'Where are we going today on the shitty bus? Your library job was short-lived. Did you lose that one already? No matter. I got a buddy in

the city who is gonna hook me up with a job, and it pays way better than that promotion I was working for. I've already got a place for us. We'll get settled, and I'll make sure you and the baby have all you need. You won't even need to leave the house.'

"Text Troy, she's on a bus," Sam commanded, but my brain was focused on her...my girl...she was being so strong.

'You think I would ever come back after the way you treated me? I could never trust you or love you after the way you made me feel. You left me out in the middle of nowhere, Dean. You made me walk all the way back to town in the dark. Do you know how long that took me?'

"When was this?" Sam asked, but I ignored him as I stared at the phone, my blood screaming for Jensen's head.

'Let's not fight anymore, sweetheart. It's not good for my baby.'

'Stop calling me that!'

I was so proud of her for standing up for herself, even as my white-knuckle grip on the dash threatened the integrity of Sam's car. A voice in the distance said something we couldn't make out before Jensen spoke.

'You know, my fiancé here is pregnant. I think she's getting a little road sick. I hate to be an inconvenience, but is there any way you could maybe drop us off at the next intersection? She could use some fresh air.'

The voice in the distance mumbled something about a store I couldn't make out.

"Did he say grocery or pharmacy?" I asked.

"Gotta be the five points intersection. It's the only thing that direction that would have both. Text Troy." I began typing a text, still listening in, as my world spiraled out of control.

'Not a gun. Please. Don't hurt my baby.'

Her voice cracked, and she sounded like the night of the fire, terror-filled and desperate. Jensen mumbled something I couldn't make out, but I could hear Moira's soft whimper just as the line went dead.

"Moira!" I screamed at the phone. "No!" My voice shattered into a primal roar as if I could will her back on the line.

"We're almost there." Sam took his phone from the dash and called Troy on speakerphone. "Tell me you are near Five Points?"

"Almost. I have two other units with me."

"Jensen has her, TJ! He has a gun!" I shouted at my brother. "He's taking her!"

"We're almost there." Troy's sirens played in the background. "Stay calm, Brother."

"No chance of that now," Sam muttered. "Better get there quick, dude." We pulled into the intersection right behind the police, and I began scanning the parking lot for a bus when I saw a flash of blonde hair. It was Moira...running.

"There!" I pointed, grabbing the car door handle.

"Hold the fuck on, Chase." Sam grabbed my shirt collar, pulling me back. "Let the cops do their job."

Running as fast as her ballet flats would let her, my girl never looked back. Unfortunately, Dean was right behind her, gaining on her every two steps with each one of his long strides.

"Let the cops do their job." Sam was pressing into my chest, trying to pin me to my seat, even as he angled the car towards them.

The police had seen the action too and were making their way towards them...too slow. Jensen yanked her legs off the ground when he caught her, but my ferocious wife spun and slapped Jensen so hard his head snapped to the side.

"Little badass!" Sam slammed on the brakes, and my world all but froze as the scene unfolded in front of me.

Moira's face contorted in pain as he grabbed her arm.

Jensen wiped blood from his lip.

Jensen cocked his hand back.

My vision went red with rage.

I barely registered someone shouting my name as I lunged from the still-rolling car. Red and blue flashing lights illuminated my runway as I rolled to my feet, vision tunneling to Dean and the arm gripping my wife. Running at full speed, Jensen never saw me coming. I plowed into him from the side, slamming us both into the ground with a bone-crunching thud as a gun went skittering into the periphery.

"Wilder?" Jensen looked up at me with confusion for half a second before I started swinging.

I landed two good hits, maybe three, as I imagined all the ways he might have hurt Moira, hurt her baby. I was crazed with anger that he dared to steal her from me...steal my baby. I heard my name from a distance, but rage drowned it out as I swung again, screaming God knows what. I hurled my fists over and over, relishing every crunch of cartilage and bone as I split his face open. He needed to suffer for what he'd put my wife through. He needed to hurt. He needed to–

Arms grabbed me from behind, pulling me off Jensen.

"No!" I lunged again as a second set of hands...my brothers... flanked me on both sides, dragging me back. "He took her...he bleeds!"

"We have him!" A voice yelled.

"She's okay." Someone echoes...Sam maybe. I couldn't see anything but red as I lunged again. I wanted him broken for the audacity to take her, to touch her. I wanted him...dead.

I'd never wished for death before—but right now, all I wanted was a cold, hard, brutal death to the man who hurt what was mine.

My brothers both fought to bring me back from the edge, reason lost in adrenaline, until Moira's voice pierced the haze.

"Chase." She sobbed, putting her body in front of mine and pressing her hands against my chest. "Please...."

My eyes snapped to her as she cupped my cheek.

"Come back to me, Big Guy."

Everything stopped as I looked her over–No bruises. No blood.

Just like that, the rising tide of homicidal insanity all but dissipated at the feel of her hand on my face.

"My god." I wrapped my arms around her as she folded into my chest. "You're okay." I held her out again, looking her over again. "You're...okay?" I rested a hand on her belly. "And the baby? God...Is the baby okay?"

"I'm okay." She sobbed and fell back into me. "He didn't hurt either one of us. We're both okay."

Out of the corner of my eye, I saw Troy mouth the word 'baby' to Sam, who just raised his eyebrows and shook his head. I knew my brothers had questions, but I didn't care. I couldn't care. All I could do was hold her to me, feeling her body pressed into mine and knowing that nothing could hurt her if I was wrapped around her.

"Well, well." Jensen's voice lilted over the chaos as he was led to a car in cuffs. I glared at the walking mistake, hating that I'd left him capable of speech. "Isn't this an interesting development?" He cocked an eyebrow at Moira, seemingly unbothered by the blood pouring from his face. "My baby mama found someone new to clean up her messes."

My body screamed to finish him off on the spot, but Moira's grip on my shirt tightened as she sent a fresh sob into my chest.

"I've got this," Troy said, holding a hand against me in warning. "We need statements from all of you, but it can wait til tomorrow." He glanced back at Sam, who was already waving a hand.

"Yeah, yeah. I'll get 'em home." Sam's glare leveled on Jensen as he tucked into the squad car. "But shut that fucker up before I decide to join Chase for the next beating."

30

CHASE

THE RIDE HOME WAS silent.

Moira and I hand in hand in the backseat of Sam's car as adrenaline gave way to the dull ache of bloodied knuckles while I played a round of 'What-if.'

What if he'd taken her phone?

What if he'd managed to take her?

What if I hadn't gotten there in time?

What if he'd made it to New York?

What if he'd pulled that gun?

My skin crawled at the thousand ways today could have ended. I didn't feel bad for beating the guy bloody; I'd seen his type during my time in the Marines—warlords or insurgents who enjoyed hurting women. If anything, I felt bad for not beating the guy a little harder, but I worried about Moira. She cried a little on the scene, but not in the way I would have expected. If anything, she'd been oddly numb... almost dissociated.

Had I scared her?

She walked into the house, dropping her bag and flopping onto the couch while fidgeting with her nails. Her face bore a look of regret or shame, which infuriated me all over again. That piece of shit had her crawling back into the shell I'd worked so hard to pull her from, and dammit, he didn't deserve to take up space here, not between her and me. Needing to bridge the gap, but feeling waves of 'don't touch me' wafting off of her, I lifted a hand toward the kitchen.

"Tea?" Moira shook her head at my request.

"My stomach is still a little queasy." Her soft words made my whole body scream to hold her. "I made myself throw up to get away from him."

"That was smart," I said, genuinely impressed she had the where-withal to think of that.

"Are you...okay?"

"Me?" I dropped onto the couch. "How can you possibly worry about me?"

"You got dragged into all this." A tear fell from her eyes, and my anger grew again. "None of this would have been your problem, Dean, any of it... if it hadn't been for me."

Guilt over my involvement with Jensen and his sordid black past rose like bile in my throat. She must not have heard him say my name when I was pounding him into the pavement, but I needed to come clean about our shared history. Tonight wasn't the time, though.

"Please don't apologize." I reached for her, grateful she didn't flinch away. Her touch was a lifeline I didn't realize I needed, as if she weren't so far away that I couldn't pull her back. I also hoped this meant I could move forward gently with the only question I couldn't shake. "How did he find you?"

"He heard about the baby and my job the night he came to the hospital." I cringed inwardly, but let her talk. "I think he'd been waiting at the library...waiting for me to start, I guess."

"And he pulled you from the library...and no one saw," I wondered aloud, imagining how he had managed to pull that off logistically without raising alarms with Moira's coworkers or library patrons. "And why a city bus instead of something more private? I mean, the man is an evil bastard, but he's stupid."

"No." Moira looked sheepishly at me. "Not exactly. He..." She shifted on the couch until she was facing me with a leg tucked under her. "I was already on the bus." She stammered nervously. "*Before* he found me."

"You...got on a bus?" My heart all but fell out of my body and threw itself into oncoming traffic. I had gone too far, pushed too hard, and spooked her. She'd planned to leave, to run, and I'd missed the signs because I was so caught up in how beautiful she was and how much I wanted to feed her onion rings and keep her forever pinned against my bathroom wall.

"Yes." She stood, grabbing her bag and dragging out papers. "I planned to go to the DMV and have my License redone." She handed me a file folder with a tentative smile. "I wanted to do it on my own, not to bother you with the drive and the wait and all the hassle." She glanced down at her nails, fidgeting again in that crazy-making way I was growing to hate. "He...Dean... got on the bus with me, or after... I'm not sure. I didn't realize until he sat next to me and..."

She clenched her hand across her abdomen, and a new anger began to flare. She'd willingly left her job, without me. She'd hopped on a bus, alone, without telling anyone her schedule or plan, in some misguided notion that it would be easier... on me?

"Okay." I willed my face neutral, hoping there was more to this that would make it all make sense. "Then what?"

"I tried to leave, but he had me sorta...pinned with his body and the bench." My stomach dropped at the visual image conjured by that little nugget of information, which did nothing for my blood pressure as I tried to balance my absolute adoration for this woman with this new frustration gnawing at my gut. "And I tried to get the bus driver's attention, but Dean convinced him we were just a regular couple in love." Jesus fucking christ. Hearing his name on her lips in the same sentence as 'in love' had my fists clenching. "I tried to call you, but he blocked my phone, and–"

"So, he stalked you at work," I cut her off, pacing to give my energy something to focus on while my mind filled in the gaps of her story with the million ways this was all avoidable. "And followed you onto a bus to take you away to New York. And he convinced the driver to drop you off at the intersection where we found you, and then what?" I needed every sick, twisted detail just to get the poison out so we could move past this and find a way to handcuff her to me for the rest of our lives...or until Jensen was dead.

"Chase. I don't want to upset you more."

"I'm not upset," I snapped, closing my eyes and taking a deep breath. "Okay...I am upset. But not because you got kidnapped... I mean, of course, I'm fucking furious you got kidnapped. It's just - ." Her worried expression halted me–I was towering over her. I slumped back onto the couch, rubbing my face with my hands. "I told you, I'm not good with words. It's worse when I'm pissed. I mean flustered, I'm -"

"But I'm okay. You saved me...again." Her gentle tone was intended to soothe me, but all it did was make me feel worse.

I wanted to lock her away in a bubble to keep her safe forever, and even as the thought flashed through my brain in vivid technicolor, I knew it wouldn't work because she wouldn't even trust me enough to get her a goddamn license.

"He didn't get me."

"But he did get you!" I blurted out. "Because you didn't trust me!"

"What?" She stepped back with a frown. "I do trust you."

"Then why would you go to the DMV alone?" I waved a hand at the file folder of documents between us, still fighting to keep my voice level as my frustration bubbled over. "Why hide your short workday from me and plan out this whole thing when you knew Jensen was still out there somewhere?"

"I was trying to save you the hassle of waiting around in those ridiculous lines!"

"I don't need you to spare me extra work or time." Calm and level gave way as the fear I'd been choking on all afternoon finally shook loose. "All I've done these past few weeks is bend over backward to help you, provide for you...to care for you. And still you hid this from me!"

"I know!" Moira snapped back, eyes glossy. "You think I haven't seen everything you've done for me...are doing for me? It's literally all I see!"

"But you wouldn't let me help you with this?" I flicked a hand at the papers now crumpled on the couch. "Didn't you think I would happily handle something so fucking small? What the fuck!"

"Because I don't need someone to clean up my mess!" The phrase triggered my memory of Jensen mouthing off those exact words. "Do you think it's been easy being so helpless?"

Helpless...not the word I expected her to use.

"'Oh, poor Moira got stuck in her apartment and needed a big, strong man to literally throw her out of a burning building cause she locked herself in." She began gesturing to the room as she ranted at an increasingly faster pace. "Oh, poor Moira was so out of tune with her own body that she didn't know she was pregnant. Oh, poor Moira has no money and needs a collection from strangers. Poor Moira has no car. Poor Moira has no job." She checked off line after line of scathingly brutal descriptions, counting them off with her hands. "'Poor little helpless orphan has to take the charity of not one, but THREE, of the town's finest fire and rescue employees just to survive from day to day and still needed you to buy me pajamas!" She stopped with a gasp just as her chin quivered despite her determined fist and single raised finger. "I just wanted to do this one thing...all by myself. To prove that I could." Her face dropped. "But surprise, surprise....I needed you to come yet again to clean up my mess."

She said those words again, 'clean up my mess, and it clicked.

She truly believed that being dangerously independent was better than asking someone for help.

That was the long and short of it.

"Okay... stop." My frustration pivoted to the invisible foe I realized had been on the scene long before Jensen arrived. "I'm not sure why you think I'm doing any of this out of charity...but I'm here with you every day, all day, because I choose to be." I started counting off fingers as I challenged each of her statements, head-on. "You didn't start a fire in your building. You didn't reverse your door lock and trap yourself. You were early in your pregnancy, and hardly anyone would have known yet. You do have money, you do have a job, you have a temporary block to them, but that will work out over time." I added a second hand and continued my rant. "You don't have a car, but I was trying to help you with that today when you decided to run off on your own, knowing full well that there is an open arson investigation, and you never once thought about how hard it was for me to listen on the phone as that son of a bitch threatened my wife and there wasn't a goddamn thing I could do about it!"

She genuinely couldn't see how poorly she'd planned all this, and I had to recalibrate her thinking.

"God...Moira. I can't protect you if you don't let me, and goddammit, woman, it's the only thing I have ever wanted to do!"

"My phone?" Moira's eyes were as big as saucers. "You heard..." She covered her mouth, tears flooding her eyes. "Oh my God, you heard him...heard the things he said." She turned her back, stifling a sob with her hand. "That's how you found me."

I crossed the room in a single stride...anger gone.

"Hey, come here, don't do that." I spun her around, holding her to me as she heaved in body-wrenching sobs—the day's events finally pushing through all her walls and pouring into my chest. "You accidentally called Sam's phone...and it connected. We heard everything... I was able to track you on the app on my phone, and I sent Troy the heads up, and he got his guys on it too."

"That's how you all got there ...at the same time." Her words were muffled into my chest, but she slid her arms around me, finally relaxing into me, and with it, my chest relaxed. "You came outta nowhere."

"Knowing he had you, it broke something in me, Moira." I lifted her chin enough to make sure I had her eyes on me. "You are not a burden. You are not a problem. And you sure as shit aren't some mess that needs cleaning." A sob slipped before she covered her mouth, but I pushed on. "Today was a stupid risk, and you just... You can't do that again. Please tell me that you understand how wrong this could have gone."

"I know." She sniffed. "I'm sorry." I pulled her to me, releasing the last of my anger as I focused on having her in my arms.

"And no more hiding your damn tears from me. I'm here for all of it, good and bad." I let my lips rest on the top of her head. "I won't lose you."

I held her on the couch til she calmed, both of us seeming to need the quiet connection to process everything. There was more to say, more to ask, more confessions I still owed her, but it needed to wait.

That night, from the couch, I replayed the day until I heard Moira mumbling from the bedroom. I listened intently, unable to make out the broken phrases. She sounded like she was talking, but I also listened to what sounded like crying. Cracking the door, I found her lying on her back with one bare leg kicked out from under the blankets. She was breathing fast, almost panting, and I stepped to the foot of the bed to see her fists clenched into the sheets, eyebrows pinched together in fear.

"Please...no..." She mumbled, tossing her head to the side.

"Moira," I whispered in the hopes of not scaring her awake. "Wake up."

"Stop....help..." Her voice carried a plea, and her fists kept grasping at the sheets, opening and closing. "No...no..." She turned, half on her side, and her legs curled up to her chest. "Please."

"Come on, Fancy." I rounded to her side of the bed. "It's just a dream. You are safe now." I gently rubbed her shoulder, trying to bring her out of her nightmare.

"No. Stop." She cried out, clenching her fists into tight balls and drawing them up towards her face. "Help!"

I stood helpless to pull her out of it, and when I reached for her again, she thrashed against me, crying for help. In my panic, to give her some peace, I did the only thing that made sense and climbed into bed behind her.

"Shhhh.... I'm here." I whispered, sliding under the sheet, my arm as her pillow. I cradled her head, gently rubbing her hip as I spoke the only words that came to mind. "I've got you, baby. You are safe with me." I let my hand rest on her waist until my palm pressed gently against her abdomen, and her breathing slowed down. "It's just a dream, Fancy Pants. A bad dream." Tugging her to be my little spoon, I nuzzled the back of her neck. "Come back to me."

"Chase?" Her drowsy voice was sleepy and sweet.

"You had a nightmare," I tucked her hair behind her ear. "But you are safe. No one is here but you and me. I've got you." I half expected her to bolt up, embarrassed or apologetic, and send me packing for the couch again, but she didn't. My heart leaped into my throat as I let myself breathe her in, soaking in every inch of her pressed against me.

"Please...." She dragged my arm around, hugging it against her, curling into a little ball. "Stay with me."

It took a minute for her hands to relax.

A minute more to stop shaking.

At last, her breathing slowed into a steady cadence, letting me know she was fast asleep. Lying there next to her, in my bed, feeling her heart beating against my palm and reveling in how perfectly her tiny frame tucked into the shadow of me, I knew.

I'd never let her sleep alone again.

WILDER BRO'S GROUP CHAT

-5-

TJ: Intel on laptop.

ME: Specialist found something?

TJ: It's….not pretty.

Samoa: Spit it out.

TJ: Jensen played the long-con. Nearly 8 months of texts, calls, video chats, gifts, trips. Consistent on a pathological level.

ME: Warning signs?

TJ: The specialist labeled him a "narcissistic so-cio-path".

Samoa: That tracks.

ME: So he just what… wore her down?

TJ: His narrative was to push her boundaries, guilt her when she resisted, and then soothe her back when she doubted him.

Samoa: So…gaslighting narcissistic socio-path.

ME: for 8 months…No wonder.

TJ: No wonder?

ME: I always feel like she's prepared to bolt.

Samoa: No way she'd trust her gut after that.

ME: She trusted Jensen. It cost her everything.

TJ: There's more….Her Camera was accessed remotely.

Samoa: dafuq?

TJ: Given what we know about his propensity for … video-logs…

ME: Fucking Hell! He watched her?

TJ: There's more.

Samoa: God man, TJ get it out before Boyscout explodes.

TJ: The job Moira thought she was moving here for…was also a fake.

Samoa: Like, fake company? No way Jensen is smart enough for that.

TJ: Maybe tied to a company in NYC - Specialist is looking into it.

Samoa: Why go through all that trouble to kill her on his own turf?

ME: FUCK SAM!

Samoa: Sorry…I just mean…

TJ: My thoughts exactly.

ME: I'll kill him.

TJ: Chase. Breathe. He's locked up. Let's focus on Moira.

ME: I'll fucking end him.

Samoa: He's in jail.

ME: He has to pay. I want him to bleed.

TJ: He's not going anywhere.

31

MOIRA

THE FOOTAGE FROM THE bus security camera showed Dean sliding in next to me, but it never captured his gun. So, while they couldn't charge him with armed kidnapping, he was officially booked on charges of arson, attempted kidnapping, and assault. Chase, Sam, and I all gave our statements to the police, and Troy managed to push the bail hearing as far back as possible to keep Dean behind bars.

For the first time in a long time...I could breathe.

The night Chase found me having yet another nightmare about the fire, something shifted. I woke up and stretched the next morning, and he ran a hand lazily across my belly and asked if I wanted tea...easy as you please. The next night, he tucked into bed as if it were the most natural thing in the world.

And I let him.

The rhythm of our days and nights felt as if we'd been together for a million years. His brothers took the news of my pregnancy in stride. I explained the timeline and how I found out, and they cursed the ground Dean walked on. Then Sam teased Chase about a car seat for the Harley, and that was that.

Instant acceptance, no questions asked, and no judgment.

Brothers were so cool.

A few days later, I walked out the front door to three smiling Wilders and a brand-spanking new SUV. At first, I worried...about the enormity of the gesture. But Chase told me he'd been in the market for one anyway, claiming I gave him a kick in the pants to finally buy a second mode of transportation for the rainy days. I vowed to pay for all gas, payments, and insurance costs, which Chase scowled at. Later that night, he admitted his real estate investments were solid, and he'd saved long enough to make the car a cash purchase.

Because, of course, the smoking hot fireman, able to bring me to a panty-melting orgasm just by touching me, was also a humble and unassuming ba-zillionaire. No inferiority complex here.

I tried to sit out the next Wilder family spaghetti night with polite concern about overstepping my bounds in their family tradition. Troy looked at Sam, Sam looked at Chase, and Chase scowled at me as they all turned to leave–returning minutes later carrying bowls of pasta, meatballs, and bread. They transformed Chase's kitchen island into an Italian buffet, then sat down and stared at me like I was the weird one for not joining. Later, during clean-up, Troy mentioned that Nonna would never have tolerated someone not feeling like they were 100% a part of the family when it was so obvious they were precious. His use of the word precious took me by surprise, but he nodded at Chase, who handed me a seltzer as if he had read my mind and delivered a kiss as he departed.

After that, spaghetti nights resumed at Troy's, and by my third one, I began introducing salad.

Insurance continuously denied my claim despite the arson suspect being in custody. However, my job was going well. I had steady paychecks deposited into my bank account, which I could access thanks to my shiny new driver's license. The day it arrived, I was surprised to find that my maiden name was still intact. Then I had a tiny aneurysm when I realized I was hoping it would read 'Moira Wilder'. I had to work harder than I thought possible that day, remembering my earlier stance on pragmatism and telling myself that our physical interactions were from proximity...and pregnancy hormones. Then my horny pregnant brain ruined a pair of panties daydreaming of all the other surfaces we could reenact our bathroom wall encounter on, and I had to have a cold shower.

My hormones were insane.

My nightly dreams had my core clenching at the very thought of Chase's body on mine. I woke up half-feral each morning, wondering if I'd ever disturbed his sleep, but he never said anything. As the weeks went by, I wanted to discuss what all of this meant between us, being married and sleeping together while not sleeping together, yet still being intimate.

Each time I tried, I froze.

On one hand, Chase had never treated me with anything other than total kindness. He had met every need he came across, unasked, and consistently showed me through his actions the kind of man he was. My feelings for him were understandable, given how intimately connected we seemed to be, but therein lay the rub. My feelings got me stranded across the country in a burning building, hunted by a raging arsonist. I thought Jensen was a knight in shining armor when he was the monster. And if I was so sure then, how could I be equally sure now about Chase when the two were night and day opposite?

I had my baby with me, and I needed to keep a level head.

But damn the part of me that ached for him to fulfill the promise he'd made when he made me cum with the force of his body against mine, paired with a well-timed bite on my shoulder. Stifling that part of me into quiet shower releases, I settled into the silence of wanting, and we continued each day the same. Rising each morning and interacting like really, really, really intimate roommates.... who cuddled to sleep each night and enjoyed passing kisses and a severe case of blue bean.

32

MOIRA

"I HAVE A SURPRISE for you." A month into my job, Chase greeted me at the door on a Friday afternoon, holding a black leather jacket. "It'll be chilly, so bundle up." He draped a scarf over the coat, handed me the pile, and pointed to the bedroom with that boyish smile I loved. "You have two options for boots. Pick your favorite and be outside in ten." Before I could so much as say hello, he gave me a peck on the cheek and walked back out the front door with a wink.

In the bedroom, I found the black leather boots, one taller with a zipper up the sides and a shorter pair with laces. On the bed was a pair of black, fleece-lined leggings with padded stitching on the thighs and knees, with streaks of pink glitter dripping down the waist like wet paint.

Fancy pants, I mused to myself.

Donning all the new clothes, I stepped in front of the mirror and admired myself in head-to-toe motorcycle gear. A far cry from my office wardrobe of pastels and neutral basics, the look was bold and made me feel sexy and powerful. Riding the high, I smoked out my eyes and added a dark pink lip to finish the look.

With a flip and a fluff of my hair, I strutted out like a total badass.

"Wow." Chase froze midway through securing the storage pack on his bike. He gave me a once-over that sent shivers of excitement all through me. "I knew you'd look good in leathers, but..." He ran his hand over his face before finishing. "You look *outstanding* in leather, wife." My stomach got all fluttery every time he used that word...wife.

"I take it we're riding your bike finally," I had hinted at a desire to ride twice before, but Chase always insisted the timing was bad. I assumed that was code for 'I don't take girls on my Harley.'

"Smart girl." Chase handed me a black helmet with a metallic pink shimmer. "You're well into your second trimester and haven't thrown up in a while. I picked a smooth route, too, so we can take our time and enjoy the ride."

"How did you know that?" I couldn't hide the surprise on my face. "About the date...I didn't even realize that with everything it was with–" counting weeks on my fingers, I realized he was right.

"It's understandable that you have been distracted. Life has been a little sideways, what with the new job and all." I was grateful he didn't mention Dean...or my blush. "I haven't ridden either; my shoulder didn't like the weight of the coat. But I'm all healed, and the doc gave you an all-clear." He mounted his massive bike and extended his hand as if he hadn't just mentioned talking to Dr. Burner. "Hop on, Fancy." Climbing on, Chase tugged close until his giant body was pressed tight against my core, essentially wrapping my arms around him like a human backpack, and we were off.

Riding behind Chase was exhilarating. At each stoplight, he pointed out landmarks around town, then pulled my arms around his waist before accelerating again. Past the town center, tree shadows stretched long across the road, and each straightaway found Chase's hand sliding up my thigh. His caresses were heady, and I didn't hate the roaring engine vibrations, either.

Taking in the world like this felt magical.

The fall colors were singing their brightest notes, and autumn's perfume filled the air. With nothing between me and nature, it felt like I could reach out and touch every tree we passed. Rounding the final turn on the one-lane black-top, we stopped at a clearing on the edge of a mountain lake so still you'd have thought a mirrored glass lay before us. The fiery leaves reflected around the hazy sky streaked with the colors of sunset, and I couldn't resist breathing in the earthy forest scents as Chase lifted me off the bike.

"Oh wow. This is kind of amazing." I shook my hair to fluff it out.

"I figured the end of morning sickness was worth a little celebration." He rested his hand on my back and drew my attention to a thick plaid blanket on the ground, complete with a basket of food and mason jars full of tea lights. "No wine or charcuterie—you're banned from all the good stuff. But hopefully, you'll like this just the same." His smile was broad as we both sat at the picnic he surprised me with. I attempted to peek in the basket, but Chase lifted a finger, halting me with a playful scowl.

"I can't believe you did all this." I waved a hand around to everything. "And apparently tracking my pregnancy, too. Even I hadn't realized I was so far along."

"I was gonna ask about that." Chase opened the basket and pulled out napkins and silverware. "When I called Burner, he mentioned he hadn't seen you yet."

"I haven't told my work about the baby yet." I gave my belly a little rub, noting I wasn't showing on the outside even if I felt the fullness invading my abdomen as my clothes tugged at my fuller figure. "I know I've put it off too long. I should call and get on the books...I will soon." I resisted sharing that part of me was terrified they'd find something wrong or that this had all been a dream.

"I don't love that you are still waiting. I know you don't like it when I..." He paused his work unpacking the plates, considering his words. "Is there any way I can convince you to make that appointment sooner? You have my insurance for a reason. I want you to use it."

"I promise I will. I want to give it a little more time. To make sure..." I want to make sure your brothers know I'm not taking advantage of you. I want you to know that I don't take you for granted. I'm scared.

"I see those gears turning." Chase began lighting the candles in each mason jar. "You're lost in your thoughts again." He then placed each one around the outer edge of our blanket and returned the lighter to the basket. "Maybe this will help pull you out of that head of yours." Chase reached into the basket and pulled out two take-out boxes. "I know how much you've been craving tacos. I had this place downtown make up a batch to go." He opened the first box and displayed a variety of street tacos; the second held rice and beans. I couldn't quiet the moan I let slip as I inhaled their delicious aroma.

"I think the baby loves tacos more than anything in the whole, wide world." I grabbed a taco, inhaling nearly half of it in one massive bite as the flavors exploded in my mouth.

"You know it's damn adorable when you do that." Chase smiled around his bite. "I could watch you eat everything, every day, forever, just to see that little wiggle you do when some flavor hits the sweet spot."

"I *feel* like I eat everything, every day, forever lately." I gave my well-rounded hips a little smack. "This past week especially. I think the baby might be a tapeworm with this appetite."

"That's normal second-trimester stuff."

"So you're tracking trimester dates, know about my sensitive nose, and now my appetite?" I narrowed my eyes at his ready knowledge of all things gestational. "Are you a closet OB/Gyn?"

"I like audiobooks." Chase laughed, handing me a water bottle. "I listen when I'm working out at the gym or in the shower. When you moved in, I snagged that book on pregnancy...What to expect something or other."

"What to Expect When You Are Expecting?"

"That's the one." He snapped his fingers and smiled again. "I figured I should be educated on what you and the baby might need since we're together." Since... we're together. Chase's finite phrasing had butterflies swarming in my belly.

"I was just thinking I should read that book," I tucked my unruly locks behind my ears, hoping to disguise the blush creeping up my neck. "Maybe it'll tell me why my ass and thighs are more pregnant than my belly," I added with a self-deprecating laugh. "My belly has yet to make an appearance, but my hips are declaring themselves so loud I'll be busting the seams of my pants before I get the joy of cradling a bump."

"Your ass is perfection." Chase's words were pointed and heavy. Laced with meaning, and he held my gaze with an intensity I couldn't look away from. Watching his eyes grazing over me, I played through everything we'd been avoiding all these weeks: the little kisses, the playful teasing, the bathroom. Now, with his gaze so penetrating, I was suddenly very aware of my body screaming for me to lunge at him. "Moira, I didn't just bring us out here for dinner." His voice was so gravelly and low that it vibrated through me. "I've been trying to give you time to process everything...and space to settle in and be more comfortable...but having you in my space has been both amazing and painful."

"Painful?" I blinked away confusion.

"I've been holding back since that morning in the bathroom." He closed his eyes, his hands clenching as the muscles in his forearms coiled and feathered under his skin. "Since you traced your fingers along my ink and begged me to–"

"Chase," I started to tell him 'me too', but he held a hand up.

"Falling asleep next to you every night is the best part of my day—and it's driving me *insane* not touching you." His jaw feathered, and it was all I could do not to grab his face and pull him in for a kiss. "Getting to touch you and feeling the heat of you against me, but not getting to *have* you–"

"Have...me?" I breathed. "Chase." My heart was pounding in full understanding of the pain I understood all too well.

"You are so damned smart." He took my hand in his, gripping my fingers like they were a lifeline between us. "You are strong and courageous." I blinked away a tear at his words. "I can't ignore how I feel about you anymore."

His eyes were pleading, and I couldn't resist shifting to my knees, bringing me a little closer to him.

"You hadn't talked about that morning. I just assumed you didn't want to go...there...with me...like this." I waved a hand around my belly, unable to say 'carrying another man's baby'.

"I was trying not to crowd you or pressure you, but...Goddamn woman," He took his free hand and rubbed it across his face with an exasperated sigh. "Do you *not* know how gorgeous you are?"

His gushing compliment caught me off guard, and I couldn't help the little laugh that escaped as I tried to sidestep my embarrassment.

"Well, we'll see if you feel that way when my thunder thighs are busting the seams of these lovely new pants you bought." I gave another playful smack to my thighs, hoping to make light of my awkwardness, even as he pulled me closer.

"I don't want to pressure you, but I can't ignore how crazy you make me. I want to do more...*be* more for you." He ran his hands across his face again, and I was drawn to his chiseled jaw, stubbled and stalwart and home to the boyish dimples I loved. "I'm saying this all wrong."

I was moving before I realized what I was even doing. Lunging, I wrapped my arms around his neck and pressed my lips to his before another perfect word could fall from his mouth. His grunt of surprise was fleeting, then gone as his hands wrapped tightly around me, and he took control. Like that first kiss we shared, his tongue caressed my lips, and lightning shot to my core. I opened for him, and his tongue plunged into me with a yearning so deep that an ache bloomed between my thighs. My whimper was fuel to the fire as Chase deepened the kiss into something desperate, ravishing me like a man too long starved.

His hands were all over me, one around my waist and the other hooked under my knees. Before I fully registered, I was moving, and Chase had me flipped onto my back in a move so smooth he never lost contact with my mouth. He leaned over me, supporting his sizeable weight with one arm, while his free hand dragged the length of my body. Everything he touched lit up, from the soft squeeze he gave my hip to his gentle caress at the swell of my breast. He was tentative and gentle, and was driving me mad. Pulling his shirt in a desperate plea, I all but begged him to move closer. When his knee pressed my thighs and his hard length ground against my hip, I rocked my pelvis into him, moaning at the friction his muscled thigh provided. Chase growled his approval into my mouth when my hands slid under the edge of his shirt.

"God. Moira." He released my mouth, gasped into my neck, and pressed against me. "I meant what I said...I won't push you."

"You're not," I breathed. "You're saying it all right...I want you."

"Oh, I want this, believe me." Chase's eyes were blown wide, heated, and crazed. "But if we don't leave now, I'll lose every shred of control—and I'm not taking you for the first time on cold, hard ground."

33

CHASE

I MAY NOT HAVE planned that picnic with entirely pure intentions. Still, I never expected Moira to lunge at me, moaning into my mouth like a woman possessed and sending all the blood in my body rushing to my cock. It was perfection, but my wife deserved more than a rushed fuck on cold dirt. So, pounding back my inner caveman, I gentlemanned the fuck up despite my aching dick and repacked the basket like a man possessed.

The ride...was brutal.

Like before, I took it slow, careful not to jostle her and the baby, mindful of curves and turns. But I could feel the heat radiating from her thighs as she snuggled in behind me. And when she wrapped her arms around me, her fingers splayed wide across my abs, and I felt her turn her head to lean her cheek into my back. I caressed her arm, and she let her hands slip under the edge of my shirt. I grazed a hand over her thigh, and her fingers grazed the edge of my jeans as if searching to go lower.

It was foreplay on wheels.

By the time we hit the driveway, I was a goddamn king with a crown of lust. Dismounting, I turned and grabbed my helmet and hers in one hand and lifted her off the bike with the other.

"Has anyone ever told you you're kind of a show-off with all those muscles?" she teased as I gently set her down on the ground, noting her nervous fidget and deflection as I unlocked the door. The drive had given her too much time to think, and I needed to remind her of exactly how I felt. "I *am* capable of—" I scooped her up in my arms in a move so quick she yelped into my mouth as I pressed her into the back of my door.

Gentler than before, I kissed her until her body went lax against me. Only then did I grab her ass, encouraging her to wrap those sweet legs around me as I carried her into our room. Her jacket hit the floor as I lay her down, trailing kisses from cheek to jaw while she yanked mine off like she owned me. Her thighs squeezed my hips as I sucked and nipped a path down her neck to that little spot where her neck and shoulder meet. My dick twitched in memory of the last time I had that spot in my mouth. Grazing it with my teeth, I peppered kisses across her collarbone to the hollow at the base of her throat, where she arched against the mattress to give me more access.

"Aren't you accommodating?"

"Chase...please." She panted my name, and my cock damn near punched through denim. "Get these clothes off of me."

Standing, I grabbed the back of my shirt and pulled it over my head while toeing off my boots. Grabbing Moira's wrists, I pulled her up enough to remove her shirt, pausing to marvel at her magnificent breasts heaving over the edges of her bra before I snapped it loose. I splayed her out below me once more, worshipping my way down her body, kissing every curve. I lingered in the valley of her breasts, tracing my tongue across one nipple while pinching the other. They instantly pebbled at my attention, and so I stayed there awhile, reveling in the way she responded to every flick of my tongue. Her fingers scraped across my scalp, but it was her hips writhing beneath me that had my cock leaking, and I could have happily died just listening to her moans.

"What do you need, baby?"

"I need..." she stuttered through a breathy whimper, and I lifted my eyes to see her head tossed back like she could cum just from me sucking her tits. "I need..." I was dying to claim her, but I needed her pretty mouth to finish that statement.

"Use your words, *wife*." Moving my way down, I kissed her belly at the edge of her pants but went no lower. "Tell me what you need."

"God...you." She gasped when I pressed my hand against her fully dressed cunt, grinding my heel down against her clit. "I need my husband." The title felt as right in my ears as her body felt underneath me, and with a growl, I popped the button of her pants open with my teeth.

Moira's breathy laugh was intoxicating, and so growling again, I yanked the pants down to her hips and trailed fresh kisses across her lower belly, nipping gently as I moved from hip to hip. Her arousal was mouth-watering, and I lingered there as long as I could, savoring every possible sound from her lips.

"God. Chase." The moan she put in my name had my dick straining the edges of my jeans. "Get these goddamn pants off of me!" Standing at the edge of the bed, I slid them clean off and stared down at her. She was naked, laid out before me, and exactly as I dreamed, she'd be.

"Perfection." Her smooth skin, the perfect fullness of her thighs and hips, was enough to have me gripping my shaft as my pants hit the floor. Her hands slowly covered her breasts, nipples tight and begging to be sucked. Then, something shifted in her eyes, and her knees began to draw up as if she were self-conscious.

That wouldn't do.

"Don't you dare hide from me, wife." I hooked her ankles and dragged her to the edge. "You are exquisite."

"Even with my big ol' pregnant thighs?" She deflected her self-consciousness with a breathless laugh, but I wasn't having it. Kneeling at the edge of the bed, and ready to put this issue to bed, I tossed her knees over my shoulders and inhaled her addictive essence.

"I'm pretty sure you mispronounced earmuffs, wife." I slid my tongue from one end of her slit to the other as Moira's gasps and moans offered the most beautiful soundtrack. I wasn't about to let any more of that negative bullshit come from her mouth, and I wasn't above using her pleasure to my advantage. I growled into her pussy, plunging my tongue inside before circling her again, bottom to top, then sucking her clit into my mouth until she was arching off the bed.

Then, I suddenly stopped...loving the few seconds of her hands pulling at my head in desperate anticipation.

"I need you to understand, it's schoolyard rules," Moira looked down at me with a whine, eyes full of confusion as that little eleven of frustration adorably crowned her face. "I licked it," I said, brushing my mouth across her folds. "That makes it mine." Nestling deeper into her heat, I flicked my tongue across her clit and felt her thighs reflexively twitch around my head. "So don't ever let me hear you badmouth this delicious body again." I slipped a finger inside but didn't move it. "Understood?"

"Understood." She panted, muscles clenching as she tried to thrust herself down on my hand.

"Promise?" I gave her another slide of my tongue with more force this time, pumping my finger in and out of her tight heat, then stopping once more.

"Yes." She threw her head back onto the bed. "Yes, anything."

"Good girl," I growled as I sealed a kiss over her swollen pussy and slid a second finger inside. Licking her folds, I set a steady rhythm with my hand, pumping in and out.

"Oh god, Chase...that feels so good." She arched her back when I circled my tongue around her sensitive clit, and I pumped a little faster, letting her slide down on my knuckles as she flexed her legs against my shoulders. "Oh God. Yes."

"You are so wet." I groaned, feeling her walls pulse around my fingers. "I wanna feel you come on my fingers before I fuck you, wife." Never wavering the rhythm of my hand, I drew her clit into my mouth and began to suck, gently flicking the tip with my tongue. Alternating my hands pumping in and out, with the suction of her clit, had her nails digging into the back of my head, but it was the little crook of my finger into her g-spot that sent her over the top with a scream.

"Yes! Yes! Oh God...Yes!"

I couldn't resist pulling back and watching as her walls pulsed and squeezed around my fingers in a sight so gorgeous I nearly came on the spot. Leaning forward, I lapped up her juices with soft, broad strokes of my tongue, pumping gently until she came down the other side of her climax and her legs went boneless across my back. Lifting myself up, I began kissing and praising my way up her body.

"That was the single," I sucked and nipped at her hip, "Most erotic," I dragged my teeth across her ribs, "masterpiece," I pulled a nipple into my mouth, nestling my cock against her still trembling sex. "Thing I've ever witnessed in my life." I dragged my tongue across that sensitive spot on her neck, inhaling her scent and savoring the moment as she continued to gasp and twitch from her orgasm. "You are so responsive," I whispered the praise in her ear, loving how she wrapped her arms around me and nestled into my neck. "I could spend all night worshiping every one of your curves if only to hear you scream my name a little longer."

"Please," The breathless hitch in her voice told me she was near tears. "Please," I loved hearing her beg even as I kissed away the tear slipping from the corner of her eyes.

"Tell me, wife?" I settled my weight on my elbows, my cock notched at her entrance with barely the tip pressing against her. "Tell me what you need."

"Please, Chase." She drew my mouth to hers and kissed me, savoring the taste of her on my mouth even as a fresh sob escaped into my mouth. "Take me."

And I was done.

My mouth still sealed on hers, I slid my cock in fully, to the hilt, in one smooth motion without a second's hesitation. Moira gasped in my mouth as her walls stretched around me, and it took all my willpower to pause long enough for her to adjust. Letting myself get lost in her lips, I ran a hand down to her knee, lifting it higher on my hip so I could nestle a little deeper. Still trying not to move too fast, I pulled back, entering her again, feeling every rippling inch of her throbbing walls clench around me. The third time I pulled back, she arched her back and thrust against me with a gasp that might as well have been a starter pistol. Increasing my intensity, I began pumping in and out, setting a pace that let her feel the full length of me while still giving me control not to blow like a two-pump chump into the heaven that was my wife's sweet cunt.

"Oh god," she gasped. "You feel... you're so..." I cut her off with a kiss to that sensitive spot on her neck, knowing that if she added dirty talk to the way her hips were moving, I'd lose all control.

I was already hanging on for dear life.

"God woman, you'll be the death of me," I growled, bending down and taking one of her nipples into my mouth.

"More." She wrapped her legs tighter around me, at once restricting my movement and forcing me deeper. "Chase, yes. More!" I didn't dare speed up as I was so close to losing my mind and my load at the same time. But shifting my weight slightly, I snapped my hips a little harder, giving my wife the intensity she craved.

"Yes. Don't stop!" Her nails clamped down on my ass as she pulled against me, grinding me to her clit as I pounded into her.

"Fuck yes, baby." I thrust a little harder, "Mark me." I kept pumping, increasing my force only a little as my self-restraint burned with each score I felt her scratch into my back.

"Chase...oh God," Her pussy pulsed around me, and sweet merciful hell, I was never so glad to lose control as I clamped my teeth down on that spot on her shoulder. "Yes, Yes, Yes!" She clenched around me as I slammed balls deep, loving the way her pulsating orgasm milked every last drop of cum out of me.

We sat there for a minute...or was it two?

Time had lost all meaning.

Breathing in the smell of her, of us, had me so drunk I barely knew which way was up. Trailing kisses up her neck and jaw, I let my body come down from the adrenaline to the sweet sounds of my wife panting in my ear. Her luscious thighs quaked around me, and every tremor of the aftershocks she was riding felt like a little piece of paradise. I wanted to live forever buried deep inside, her heart pounding against my chest and her scent covering me. The very idea of it had my cock hardening, but she needed time. When her breathing steadied, and only when her body was quiet, I lifted off of her.

"Don't move." I grabbed a towel from the bathroom and soaked it with warm water. When I returned, I set about worshipping her body differently–gently cleaning, starting with her thighs, then down to her pussy, minding the pressure and wishing I could be in her again, and again, and again.

Moira let her fingertips graze over me as I cleaned all the juices from our time together. Part of me was almost sad to wipe away the evidence of what we had done, a feeling I'd never experienced with any other woman. Then again, I'd never taken a woman raw, and the sensation of having Moira without any barrier was the drug I never wanted to be free of. When I was done, I tossed the towel to the floor and grabbed the blankets to cover us, tucking her warm, pliant body against me.

"That was way better with our clothes off." She said with a giggle, her voice already sounding sleepy. "Not that the bathroom wall won't forever be a favorite memory of mine."

"We'll have to revisit that sometime," I brushed her hair back from her cheek.

"You were so.... are so...good to me." Her voice trailed into a stifled yawn.

Tucking my little spoon in close, I thought of a million ways to say what I was feeling. Lucky, sure. Unimaginably happy, absolutely. But those didn't convey the depth of what burned inside me. The bone-deep contentment of Moira burrowing into my life was like finding the missing piece of a puzzle I didn't know was incomplete.

'Happy' was too damn small a word.

Her breathing slowed, that familiar cadence of sleep telling me she was at peace. My chest tightened at the word that came into my mind then. The perfect word to encapsulate how she made me feel whenever she was near, smiling at me, or laughing for me.

She was that forever happy place reserved just for me.

She was the oxygen I was starved of.

She was the peace I craved.

Moira...was Home.

34

MOIRA

I SLIPPED OUT FROM under Chase's massive arm the next morning, padding into the bathroom quietly so as not to wake him. It was technically the weekend, but I had a quick meeting at the library to attend. Waiting for the shower to heat, I took a moment to admire my reflection. I was prepared for the pregnancy to bring changes to my body. Still, my appetite was recently large and in charge, making my swells and curves more pronounced. My breasts were fuller, my ass a little rounder, and I found...I didn't hate it. Resting my hand on the firm swell of my belly, I smiled.

My baby was healthy—so was I.

Standing under the hot water, I drenched my hair as the glorious heat soaked into my achy hips and thighs. Chase was a big guy in every way, and having him work my body was a stretching glory I was all too happy to massage away this morning. As if on cue, my core throbbed at the soap-slick way my hands glided over my body, remembering him luxuriating on my breasts, softening for him again. Sliding my hand across my collarbone, I imagined his teeth at the erogenous spot on my shoulder, and my thighs squeezed.

"Mind some company?" His voice snapped me out of my reverie with a jolt, and I glanced over my shoulder to find him watching me with sleepy, lust-filled eyes.

"Sure," My voice was far more confident than my blush let on, knowing what he'd almost seen my hands do. "It might be kind of a tight fit with those big shoulders, though."

"A problem I will remedy." He stepped in with a mischievous grin and a raging hard-on.

"I hope I didn't wake you?" I turned into the water to resist openly staring at his cock.

"Waking up without you was terrible." He slid his hands around my waist, grabbed the soap, then massaged the suds into my shoulders and back. I braced my hands on the wall with a groan as he worked his way down to my butt and hips. "When will you be home today?"

He tugged me around so the water could wash me clean, and I couldn't resist the peek down at his massive length.

"I uh.. have an early meeting with the children's department to discuss my social media plans." I hardly realized my arms had drifted up to cover my breasts until he narrowed his eyes and gently lowered my hands before continuing his work, soaping my body. "I shouldn't be long, maybe an hour or two?"

"Don't hide from me, gorgeous." His voice, still sleep-graveled, made my belly do a little flip. He tugged me close enough that our bodies were pressed together. "Unless you're looking for another lesson on the rules, that is."

"Oh no." My slippery hands glided across his tattooed pec, and memories of our first bathroom encounter had my pussy clenching around nothing. "I suspect your lesson would make me late for work."

"Hm," He pulled me against him, his hard length pressed against my belly. "I was hoping to get a little breakfast before you left."

It took me half a second to realize the hidden meaning in his words before my belly clenched again with a flutter.

"Whoa?!" Chase's head jerked up, his eyes big as saucers. "What was that?"

"Wait." I looked down at where his body had pressed against my belly. "You felt that, too?"

"Hell Yeah!" He pressed his hand against my belly, kneeling before me. "Do it again?"

His face lit up like a kid at Christmas, and I couldn't help but laugh at his huge, full-dimpled smile.

"I think the baby kicked."

"Has that happened before?" The wonder and awe on his face were magical, and I worked to memorize every detail, not wanting to forget a moment.

"I thought I felt something last night, but wasn't sure." He stood, pulling me in for a kiss that pressed us into a tight embrace, and another little flip in my belly had us both giggling.

"There it is again!" He kissed me again, half laughing as his face held a heart-melting expression of pure elation. "But you aren't even showing yet. The baby was kicking me...I mean you?" Kneeling again, he pressed his mouth to my belly in a muffled half-yell. "Hey baby.... kick me again?" Hugging me close, he pushed his cheek into my belly and waited. As if on cue, the flutter thumped me again, and I swear if it weren't for the shower, I would have seen tears in his eyes that matched my own.

I let my mind nest in the moment as I drove into work.

The scenery was showing off as the autumn colors blazed, and I couldn't help but drive a little slower, opting to detour through the small coffee kiosk for a decaf latte to round out the perfect morning. Sitting in line, I played through the shower in my mind and couldn't believe I was feeling my baby move. Even Chase said his books predicted it would take longer. Then he bragged that it must have meant my baby was some muscle-lifting prodigy, and my heart soaked up the idea of my baby having Chase's traits. Sadly, my brain then went to wondering how much of its characteristics would belong to Dean, and I hated the shadow it cast over such a magical moment. I hated how even my happy moments felt borrowed, as if joy would never be my own.

I hated that Dean lived in these spaces.

I wanted to focus on Chase and me, unfettered. He deserved that.

Pushing Dean out of my mind, I ordered my drink and vowed to actively shift my thoughts to happier Chase memories anytime Dean snuck in. I floated on that happiness all the way through my meeting prep, until an oddly distracting scent drifted through the air. It wasn't unpleasant, per se, but it nagged at me until I was forced to get up and find the source to assuage my curiosity.

Stepping out of the administrative corridor of offices, I entered the children's book section but didn't find the origin of the cloyingly sweet scent. Following my super-charge pregnancy nose, I tracked the odor like a bloodhound until I walked into the main lobby of the library to find a giant cascading arrangement that made my stomach leap into my throat. There, on the round table inside the front lobby, was a massive arrangement of white roses.

Not pink, not red, not even another accenting color to round them out.

All bright white, and at least three dozen of the same giant pristine flowers Dean used to send me when we dated. The same flowers he graced me with before I moved. My mouth went dry as I slowly scanned the room, blood thumping in my ears, half expecting to see Dean watching me. He wasn't there. No one was there. Until a volunteer walked by pushing a squeaky cart full of books.

"Where did those flowers come from?" I halted their cart with my hand.

"Aren't they gorgeous?" The woman gushed. "The library sometimes has arrangements when special guests are coming for book signings and stuff." It was plausible, reasonable, even, but the answer didn't slow my pulse in the slightest.

"So this is for an author event?"

"Yeah, I guess." The volunteer shrugged and walked away, leaving me feeling foolish for my brief moment of panic. Still, the smell lingered in my nose, and my lungs burned as my heart raced from the shock of seeing them.

"It's not Dean. He's not here. He can't reach me." I whispered to myself, forcing my feet to take me to the flowers. If I inspect them up close, I reasoned, I'll relax, and everything will be fine.

Getting closer to them, I focused on the lovely parts and tried to convince my mind we weren't running from a live bear. The greenery was a soft, ashy color, and it complemented the creamy blossoms perfectly. And their blocky glass vase was a lovely addition to the otherwise dated library décor. If not for my personal history with them, I would have been all too happy to sit and admire them. As it was, I was happier to hide in my office and ignore them completely.

A small card tucked inside the arrangement caught my eye. I glanced around to see if anyone was watching once more before my curiosity pressed me forward to read the card.

Courtesy of
The Apex Society

"Apex Society?" I flipped the card, reading the florist's shop info on the back. "What's that?"

"Our new patron!" The head librarian, Todd, startled me, and I nearly dropped the card as I jumped with a yelp. "Oh, sorry." He steadied my balance with a kind smile. "I didn't mean to scare you!"

"I didn't hear you walk up." I pointed to the flowers with the card. "Is Apex Society a literary group? Are they doing an event?" Todd shook his head

"They are an outside organization that's begun investing in several small upstate libraries to try and revitalize the towns. Our library was their latest recipient." He nodded at the flowers. "They sent these over in celebration of the handshake deal; They plan to fund a new tech lounge to expand the children's department into something more teen-inclusive." Todd beamed. "Isn't it great?!"

"Yeah. It's great." I stared at the white roses, a foreboding sense of unsettling nerves still weighing on my chest. "White roses are kind of a weird selection for a library, though, isn't it? Especially for a teen lounge?"

"Meh. It's a little funeral-ish. Wouldn't have been my first pick." Todd shrugged. "I would have gone with something fun...like a cookie bouquet!"

"Same," I mumbled down at the card again, hating that I couldn't shake the lingering fear in my stomach.

"Speaking of...Are you ready to meet with June?" Todd's voice held a hint of concern until I finally let my eyes leave the card.

"Um, yeah." I shook my head to refocus. "I can see now why she was so insistent we meet. I'll be there in five." I headed back to my office, mindlessly pocketing the card and trying to convince myself they meant nothing.

The flowers' ominous foreboding followed me the rest of the day, even though I gave the arrangement a wide berth. On the way home, I stopped by the pharmacy to refill my prenatal vitamins and found myself lingering at the infant first aid section. I got a little lost in my thoughts, comparing the various items and debating if I should buy them now or later, when someone bumped into me with a loud 'Oof.'

"Oh goodness." A strong hand grabbed my arm, preventing me from toppling completely. "I am so sorry." Looking first at the hand, my eyes drifted up to the icy, pale-blue eyes of strangers with slicked platinum hair. "Distracted as I was, I wasn't watching where I was going." The man was taller than I and had a slim build, noticeable only in the way his black suit hung off his shoulders as if it were tailor-made.

"I'm okay." I anchored my feet back under me and went to step away, but his hand remained firmly around my arm. His face seemed genial enough, but his smile was thin-lipped and tight and didn't really reach his eyes.

"Damn, these devices that snare our every waking hour." His voice was smooth, almost melodic, but it dripped with a sugary venom that set my teeth on edge. I hardly noticed the cell phone he waggled in his other hand. "Are you sure you are alright?" His gaze wandered down my body, surveying me for any bruise...or just surveying me?

"It's fine, really." I successfully tugged my arm away, stepping back to put some distance between me and the stranger. "No harm done."

"So glad to hear it, my dear." His eyebrows gave a bemused lift as he dripped the endearment from his thin lips. "Take care of yourself—*and* the baby."

My heart...stopped.

The man in the suit turned to leave, and I clutched a hand to my barely baby bump, wondering how he knew. I exhaled until he disappeared out the front door, and I felt a cold panic build as I considered he could be a friend of Dean. Lifting my phone, I started to call Chase when I realized I was still standing in front of Baby Cold Remedies. Lowering my phone, I felt like a fool. I thought about the flowers and realized I had let them get into my head.

Get a grip. I chastised myself. Sometimes, flowers are just flowers...and strangers can be weird without being nefarious. A speaker announced my name, and I headed to the pharmacy counter, promising myself I'd stop being paranoid.

I couldn't embrace the future if I was still jumping at ghosts from the past.

Wilder Bro's Group Chat

-6-

TJ: Heads up. Jensen's lawyer is in play.

Samoa: Anyone you know?

TJ: NYC suit. Never heard of him.

ME: New York? Poker buddy?

TJ: Perhaps.

Samoa: What does this mean?

TJ: He's making a case for unlawful detention and petitioning for quick release, speedy trial, etc.

ME: The FUCK!

TJ: This isn't a surprise. It's all noise. However, he's casting doubt on the arson by blaming Jensen's former colleague.

Sam: Which one?

TJ: The one now married to Jensen's former flame…seated in line to replace Brandt.

ME: ME?!?

Samoa: Fuck that shit!

TJ: It's a ploy for leniency, nothing more.

Samoa: And Moira?

ME: He CAN'T talk to her. No fucking way. She doesn't even know everything.

Samoa: What do you mean she doesn't know?

Troy: Chase, stay calm.

Samoa: Calm has left the building.

TJ: Let me do my job. I'll keep you updated. I'm using the video footage and her written statement to shield her as best I can.

ME: I'm crawling outta my skin, TJ. Gimme something to do before I go crazy.

Samoa: Maybe it's time to get back to work. Your shoulder was cleared.

ME: I can't.

TJ: You can.

ME: With four 24s in a row? She won't sleep while I'm gone

TJ: Help me understand.

ME: She gets nightmares. If I tell her about Jensen and then leave for days on end …

Samoa: We can fix this…I can sleep on the couch at night.

TJ: And I can drive by the library during the day.

ME: Fuck. I've waited too long to tell her.

TJ: She's stronger than you think.

Samoa: So are you.

TJ: Let's talk over dinner. We'll help you.

Samoa: She'll understand.

Me: What if she doesn't?

Samoa: We'll help you.

ME: Fuuuuccckkkkkk

35

MOIRA

THE SECOND TRIMESTER KILLED the nausea but brought on a new enemy I referred to as: Prenatal Narcolepsy.

I worked barely 6 hours a day, and still, I needed a catnap when I got home. Today, it was essential since Sam was hosting the Wilder Family dinner, and while these were full of fantastic food and laughs, they weren't short. Even thinking about the hours of conversation had me yawning over Chase's note he'd left on the bar.

Ran to the station for a PT check. Home soon. XO

I smiled over his 'XO' as I stretched out on the couch...falling instantly into a heavy sleep.

"Hey, baby," Chase's voice tugged me from sleep, "I'm home."

"How long was I out?" I yawned at my watch, surprised I'd slept for 2 hours.

"Nap all you want if it means I come home to a vision of you splayed out on my couch." He slid his hands down my bare thighs until he reached my boots, unzipping and removing them before smoothly rolling my knee socks off to the floor. "This sweater dress might be my new favorite." Chase knelt on the couch between my knees, his broad shoulders crowding out the rest of the world.

"I should get the bread started for dinner?" I moaned as he massaged my feet and then calves, delivering a decadent promise with his smouldering eyes. The man was ravenous and had taken me every day this week.

"Nope," Chase mumbled between kisses to my knees.

"But dinner." I laughed as his stubble tickled my thighs.

"Nuh-uh." Chase slid my dress high enough to expose my panties. "Can't hear you." Lowering his head to my core, he inhaled deeply, sending a shiver of cool air flashing across my pussy.

"But Sam..." I breathed. "And Troy..."

"Woman." Chase draped my legs over his shoulder. "Keep my brothers' names off your lips while I have my appetizer." He ripped yet another pair of panties clean off my body and buried himself in my center.

I gasped as he dove into me, his tongue sliding quickly in and out of me in an urgent fucking that had me instantly arching up off the couch. Unlike the other days, where he slowly teased me, tonight he moved with urgency, fast, and animalistic. I swear the man growled as he sucked my clit into his mouth, hands wrapping around my hips to pin me in place as he worked me over.

"Oh god." I moaned, shocked at the tension already building inside. "God, Chase, yes, yes!"

"That's my girl," Chase growled into my core. "Show me how hard you can cum." His voice rumbled through me, and just as I was about to climax, he slid one finger inside me and hooked a come-hither motion, sending me over the top in a shattering orgasm.

Barely a moment to catch my breath, Chase sat up on his knees and unzipped his pants.

"Come here, Fancy." He pulled me up to my knees, turning me until my belly pressed against the back of the soft couch. "Open for me." His hands gently slapped my thighs further apart as he positioned himself behind me, his cock notched at my entrance as he grazed his teeth down my spine. "I've wanted you all day." He growled. "But coming home to you laid out like a buffet...perfection."

He pressed into me, just the tip, and I leaned back against him.

"If this is how you come home... I'll nap on this couch daily." I pressed my hips back against him with a whimper as he entered me, inch by breathtaking inch.

"God...I need you...so bad." His voice was thick, and for a split second, I could hear the echoes of a thousand things he wasn't saying as he stilled his body. But only for a moment, before he slid back and pumped into me again.

And again. And again. And, God yes, again.

His need rocked into me over and over, increasing in speed and intensity as his hands peeled my dress over my head, and he found my breasts. Pinned to the back of the couch, I was helpless to do anything but lean my head back and feel the delicious warmth that grew with every deep slam.

"Oh god...Oh God..." I was so close, and his thrust became faster, more potent as he banded his arms around me. I was so close, but my orgasm was just out of reach, and the frustration of chasing it was maddening. But Chase played my body like a master musician, sliding a hand down and cupping my mound.

"Cum with me, wife." His command flipped a switch as his thumb and forefinger pinched my mound closed with the perfect pressure, and I...was...gone.

"Yes! Yes! Yes!" The orgasm was so powerful, so fast, that for a moment, I felt lightheaded at the intensity. Releasing his grip on my mound, he kept pumping while sliding a finger down against my clit, sending me into the stratosphere again. I don't even know what else I screamed then or how long or loud I was. I only know that when I hit my peak for a third time, I felt him tense and slam into me with the force of his climax as he roared in my ears. His climax sent me over again—so big, so blinding, I couldn't stop the tears from emotions pouring out as hard as my orgasms.

Chase sprinkled kisses across my shoulder, then collapsed his head on my shoulder, one hand on my belly, and I realized with startling clarity...I loved my husband.

36

CHASE

WE WALKED INTO SAM'S house a solid half hour late, he and Troy both shooting cheap-ass grins at me. I had wondered if they could hear her screams from across the yards, our homes were in fairly close proximity. The debate all but settled when Sam snarked in my ear, 'don't you ever give the woman a rest?'

I couldn't help it.

Feeling Moira wrapped around me, her body coming undone for me, was a drug. Every moan, every whimper, was a symphony, and I didn't care who heard. Still, I made a note that a property with some extra space wouldn't be a bad idea.

"Each of you has such different styles." She gestured around Sam's place between bites. "Your homes are all so unique."

"You have a favorite?" Troy asked over the edge of his beer. "And may I remind you that I hold the recipe to that sauce you love so much?"

"Hmmm." She wrinkled her nose, and I swear my dick twitched at the cuteness. "Hard to say."

"Um, hello," Sam gave a little wave. "I gave you my car for *weeks*."

"Fellas..." I flicked an invisible piece of lint from my shirt, then flashed my cockiest grin. "I pulled her from a burning building."

"Old news!" Sam and Troy said in unison.

Moira tossed her head back in laughter, one hand over her belly and another over her mouth. It sparkled in her eyes and rang through the whole room, catching us all up in happiness as we laughed with her.

"OK, OK." She patted her hands through the air, quieting our amusement as she sat upright, squaring her shoulders in all sincerity. "Troy's place has a homey feel, with big overstuffed furniture and that gorgeous wall of memories. I adore the pictures of you three as kids and your beautiful Nonna."

"Here, here." Troy tipped his beer. "The woman has excellent taste."

"But," She lifted a finger, drawing out the one word with a glint in her eyes. "Sam's place has charm. A laid back, casual, 'kick off your shoes, come as you are, zero bullshit or pretense' kind of vibe with its leather furniture and dartboard on the wall." She gave Sam a nod and added, "And don't think I didn't notice the memorabilia from all the weird roadside attractions you frequent."

"Why road trip if you aren't gonna stop and see the world's biggest ball of yarn?" Sam tipped his beer at Troy with a smirk.

"And yes..." She turned to me with a soft expression–my whole world stood still. "Chase saved me...in eleventy-billion little ways. And his home is filling with memories day by day that I'm growing quite fond of." She grazed her thumb over my chin, a look in her eyes that nearly had me lifting her over my shoulder and running us both back to my bedroom, before shooting her hands in the air. "But I'm GOING WITH DARTBOARDS!"

"Hell Yeah, she is!" Sam shot to his feet, giving Moira a high-five as Troy rolled his eyes, and all I could do was take it all in. How well she blended in with them, how easily they accepted her, and how she accepted them in return, made me think that maybe she had healed something in them, too.

As the meal wound down, Troy and I shared a silent look, noting it was time to have the hard conversation. Reading the room, Sam shut off the water in the sink, and we all moved into the living room in unison. I'd been thinking over my words all week, considering the best way to say what needed to be said, and I was still coming up blank.

"Now that our meal is done," Troy began. "There is news to discuss." He gestured to the recliner, inviting Moira to sit.

"News?" Moira looked at Troy, and then her eyes turned to Sam and me as we sat around her. I physically ached when she slumped in the chair with a huff. "It's him, isn't it?" I sat on the coffee table across from her, needing to touch her. "Might as well get it out."

"Jensen's lawyer arrived earlier this week, throwing his weight around. Filing motions, asking to move up trial dates, accusing the department of mishandling things." Troy waved a hand as if swatting a gnat. "It's nothing we didn't anticipate. No cause for concern there."

"OK," Moira sat up, tipping her head from side to side. "So he's lawyered up, we knew that could happen, right?" Straightening her shoulders, she put on that little scowl of resignation. "What do I need to do?"

My brave little badass.

"Right now. Nothing." Troy took a seat in the second chair, turning to face her in a show of gentleness I was grateful for. "But you should know, there is a good chance Jensen will be released on bail...soon."

Moira's face was a mask of calm, but her hand slid to her belly. Sam noticed, his eyes closing as his jaw flexed; even Troy gave that almost imperceptible lift of his brow in acknowledgement – her fear... was shared.

"There is a restraining order in place," Troy continued. "But Jensen's previous actions show a clear disregard for the law. As such, we would like to make a plan so you are never alone."

"Never?" Moira's head snapped back; her eyes were locked onto Troy's face, body frozen, and her breathing grew shallow. Each tiny breath was a flicker of panic that sliced into me. I couldn't take this away from her...and I should have hit Jensen harder. "Will he come after me...again?"

"That's *not* happening." I put my hand on her knee, and she blinked as if snapping out of a trance. "I'm not letting anything happen to you. It's just..." I fumbled for the right words to rip this Band-Aid off. "Jensen has a history... of crossing boundaries."

"Like stalking me at the Library," Moira huffed in frustration. "I know."

"No, Baby." God, this was going to hurt her, and it was my fault. I didn't know if it would embarrass her or make her scared, and I didn't know how to begin, that we've known all along.

"It's more than that. It's..." I searched for a word I could use to soften the blow. But what word could sugarcoat non-consensual recordings and a husband who hid it from you for months? The longer I sat, the more my world caved in around me as my mind remembered how hard I'd worked to get her to trust me, and how easily I could lose that trust now.

"What our brother is struggling to say is that Jensen has a history of crossing boundaries with women," Sam interjected, giving me a nod of reassurance before he continued. "Before we all met you, Jensen was fired from his job at the firehouse for blackmailing women with videos taken...*without* consent."

"Recordings, with other women?" Her voice was firm, but her chin trembled as she began reasoning it all out. "You mean, he made secret sex tapes? As in plural...more than one."

"Chase uncovered it." Troy squeezed my shoulder. "Put his job at risk to help bring him down."

"Even had to suffer a few weeks desk duty and board review for cold-cocking the asshole", Sam added with a proud smile. "His first fire back on duty was your apartment."

Moira's eyes held that chilling thousand-yard stare that I knew meant her brain was working overtime.

"You." A dozen emotions flitted across her eyes as she suddenly focused on me. But it was anger that resonated in her voice. "You *really* knew him. You worked with him."

And here it was, the moment I had dreaded since learning about that damned partial fingerprint that linked her past and mine together.

"Yeah, baby." I slid forward, touching our knees together, with both of my hands resting on her leg; to hug her or keep her from running away, I wasn't sure. "He was a member of my team at the station. I stumbled across the recordings on his computer by accident."

"Oh God," Moira's hands shot to her mouth, face ashen, tears welling in her eyes.

"I don't know, I don't think so. I only saw a few seconds of the one I stumbled on." I answered, squeezing her knee as if that could keep her dignity intact and make her not hate me for hiding this from her.

"I instantly shut off the recording, reported the issue, and confronted Jensen. What I did see wasn't you–I swear it."

"That's why you wanted my laptop." She fired at Troy. "You were looking for recordings of me."

"I can attest that I, nor any male officer, watched any recordings. A female specialist helping my department viewed them and, to date, your name is not listed as one of the victims, so I don't believe you were recorded." Troy hesitated for a fraction of a second, his eyes never leaving Moira, even as his voice dropped to a calm, soothing tone. "But...your laptop–"

Moira silenced Troy with a raised finger while clenching her eyes shut. Taking a deep breath, then another, steadying herself before leveling her eyes at me with ferocity I hadn't seen before.

"You know what they found on my laptop?" Her clipped words felt like a cavernous divide being spoken to life between us as I nodded my confirmation. "Seems you owe me a little more transparency...so you tell me."

Cold, flop-sweat, panic.

I scrambled for some way to reassure her that I never wanted to keep this from her. I wanted to take her and hold her and swear that I was trying to protect her in my secrecy. I wanted to vow to never keep anything from her again, and pledge my undying devotion to her if she'd just forgive me and, please, please, please, not retreat behind a wall of elephant shields and fake smiles.

"I wanted to tell you all of this, before–how Jensen knew me, and what he was fired for." I ran my hand across my face and tried to find the right words. "The camera was accessed remotely a few times so we think he may have watched you but baby, I swear, I should've told you sooner but the timing was never right...so many things...so many good things were happening...and when I thought about the fire and what he'd-" I was rambling, near incoherently, but the thoughts were too fast for me to filter and all I could see were the eyes filled with hurt and anger and betrayal and I...had done that. "I wanted to kill him for you, I should have at the pharmacy, and please-"

"What my brother is choking on," Sam mercifully halted my word-vomit. "Is he only kept this from you because he was taking it all on himself and trying to fix it?"

"Less keeping it secret, and more sparing you from it," Troy added.

I was beyond grateful for their words, but the look in her eyes told me that if I didn't tell her everything, open and raw and brutally honest, she'd never trust me again.

"Baby," I edged closer, nearly kneeling at her feet. "Until that day, the day Jensen," I clenched my jaw at the memory. "Jensen hated me already. But didn't have any reason to connect me to you until he saw us together after the bus."

"When you plowed him down and nearly beat him to death." Moira's eyes held a sliver of light that gave the first inkling that she didn't entirely hate my guts-I clung to it.

"He knows about you and me and the baby. He has every reason to break that restraining order. Especially if he thinks it'll hurt me and scare you into siding with him-ending his legal troubles." I looked down at the floor. "He blames me for losing his job, but he wasn't facing jail time before your connection brought arson into the picture, and now he's up to his eyeballs in the shit he shoveled and looking for someone to blame."

"That's the other part of this," Sam said. "Jensen's attorney is a piece of work, and he's fingering Chase for conflict to cast doubt on Jensen's involvement."

"While he's been cleared medically, his PTO is out." Troy gestured towards me as he spoke. "Hiding here with you...The optics are bad. It could fuel rumors of a witch hunt if Jensen's arson accuser is the wife of the man who shut his career down, as it is already a tangled web. Chase needs to appear clean as a whistle to avoid a conflict of interest." Giving my shoulder a pat, Troy added on. "He needs to go to work."

I could have killed Troy.

He was right.

But I could have killed him.

I had used my mandatory leave for my shoulder, and my paid leave was dwindling by the day. I did need to get back to work, if for no other reason than to keep the internal investigation as far from Moira as possible.

But leaving her might kill me.

"OK. So, you go back to work. That's easy enough, right?" She glanced at Sam and Troy, then back at me. "Does that warrant a family pow-wow like this? What am I missing?"

"Baby...Firefighters work four days on and three days off. That means I sleep at the station and don't return home for four days at a time."

"Sometimes more than that if your account for training, dev work, and that promotion Chief is grooming you for," Sam interjected, ignoring my best 'shut-the-fuck-up' look.

"I don't need to do all the extra stuff right now," I waved a hand in Sam's face to silence the eager bastard. "But it still means nights at the station."

"Oh." Moira took on that distant look again, no doubt deep diving into plans to be alone, taking care of herself, needing no one.

"If you would allow us," Troy said calmly. "Sam and I would like to help."

"How?" Her voice was an echo of the fragile timbre she had in the hospital, and it made me realize how far she had come out of her shell during our time together. A reminder, too, of how close that fragility still was when her safety, her baby's safety, was at risk.

"I can check in on you at the library." Troy answered, "And the restraining order lets me order a few Unis to patrol without raising eyebrows."

"And I'll help at home." Sam strolled over, propping himself on the arm of her chair. "I'll work my shifts opposite of Chase. I'll keep you company on any errands, and sleep on the couch so you don't feel alone in that 'big ole house'."

I was grateful for Sam's effortless humor when Moira's lips gave the faintest hint of a smile. I could see the million questions drifting through those beautiful river blues of hers, but there was nothing more to be said. So we sat, holding our breath and silently acknowledging that we were here for her while my brave wife worked out all the things in her mind before finally voicing them to us.

"I have one condition."

Troy and Sam both shot me a look, and I shrugged, having no clue where she was going.

"You have a condition?" Sam cocked up an eyebrow to match his smirk. "For letting us protect you?"

"Name it." Troy gave the command, but she never took her eyes off me as she spoke.

"You don't hold back on your career for me. Not now, Chase Wilder...not ever."

"It's not like that, Fancy." I pleaded. "I don't - "

"Then no deal." Moira crossed her arms, jutting her chin out in a surprising show of defiance. "And you can all stare at me all you want, but I won't budge. So, when you're ready to pick that big ass jaw off the floor, you let me know."

"All that extra stuff was just filler - "I tried again, but she lifted a finger and pointed it at me.

"You have a family, Chase. Brothers who love you and have been with you your whole life. I never had that, but you do!" She thumped her finger into my chest.

"Yeah, but - "

"I'm not done!" She scooted forward on the chair until she was nearly in my lap, her face inches away from mine. "Dean Jensen played me like a fool." Her voice dropped to a near whisper. "But from what you say, he's done that to way more women than just me. I nearly lost my life to that psychotic piece of shit, and I'll be damned if I let him steal one more second of my life, or any other woman's life, Or. Yours," she thumped her finger into my chest again, punctuating her words. "Because you're afraid to trust your brothers to help me!" She placed her hand on mine, her countenance softening towards me. "Trust them with me, the way you've trusted them with everything else." Leaning forward, she pressed her forehead to mine and closed her eyes, whispering, "And I will too."

Pride.

Chest-bursting pride flooded me as my wife commanded a room with her confidence despite what I knew was the scariest thing she'd ever faced.

"I like her, Chase," Troy clapped a hand on my shoulder. "I really do."

"Pretty badass," Sam gave her an encouraging nudge. "And she's right. At some point, this will all pass. Don't let Jensen derail either one of you." He nudged her again, getting her attention. "Make your doctor appointments, keep your job, we've got you."

Hard as it was to admit, I couldn't do everything for Moira on my own, and I knew without a doubt my brothers meant every word. They would keep Moira safe, so I could put Jensen behind bars.

Then maybe, finally, we could all move forward; Moira and I and the baby.

"OK. I'll call Chief in the morning and schedule my return to duty." I resigned, squeezing Moira's hand. "Let's add her to the group chat to stay in the loop on scheduling."

"There's a group text?" Moira asked.

"Finally, someone to muzzle those dick jokes," Troy quipped, standing to clear the table.

"Great." Sam stood and mumbled his way to the kitchen. "First, I gotta eat salad, and now I have to censor my texting."

"You know you weren't complaining about the salad when you scarfed down your second bowl!" Moira teased.

"You're amazing, you know that, Fancy Pants." I marveled at the return of her smile.

"Perhaps...but don't do that again."

"Do what?" I asked, letting my hands rest on her thighs as her arms draped across my shoulders.

"Underestimate me." Her tone was flat, steady, and pure power. "I know our time together has been short, and I needed an awful lot of rescuing at first, but I meant every word I said. Jensen doesn't win. Not with your work, not with me, and not with my life or my baby." The faintest shimmer of tears in her eyes was the only indicator that she held more under the surface...and that made her bravery all the more amazing. "He. Doesn't. Scare. Me...so don't let him scare you either."

"God, woman. You are a marvel." I pulled her into a hug, soaking in the way her body melted into mine. I knew I had more work to do; my withholding information was a betrayal. I would do the work, but for now, I wanted to bring her smile back before the night ended. Leaning down, I mumbled in her ear. "But this four-on-three-off shit is gonna cut into my snacking habit, though."

Her blush and its companion giggle were all I needed.

She'd be OK–we'd be OK.

We weren't just going to survive—we were going to build something.

Together.

37

CHASE

I MET WITH THE chief a few days later to discuss my return to duty. Walking into the station, I found him leaning back in his chair, his boots propped up on his desk, scanning the logs.

"I got the papers you were cleared from the shoulder weeks ago, and then suddenly you asked for extended PTO." He quirked a wry smile from the side of his mug as he swigged back his coffee. "I take it things are...going well with the Missus." I expected the Chief would ask about our relationship status, but I was still at a loss as to how to define us.

We hadn't discussed what all this meant, or where it was going, and the fact that I was too cowardly to instigate that conversation said more about me than I liked. On one hand, we lived together and were fucking like bunnies. My brothers rallied to watch over her, and a baby was on the way we were all excited to meet. But Moira still guarded her independence, and since she found out about Jensen and mine's history, she'd begun resisting my efforts again. Little things like refusing my offer to bring her lunch at work, and bigger things like insisting she'd pay the cell phone bill when it arrived. I swear I caught her checking out apartment listings at one point, and it gutted me.

Label or not, I couldn't let her go, but what did that make us?

Oh, right, married.

Goddamn.

"It's good." I managed to say. "But it's time I got back to work, back to the gym, and back on track." I thumbed over my shoulder and added, "Besides...the station is a fucking wreck. How the hell are you letting these guys live in their filth?"

"We ain't all OCD-level cleaners, Wilder."

"I'll get it whipped into shape. Just as soon as I start." I propped my elbows on my knees, aiming for a nonchalant look. "I can help move the needle on the arson investigation, too."

"I can put you on schedule in, say, a week, but you aren't going near that investigation."

"I gotta help," I began, but the Chief stood up, effectively cutting me off.

"Start in a week. There will be no investigation involvement. There will be no ifs, ands, or buts, kid." I was surprised at the swift shutdown, having expected more dialogue on the issue. However, the Chief grabbed a file, appearing to be ready for another meeting.

"Yeah, ok." Standing, I stretched a hand across to him. "I'll come in between now and then and use the gym. Try and get my muscles past the hurt."

"Shut the fuck up with that hand." He pulled me over for a brisk hug. "It's good to have you back, kid." He walked towards the door. "I'll walk you out." As we walked, I tried to remember the last time the Chief escorted me out, and I decided it was the fifth of never. And yet, here he was, strolling confidently down the stairs as if we did this all the damn time. He seemed stiff and clipped, and didn't speak again until we neared my bike in the parking lot. "The whole station is on edge. The idea that one of our own could have started fires hasn't set well...even if they already hated the son of a bitch."

"Makes sense." If it wasn't for what I learned about Jensen before all this, I might not have believed he could do it either. "What can I do?"

"I'm trying to help move things along so we can all heal, but I'm hitting a brick wall." Chief scanned the lot around us as he spoke. "I know you and your brothers are close. And Troy's a good egg." The chief handed me the folder from under his arm. "Before shit hit the fan, Jensen kept inviting me to this group of his."

"Poker night?"

"That's what I thought at first...but nah. More like a lodge or fraternity group thing in the city. They call themselves Apex." The chief crossed his arms and pointed to the file. "I went to one meeting with him, and this is all I got on it. But when I brought it to the arson investigators, they blew me off."

"And you think Apex has something to do with Jensen being a misogynistic pyro?" I thumbed through glossy, generic pamphlets on leadership, community, and brotherly support endeavors.

"That whole meeting gave me the heebie-jeebies. The way these guys talked about their lives...it was off. But their keynote speaker was some bigwig lawyer who really liked the sound of his own voice." Chief leveled his eyes in that familiar way that always meant business. "His pitch? That men were the rightful apex of society. That women...well, women were the weight holding us down."

"No shit." I scowled down at the documents, which suddenly took on a more sinister tone with their glossy covers and homogeneous audience. "Second-class?"

"The guy was a smooth talker, no doubt, but the pyramid scheme vibes were wafting off of him like flies on shit, and I couldn't get out of there fast enough."

"Jensen was recruiting you?"

"Maybe. Trying to elevate his status by bringing someone higher up as a guest. But that's not all." Chief pulled out a simple slip of paper that had one sentence typed in all lowercase letters on it. 'Membership gained with emphatic assertion.'

"What the hell is 'emphatic assertion'?"

"If I was reading the room right, and God, I hope I am wrong, but if I'm right, it's some sort of act of dominance." Chief sighed, rubbing his hand across the back of his neck. "Dammit, Wilder, I think he was using those videos, those women, as his currency to get in."

"Jesus Christ," I mumbled, looking at the file again. "What the hell kinda group is this?"

"That's where I hit my first dead-end. This meeting was a week before you busted Jensen with the recordings. The shit hit the fan, and I forgot all about this until I was at the library the other day, dropping books off for Carol and doing a quick inspection on some expansions they are looking to build out." Chief leaned a little closer. "And walking out of the children's wing? That same skeezy bastard from the Apex meeting."

The Children's wing...where my wife was.

"Fuck." I hated the new layer of complexity to this shit-show.

"I went straight home and dug out these docs and tried to take them to the investigator, but he stonewalled me. Said Jensen's extracurriculars had nothing to do with the arson case."

"But you think that keynote from that meeting..." I lifted an eyebrow, waiting for Chief to finish my thought.

"Dollars to donuts...." The chief thumped the file in my hand. "It's Jensen's lawyer."

"Can I keep this?" I waved the file, tucking it into my bike when he nodded in agreement. "I'll see what Troy makes with them. If you find anything else..."

"Yeah, yeah. I know where to find ya." Chief clapped me on the shoulder again. "Keep your head on a swivel. We already knew Jensen was a slimy son of a bitch, but if he has connections to some big city law firm, he could be walking free in no time, and your girl would be exposed."

"We had the same thought. Got a plan in place to keep her covered so I can return to work."

"I'm here for you, kid. I can help." The chief gave me a half smile and another slap to my shoulder. "Carol, too." The idea that Jensen was a part of some fraternal men's group that thought of women as second-class, tracked completely with his treatment of the women on those videos. But to believe that a group supported, even by the thinnest of threads, acts of violence like arson was enough to make me see red. Hoping Chief's information was wrong, I texted Troy.

Me: Work or home?

TJ: Work.

Me: Headed your way.

315

38

CHASE

I FOUND TROY HOLED up in a conference room upstairs at the station, surrounded by files and coffee cups like he'd been buried there for days.

"Hey, man." I tapped on the door frame.

"Come in." Troy never looked up from his notepad as he motioned to a chair opposite him. "You haven't been up here in a while. Does this have to do with your return to work?"

"No...and Yes." I leaned my elbows on the table and took a deep breath. "I'm hitting the gym for a week or so, and then I'm back on schedule. Can you cover Moira that soon?"

"And?" With a sigh, I slid the file that the Chief gave me across the table.

"The Chief handed me this. Said arson investigator ignored." I gave him a minute to look through the marketing materials, pausing when he lifted the slim piece of paper with typed letters.

"Emphatic assertion?" Troy's brows lifted in question, which I took as my cue to share everything about Apex. About their twisted ideology—and how Jensen tried to drag Chief into it. Troy listened intently, making a few notes, as I rattled it all off.

"I can see why arson turned it away. It's hearsay at best. What am I missing?"

"The self-important blowhard Chief heard that night is here...now." Troy leaned forward, halting his notetaking to look at me. "Chief says he saw him at the library."

And he's sure it was the guy...even from months ago? Troy resumed jotting down notes.

"He swears by it." I ran my hand over my face and leaned back in my chair. "We knew that Jensen had something going on in the city already. Maybe this Apex group was 'poker'."

"It's thin. But I agree it's connecting dots I had myself."

"Dots?"

"I told you that Jensen's lawyer showed up. Flashing his New York swag and generally pissing everyone off."

"And?"

"I checked into his firm's billing rates...there is no way Jensen could afford a lawyer of this caliber on his salary. Private defense, like that, would likely have to be established pro bono. Maybe networked in at a meeting where women were treated like chattel and leverage came in the form of blackmail."

"Dots," I sighed.

"Dots, indeed." Troy pulled his laptop over and started typing. "This," he spun the laptop around, displaying the profile of a Manhattan attorney with ice blue eyes, pale blonde hair, and an expression I could only describe as moderated disdain. The kind of face that belonged in a courtroom—or a cult. "Is Jensen's attorney. Let's call the Chief and see if we have a match." I opened a video chat and flipped the camera around so the Chief could see the screen.

'That's the fucker, alright.' He confirmed. 'Real slick piece of shit. Smiling praise out one side of his mouth and spewing bile out the other.'

"I'll look into it, Chief. Thank you for the tip." Troy looked at me. "I encourage you both to keep it quiet for now." The Chief agreed before disconnecting.

"Have you ever heard of this Apex group?" I asked.

"Only one other time." Troy nodded. "That cyber specialist I had here found connections for an open case they were investigating. It involved an organized group that had their hands in a variety of crimes but always seemed to slip through the cracks of red tape."

"And it was Apex?" My stomach began to knot at the complexity of all this.

"I saw it in a written statement log for a low-level thug and only in passing as part of another investigation I wasn't involved in." Troy shut the laptop. "This may be bigger than just Jensen."

"What did the specialist find out?" I asked, half distracted as my mind went in a thousand different directions.

"I didn't get a full report before they were called back to the city, but I will reach out." Troy waved a hand over the paperwork in front of him. "As much as I can with my hands half-tied, that is."

"Half-tied?" I swallowed the ball of panic that rose in my throat. We banked on Troy having the freedom to do what he needed to keep Moira covered. "I thought you had grounds with the restraining order to do what you needed."

"My Captain hasn't officially sanctioned anything other than a protective detail for Moira. He has turned a blind eye to any extracurricular work I do as long as I don't ruffle any feathers." Troy leaned forward, resting his elbows on the table and lowering his voice. "I'm working within the lines, but I have to tread lightly until I have more concrete facts."

"Jesus...how does all this connect to Moira?" I ran my hands over my face in exasperation. I was already drowning in the Jensen shitshow. Now this?

"I wish I knew, brother. Apex is a surprise complexity." He offered a small smile as we both stood. "Give me time to dig around. I'll let you know what I find."

39

MOIRA

T HE FOLLOWING WEEK OF work was nerve-wracking. Chase made it his mission to ensure my good sleep via multiple orgasms each night. But the mornings brought a fresh set of nerves that made no sense. When I was closed in my office with my headphones in, I was okay. But when I needed to walk about for a meeting or to grab documents off the printer, the hairs on the back of my neck stood on end as if I was being watched. Add in the stupid flowers and their cloying sweetness permeating every inch of the Library, and by midday, I'd be jumping at random noises and crawling out of my skin. By Friday, it was so bad that I opted to grab lunch out instead of eating at my desk, needing a reprieve.

As I drove, I let my nose clear of the sickly-sweet rose smell, and I admired the beautiful fall scenery around the town I was becoming so fond of. The tiny main street where the Library sat was decorated with giant potted mums in every color, and bales of hay piled around pumpkins and gourds. The shop windows were painted to advertise an annual turkey trot, and I could practically taste the apple cider offered to shoppers by every other artisan on the strip. The warmth and color of fall exploded all around me, and with it, I realized how much more color my life had, too. As much as I'd lived in this town before Chase, I wasn't really living. Like the fire portaled me into a new world, my time with Chase had opened me up to all the beauty this town had to offer. Through him, I could imagine a life here, a family – me, my baby, and Chase.

The main drag was picture-perfect, but the residential area was in dire straits. For every revitalized house, three others needed remodeling. Even the commercial properties begged for a reinvention worthy of a town so filled with kindness and charm. This made NB Realty's origins more understandable, given the brothers' feelings.

They'd all come here as orphans and found a home–they wanted to pay that forward.

The whole town had a sort of raw beauty to it that cried out for the new life–Chase and his brothers were trying to breathe into it. Fixing up houses was one small way the brothers could give back to the community. But they could do more and invest more widely if they could gain exposure in the right areas. So many neighborhoods in disrepair, as well as numerous commercial properties, were abandoned, leaving the entire county economically struggling. It sparked my interest enough that when I parked my car to eat lunch at the park, I took a dive on the internet with my phone and did a little research. I had just finished up my sandwich when an incoming call splashed Sam's goofy face across my screen.

"Hey there!"

"Where are you!" Sam's voice was urgent and sharp, firing off all my alarms.

"I'm at the park. What's wrong?" I scanned my surroundings for signs of Dean, my panic rising.

"Call Chase so he doesn't worry!"

"Sam. What's wrong?!"

"I needed to make sure you were okay. I'm on the rig, we've been called to the Library." Sam paused, listening to someone in the background. "Steer clear of it. I gotta go, sis."

My mind was racing.

I tossed my remaining lunch on the floorboard and headed for the Library, wondering why Sam would demand I set Chase's mind at ease. Dean was still in jail, and a library isn't known for risky shenanigans. Did someone from the weekly knitting group break into hysterics? Did a particularly tall pile of books fall over and take out a small child? Would could go wrong in a quiet building full of inanimate books?

Getting closer, however, my heart sank.

Billowy black smoke poured out of the building, and the fire department had already blocked off the parking lot and side street. People lined the opposite curb watching as the crew expertly went to work dousing the flames, and my chest seized with flashbacks.

I could practically taste the sour smoke filling the sky–the grime of soot and gritty water rough on my skin. Rushed images of heat and fire had me practicing all my deep breathing techniques to quell the panic clawing at my throat as I repeated my mantra in my head–I'm okay... I'm okay... I'm okay.

My tunnel vision finally cleared, but the sour taste of panic still coated my mouth.

Moving slowly, I exited my car, letting the dizziness clear as I scanned faces in the crowd, noting the ones I recognized who appeared unscathed. I walked to the side for a better view, and my stomach lurched at the huge plumes of smoke roiling out of my tiny office window. It was all I could do not to throw up my lunch at the terrifying reality that washed over me.

I could have been trapped in a fire...again.

Terror gripped me as I dialed Troy's number, but it went straight to voicemail, so I sent a text.

> ME: Is Dean still behind bars!!!

> Troy: Yes.

I sighed in relief, pushing through my fear and closing my eyes to calm my nerves.

This wasn't Dean. He's in jail. Fires happen all the time. This is terrible...but unrelated.

I settled into a swaying rhythm, letting my inner cool collect itself, when my pocket vibrated with a call. Chase's easy smile stared up at me, reminding me I'd forgotten to text him.

"I'm okay," I answered. "I was out at lunch. Not even near the building."

"WHAT!?" His voice was shrill...alarmed. "What do you mean you are okay? What building aren't you near?"

Shit shit shit. He didn't know.

"I figured you heard from Troy." I could hear the tell-tale sounds of Chase's heavy-booted pacing and felt terrible for worrying him again. "There's a fire at the library."

"WHAT THE FUCK!"

"I'm okay!"

" I tried to reassure him quickly. "I'm seeing it from the sidelines like everyone else." Chase's jingling keys sounded above his steps.

"I'm on my way...I want you out of there. Now, Moira!"

"Chase...Wait." I began pacing, trying to find the words to soothe him. "I was away at lunch, at the park, when this happened. I wasn't even near here. I texted Troy and confirmed Jensen is still behind bars." Chase let out a resigned sigh. "Sam is here working, and I'm safe." I rested my hand on my belly. "The baby, too."

"No." He sounded so angry, or was he scared? "I need you home. I'm coming for you."

"Wait...please." I could hear a small sigh of resignation. "If you come, your bike will be stuck here. I promise I'm okay."

He growled in frustration, but his stomping steps halted.

"Please just...come home to me." I could practically hear his jaw clenching, and my heart fell at the realization that all the stress and worry over me had taken a bigger toll on him than I first imagined. I made a note never to forget that the man's heart might be the biggest muscle of all.

"I am...I will...Right now." I kept my voice smooth and steady, the way I'd heard Sam do so many times. "I'm getting in the car. I'll come straight home. You can even stalk me on that app of yours." I hoped a little humor would break the tension before his teeth ground to nubs.

"Just.... come home."

"I'm on my way," I pocketed my phone and headed to my car.

"Oh, Moira... thank God!" Todd trotted over to me. "I had put eyes on just about everyone but you, and I was starting to panic."

"I was out at lunch." I happily took his reassuring hug. "I'm so glad everyone is okay."

"Can you believe this?" He waved a hand over the cacophony.

"What do they think happened?" I hoped for a plausible excuse to put Chase and me both at ease.

"No one knows! One minute we're all working, the next the alarms and sprinklers go off, and we all evacuate."

"But everyone got out...safely?" I was relieved to see Todd nod, eyes locked on the building.

"No one hurt but the books...the water and smoke will ruin the lot of them." He turned to face me then, and his eyes were full of heaviness. "I'm not sure how long it will take even to repair the building, much less the salvageable books. And that's nothing compared to how long it will take to get restocked again."

Realization washed over me like a cold bucket of water. If they didn't have a building, they hardly required a social media person, and my pragmatic cynicism was winding up for the pitch.

"And since I'm part-time and on contract..."

"I'm so sorry." Todd gave my arm a reassuring rub, his head cocked to the side in a pitiably expression. "I'm sure personnel can help you find something else in city services."

"Let's be real, Todd. I hadn't even made it past the 90-day probationary period." So much for any future gainful employment potential–Hello, rock bottom. "I doubt I'll be on the city's radar with this mess." Todd opened his mouth to speak, then closed it again. I could feel my self-esteem circling the drain as the title 'unemployed' loomed once more. "Don't sweat it, Todd. I'll bounce back. In the meantime, if you need a few infographics for social media, such as to announce closure dates, please let me know. I can whip those up free of charge." Why not hand out freebies while you are out of work?

"You're the best." Todd hugged me again and scurried back over to the gaggle of full-time regulars, leaving me in a sinking pit of self-pity.

Unemployed, pregnant, and pissed off. Fan-fucking-tastic.

40

MOIRA

THE DRIVE HOME WAS one long anti-pep talk. I'd just started to pull myself up—job, life, maybe even a family—and now? I was heading home jobless. Again.

After a fire...again!

When I left this morning, Chase was smiling and flirting, and we had dinner plans, and life was extraordinary. And now...what? I was coming home with no benefits or income on the horizon, again...only now it was worse—because this time, I wasn't failing alone. I'd entangled myself so deeply in Chase's life, his family, his home... they'd all feel the impact of me unraveling. Even Troy and Sam were rearranging their lives to watch over me because I was so fragile that Chase nearly jeopardized his career for me, and that was before I returned to my homeostatic state of vagabond.

God, I suck.

Pulling into the driveway, Chase exited the house and half-pulled me from the car. He wrapped me in his arms, and the comfort was as heartbreaking as it was soothing.

"God, baby." He took my face in his hands. "I was worried sick." He placed a kiss on my forehead, then pulled me to his chest. His heart was pounding so hard I could feel it thumping against my cheek, and I ached to put his fears to rest.

"I'm okay." I leaned back so he could see that my eyes were clear and bright, free of smoke or soot. "Todd said that everyone was out even before there was any smoke or fire...so, this was minor, right?" He searched my face, no doubt looking for cracks in my armor. I willed myself to neutrality, and I let my hand calmly rest atop his. "I'm safe. No injuries of any kind."

"And the baby?" He placed his hand low on my belly, his brows creased in worry as he stared at my stomach.

"I felt a kick on the drive home." I lowered my head until he met my eyes again. "Baby is tucked in nice and cozy."

"Jesus." He sighed into the top of my head as he pulled me back into him. "I was out of my mind waiting for you to get here." He guided me towards the house and pulled out his phone. "We need to start that group chat sooner rather than later. Might have saved a few steps today in all the back and forth."

He opened the door, shoving aside a pile of boxes and Styrofoam.

"Been...busy?" My guilt spiked in the face of yet another potential grand gesture I'd never be able to repay. "Tell me it's not something frivolous for me."

"Busy.... yes. Bought something...yes again." He took my hand with a smile, tugging me through the boxes to the bedroom. "But frivolous....

no." Everything in the room was much the same as before, only moved around to make space for two new additions.

"Oh.... Chase." I gasped at the new crib and rocking chair, both fully assembled and waiting...for me.

"I'd planned to clean up before you got home." He stepped to the end of a beach-washed grey wood crib. It was a contemporary piece with smooth lines, and a little baggy of paints and stencils hung off one side. "I thought we could stencil the baby's name on the end panel when we find out if it's a boy or a girl." He beamed with pride, and my heart broke.

Here he was again, selflessly pouring so much of himself, his life, into my baby, and I hadn't even had a chance to tell him I wouldn't even be able to help with groceries soon. I let my fingers graze the crib rails before lifting the soft blanket he draped over the edge. I grazed the fluffy softness across my cheek, taking in the rocking chair.

"I know it's not the trendy gliders, but Nonna had one like this." He put a hand under my elbow, encouraging me to sit. "But if you don't like it, we can swap it out. I'm not attached..." I rested on the vintage-looking chair; its smooth wood hugging my back perfectly.

My heart splintered.

Chase selected something for my baby that he attached to his mother.

"It's beautiful," My voice was barely a whisper as I held the blanket protectively to my chest, a barrier against the emotional onslaught.

Embarrassment and shame at losing my job, humiliation that I was again jobless and pregnant, and here across from me was a man who brought the biggest emotion of all...love. I loved him. But how could I love him and put him through all of this...all of me? The intersection of overwhelmingly blessed and despairingly broken spiraled into a cascade that tore me in two.

"Hey, Fancy Pants?" Chase knelt in front of me, his hand resting on my knees. "I'm not attached to any of this if you don't like the color or the - "

"Oh, Chase." I buried my face in the blanket as muffled sobs spilled out in waves. "I'm so sorry."

"Sorry? Baby. What..." I could hear his worry, his panic even, and it only made me cry harder. "Are you sure you are okay...maybe we should have Sam look you over after the fire, or–"

"God, No!" I shouted louder than intended, desperate to alleviate at least one of his worries that I was physically okay. Then I took a breath, willing the heaving sobs to slow beyond the jerky breaths I was sucking in. "You have been so good to me...so amazing all this time...and you took me into your home...and your family...and helped me get back on my feet and –"

"And I would do it again." He assured me, his face a picture of painstaking worry, which only made me feel worse.

"You don't understand." I dropped the blanket onto my lap, waving a hand towards the crib. "I love it. All of it. I love you, your brothers, the crib, the chair, the groceries, this ridiculously perfect little town, and dammit, I really do love that stupid dart board! And you've *never* asked for anything in return. Do you know how amazing that is?" I put my hand on his cheek, willing my emotions to slow down, but the tears fell so fast it was a wasted effort. "I can't repay you, Chase, not for any of it. I can't pay for the *car* or the *furniture*," My breathing quickened as my volume increased. "I can't pay you back for the clothes or the make-up, and now...NOW...I can't even cover the insurance or groceries since today's fire has put me back out of work *again*."

The worry in Chase's face melted away as the most adorable grin spread across his face. Not that it helped my panicked spiral, as anger decided to join the party.

"So, in case you are keeping count, this would be *twice* you have found me unemployed and destitute from yet *another* fucking fire, and I have *zero* back-up plan because who is gonna want to hire a pregnant woman a few months out from maternity leave!"

"You love me," Chase whispered, and I clapped a hand over my mouth at the truth that slipped out amidst my rant. "You just said you loved me." He pulled me to the edge of the chair, nestling himself between my knees. "I don't need you to repay me, I never did. I never saw us being that transactional. I only ever - "

"But you don't understand," I whispered hoarsely. "The baby will need diapers and formula, and pacifiers and blankets, and baby clothes and a car seat and a high chair, and this crib is absolutely beautiful and I can't even enjoy it because all I see is the eleventy-billion little ways you are providing for me and my baby that I can't ever repay and - "

"Marry me."

41

MOIRA

"MARRY ME, MOIRA. AGAIN...FOR real this time." I stared, slack-jawed, into Chase's hope-filled eyes. "You love me, you just said it, and it's all I've ever wanted from you. I'm crazy mad in love with you, too. Marry me, woman."

"Chase. You don't mean that...you can't." I struggled to find words, but my brain was still frozen in shock that he'd proposed to...again. "I mean, we already did...or are–"

"I do. And I can. And I don't care." He took my hands in his, grinning so big his dimples looked deep enough to swim in. "I felt a connection the first night I met you–unexplainable but real. And when I first saw those gorgeous eyes of yours, I was so gone over you."

"River blue," I breathed, remembering the words he said when I woke up. "You called them river blue."

"I have never felt this way about anyone in my life, not once, and while I never expected things to move so quickly, every step was easy and right. I don't ever want to be without you." Tears began to well in his eyes even as his words sank into the tiny dark crevices of my battered heart. "You have this misguided idea that we are transactional, but I've never–not for one second–seen us as anything other than a man providing for his woman, and that's what you are to me...mine. You are mine to love and cherish...body and soul. Taking care of you is not only my duty but my honor, and dammit, Moira, I'll do it till the day I die if you'll please say that you'll have me."

"But, the baby and..." I swallowed, and the one fear I hadn't put words to formed in my mind.

"No. Not anymore." He scowled with that face that I knew meant stubborn resignation. "I don't want to hear *A* baby or *The* baby ever again. This," He put a hand on my belly, pressing gently around the bump. "Is now and forever *MY* baby. And just as I've loved you from the moment I held you on that hospital bed, I've *loved* our baby. I plan to be here for both of you every day for the rest of my life if you will please, please, for the love of God, woman, Say yes and make me the happiest man... husband...FATHER in the world!" A tear slipped down his cheek, and I shattered into a million tiny pieces as his words broke through the last of my self-imposed isolation.

Breaking and reforming again in the span of a breath, I knew both my baby and I had found forever.

"Yes, husband. I will marry you."

The words hardly had time to escape when he jumped to his feet, taking me with him in a room-swirling hug that had us both laughing past the tears we both shared.

"You are my world." He lowered me to the floor, his forehead pressed to mine. "I won't ever leave you. I will always be here for you." Then, dropping to his knees, he wrapped his arms around my waist and pressed his face into my belly. "And I'm gonna be the best damn dad in the whole world. You will never doubt how very wanted you are." His voice was so rumbly it must have reached the baby, who chose that moment to give a good, swift kick. "God... I'll never stop loving that feeling."

"Well, that's good, the little thing is growing stronger every day." I loved seeing Chase's eyes filled with contentment. "I swear, the other day I felt it stretch to hit me in two places at once." Chase placed a kiss on my belly and then, lifting the bottom edge of my shirt, he placed another. Slowly, he buried his face under my shirt and started trailing kisses across my bump, causing flutters of a different kind. He paused when he reached the button of my pants.

"Tell me this isn't a rubber band holding your pants up, wife."

"It's a practical way to stretch the wardrobe." I laughed, feeling the band snap.

"Tomorrow," he grunted. "Maternity shopping." He tugged the back of my knee in a silent demand for me to lift my foot. He removed my pants, kissing each hip and thigh as he went.

"Doesn't seem like a smart buy when you keep pulling things off me every time we're together." I giggled, a thrill rushing through me as he began lifting the edge of my shirt. "Might as well hang around naked all day and save a buck."

"Well now," Chase's devilish grin made my pulse stutter just as my shirt hit the floor. "There's an idea I can get behind." Chase swept me off my feet, crossing the room in a single stride to toss me onto the bed.

Chase was a big man, tall and broad, muscles for days, and panty-dropping tattoos. But now, watching as he undressed at the edge of the bed with a feral look in his eyes, I saw so much more. Now he wasn't just a man who saved me from a fire, or a shitty motel, or a nightmare of an ex. Chase was the man I loved, and who loved me. All of me. The me who had a job and the me who had no job. The me that was independent and stubborn, and the me that was sometimes needy and scared. Chase was my proper fiancé, and as he peppered kisses up my body, I realized I was irrevocably changed because of him.

"Chase," I panted. "I..." but the words to convey how I felt escaped me. I want you...was too small. I need you...was too simple. I struggled to find the words that could tell him how much he meant to me.

"Me too, Fancy." He nestled between my thighs, letting his weight settle on me as he looked into my eyes. "I love you, too." He crashed his mouth to mine, his cock nudging my entrance. That was when the right words finally took shape in my mind. Hooking a leg around his knee, I gave his shoulders a shove, rolling us over til I straddled him.

"I need you to understand something, Chase Wilder." I slowly rocked my hips, sliding my wet slit back and forth across his cock, not letting him enter me. "I am not marrying you out of convenience, or obligation, or any other reason," I added a little pressure. At the same time, I thrust back and forth, letting my wetness coat his shaft as he groaned in approval. "You have saved me in eleventy-billion little ways. But none of them matter."

I leaned in for a kiss, then released my bra. His hands lifted to my breasts as he thrust against my growing ache. Little tremors rippled through me each time his head tapped at my clit.

"I'm not marrying you for anything other than how very much I love who you are." I leaned again, placing my forehead on his forehead as I lifted just enough for the tip of his cock to notch at my entrance. "I love you, Chase." Inching down, I let him slowly fill me. "I love your smile and your heart." Another inch down, his hands gripped my hips with bruising intensity as I slowed my pace even more. "I love...your bravery, and your...sincerity." My voice strained as I took him in only an inch more. "I love you, body," drop, "and soul," drop. I finally reached the base of him and lingered in the fullness and stretch.

The girl who walked into that fire was gone.

This woman—the one who chose love, safety, and joy—was here to stay.

"I can't imagine my life without you, Big Guy. You're my home." I heard his breath catch, and I opened my eyes to see the tears in his. Kissing him, my body screamed for friction, and I couldn't take it anymore. I sat tall, arched breasts to the sky, and began grinding back and forth his considerable length.

"Fuuuuuuck." Chase's growl was primal as his fingers dug into my hips, urging me to move faster, harder. I liked the control this position gave me, so I resisted his push and pull, setting a languid pace of hip-swiveling rocking. Each forward thrust echoed through my clit, and each backwards rock slammed his cock into that spot deep inside. The combination sent wave after wave of pleasure rippling through my body. Abandoning my hips, Chase ran his hands up to my breasts, cupping their weight and pinching my nipples.

"Oh God." The little bite of pain sent a jolt straight to my core. Increasing my speed, I was climbing, rocking, and swirling my hips on his cock. My orgasm was building when suddenly Chase sat up and jolted me into a different angle.

"Wrap your legs around me, baby." He buried his face in my cleavage as I obeyed, holding onto his shoulders for balance. "You feel so perfect. ..wrapped around me." He feasted on my tits like they were his last meal, and every lick and suck had me aching to rock into him. The new angle put me entirely at his mercy, all traction lost as I hung off his shoulders and panted for want of friction. Seeming to know what I needed, his hands returned to my hips, pulling me into him with a hard thrust that slammed his cock deep into my back wall.

Shockwaves of ecstasy ripped through me.

"God...Damn...Woman." He thrust into me between broken words of pleasure, and all I could do was surrender to his powerful arms. Each drag went a little deeper, his arms moving a little faster, making the thrusts a little harder, as he slammed into me again.

Again. And again. And again.

I wanted to scream—his name, his praises, anything. But I couldn't. Each word was lost to the heat building in my spine as I gasped for air between animalistic movements. Flexing his hips, Chase got a little deeper, pressing my body so tightly against his that I was lost in the feel of his mouth on my breast. Then he bit me...and I shattered.

"Yeah, Baby!" Billions of tiny stars exploded behind my eyes as Chase pulled me down on his cock. "Fucking cum all over me."

Wave after wave of pleasure burned through me with an intensity I had never experienced, and I could feel my climax dripping out of me even as he thrust again and again. Just as I thought I might be done, Chase rolled us again, pinning me to the mattress, his cock never leaving me as he set a new rhythm.

"Oh god." I cried, finally finding my voice. "Yes, Yes!" My cries were a sob of relief as tears spilled over my lashes when a final climax overcame me.

Chase never slowed, never wavered, as he pulled himself into me over and over, riding out the final pulses of my orgasm before shuddering into me with a staggering grunt. I felt his cum fill me, sliding down the walls of my stretched and aching sex, then dripping out and between us. Both sated, gasping, and happy, I had never been more blissed out in my life.

I'm not sure how long we stayed like that, breathing each other's air as we reveled in the aftershocks, before he pulled out of me.

"Don't move, baby." He shuffled to the bathroom, returning with a warm towel in one hand and both of our cell phones in the other. I gave him a confused look, but he just smiled, setting the phones aside before gently cleaning my sopping and sensitive sex while kissing me stupid. Once he was done, I rolled to my side, facing him, and watched him plop onto the bed beside me, our phones in his hand.

"I can't think of a better time to start the new Group chat with my brothers. You wanna type it up?" He handed me my phone, grinning like a Cheshire cat.

"Are you sure post-coitus is the best time for a family chat?" I wondered if a text message could convey the naked aftershocks. "Maybe we should wait -"

"No chance." Chase lifted his phone, rapidly tapping on the screen. "I asked you to marry me and you said yes...I want everyone I love to know it."

Wilder Family Group Chat

-1-

Me: Hey guys---> NEW group chat.

Samoa: So I see. Welcome to the crazy, Moira.

TJ: Welcome. I assume you are well despite today's stress.

Fancy: I'm good. Sorry I worried you. I wasn't even in the building when it started.

Samoa: No apologies necessary.

TJ: Agreed.

Me: We have news!!!!

Fancy: Chase said you normally discuss big things via text…

Samoa: He's right.

TJ: News?

Me: I asked Moira to marry me.

Fancy: And…. I said yes.

TJ: I knew it. Pay up, Sam.

Samoa: I've never been so happy to lose 300 bucks. Congrats guys!

Fancy: You had bets …On marriage?

TJ: Technically, we had bets on the proposal. The payout started smaller. Sam kept adding to it when he kept losing.

Samoa: I figured Boyscout would pop the question a little sooner.

Fancy: Boyscout?

TJ: Chase's nickname. He's a bit of a rule-follower.

Samoa: I'm happy for you both.

Fancy: I want you to know I truly love your brother.

TJ: I am quite lovable.

Me: She means me dipshit.

Samoa: Um, I'm a brother too. Maybe Moira loves me.

TJ: Not possible.

Me: Guys!

TJ: Celebrating is in order.

Me: YES!

Samoa: And the bride chooses...

Fancy: Um, the baby seems only ever to want Tacos these days.

Samoa: OMG

Me: Hey! My baby wants tacos...so we celebrate with tacos.

Samoa: We're gonna be uncles!!

TJ: Dear God…we are.

Samoa: I'm gonna be the funnest uncle… I'm gonna be the FUNCLE!

Fancy: Funcle Sam?

Samoa: Still better than Uncle Grandpa.

Me: STOP

TJ: STOP

Fancy: OMG what is even happening?

TJ: Where will the ceremony be?

Samoa: And when…I gotta get my PTO lined up.

Fancy: Oh…no…we don't need to do all that.

Me: As soon as possible. I've already got a place in mind.

Fancy: WHAT!?

42

CHASE

SAM DANGLED A VEGAS elopement in front of us that night, but I wouldn't hear it. Moira deserved a real wedding this time and no way was I sharing my time with her and some magic rainbow rock pit-stop Sam was dying to check off his bucket list.

I told my Chief I'd need to postpone my return, and when I told him why, he whooped so loudly that I had to pull my phone back. We planned the ceremony to take place at the end of the week, after which I was whisking Moira away to a cabin we owned for a two-week honeymoon. Leading up to the wedding, my brothers and I rented suits, and Moira found a dress. She still insisted on using all her own money for any wedding purchases, and I made a mental note to use our honeymoon time to show her all the financial side of our lives.

All I had—now and always—was hers.

I had one more surprise up my sleeve to make the day memorable for her, and I couldn't wait for her to see it. But the night before the wedding, I came home from the gym to find Troy on my porch wearing an expression that instantly set my teeth on edge.

"What happened?" I cut the engine, and Troy got straight to the point.

"Jensen's out. His lawyer used the library fire as proof that Jensen couldn't be the arsonist since Jensen was detained."

"Fuck!" I looked at my closed door, knowing Moira was inside. "What about the bus? We have proof he tried to kidnap her."

"And he's been jailed for weeks and posted bail." Troy kicked his shoe on the ground. "I don't like it, but he's claimed it was all a misunderstanding. Maddening, but he will stand trial for that eventually."

"Where is he?" I gritted my teeth. "Is the restraining order still in place?"

"Restraining order stands. But Jensen's...in the wind." He lifted his hands in surrender when I opened my mouth to protest. "I tried to get a unit assigned, but we had no grounds. I tried talking to my boss about off-duty units to track him, but his lawyer did a preemptive strike. My Captain stopped me at every turn with a clear and present warning about crossing Jensen's attorney."

"He *took* her." My fists flexed and pulsed, wanting to punch something. "He took her and my baby and he - "

"Going there won't help you, brother." Troy placed his hands over my white-knuckled fists. "Even without sanctioned units, Sam and I are here. You are here. Jensen can't get near her." I closed my eyes, knowing and hating that he was right.

"What happens now?"

"The trial is a month from now. His attorney will undoubtedly file every document possible to have the charges dropped. That'll push the trial 6 months or more. This is how it goes."

"That bastard walks free!" My anger burst out louder than intended, and I took a painful breath to rein it back in before Moira heard me. "He tried to kidnap her. He tried to kill her in that fire. How does that waste of skin get to walk?" My head hurt from the pressure building as memories of Moira cowering in the corner of a burning building flooded my mind. "Wait." A memory punched through the haze. "How did the library fire clear Jensen?" Troy sighed, deep and long, while he chose his words. The wait did nothing for my anger. "How, TJ?!"

"The library fire had gunpowder residue." Troy lifted his hands to soothe me. "Thus, his attorney reasoned that whoever started the other fires was on the loose."

"BULLSHIT!"

"I agree. I suspect another Apex associate did the library, but you have to pull it together." Troy glanced back at my front door, a reminder that Moira was inside. "Tomorrow is the wedding, and then you are taking her away for a few weeks. This is good. No one will know where you are except Sam and me. During that time, I'll try to get a bead on Jensen, track his whereabouts, and find out more about this Apex group. By the time you get back, we'll have answers, a solid plan, and we'll focus on getting you a house big enough for Moira and the baby." I stopped my pacing and shot a sidelong glance at his smirk. "You have the smallest place among us. It's ridiculous. Where will my new nephew or niece run and play when you're yard is too small for a proper swing set?"

"Whatever." I brushed off his brotherly distraction. "How am I going to tell her?" I stared at the door again. "It'll break her, Troy. She'll sink. There'll be nightmares, hell, she might even back out of the wedding with some crazy nonsense about her putting me at risk."

Her words echoed in my mind. 'Don't underestimate me.'

"She's strong, but knowing that asshole is cleared from a fire we know he set for her...Jesus, I'm freaking the fuck out and I wasn't even the target."

"Don't tell her." I snapped my eyes wide, having never once heard my straight-laced, rule-following, upfront, blunt, and taciturn brother propose someone withhold information. "Not a lie...per se...Just a delay. Let her have the day. Enjoy this moment. Get Married. Be Happy." He clapped a firm hand on my shoulder. "You deserve to be deeply happy, Boyscout."

I couldn't help but lean into his hug before he left, and I had to find a way to pack all this up tight.

Entering my house, I heard the shower running. The door to the bathroom was half open, and inside the shower stood the steamy silhouette of my bride. 'Get Married. Be Happy.' Watching her made my heart swell. She was graceful, every move like a delicate dance. She had long arms and curvy legs with juicy hips. Soap slid in slow rivulets down her curves, fueling my growing hard-on, and that was before she gifted me a view of that gorgeous belly.

Gone was the too-flat stomach she had when we met, and in its place was the roundest of baby bumps. Large enough that she could barely hide it behind baggy shirts anymore, it was beautifully displayed when naked. The bump was so goddamn sexy with those heavy breasts above it, and my hard-on twitched imagining how big she'd get in the final months.

I couldn't wait to see her body change as our baby grew.

I couldn't wait to taste the sweetness.

"You know, if you wanted a show, husband, all you had to do was ask." I caught her peeking back at me through the mirror's reflection, and the fire in her eyes had me stripped in five seconds flat.

"I hated to interrupt such a beautiful scene," I stepped in, soaping up my hands and letting the hot shower warm my skin before touching her.

"Carol came over. I tried prenatal yoga and got sweatier than anticipated. I needed a clean-up before dinner." She outlined my tattoos with her nails, sending shivers straight to my cock.

"Yoga, huh?"

"I read it was good for the baby, and Carol offered an in-home session to try it out." She cut her eyes up from under her lashes and let her fingertips drop to the sensitive spot at the base of my dick. "It might help me be more flexible, and" Grabbing my shaft, she squeezed. "Bendy."

The whole day fell away as I took her mouth with mine. Holding her to me by the back of her neck, I let my other hand slide down the globe of her perfect ass. She stroked my dick at the exact moment, and I ended up squeezing harder than I intended. But the way she pressed into me, gasping a little moan into my mouth, unraveled me. I lifted her fully, wrapping her thighs around me and positioning her right on the head of my cock. Pressing her into the wall, I lowered her inch by inch until she was fully seated, and all my worries melted into her soft body.

"Promise me," She gasped as I licked her neck. "It'll always feel this good."

"Being with you will forever be the highlight of my life." I sank my mouth down on her neck and began driving into her with slow, steady pumps. Her legs squeezed, sending chills straight to my balls as her moans and whimpers hitched every time I bottomed out. Her noises alone had me nearly busting, but I needed her to cum first. Holding her ass with one hand, I cupped her breast with the other, pinching her tight and ever-sensitive nipples.

"Chase. Yes." Her hands were frantically pulling at my shoulders, my neck, and I loved the little scratches I felt as she clenched around me. "Yes, please, don't stop. Yes, Yes!" My legs burned, but I didn't dare change my speed or my angle. My girl was going over the top, and I was gonna hear her scream.

"Oh Fuck, Moira. You feel so..." My balls tightened, and I could feel my orgasm building.

"Chase! I'm coming!" Thank God.

I held out for two more pumps, her screams echoing off the tile as I slammed deep into her, grunting my release.

I'm not sure how long we stayed like that, me buried in her, her wrapped around me, before I finally let her down. My head swam with pleasure from what we did, battling it out with the knowledge that Jensen was out. I hated keeping this from her, but watching her lotion her belly with pure contentment on her face, I couldn't bring myself to ruin the moment.

With a sigh, I clung to Troy's plan, swearing to myself that Jensen would never get anywhere near her, and I'd tell her everything as soon as we were safely on our honeymoon.

43

CHASE

THE NEXT DAY, SAM and Troy whisked me away at o-dark-thirty so that Moira could get ready. I hated the idea of leaving her, but she insisted on surprising me with her dress, and Troy had an off-duty buddy camped at his house keeping watch.

"I didn't tell her about Jensen being out," I confessed over coffee. "I hate keeping it from her, but I want her to have this day."

"So you heeded the wiser brother's advice." Troy clinked his mug against mine. "Smart boy."

"It's a good call." Sam agreed. "That pantywaist doesn't get to ruin your day either."

"Here, here." He and Troy clinked their mugs together as well.

"I can't thank you guys enough, seriously." I sat back and ran my hand over my face. "Moira was... unexpected. But I swear she's the piece that made me whole. As much as I love her, you guys accepting her makes it all so much better."

"Stop. You're gonna make TJ cry." Sam waved me off. "Besides. Any idiot with eyes can see how happy she makes you."

"And how happy you make her," Troy added.

"One of us had to go first," Sam added. "It was easy money that it'd be you."

"It's scary how often I find myself agreeing with the man-child lately," Troy teased. "But he's right. You've always had the biggest heart of all of us. Even if you did hide it behind all those ridiculous muscles."

"So you've heeded the wiser brother," Sam smirked over the rim of his coffee.

"My money says you'll be next," Troy said, stealing the last piece of bacon from Sam's plate.

"Ugh. Why are we talking about me?!" Sam deflected with an eye roll, "Did you get the cabin ready for your honeymoon?"

"Yep. The cleaners did a once-over, and I had the florist deliver flowers to every room and paid a probie from the station to stock the kitchen."

"All out, indeed," Troy nodded in approval.

"I hope she likes it. I know it's only a half hour from here, but she hasn't been up the mountains yet, and the scenery is so awesome up there."

"More importantly," Sam deadpanned. "It's far enough away, we won't hear you fucking your brains out in the shower."

"Or the couch," Troy added.

"The kitchen island...the back deck..." Sam counted off fingers.

"Do you *ever* use your bed?" Troy teased with a smile.

"Holy god, I swear I'll kick both your asses!" I looked around the diner for anyone listening, but my brothers just laughed as they continued to tease me. "You shoulda told me you could see us?"

"See?" Troy choked out, "Baby sister has lungs like a banshee...wailed right through the paper-thin walls of your tiny tiny house." I clenched my eyes shut, from embarrassment or the need to punch their lights out...I didn't know.

"Don't be ashamed, brother. It's not your fault, God's got you walking around swinging what is apparently a dick long enough to knock her lungs loose." Sam slapped my shoulder.

"Oh my god." I groaned.

"Yes... that's a favorite phrase of hers," Troy laughed.

"Yes," Sam added. "Yes. That's one too. How does it go?" And Troy joined him in a resounding chorus. "Yes...Yes...Yes," they jeered as Sam waved his arms like a conductor, ending in a far too rowdy, "Oh Chase!" before falling into peals of laughter.

I loved those idiots.

It was another hour before we paid the check, and I was remanded to Sam's house for wedding preparations with promises that Troy would get my girl there on time. By noon, we pulled up to the little chapel I'd seen Moira eye more than once. It sat in the center of the town green and wasn't usually used for weddings, but having a brother in every branch of city services has its perks. Troy secured clearance for us to use it since the ceremony would be small, and Sam made a charitable donation from NB Realty into the trust set up for the maintenance of the historic grounds. Walking in, I expected the place to be clean but otherwise untouched. I was pleasantly surprised when Sam and I walked in to find it fully decorated.

"Did you buy *every* flower in town?"

"What kind of brothers would we be if we let our sister get married without merry fucktons of flowers?" Sam gave a concentrated scowl as he pinned a flower to my jacket's lapel. "We knew you were busy getting the cabin ready, so we took care of a few details for you." With a swift slap to my shoulder, he added, "You deserve it too, brother."

I couldn't hide the swell of pride at their attention to detail. Every shade of pink flower known to man was arranged and draped over every flat surface in the place. They'd caught on that it was her favorite color, and there was even a box holding a bouquet for Moira, along with two more boutonnieres for Troy and Sam. Only then did I notice the preacher was wearing one on his robe, but I hardly had time to take it all in before Carol appeared from nowhere, grabbing Troy's flower and bouquet and waltzing towards the front door. I opened my mouth to ask why Carol was here, but Sam spun me around to face the back of the chapel.

"Showtime."

In the back, Carol stood beaming at the door as if waiting for some cue. Then my Chief entered from a door behind me, wearing his guitar. My mouth opened in question as he started playing.

"Did you think I'd miss this, kid?" The simple sounds of his hobby folk music filled the air as his wife wiped away tears from her perch at the other end of the short, center aisle.

"You thought of everything," I gaped at Sam, but he shook his head.

"Moira figured you'd want Chief and Carol here. She did that part." My chest squeezed knowing she'd done that... knowing I'd want that...for me.

"God...she's...." My words stuck in my throat. I could feel the sting in my eyes as the click of the door pulled my focus. Carol tugged the double door open, and Troy entered, donning the same suit as Sam and me. Once he was through the door, he reached a hand out to Moira, who stepped smoothly beside him.

She draped her arm through his–the whole world fell away.

44

MOIRA

MY WEDDING DAY. My real wedding day.

Other than a few sweet texts from Carol, it was a quiet morning. I missed the constant playful banter Chase usually sent if we were apart. Still, I spent my time considering every detail to make this day memorable for Chase. That included doing my hair the way I knew he loved. He'd never actually said, but anytime I wore my hair down in big loose curls, he'd sneak passing moments to touch it, brush it behind my ear, or wind his fingers through it in bed.

What better day to lean into those quiet touches?

I indulged myself too, with a splurge on a pretty pair of earrings and a smattering of glittery accessories I'd hidden in my hair. Both of which perfectly accentuated the vintage gown I saw in the consignment window that called to me. The simple scooped neckline featured gold glitter netting across the bust, giving way to a bodice of dusty pink appliqué flowers that cascaded down the fitted waist. From there, the

355

flowers scattered across the length of draping, shimmery, gold tulle that fell in a simple A-line, creating a rose-gold waterfall that made me feel like a million bucks. Sure, it wasn't a traditional white gown, but it fit like it was meant for me—even with the baby-blessed boobs. I polished my nails in a deep pink that matched the lip color Chase smiled biggest for, and when Troy's jaw dropped, I figured the look was pretty good.

"Think Chase will mind a nontraditional gown?"

"I think my brother is a very fortunate man," Troy held his hand out for me. "Now, to the church with you, fair lady."

I'd managed to avoid any nerves while getting ready, but as we rode, butterflies the size of Texas set up shop in my stomach as familiar worries gnawed at me. Worry we'd moved too far, too fast, or the ever-present nag that I was somehow trapping Chase. Using him to take care of me...the way Jensen claimed. I was so lost in my thoughts, I didn't realize we'd passed the courthouse until Troy's voice brought me to the present.

"We're here." Smiling at me, Troy rounded the car, opening my door as I took in the venue change. It was the little chapel at the town center I'd admired so many times, and I couldn't stifle the gasp that left me when I realized what had happened. "You will find, Chase doesn't miss much, and he wanted to make the day perfect for you."

Troy took my hand, leading me to the outer door as I sifted through the million moments I had shared with Chase. I shuddered to imagine what my life would have been like if Chase hadn't found me and saved me over and over again, healing my heart and gifting me a family of brothers. I searched for anything I could have done differently to reassure them all that I wanted to be with him for him...not for what he provided for me. I wanted to protect the integrity of this man, his life, and his family, more than anything in the world. I was lost in my thoughts until Troy's warm, strong hand slipped onto mine, both of us cradling my bump.

"I don't know what kind of wedding you had dreamed of," Troy stared down at me with a soft kindness I hadn't seen before, "But you should know that he is one of the truest souls I've ever had the privilege of knowing. Your heart could be in no safer hands than Chase's." He put his other hand around mine and added. "And you should also know, before you walk through that door and take vows with my brother, that you gain not only a husband today but a family. Sam and I are as happy to have you two together as anyone, and frankly, we've all benefited from your presence in our lives. You are very welcome here, Moira. And very loved."

"Really?" A tear fell in relief of the question I never knew I needed answered.

"You have brought our brother out of his shell in a way we never could have. He is more alive with you than ever before in his life." Troy dabbed gently at my tears with a handkerchief from his pocket. "This might not have been the wedding you dreamed of, but it will most definitely be the marriage you so *richly* deserve."

Without another word, Troy turned and stepped through the door, holding out a hand for me as guitar music filled the air. I stepped in and draped my arm through his, and only when I was able to swallow past the rising tide of more tears, did I look up and find Chase.

He stood at the end of the narrow center aisle, hands clasped in front of him in a simple black suit with clean lines cut to both display his ginormous arms and hang pristinely around his chest. Sam was next to him in a similar fashion, but I hardly saw him when I met Chase's glistening eyes. There was that boyish, close-lipped smile I loved that hinted at the dimples he held back from the world. His eyes grazed over me from head to toe with streaming tears that melted every worry away. I wanted to tell him how happy I was, how safe I felt, and how very blessed

I was to have found him and his brothers, as well as this family I was joining. But I didn't dare speak for fear that every tear I held back would fall. And so, I rested my palm on his cheek. A silent message of how proud I was to marry him. A quiet prayer of thanks for the miracle that his love was.

A silent promise to be the miracle for him, too.

"You...look..." He stifled a sob, and I brushed the tear away with my thumb. Planting a kiss in the palm of my hand, we might as well have been the only two souls in the world as everything and everyone fell away, and it was just me and him and our baby and this love and–

Marriage is a public declaration of two people. The preacher began. *But beyond that, it means you are committing to each other.*

My heart fluttered in excitement because I was committing to this man, and I knew without a doubt that Chase was wholly dedicated to me. He'd shown it time and again in his every action, and I finally understood how real it all was for him.

Beyond that commitment, marriage also means that you will be there to share in each other's joy during happy times and bear each other's worries in times of difficulty.

Chase displayed his heart for me the first moment I met him. Despite all my brokenness, he had consistently been there for me in big and small ways.

Marriage means you will walk the path of life side by side, one with another, and experience all that life brings you together as a single unit. Now and forever, you against the world.

Chase and I, now and forever–us against the world. That is what we were.

"Do you, Moira Vanderbilt, take this man, Chase Wilder, to be your lawfully wedded husband? To honor and cherish him, in sickness and in health, for richer or poorer, and will you be faithful to him for as long as you both shall live?"

"I do," I beamed at Chase.

"And do you, Chase Wilder, take this woman, Moira Vanderbilt, to be your lawfully wedded wife? To honor and cherish her, in sickness and health, for richer or poorer, and will you be faithful to her for as long as you both shall live?" The judge hardly paused before Chase blurted.

"I DO!" I saw Sam stifle a laugh over Chase's shoulder. "I Do...I definitely do."

My heart soared at his enthusiasm, and that moment of levity was the perfect addition to a brief yet profoundly meaningful ceremony. Because we'd shared so many laughs, happy times, and laughter, and we'd built sweet memories.

"Your wedding rings are an outward and visible sign of your eternal love for each other."

I blinked and looked at the Preacher and back at Chase. We hadn't discussed rings, and I wasn't sure how to stop the judge or let him know. But Chase squeezed my hand, drawing my attention to him as he gave me a little wink.

"As you look upon them from day to day, may they remind you of the promises you have made together in front of these witnesses."

Chase turned a little to Sam, who stepped forward and placed a box in Chase's hand. Chase turned back to me and opened it to reveal a simple rose-gold band topped with a giant oval stone of the palest pink encircled by a halo of small white diamonds.

"I hope you don't mind a pink stone," Chase whispered. "It reminded me of you."

"It's perfect," I answered, awestruck by its classic beauty. "When did you possibly have time–"

"I, um," Sam cleared his throat. "I've been sitting on that ring for weeks." I looked back at Chase and lost all capacity for words as he slipped the ring on my finger.

"With this ring, I thee wed, and pledge you all my love, for all my life, for as long as we both shall live." More tears fell as Chase spoke. The Preacher then looked to Troy as he presented a box to me, slipping my bouquet away with his other hand.

"Don't worry... little sister. I've got you."

Little sister.

The box held a matching rose-gold band, smooth and wide. I lifted it out of the box and marveled at its heft. Chase leaned forward and whispered, "Check the engraving." And when I spun it slowly, I found the tiny writing on the inside.

'Property of Fancy Pants.'

I couldn't hold back the laugh that bubbled out of me as I slid the ring on his finger. "With this ring, I thee wed, and pledge you all my love, for all my life, for as long as we both shall live." When I looked up, I saw at last that big, broad smile of Chase's that showcased those gorgeous, deep dimples, and my heart was flying again.

"I understand there is one additional token that is being bestowed today." The Preacher stepped back as Sam produced another, larger box from his coat.

"It didn't seem right, on a day when you've made me so wildly happy, not to acknowledge that our baby has played a part in my happiness too." Opening the box, Chase presented a necklace that was a perfect match for the ring on my finger. A shimmering pale pink stone, again circled by tiny diamonds and dangling from a rose gold chain. "So today, this matches our wedding ring because this is the day our family begins. And when the baby arrives, we'll add a birthstone and start building new traditions." Sam handed a fresh handkerchief to Chase as Troy did the same for me, all four of us crying. "Our family is perfect. Thank you...for giving me this." Chase lifted the necklace to my neck, Troy took over, finishing the clasp as Chase leaned in and whispered, "I can't wait to meet our baby...you are going to be the best Mama."

I couldn't speak.

I could only gaze into the loving eyes of a man who had surely been carved straight out of heaven for me.

"Chase and Moira," The Preacher continued, "Because you have now declared your intention through these vows, and you have both accepted these rings, and necklace, it is with great joy that I, with the authority vested in me by the state of New York, do pronounce you husband and wife. You may now - "

Chase's lunging excitement cut off his final words as he swept me into his arms, kissing me deep and long as he spun us both around to the whoops and cheers of the room. When my feet finally hit the ground, he rested his forehead against mine.

"I love you so much, Chase....I...hardly have words." I couldn't hold back the tears as joy poured from my heart.

"We don't need words." Chase planted a hand on the back of my neck and the other on the side of my belly. "I'm lousy with 'em anyway." And again, as if on cue, our baby gave a mighty wallop so strong we both flinched a little. Sam and Troy instantly elbowed in, placing their own hands on my belly too.

"That's our nephew in there." Sam beamed.

"Or niece, God help us," Troy added.

"Say cheese, guys." Looking up, Chief snapped a picture with his phone, forever freezing the single happiest moment of my life. I was utterly at peace. My husband, before me, and two brothers doting on the baby in my belly.

A family.

My family.

We stepped out of the chapel to a roaring chorus of hollering cheers as the whole fire department was turned out in full dress, blocking the road with their rigs.

"Did you do this, too?" Chase asked, face beaming.

"Come on, kiddo." His chief clapped his shoulders, and Carol hugged my neck. "You think we were gonna let one of our own get hitched without a little fanfare?"

With a wave of the Chief's arms, the truck lights flashed, and horns honked, and my husband was a kid at Christmas.

His chief hugged me then, welcoming me to yet another family, before sending us through a row of firemen and women holding bright silver axes in an arch over our heads. At the other end, a firetruck held a giant 'just married' sign off the back as one of the guys held out a hand for me to climb onto the back of the truck.

"No way probie." Chase slapped the man's hand away. "My wife isn't hanging off the back of a filthy truck." He lifted me into his arms and walked to the front, "But she sure as shit gets to have the full escort as I take her home."

And so we were given full fanfare through town, with well-wishers waving as we passed, until the rigs peeled off at our street and we pulled into the little driveway of our little house with my little family.

My little slice of perfection.

45

MOIRA

I COULDN'T STOP STARING at my ring, still marveling that Chase had chosen something so perfect for me. His hands slid around my waist from behind me, and I tilted my head to the side, giving his mouth its resting place on my neck.

"Happy, wife?" He mumbled against my skin.

"*Very*, husband," My cheeks ached from all the smiling I'd done. "Today was perfect." I turned in his arms, resting my cheek on his chest. "So much more than I could have ever hoped for."

"I hope you aren't worn out, though. I have more surprises planned."

"More!" I popped my head up. "Chase Wilder, you've given me a fairytale wedding, complete with tears and jewelry and a full fire brigade with axes! Even your generosity has to be spent by now."

"Doesn't every groom give his bride a honeymoon?" Mischief danced in his eyes as he tapped my nose with his finger.

"Honeymoon!" Before I could say another word, a loud growl rumbled up from my belly.

"Please tell me you didn't forget to eat all day?"

"Not exactly," I shrugged sheepishly. "I snacked a little this morning. My stomach was a little nervous. Then I was distracted, and by the time I was hungry, it was ... well, now!" He crossed into the kitchen, and I followed behind him. "You said honeymoon?"

"That's what I thought." He sighed, opening the fridge with a grimace. "I did too good a job cleaning out the fridge. I'll run and grab us a bite while you pack for the cabin."

"I'm okay, it can wait until dinner." He changed out of his suit and into his jeans and leathers. "Wait...did you say cabin? As in, you rented a honeymoon cabin?"

"Surprise." He winked, giving my backside a little smack as he passed me to grab his boots. "It is a rental, but no...We own a cabin near the Whiteface mountains, and we'll be honeymooning there in just a few hours." I was speechless. "I keep telling you we should review our portfolio to familiarize you with the business." He smiled at me again and stood to kiss me. "It's half yours now, too." He grabbed his helmet and headed towards the door. There's more snow up there, so pack warm." Stunned, I stood frozen as he left, only moving when I heard his bike roar to life outside.

A honeymoon...at a cabin...in the mountains.

With a giddy clap, I skipped into the bedroom to change, taking a moment to give the newest family heirloom one last look before zipping my dress into its secure garment bag. Snagging my favorite comfy jeans, I pulled them on but found I could hardly pull them over my hips. Buttoning them was a definite no-go, so I reached for a soft pair of leggings that were stretched to the max around my bump.

"Geez, baby, guess you decided to pop out overnight, eh?" Rubbing my belly, I reached for a soft, oversized sweater and grabbed a duffel to start packing. I checked the weather near the mountains he mentioned and decided I might need two bags to hold thicker sweaters and other essentials, as well as toiletries and shoes.

I lost myself in the happy task until the click of the front door told me Chase had returned, my stomach growling its approval.

"When we get back from the cabin, I'm going to need new pants. My bump will *not* tolerate these jeans anymore." I waited for Chase's reply while chastising myself for not thinking to purchase lingerie for tonight. Then smiled, remembering he'd just rip it off me with his teeth and I'd end up naked. That's when I pulled my robe from the edge of the crib, and all the air was sucked from the room.

There, inside the crib, lay a single...long-stemmed...white rose.

The world tunneled into a perfect circle framing the dread-filled omen as my mind scrambled to think of any reason, any explanation, to explain it away. Chase knew I hated white roses. He wouldn't have left me one. And Sam and Troy certainly weren't the type to leave random flowers around in cribs.

In my baby's crib.

"No," I whispered, trying to regain my senses or make my feet move. "No, no, no," I clenched my eyes tight and shook my head, trying to clear the cobwebs. Only then did I remember the front door click, the sound I thought was Chase coming home, but he didn't answer when I spoke, he didn't come help me pack, or wrap his arms around me, or try to make me sit and eat while he did all the work. "No no no no no." I turned to the front door. I could see it through the living room. The path was clear, no Chase in sight, and a bone-chilling clarity resonated through me; I couldn't hear him either. No rustling take-out bags, no low baritone humming around the kitchen. The house was silent. Too silent...until a metallic snick-snap cleaved the air.

My blood iced over — that sound didn't belong here.

Alarm bells blared in my head as I looked at my cell phone on the bed. Running, I reached out to call Chase...or Troy...but I was too slow. Time slowed to a glacial pace–familiar rough hands surrounding my waist.

"Ah...Moira, Moira." My vision went watery as Dean took my phone, firmly canceling my dial before slipping it into his pocket and palming my belly. "How's that baby of mine doing?" My stomach twisted into a heaving knot that made me wish I'd eaten something I could vomit now.

"Chase will come back. He'll be home any minute. If he finds you here, he'll kill you." I hated my shaky voice, but I prayed my words would make him flee. "Just leave, Dean. Leave now."

"Moira, Moira." He drawled in my ear with a predatory growl. "You think I'm letting either of you go after the stunt you pulled on the bus." Spinning me, Dean pushed his mouth down on me so hard I could feel the bruising set in. I pulled back, gasping, shoving with such force that I hit the bed and toppled back onto the mattress. His sneer had me scrambling backward, knowing I'd made a crucial mistake. "You think," Dean grabbed my ankles and yanked me towards him with a yelp. "I'd let good ol' squeaky clean Wilder get off scot-free after he broke my nose and stole my girl?" Dean crawled over me, spreading my knees with his legs as if I were a rag doll, helpless and at his mercy. I slapped and scratched at him, fighting to stave off the inevitable, even as he laughed at me. His body leaning into mine, his breath sick and moist in my ear, he hissed his threats. "You think I'd let you ride off into the sunset after watching you rut onto him like a whore." His weight dug into my abdomen, cutting my breath short as he thrust his erection against me to punctuate his final words. "With. My. Baby!"

"Stop!" I pushed at his shoulders with my useless, weak arms. "No...Dean...Why are you doing this?"

Dean sat back on his heels, staring down at me with a mix of lust and hatred on his face. He lifted my sweater, and I instinctively pulled it back down, slapping at his hands, which only angered him more. He pinned my arms above my head with one hand, leaning over me as he traced his fingers across my belly like he owned it. "This is my ticket, you know." He brushed his nose against my cheek like a lover, slow, deliberate, and wrong. My bile rose as he nestled between my thighs, resting an erection against my core. "I thought getting you to move, and fucking with your career was enough." I tried to hear his words, but they dissolved in the rush of blood pounding in my ears. My body screamed the wrongness of his touch, every inch of skin he caressed felt stolen, like he was prying ownership from my bones. Then, just as his fingertips reached the edge of my leggings, he jerked back, yanking me by my wrists as he exited the bedroom.

"Where are you taking me?" Relief at being away from the bed warred with a new panic. My balance forever shifting against his yanking arms as he dragged me through the house. "Dean, what-" He spun me to face him, the movement jarring enough to rattle my teeth. Then, his mouth was on mine—bruising, greedy. One hand tangled in my hair, anchoring me like a puppet, the other forcing my head back as he dragged his tongue across my lips, my jaw, my neck—marking territory I never offered.

I kicked. Scratched. Clawed.

It wasn't enough.

Not even close.

I sobbed, helpless and shaking, while he sneered like a monster, savoring the silence before the scream.

"If you had just come with me that day on the bus, things would have been different, you know." He dragged me to the kitchen and produced a pair of handcuffs. "I was gonna give you the life you always wanted, you know. I was gonna marry you - good and proper. Let you have the baby, stay home, and raise the little brat and everything." He slung the cuffs through the oven door handle and cuffed both wrists in place.

"Dean. No!" The metal bit into my skin as I yanked helplessly against their cold restraint.

"But then you spread your legs for good ol' Chase, who already fucked me out of a job." Dean grabbed a kitchen chair, its legs screeching across the floor, before he slammed it down in front of me. I flinched, my cuffs biting into raw skin as I twisted against them.

That's when I saw it—the duct tape, and the tiny baggies of black powder lined up like little warnings on the counter...and his Zippo lighter. My stomach turned as he reached for it.

"That dumbass came riding in like a hero on a white horse to save a bunch of women he didn't even know, and it cost me my goddamn promotion, Moira!" He paced like a caged animal, shoulders coiled tight, every step a stomp while he rolled the lighter over his knuckles like a coin trick. His breath came sharp and ragged, his face mottling with fury as he ranted about losing me, too.

He wasn't looking at me when he yelled—not really. He was shouting into the room. Shouting at the version of himself that didn't get what he wanted. I might have taken pride in that, in having stolen something from this petulant man-baby, until he turned back to me.

"But then again, apparently saving strangers is this guy's kink, isn't it, baby?" He strolled over with a smug swagger and slapped my ass—a white-hot sting knocking the air from my lungs. I jerked against the cuffs, uselessly, and he laughed, grinding his dick against me like he was owed the right.

The nausea rose fast and ugly, but I didn't look away.

"Having a man swoop in and rescue you was always kinda your kink too, wasn't it, sweetheart?" I needed to watch him. Every second. Every twitch. Even when his hot breath choked the side of my neck, when his tongue dragged across my skin, and his teeth clamped down on my jaw, not playful, but punishing. I cried out, the sound raw and involuntary, but I didn't dare look away.

Monsters grew bigger in the dark.

He covered my mouth, muffling my cries, to address my phone, which was chirping a text from Chase. He read the words as if reciting poetry to a crowd of adoring fans.

"How many tacos do you want today? 2...or is my baby starving and needs 3?" Dean sneered down at my belly, gripping his hand painfully over my mouth in a needless display of dominance. "Hmph, seems my Baby likes a lot of tacos these days." He fired off a text and pocketed my phone. I forced my panic down, one shallow breath at a time, as he released my mouth. I couldn't afford to lose my grip—not when he was watching. When I finally spoke, my voice didn't shake. I didn't let it.

"Dean. What do you want?"

"Ahhh, Moira, Moira." He hummed my name into my neck, grinding against my ass and smelling me like a feral animal, the grind of the lighter's wheel whirring in my periphery as he resumed toying with it. "A home, a wife, a family. Isn't that what all men want?" He shoved me away, snarling under his breath like something barely human. "It's what men deserve." My stomach turned.

"You made it clear you didn't want me." I snapped, heat rising to the surface—anger and disgust in equal measure. "So why try to take me *now*?"

"POWER, MOIRA!" His voice exploded beside my ear, shattering the breath in my lungs as he thunked the lighter into his thigh, slamming the metallic lid shut. Grabbing my head, he shoved me forward, violently folding me in half until my cheek pressed against the glass stovetop, wrists screaming from the wrenching twist. "I was supposed to be the next Chief! Apex had plans—I put them on the map up here, and in return, my career shoulda been fast-tracked after you anchored me in."

From the corner of my vision, I saw his free hand crank the stove dial. My heart stopped at the tell-tale click and hum I heard under my ear.

"And you know what would've been the cherry on fucking top, Moira?" My cheek burned. Not metaphorically—literally. The glass beneath my face was warming fast.

"Dean... no." I thrashed against the restraints, wrists tearing at the metal as my back arched in pure survival instinct, trying to lift my face even an inch. But Dean was too strong.

"The sheer amount of money I'd be bringing in helping move product!" With a disgusted huff, he released me. I collapsed backward, gasping against the panic of a burned face I only narrowly avoided. "I woulda been fucking rolling, Moira!"

He was unhinged—like I'd never seen and I didn't know if I'd survive the next five minutes. I'd never known him to be so violent, but now, this raw and raging insanity seemed so effortless for him, and I knew–this was the real Dean. Standing shakily, pins and needles screamed through my hands as blood slowly returned. But somehow in the chaos, clarity cracked through.

Apex...I knew that name...But how?

Dean hunched over the counter, working fast with his baggies of black powder, and an acrid sting of sulfur hit my nose, just like my apartment.

My stomach dropped.

The scent wasn't just familiar—it was a signal—a trigger. My mind flashed to flames licking the walls, to smoke clawing down my throat, to the sound of my screams. He was going to burn it all down. Again. Panic surged—sharp and blinding—but it wasn't chaos this time. It was purposeful. I couldn't survive another fire, and neither could my baby. I had to stop him. Or at least slow him down. There was no way out—not yet. I couldn't run. Couldn't fight. Not cuffed, not like this.

But I could talk.

I could keep him looking at me. Not the fuse. Not the fire. Me. If I had to bleed for his attention, I would. I could survive pain. I could survive him. I just had to make him forget what he was trying to light. I just had to make him put that lighter down.

I'm okay... I'm okay... I'm okay.

"Apex?" I put the pieces into place. "So, the library fire was you, too!"

"I can't claim that one, sweetheart," he answered with a glint in his eyes. "I was still in jail thanks to your new brother." He reared back and slapped me across the face, scattering stars behind my eyes from the force of the blow. "Thanks for that, by the way." He stood back, straightening his shoulders. "Apex is men reclaiming our dominance in a world determined to bring us fucking down. Not that you deserve to know about it." He spat the answer at me like I was vermin, but he didn't start a fire, so I kept focused on his face, never shying away from his eyes. "It's the answer to all the world's problems by placing us at the top of the fucking food chain and with it, putting all of you back where you belong." He sneered at me. "Serving...with your legs spread and your mouth shut."

"So, you're not just a gaslighting pyromaniac—you're a misogynistic piece of shit, too." I wanted him angry. I needed his focus on me. But the second his eyes snapped to mine—feral, burning—I knew I'd gone too far.

He moved. Two steps. Fast.

I opened my mouth to apologize, to walk it back, but the words tangled behind my teeth. Squeezing my eyes shut, I braced for the blow—but instead, I felt the click of metal. He was uncuffing me from the oven.

That was worse.

"You didn't think I was nasty before, though, did ya, sweetheart?" He yanked the cuffs hard enough that my shoulders screamed. I stumbled forward, forced to follow or hear a bone snap, and it was only a few steps to know where he was dragging me–the bedroom.

Dean flung me to the bed. The mattress caught my body with a dull thud before he hauled my arms over my head and cuffed me to the headboard.

"You thought I was some magical knight in shining armor when I flew you around the country, dropped cash on dinners and flowers. Remember that?" I pulled against the cuffs, wrists already raw. Dean unbuckled his belt. Climbed onto the bed. "Maybe you just need a little reminder of how good it used to be, huh, sweetheart?"

"No. Dean. No!" I kicked—wild, panicked—but he caught my ankles in one violent jerk, lifting my hips clean off the bed. The cuffs clanged and bit down on my wrists, a trickle of blood slithering down my arm.

"Ah! No, stop! No!" Dean wedged himself between my knees. Smiling. Palming his dick through his jeans like it was a show.

"Yeah... I think you need a good fucking reminder of how great we were when we made that baby." He shoved my sweater up, exposing my belly. Cold air met skin. I sucked in breath after breath, heart jackhammering behind my ribs. "Maybe after a proper dicking, you'll see that do-gooder for what he is... a Beta." His fingers hooked the waistband of my leggings, then his teeth sank into my belly.

I barely recognized the scream I let loose.

Not from pain—something deeper. A scream that recognized this danger, this man, this bed. Twisting on me, he bit me down again, higher up on my ribs. And for a sickening moment, I was grateful. As long as he was biting, he wasn't...

"Who knew you liked it so rough?" he muttered, leaning back, studying me like I was a puzzle, and he had all the time in the world. "Maybe we were more compatible than I thought."

"Dean... let me go." My voice cracked. "You don't need to do this."

His hand slid to his zipper. I began to beg.

"You'll hurt the baby, Dean. Please. You don't want to hurt the baby, do you?" He sneered. Licked my stomach. Whispered something I couldn't hear over the blood roaring in my ears.

And in that moment, something gave way inside me.

The panic was still there, but distant. I wasn't in my body anymore. I was floating above it, watching the scene I was no longer a part of. Maybe if I let this happen... if I stop fighting... he'll stop. I thought. Better raped than burned.

I'm okay... I'm okay... I'm okay.

The thought sliced through me like a blade—my mind split.

One part watching.

One part calculating.

"Okay," I whispered. "I'll go with you." Dean paused. "We can go to New York. Like you wanted. We can be a family. You can have me. Anytime, anyway you want."

I was lying through my teeth. But if I could get him out of here before Chase returned, I could spare him the pain of witnessing this. I could save Sam and Troy from losing a brother. I could disappear. They'd be sad, but alive, and Chase could move on.

Dean's expression turned calculating. If the keys hadn't jingled in the front door, I might've convinced him.

Chase.

The sound of him coming home cracked the air like a gunshot. Dean moved fast—A hand clamped over my mouth as Dean glared at me. My eyes dropped, following his gaze to the knife now pressed against my belly. The message was crystal clear: Make a sound, and the baby dies.

"Hey, baby! You said three tacos!"

Dean's knife pressed deeper into my belly; the sting was tight enough, I knew there was blood, but I couldn't look. He unlocked the cuffs slowly, silently, careful not to let them clink.

"Figured it's been a big day, so I got you three tacos," Chase sounded light, full of peace. I could hear the smile in his words. "And I got the baby rice and beans... and chips." My heart shattered. In seconds, he'd see me, and his world would shatter like mine had.

And that meant Dean would have him, too.

I was frozen—terror anchoring me in place—as Dean pressed his front to my back, shoving me toward the bedroom door. The knife didn't waver.

"Hey, what's with the tape and—" Chase's words died in his throat as Dean pushed me into the living room—Straight into his line of sight.

46

CHASE

"**H**ey, what's the tape and..." Time stopped when the scent hit me.

Sulfur.

My brain kicked into trained overdrive as I looked around—gunpowder, duct tape, silence.

Where was Moira?

My fingers fumbled over my phone to the messaging app.

> Me: Flashpoint. Code Red. On me.

Old Corps code was all I could manage before I saw my wife stumbling out of our bedroom, barefoot, and bleeding.

"Moira!" Dean Jensen, that sick fuck, tucked in behind her.

"Chase, No!" Her cry cracked me in half. My eyes locked on the blade at her belly first, then the blood. A small dot, but growing. The kind of bleed that meant a puncture. Pressure. Threat. And then my gaze traveled. Her wrists—swollen, raw, cuff-burned. Her clothes—askew, twisted, pulled halfway down her hips. Her mouth—smeared lipstick, split lip, a bruise blooming across her cheekbone.

The woman I made vows to. I left her alone. How could I? My wife. Tortured. Violated. Used. I couldn't breathe. Rage flooded every vein.

"Kinda makes your blood boil, doesn't it, Wilder?" Dean sneered into her shoulder. "Seeing another man's hands on your woman." His belt dangled off the edge of his pants. Jesus fucking christ.

"I'll kill you, Jensen." My fists clenched so hard my nails dug into my palms. Every part of me screamed to launch forward, to rip him away from her with my bare hands. But the knife—that fucking knife—pressed against her belly like a live wire, and I knew one wrong move could end everything. "Your only chance to walk out of here breathing is to give her to me now and run." I inched forward anyway, rage thrumming through my blood louder than logic.

One more step. I could take him. I was fast.

I had to try.

"Chase." Her voice stopped me like a chain around my chest. My Moira. "He'll kill you... the baby. Please." Her sob might as well have been my own. She saw it in me—the breaking point. The man I was about to become. And she pulled me back with nothing but her voice.

"Better listen to the old ball and chain." Dean flicked his chin to a chair. "Have a seat."

"Fuck you," I spat, jaw clenched so hard my teeth ached. I didn't move to the chair. No way was I giving this sick bastard a position of power—not when it came to my wife and child. "What the hell do you want?"

"What I wanted," Dean's voice was calm, almost nostalgic, "was to run this town's emergency services. Perhaps become a battalion chief...

or even a fire commissioner someday. Buy a little lakefront cabin. Retire with a wife who serviced my every need." He fisted Moira's hair, yanking her back until she cried out.

"LET HER GO!" My vision went red; my pulse was a pure white noise in my ears. "You want to blame me for torching your career? Fine. Blame me, Fuckwad, I'm *right* here!" I slammed my hands to my chest in invitation, every muscle in my body screaming for him to come for me. Not her.

"You think I'm stupid?" Dean flicked his chin toward the duct tape on the counter, his smirk curdling into something darker. "I know how much time you spend at the gym. I know better than to go toe-to-toe with all those shiny muscles of yours." He leaned into Moira and breathed her in like a goddamn predator, stealing away her scent. "Even if you've gone soft lately, buried in this snatch for the last few months..."

Moira groaned, and I moved—just a fraction—but he caught it. His eyes snapped to me with hard calculation.

"Sit down." The knife pressed to her belly, just enough to make her flinch. Just enough to stop me cold.

Primal terror slipped down my spine.

He'd do it. He'd kill her and my baby before I could take one whole step.

My hands shook as I looked at her. My wife was in pain. She was fighting to stay still and looking at me like I was the only thing tethering her to this world.

I had no choice.

"Okay," I said quietly, backing toward the chair. Behind me, her cry tore through the air—high-pitched, strangled—as Dean yanked her head back again like she was nothing more than a prop to hurt me with. "Okay! I'm sitting. I'm taping." I acquiesced, quickly rolling tape around my knees to the chair. "Now let her go and handle this shit with me. Be a fucking man for once." I knew it was risky, taunting him, but it was my only play. Make him mad and hope he makes a mistake. Even taped to a chair, I could take him on vengeance alone.

Just give me a fucking opening, asshole.

"Now...my baby mama here is gonna finish the job and tape your arms down, aren't you, sweetheart?" He shoved her forward, and she lunged for me, throwing her still-cuffed arms around my neck.

"I'm so sorry, Chase. I couldn't call for help in time." She clung to me, kissing my cheek in frantic bursts. I reached for her—and felt the slice of Dean's knife across my shoulder as he yanked her back.

"Now now," he mocked. "Where were all those promises you gave me in the bedroom to do whatever I wanted, sweetheart?" He shoved the duct tape at her. "Tape him to the chair. Around that fucking chest of his—before I start feeling stabby with Hero here." He shifted the knife to my neck, just enough to break skin.

Moira sobbed as she worked the tape around me. Her hands trembled. When she saw the blood spilling from my shoulder, she broke.

"Oh god. Chase."

"I'm okay, baby," I whispered. "First chance you get, you fucking run." I kept it low, just for her. She shook her head—and kissed me like she'd never let go. "You run. Do you hear me?"

"Never."

Dean yanked her back by the hair.

"God, you really are a harlot, aren't you?" The knife pressed to her belly again. "The way she threw herself at me, then fell into your bed like a bitch in heat. Promising me the world just a few hours ago. You sure this baby's even mine?" My stomach twisted. I'd kill him for that. For saying it. But if he touched her…"She could've fucked her way across half the country for all we know."

He grabbed the hem of her sweater and started lifting. Moira flailed even as he shushed her. His eyes never left mine. The first bite mark appeared—deep, raw, just below where the knife had punctured her. Then another, higher up.

Bruised. Swollen. From his teeth.

"You sadistic piece of shit!" I thrashed, pain searing through my shoulder. "What kind of monster—"

"Seems like I marked her pretty well, didn't I?" His eyes were glassy now. Cold. "Guess I claimed her after all." Then he kissed her hard. When he pulled away, blood slicked her chin.

"Goddamn you!" I flailed again, teeth clenched, fury rising like fire. "You fucking piece of shit!" I hated him. I wanted him to bleed. I wanted him dead. But worse than anything, worse than the kiss and the blood, the look on her face.

She looked shattered.

Eyes shut. Face turned from me, like I was the one who'd failed her.

"You know, you getting me fired almost derailed all my plans." Dean slid over another chair and cuffed Moira to it as he talked. "I was wicked pissed when the board opted to oust me from my job and take away my standing on the force along with my pension." He lunged at me and punched my face with his knife still fisted in his hand. Moira cried out at it, but all it did was fuel my rage. "I'll admit I was so pissed I got a little sloppy trying to take my girl on the bus like that." Jensen swung at me again, punching me in the stomach so hard it knocked the wind out of me. "But I gotta say you did me a solid when you had me arrested."

He swung again, landing a blow that cracked ribs—pain blooming like fire through my chest.

"Dean, please." Moira pleaded. "Don't hurt him. I already told you I'll go with you, I'll do whatever you want." She looked at my face with so much sadness in her eyes that I could hardly breathe. "I'll annul the wedding to Chase. I'll marry you. I'll stay home and we can raise this... *our* baby.... together."

"No!" I growled, but Jensen just leaned over and winked at me before he turned to the island.

"Being in jail gave me time to think, and when I called my lawyer, we hatched a little plan." Dean grabbed the bag of gunpowder and sauntered to the electrical panel inside the laundry room. "You see," He wadded up what looked like cigarette papers around a trail of gunpowder. He tucked it into the electrical panel after popping a few of the circuits loose and lacing the wires with more of the same. "I couldn't be the arsonist if I were behind bars when another fire started. That made the library my easy out." He winked at Moira and added, "Bonus points that I fucked you out of yet another job in the process, ain't it, sweetheart?"

"You sick bastard." Moira spat. "People could've been hurt!" Dean just shrugged.

"But if I'm cleared of all arson charges..." He stacked a pile of clothes beneath the electrical panel, sprinkling gunpowder across the top like he was seasoning a dish. "And another fire, linked to that same arson, conveniently takes out the guy who tanked my career and—" He skipped over to Moira and backhanded her. "—stole the mother of my child to boot?" He spun to face me, lowering himself to eye level. "Wouldn't that tie up all the loose ends in one tidy little blaze?"

"I. Will. End. You." My voice was a screaming rage, drowning the pain in my shoulder. I twisted hard against the tape, felt it stretch. "You'll die knowing I took your job, your girl, and your baby." I kept talking.

Pushing buttons. Not to win. To buy time. My brothers were coming. They had to be. "How's that for *Emphatic Assertion?*" That hit a nerve. Jensen's eyes flicked, darkened. "Maybe Apex will pick me up now. Since I stole all the goods from the pussy with a bad case of failure to launch."

"Fuck you, Wilder!" Gunpowder spilled from his hand as he lunged and punched me in the gut. I didn't have time to brace. Air shot from my lungs, sour heat rising in my throat.

"Chase! Stop!" Moira's voice cut through. She met my eyes, tears already falling. "He'll kill you." I swallowed hard. I couldn't stop. I wouldn't.

"You think you're better than me," Jensen sneered, draping an arm across my chest, knife digging beneath my chin. "You think Apex wants a guy who settles for secondhand pussy and leftover babies?"

"Dean, please! Stop."

"What you had with her?" Dean's breath was rank in my ear. "That was just intermission. I had her first. You're sloppy seconds. And my dick will be the last thing she feels—before I cut my baby out of her."

Then he moved. Fast. The knife pivoted and slammed into my thigh—to the hilt.

"CHASE, GOD NO, DEAN PLEASE!" Moira's face was white, and her breathing as ragged as the roar I let loose in the room. That is, until Jensen shifted his attention to her and backhanded her once more so hard that her head lolled to the side a moment before she shook herself to refocus on me again.

"That's about enough out of you, don't you think, sweetheart?" Jensen caressed the cheek he had hit, wiping his thumb through the blood on her bottom lip, licking it off as he disappeared into the bedroom. Moira's face slowly dropped, and I knew I was witnessing the light begin to dim in her eyes.

I broke.

The confidence, the fire I'd watched bloom in her... it was gone. She was folding inward, rebuilding walls that had long been torn down. I could see it happening in real time, piece by piece. And if I did nothing else before I bled out in this goddamn chair, I had to stop her from disappearing behind them.

"Baby," I said, gritting my teeth against the searing pain in my leg. "Moira, look at me."

Her head bobbed like a marionette, dazed from the hit. Her eyes dropped to my thigh—to the knife buried in it, and the blood running down my jeans in twin rivers. Her chin quivered, but no words came. I felt it too—the blood was coming fast. Too fast. I was bleeding out. I was running out of time.

"Moira, come on, baby. Look at me! Look at my eyes." She dragged her gaze up from my leg to my shoulder and the blood streaming down my arm. "Not there, baby, ignore that. Look here. Find my eyes, dammit!"

She closed her eyes. A fresh tear slipped free.

No. I couldn't let her fall.

"Don't cry, Fancy Pants." She sobbed through a half smile at that. I had her. "Come on, wife." She opened her eyes and slowly pulled her head up to meet me. "I love you. You're going to get out of this. You are gonna be okay."

"I'm so so sorry." Her voice was breathy and weak. "I should have left when he found me on the bus and saved you from this."

"Don't you fucking dare." The force in my voice hooked her. "Don't you dare regret a second of our time together. I wouldn't trade a single breath." She stared at me, fully locked in. I didn't have long.

My body was going heavy. But she needed to hear me.

"He's a psychotic piece of shit. He won't win. He *can't* win. Not while you're still breathing, and definitely not while I'm still here." The air reeked of sulfur–time was short. I could feel it. "Moira Wilder," my voice was ragged, "you were always the missing piece. The space in my chest I didn't even know was hollow until you walked in and filled it."

Tired. I was so tired.

"Chase..." She sobbed, wrenching at the cuffs already bloodying her wrists. "Chase, stay with me!"

I was trying. God help me, I was trying.

"You always dreamed of being a princess with a hero coming to rescue you from your life and take you away to a better world."

"It's you, it's only ever been you." She cried out, her voice taking on a new urgency that didn't make any sense.

"No, baby, you had it backwards." Salty tears slipped into the corner of my mouth, but I pushed on, my head getting thicker with a haze to it. "You never needed a hero to rescue you 'cause you did that yourself. You never needed someone to take you away to a better life; you just went out and built your own damn life. Over and over, as many times as you needed to. And I was the lucky bastard who got to watch you blossom into your true self, right before my eyes."

"I'll get us out of this somehow." She squirmed again, wincing. I hated that she was hurting herself.

"Amazing... that's what you are...and you sure as hell were *never* the princess in a fairytale, cause, baby, you've always been a *goddamn Queen*." Jensen rounded the corner behind her, but I held her eyes. "You'll be okay. You'll get through this. And you'll be the best mama. Don't ever stop fighting."

"Aw, loverboy." Jensen dangled the stuffed elephant in Moira's face. "Big words from a man who is kinda slurring his words now." He crouched down between us and got her attention. "I know this all looks bad, sweetheart." He ran the elephant's ear down her cheek. "But soon enough you will forget all this when you see the nice big house I have for you, all set up with a nursery for our baby." His hand rested on her belly, but she never flinched. "This will all be a distant memory and we'll be happy, won't we, sweetheart?"

"No." Moira's voice cut through my static. She faced Jensen with dry eyes and more fire than I'd seen since this nightmare began. I blinked hard, trying to keep her in focus as the room blurred. She was my anchor; the only thing keeping me conscious.

"Excuse me?" Jensen stood slowly, towering over her, but she didn't flinch. Answering him in calm, sharp words that made me want to cheer and cry at the same time.

"You heard me. I. Said. No." That smirk—God, that smirk. It was defiance and survival all rolled into one. I would've stood in applause if I weren't bleeding out. "Even if you set this place on fire and steal me away," she huffed with a cocked eyebrow, "you think your life will be worth the air you breathe when my brothers hunt you down?"

Her chin tipped up like the goddamn queen she was.

"You won't look much like the top of the food chain when you're screaming for mercy with their boot on your neck while you eat pavement."

Goddamn. That's my girl.

Dean tossed the elephant aside and pulled a Zippo from his pocket, flicking it to life in front of her face. She didn't blink.

"Chase is *twice* the man you'll ever be," she sneered. "And you've got *half* the cock to prove it."

Her words were venom and steel, and I watched them land in Jensen's soul like a physical hit.

"So go ahead, big man," she cocked her chin a little higher, defiance dripping. "Tie up the pregnant woman. Beat me. Bite me. Kidnap me. But don't ever forget—you *had* to do all of that to win me. Because you will always be the smaller... more pathetic... bottom-feeding...Beta."

Jensen sneered down with hate in his eyes and flicked his lighter to life once more, tossing it over her head into the bedroom behind her.

"NO!" I arched back, tape tearing at my skin, pain screaming through my legs as I tried—God, I tried—to break free. The knife in my thigh screamed as I yanked at it, desperate to stop what was already happening.

Too late. Too fucking slow.

"Say goodbye, sweetheart." Jensen grabbed my face, fingers crushing my cheeks until I tasted blood. "If you're lucky," he sneered, "you'll pass out before the fire gets ya." His fist cracked across my jaw, and stars exploded.

I fought to stay awake. Just one more second. Just one more look.

Please—let me see her one last time.

Jensen turned toward Moira. Reached for her, and she moved. Her leg snapped out, catching his knee with a brutal crunch.

He howled.

Then his head hit the corner of the bar with a sickening thud.

He dropped—dead weight.

And then she was there.

Kneeling in front of me like the goddess who'd felled the monster.

My warrior.

My wife.

47

CHASE

ARM.

God, it was so warm.

My body was heavy. My arms limp. My fingers didn't twitch. My legs were buzzing and far away—gone, maybe.

It felt like sleep. The best kind. The kind you never wake from.

But I remembered...

Moira.

She'd broken free. I saw her rise. That ass didn't stand a chance.

Jensen was down. My wife—our baby—was free.

That was enough. That was everything.

So, what if I couldn't move? So, what if the room was so...

Loud.

Roaring. Like wind through trees. Like wood snapping in the cold. Like fire.

Wait—

Fire.

The room wasn't warm. It was hot. Too hot.

My head spun. My skin burned. My throat closed in on itself.

Then came the voice.

That voice.

Cutting through everything—

"CHASE!" My eyes flew open.

Moira was in front of me—over me—shaking me, kissing my face, shoving at me like her body could will mine back to life.

Behind her, fire devoured the bedroom, licking up the walls and clawing toward us. The bathroom glowed orange. The laundry room was already gone.

We had seconds.

She was still cuffed, face streaked with soot and tears.

Alive.

"Moira," My throat was dust. "Why are you still here?"

"I'm not leaving without you!" she sobbed, pulling at my restraints. "Chase. Wake up! Tell me what to do—help me!"

"The fire..." My eyes dropped again. "You have to go. Please, baby."

But she didn't.

Of course, she didn't.

CHASE WILDER!" Her voice cracked like a whip, slicing through the roar. She slammed her shoulder into me again. "You're too heavy. I can't move you..." Coughing.

The smoke was thick.

"You're a fireman. So do your fucking job. Nod if you understand!"

"Brothers...coming," I slurred.

"Good!" She was mad. Why was she screaming? "Then we buy time! Tell me how!"

"Get... low..."

"The floor?" Her hands on my face felt good. There was that eleven I loved between her eyes.

"Smoke rises..."

I felt her body slam into mine again.

Once. Twice. I shifted, barely.

"Come on, big man." Her voice cracked. "Don't make me do this by myself." I fought to help. I tried. I did. "Get your ass on the floor, Boyscout!" God, she was cute when she was mad. "You gotta keep me and our baby company. Nod if you understand!"

Our baby.

"Nod if you understand!"

I smiled.

The world spun.

"Our baby. My wife..." My shoulder hit the floor. Pain jolted my eyes open. There was Jensen, sprawled out, blood under his head. Fucker.

And then Moira.

My wife. My fighter.

Crawling to me through hell.

"That's it. That's good," she scooted close, mascara bleeding into soot. "Look at me. Nod if you understand. We're gonna be okay." She coughed, and it was wet.

"Hey, Moira..."

"NOD IF YOU UNDERSTAND!" I blinked. She was shouting. I could see it in her face. But all I heard was wind and fire and her.

Beautiful. Fierce. Mine.

"Wife," I whispered.

"Yeah, baby, yeah. Keep talking." She was almost on top of me now, her body curved over mine, shielding me. Trying to protect the protector.

"This is how we met," I slurred.

"Chase..."

"You... and the fire..."

"CHASE!"

"Stay with me, baby."

My warrior. My wife.

I'd love her for the rest of my—

48

MOIRA

CHASE'S BROTHERS BURST THROUGH the front door the second he slipped under.

Time froze.

Troy grabbed me—cuffs and all—and carried me out of the burning house. Once outside, he turned and ran back in. He and Sam carried Chase out, still strapped to the chair.

By the time someone had cut off my cuffs, an ambulance was pulling up, fire engines right behind it.

I heard one of the EMTs shout, 'Clear!' and the scream that tore from my chest didn't feel human. Troy held me back as Sam moved on autopilot, pumping Chase's chest. The world around me blurred into noise and lights and fire and smoke.

I'd never seen someone cry while performing CPR.

Chase was rushed into emergency surgery for the nicked femoral artery in his leg, a sliced shoulder, and a collapsed lung. Sam wasn't allowed into the OR, so he poured every ounce of his worry into me, demanding I be checked out. I agreed, only to make sure the baby was OK. When the OB nurse found a heartbeat, I screamed at her to leave me alone—I needed to be with my family.

My family.

Sam scowled at my return to the waiting room, but I told him he could keep bossing me around from there. Within minutes, he had fluids, oxygen, and a triage team on the scene.

I paced.

Sam paced.

Troy paced.

The waiting room turned into a circuit beneath our feet. Chief and Carol brought coffee, water, and food that we didn't touch. Every time I asked for updates, the nurses came up empty. Even Sam's contacts couldn't get us answers.

At the three-hour mark, I caught the look Sam and Troy exchanged. My tears returned. Chase had lost so much blood. The ribs, the smoke, the concussion—bad enough. But the blood loss... it was terrifying.

Our home was gone.

My home was dying.

Word spread. One by one, the fire department, police department, and EMTs all began to show up. On-duty. Off-duty. The waiting room overflowed into the hallway. Everyone who loved him waited. Everyone who owed him stood shoulder to shoulder in silent worry.

Two women from Chase's station came to me. They winced when they saw my face—my split lip, the bruises—then hugged me gently. They shared their stories of Dean — we'd survived the same predator.

They called me brave. They said I saved them.

No. It was Chase. It was always Chase.

His strength. His heart. His quiet heroism. Looking at them, I understood. That station wasn't just coworkers—it was family. And their voices rose into one mighty roar when the surgeon emerged.

Chase was OK.

He was OK... he was OK... he was OK.

A day later, we all sat sentry by his bed, waiting. He slept deep and still, half-sedated. I was grateful his body could rest. But God, I needed his eyes. I needed to see him see me—alive, whole. To know the baby was OK.

Almost twenty-four hours passed before he stirred.

His brow twitched–A shallow breath.

Then his hand lifted, tugging at the oxygen mask. I caught it and guided it gently away.

"Boy, you *really* hate that thing, don't you?" A tear slipped down my cheek as his lips twitched into a ghost of a smile. "Take it slow, husband. You're OK. We're OK."

Sam and Troy appeared at my side in seconds. Sam grabbed his wrist, counting his pulse.

"You're in the hospital. You're doing real good, brother." Troy pressed a hand to Chase's foot, a quiet grounding. They both looked like they'd been holding their breath for days.

"Moira." Chase's voice was hoarse, nearly inaudible.

"I'm here, baby." I slid closer, lifting his hand to my cheek. "We're all here." His fingers grazed the edge of my swollen eye, my bruised cheek. Even barely conscious, he was cataloging every mark.

"How's my wife... and baby?" he whispered.

"There you go... surprising me." I smiled through a sob. "Waking up in a hospital and your first questions about us." He huffed a laugh, then winced, coughing rough and raw.

"Easy," Sam said, adjusting the oxygen. "The smoke didn't do you any favors. Neither did emergency surgery. No singing for a while."

"Moira... baby..."

"We're OK." I pressed my hand over his. "The baby's heartbeat was strong."

"She's good," Sam added. "I oversaw it myself. Little banged up, but strong. Stubborn, this wife of yours."

"Your brothers are a pain in the ass," I grinned through tears.

"*Your* brothers," Sam corrected. "You're stuck with us now."

"How..." Chase's voice cracked.

"You mean how we got out?" I kissed his palm. "Your brothers showed up in time. Troy pulled me out first, then he and Sam carried you out. Sam packed your leg and got us both in the ambulance before the fire crews doused the flames."

"You lost a lot of blood," Troy said. "But half the department donated while they waited. The banks are full."

"Your leg will heal. Your shoulder's just stitches. Your lungs are recovering, but they're watching it closely. And Sam said there was no smoke damage." I smiled, willing my husband to feel my love even if his eyes could barely stay open.

"Smart move getting low," Sam said. "It saved you both."

"You should've left..." Chase's peered from under half-closed lids.

"No chance." I choked on a sob.

"Jensen?" His gaze shifted to Troy.

"Alive. ICU. Coma." Troy held up a hand before Chase could argue. "Your wife took him down. Hard. Even if he wakes, he's toast. They found the gunpowder and prints. He's cuffed and guarded...but there's no walking away from this."

"Not enough." Chase's eyes shimmered, arm flexing like he might rise, but his body wasn't ready.

The coughing returned.

"Breathe, baby," I whispered. "He's not touching us again."

"Your wife told us everything," Sam added. "Little badass took out his knee."

"Then she got you to the ground," Troy smiled at me. "She kept you safe 'til we got there."

"My badass wife." Chase's dimple surfaced faintly.

"We're OK, Chase. We're all OK."

"Baby, too?"

"Yes," a new voice said as it came through the doorway. "Hope I'm not intruding." Dr. Burner rolled in, dragging a sonogram machine.

"You did a brave thing, young lady," he smiled warmly. "It's the talk of the hospital."

"That's my girl," Chase whispered, still holding my hand. "And my baby?"

"The nurse said there was a good heartbeat," Dr. Burner peered at me with a skeptical expression. "But that she didn't get to finalize things before being 'run out of the room,'?" I shrugged, not even feeling bad for my outburst. "I'd like to take a closer look myself." He rolled the machine beside me. "Missed a few appointments, after all?"

"Should we leave?" Troy asked, glancing at Sam.

"Hell no," Sam grinned. "I'm not missing my niece's debut."

"Could be a boy," Chase rasped.

"We could bet on it," Troy offered.

"Privacy, anyone?" Dr. Burner raised a brow at them. "Perhaps Mama can decide who stays?"

"It's OK," I said. "They're family."

I lay back in the recliner next to Chase, as Dr. Burner swirled the wand through the cool gel on my belly. We all leaned in as the screen flickered to life, grainy and gray, until an image formed.

A perfectly round head.

Tiny fingers.

The unmistakable flicker of a moving hand.

And then—whoosh, whoosh, whoosh—the heartbeat filled the room like a drumroll from heaven. Sam grinned like a kid at Christmas. Troy wiped his eyes. Chase's whole body melted into the bed.

"That's our baby," he breathed.

"You see the little nose?" I whispered.

"Actually..." Dr. Burner shifted the wand slightly, his tone playful. "Would Uncle EMT Sam like to try his hand at some anatomy?"

"Hell yeah!" Sam leaned in as Dr. Burner pointed to the screen, sliding the wand slowly to the side. "Wait... that's a...."

"A what?" Troy looked over Sam's shoulder, both their eyes going wide.

"Twins." Dr. Burner said with a smile. "There are two healthy babies in here."

"Twins?" I gasped.

"Two?" Chase squeezed my hand, trying his hardest to sit forward to see more. Dr. Burner angled the screen for easier viewing, pointing out two heads. Two spines. Four perfect little hands, waving through the fog.

I thought of every moment I'd felt a double kick, every craving, every early maternity shirt that suddenly made sense.

"Baby..." Chase whispered. "I love you so much."

"I love you more," I whispered back.

"They're both strong," Dr. Burner said gently. "I'll want a full scan in-office soon—no more skipped appointments. But yes. Two healthy babies. With very familiar noses."

"You're gonna need a bigger house," Troy said.

"And more arms," Sam stood back, his arm around Troy as they smiled at Chase.

"Would you like to know the sex?" Dr. Burner peered over the edge of his glasses. I looked at Chase, who nodded.

"Get ready, Wilders," the doctor said softly. "These girls just evened the odds."

I held Chase's hand and watched the grainy screen in front of us, our daughters curled safely inside me, tiny and alive and ours. Around us, brothers and doctors and the slow rhythm of recovery buzzed like a hive—but in that moment, all I saw was light. After everything we'd lost, after everything we'd fought through to find each other, this was what survived the fire.

Love.

Family.

Life.

Two hearts beating in promise: This was my reboot, and never again would I do it alone.

EPILOGUE

CHASE: SEVERAL MONTHS LATER

AFTER I LEFT THE hospital, Moira and I spent the rest of her pregnancy at the cabin we'd initially planned for our honeymoon. My house was damn near razed in the fire, and our new build had just begun, so the cabin made the most sense. Troy and Sam had no space to spare anyway.

Honestly, it was heaven.

The first couple of weeks were all about getting Moira and me both healed up. She had a mild concussion but otherwise suffered only bruises from that animal. My rage didn't fully settle until the last bruise fully faded.

She was a trooper, taking care of me even though I couldn't keep my hands off her. Watching her play nursemaid was stupid hot. At first, she tiptoed around my injuries, and while I was starving for her, I got it—my body had taken a hit. But after a few green lights from the surgeon and physical therapy, I found ways to work around my limitations. Then, once I could move more freely, I made it my mission to fuck my wife on every surface she could reasonably bend over, sit on, or grab.

Her belly grew by the day, and I was obsessed with her breasts, her hips, the thighs carrying our daughters like they were forged for it. As the snow rolled in, each snow day another excuse to worship every inch of her. I could've stayed there forever, her moans the soundtrack of my life.

Life moved forward.

We discovered Jensen's attorney—the one Moira ran into at the pharmacy—was dirtier than we realized. Troy tried to track him down, but the guy vanished after Jensen was booked again. And Jensen... still comatose, housed in the secure wing of the prison hospital. Couldn't be tried until he woke up—some legal technicality. The whole thing made my skin crawl.

Troy's tech contact, digging into Apex, skipped town, too. The best lead we had dried up overnight, and while Troy kept working his angles, it was like Apex vanished into the mist. I tried to focus on what I could control—my healing, my wife, and the babies growing in her belly.

Chief and Carol visited weekly. He brought rehab gear and updates on the arson case, while Carol doted on Moira like a proud grandma. The investigation stalled with Jensen unresponsive, but the Chief didn't trust how neatly the whole thing had wrapped up. I didn't either. He hinted more than once about me taking over for him down the road, but I wasn't sure I wanted a desk job—not anymore. I needed to move, to protect what was mine.

Moira, in between doctor visits and keeping me in line, took NB Realty and turned it into a damn empire. She overhauled our website, rebuilt all our branding, and ran ads that doubled our seasonal bookings in months. We had waitlists on the newer cabins and bought the two flanking ours to expand. The woman is a genius. I told her to slow down before she hit maternity leave, and she rolled her eyes at me like I was the one pushing too hard.

After the shock of the twins wore off, I started reading every book I could find. Troy pretended he wasn't freaked out, constantly checking his phone when the topic came up. Sam, on the other hand, was obsessed—buying onesies, pitching baby names based on EMT calls, and showing up with rattles like he was already Uncle of the Year. For all his playboy reputation, nobody was surprised. Sam was born to care for people, and he loved a captive audience.

Spaghetti night survived the chaos. First, takeout in the hospital, then at the cabin. We never officially moved it, but none of us questioned it either. The bigger table, the bigger family—it just fit. We'd gone from three bachelor brothers to a whole tribe overnight. I barely recognized my life anymore.

And I'd never been happier.

Tonight, I was planning to suggest we rotate dinners to Sam's or Troy's place for a while. Moira was almost full term, and I didn't like how much she'd been pushing herself to clean and nest and prep every little detail.

"Woman," I growled from the stove, "if I have to tell you to sit down *one* more time, I swear I'll glue your ass to that chair."

"Yeah, yeah." She rolled her eyes and kept setting the table. "I just wanna get this part done. Do you think we need a centerpiece?"

"We need you to sit before your feet blow up like balloons. I care more about how pregnant you are than how the table looks."

"He's right, sis!" Sam hollered, walking in with bread and salad. "I already caved on that stupid vinaigrette you love. Don't push your luck with flowers."

"Troy's late," he added, dropping the food on the table. "Had a pitstop to make."

"Like it matters," Moira mumbled, stretching her back. "My feet can't possibly get any bigger than these hips of mine."

"Stop insulting my favorite pillows." I came up behind her and popped her ass.

"Any more contractions lately?" Sam rubbed her belly like he was looking for luck.

"Back pain. Hip pain. Ribs feel like I've been drop-kicked by a horse...but no contractions."

"All normal." Sam's EMT brain kicked in as his eyes got a distant stare while he massaged her belly. "They're still heads down. Good job, girls." He smiled at her belly. "But give your mama a break."

"Get off my wife," I snapped a kitchen towel at him. "You're not her OB."

"I'm qualified," Sam said proudly. "I'll deliver 'em myself if I have to."

"You are not seeing my wife's vagina!"

"I just wanna be the first to hold 'em!" Sam laughed as Moira winced, hand on her side.

"I think they like Uncle Sam's voice as much as they do their daddy's," she groaned. "I'm getting a bruise from all the kicking."

"Sorry I'm late," Troy came in juggling a case of seltzers, a six-pack of beer, and a bakery box. "Bakery line was ridiculous."

"Bakery?" Moira's eyes lit up. "*You* are officially my favorite person." She opened the box and made the happiest little sound I'd ever heard.

"Winner and still champion," Troy grinned as she squealed at the decadent multi-layer chocolate cake.

"Chocolate craving, baby?" I muttered. "You could've told me."

"You do everything else," she said around a mouthful. "I can't bend, can't twist, can't drive. You even have to shave my —"

"Dear God," Troy groaned. "Spare me the visual."

"Delicate flower." Sam teased.

"I just figured I'd spare you another craving run for something I won't even finish," Moira muttered, wiping her eyes. "I'm starving and full. All the time. I hate it,"

"All normal," Sam assured. "They're hungry but taking up all the space."

"Come here, Fancy Pants." I pulled her into my lap, cake and all, hating that I couldn't make her more comfortable. Even sleeping was a chore, and I could see the exhaustion in her paper-thin emotions. "Eat what you can. Then I'll float you in the tub, oil you up, and get you horizontal to relax for a foot rub, how's that sound?"

"That sounds like—"

I felt her freeze. Watched her eyes widen as a spreading warmth seeped into my lap.

"My girls kicking again?"

"I think my... water just broke." She looked at me, alarmed.

"Your...what?"

"I think they're coming."

"The girls are *coming*?" Troy echoed.

"YES!" Sam whooped, throwing his hands in the air like he'd won a damn trophy. "Go time! Chase, hospital bag—front seat. Troy drives. Moira's with me in the back in case I have to deliver."

"You're not seeing my wife's—!"

"Chase." Moira clung to me, her chin trembling, and I could see the excitement and fear in her eyes.

She trailed her fingers gingerly across the place on my shirt that hid the newly inked tattoo. Elaborate flourishing font that spelled Fancy, with two tiny pink crowns atop the Y representing my baby girls.

My family.

She wanted me to wait until they were born and get it all done at once, but I didn't dare. She didn't want to settle on names until she met them face to face, and I was happy enough to have her in my arms as it was, much less getting daughters ta-boot. Going through the pain of two ink sessions to add in the girl's names later was just fine by me.

Holding her close to my chest, I wrapped my arms around her for just a moment, then two, willing my heart to slow down in the hopes it would help her have one last moment of true calm before the hard work ahead of her.

I was a very, very lucky man.

Luckier than I dared to dream.

Luckier than I deserved.

"Deep breathe, baby." I hugged my wife, thankful for Sam and Troy running around and throwing things into bags so I could whisper soft promises into Moira's hair as she slowed her breathing. "You are now and forever never alone. I'm here. I've got you now." When I felt her belly tighten rock-hard as she gasped, I knew that was all the time we'd get. Taking her face in my hands, I whispered, "Come on, baby. Let's go meet our girls."

Walking out, we passed the wall of pictures. Some of us and Nonna, others with my brothers and me, all together in our military gear, and then our biker attire. Finally, my wedding day, when they all gathered round, hands on Moira's belly.

God, my life is so damn good.

Acknowledgements

Stories may start alone, but they reach readers because of the people who show up along the way.

Thank you to Jonathan House at Candlelight Creative LLC for artwork that spoke before my words did. To Laura Matney at The Writers Life, LLC, thanks for your sharp eye and steady encouragement made every page stronger. Vision became visibility thanks to Aimee Ravichandran at Abundantly Social, and to Rex — the best assistant, keeping both the words and the whirlwind in check.

These books bear my name, but your fingerprints are all over them.

About the Author

Rhone Atleshen is a multi-award-winning author writing under a pen name to explore the various corners of the thriller genre. After more than fifteen years crafting stories, Rhone launched this brand to focus on what truly haunts the page: domestic danger, emotional reckoning, and villains you love to hate.

Known for strong voice, cinematic pacing, and deeply flawed characters, Rhone's work delivers slow-burn tension with explosive payoffs—and sometimes a little spice. Whether writing psychological thrillers, romantic suspense, or twisted moral dilemmas, the common thread is always this: the bad guys burn in the end.

You won't find personal details here—but you will find stories that strike a match and walk away while they burn.

READ MORE RHONE

The Apex Society Trilogy

Gaslight (Book One) — You're holding it.

Matchstrike (Book Two) — Coming November 2025

Burn (Book Three) — Coming December 2025

Follow Rhone Atleshen for sneak peeks, behind-the-scenes chaos, and updates on future releases.

Sign up here for first looks, special extras, and reader-only perks: rhone atleshen.com

Instagram / TikTok / Facebook:

@RhoneAtleshen

Sneak Peek: Matchstrike

Book 2 of the Apex Society Trilogy

"**I**'M AN UNCLE!" I shouted over the din of my favorite bar. "Next round's on me!"

Cheers and congratulatory shoulder smacks followed me to my barstool at the back corner of Scaled Back — a seedy joint on the old logging highway, once a truck stop and weigh station, now a glorified watering hole marking the county line.

"Congrats, Sammy boy. Boy or girl?" Marge, the owner, had been a friend since I responded to my very first 911 call as a probationary paramedic–bar brawl gone south. We arrived to find two unconscious men and a baseball bat-wielding Marge standing over them, smoking a cigarette with a bloody forehead she made me stitch up right there in the bar. I returned to check on her when my shift ended to find her serving shots to the men she'd knocked unconscious earlier. My shocked face gave her the 'best laugh of her life', so she poured me a drink on the house.

"Nieces!" I accepted the mug of on-tap lager. "Two nieces, can you fucking believe it!"

"Both girls!" Marge exclaimed. "How's Mama doing?"

"Moira's great. You should see the girls...they're absolute dolls." I took out my phone, showing a picture of a teary-eyed Chase holding one of the girls as he sat beside a besotted Moira holding the other baby, both of them beaming. "They take after their mother...thank God." I swiped to another pic–me holding both my nieces at the same time, pointing them out. "That's River...and that one is Blue."

"River and Blue?" Marge scrunched her face at the monikers.

"Yeah...I don't get it either. Chase came up with the names." I flipped through a few more pics of Troy, and then one of Chase's face when we announced they were here. "Chase is wrecked."

"And did you lose your marbles holding those babies?" Marge prodded. "Blowing in here and buying a round for the whole fucking house?"

"C'mon, Margie girl." I teased the nickname she hated. "You know I gotta to celebrate."

"You mean blow money in this shithole...Yeah, I know." She whipped her towel at me before strolling to serve a few patrons, leaving me to scroll my photo album.

The twins hadn't been here 24 hours, and I was utterly smitten.

Being a bachelor was great.

But seeing Chase happy was better. I swear, watching the bulkiest tatted-up biker in town give googly eyes to those two tiny bundles of pink made my goddamn heartache.

And, a part of me was envious.

Of the three of us, I was the Wilder brother voted most likely to grow into a full-on man-whore. I subscribed to the 'work hard...play harder' school of thought. When I was at work, nothing distracted me from caring for a patient, whether stitching up an angry bartender wielding a bat or comforting a woman pulled from a burning building. I was never rattled, never caught off-guard, and never backed down from doing whatever I needed to do to help take care of the person in front of me. I loved being the person who could help someone when they were hurt, broken, and scared. I loved being an EMT.

But when I was off-duty, I wanted to party with some soft curves. Or rather, I used to.

Snagging the eye of some hottie passing through town, buying a few rounds, and hooking-up was easy. I never brought them home, and I rarely saw any of them more than once, much less snuggled up for a sleepover. Outside of the bar, I was friendly with just about everyone I met, and with my job as an EMT, that meant I saw the nurses and doctors at the hospital near daily. I tried not to dip my pen in company ink, but occasional hook-ups happened there too.

At some point this past year, my standard off-duty fare of easy tail batting lashes for a hook-up lost its appeal. It was subtle at first, me being too tired, or a shift was too bloody. Then, closing down the bar took a backseat to a hot shower and soft bed. I suddenly preferred drinking and playing pool with my brothers more than the random women who asked the same questions over and over.

A drink alone was more enjoyable than scratching an itch that was going more dormant by the day. If I let myself think too hard about it, I might worry I was broken. Hell, if I were counting the days since my last good lay, I'd schedule a physical to make sure my dick still worked. But I knew the issue was just me being generally dissatisfied with life. Sick of the solo road trips and notched-belt lifestyle I had cultivated around a reputation I had once preened over.

"Hey, Uncle Sam!" Marge's voice snapped me out of my revelry. "Were you serious about buying a round for the whole place?"

I glanced at Marge, who was talking to a few guys who walked in looking like they'd just hopped off a long-haul in their rumpled flannel and trucker hats.

"Absolutely!" I shouted up to Marge. "Beer's all 'round in honor of my nieces!"

The bar cheered again, and the two newcomers gave me a wave of appreciation.

"It's like you don't like keeping your money, Sam." Marge sauntered over, grabbing my credit card. "Figured I'd taught you better than that."

"How many times am I gonna become an Uncle, Marge?" I asked, tossing the last of my drink back. "Troy's wound so tight he'll never marry. If that control freak sat on a lump of coal, he'd shit a diamond." I palmed a fresh mug. "Did I tell you the girls are identical?"

"How can you tell them apart?"

"When I left, they were painting their toenails different colors. Doctor said little differences will emerge as they grow." I got lost in pictures of my brother's growing family, laughing at one of Troy awkwardly holding the girls. "Check it." I turned the screen to Marge, who lifted her reading glasses and then laughed.

"He looks damn near terrified."

"100%." I swiped through a few more pictures. "It's hysterical."

"When you cutting off that tab?" Marge nodded towards the bell jingling over the door. "Want me to cut it off now or wait 'til you come crying over the bill?"

"Go ahead and close it out after this one, I sup..." My response trailed off as I got an eyeful of the newest patron to walk in, door bouncing off the rounded ass of the hottest, and angriest looking, woman, I'd ever seen.

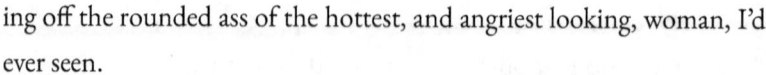

Want more of 'Funcle' Sam and the woman who just walked into his life? Preorder **Matchstrike** now — Book Two of the Apex Society Series. [link/QR code]

www.ingramcontent.com/pod-product-compliance
Lightning Source LLC
Chambersburg PA
CBHW072336020726
47506CB00004B/904

* 9 7 8 1 7 3 5 5 3 5 5 7 9 *